# The Queen of Bloody Everything

**Also by the author for adults and older teens**

*Wonderland*
*Undertow*
*Eden*

# The
# Queen
## of
# Bloody
# Everything

Joanna Nadin

MANTLE

First published 2018 by Mantle
an imprint of Pan Macmillan
20 New Wharf Road, London N1 9RR
Associated companies throughout the world
www.panmacmillan.com

ISBN 978-1-5098-5310-6

Copyright © Joanna Nadin 2018

The right of Joanna Nadin to be identified as the
author of this work has been asserted by her in accordance
with the Copyright, Designs and Patents Act 1988.

1 3 5 7 9 8 6 4 2

A CIP catalogue record for this book is available from the British Library.

Typeset in Sabon LT Std by
Palimpsest Book Production Ltd, Falkirk, Stirlingshire
Printed and bound by CPI Group (UK) Ltd, Croydon, CR0 4YY

For Henny

# Now

So how shall I begin? With *Once upon a time*, maybe. The tropes of fairy tale are here, after all – a locked door, a widower, a wicked stepmother, or a twisted version of one at least. But those words are loaded, tied; they demand a *happily ever after* to close our story, and I'm not sure there is one, not yet.

Besides, *Cinderella* was never your scene: 'Don't bank on a handsome prince, Dido,' you would sneer through the cigarette smoke that trailed permanently in your wake; that cloaked you, tracked you, like a cartoon cloud in *Bugs Bunny*. Like Pig-Pen's flies. 'If they do bother to show up it'll be late, and then they'll only beg or borrow. Or worse.' And the twelve-year-old me would roll her eyes, like the girls in books did, and think, Those are your princes, Mother, not mine. And I'm not you.

But I am, aren't I? Though it's taken me four decades – half a lifetime – to admit it.

I used to rail against my inheritance, the pieces of genetic jigsaw puzzle that make up half of me. I thought I could overwhelm them, drown them, if I found him – the man

1

who'd given me his pale skin, his plumpness, his pathetic hope in one true love. When he failed to show up on the doorstep or in any of the faces I followed in town, I turned to friends to fill the gap – stole their habits, their hair colour, their hatred of soul music. I turned too to characters I borrowed from books in the hope I could carry off their courage, their capability, or at least their slick, smart one-liners. But acting was your forte, not mine, and one you failed to parcel up and pass along, offering me instead small ears, an extended second toe, and a lifelong dislike of marzipan. Amongst other things.

But back to the story. I know how it begins now. And where. *This*, the first words will spell out in black-and-white Times New Roman, *is the story of us, of you and me. And how we got here – to this strip-lit room on the fourteenth floor of a hospital in Cambridge.* Some parts of the tale you will not know at all, or even be able to spot yourself in the cast. But, as Pied Piper, that is my prerogative – I can dance a merry dance to other houses and other cities to show you scenes that shaped our path. And, though you might not take a starring role, you are ever-present, your influence reaching across years and oceans. I know that now.

Some parts you will recognize, though they will appear distorted, skew, as if seen in a fairground mirror, or through time-thickened glass, told as they are from the haze of memory and my myopic gaze. If you asked Tom, or Harry, they'd give you a different version: a shrunken picture, like a view through a wrong-ended telescope; or rose-tinted, perhaps, embellished with sequins and a glitterball that dapples the scene with some kind of magic.

But this story – our story – has no enchantment. There is no fairy godmother, no genie, no amulet or grail.

There is just us. Me and you. And a tangle of secrets and lies, of second guesses, of half-formed hunches Chinese-whispered into tangibility; of poorly timed honesty, and misplaced blame.

But I am getting too far ahead of myself again.

Let's go back to the start, to the seed of it all.

Are you listening carefully, Edie? Then I'll begin.

# The Lion, the Witch and the Wardrobe

## August 1976

It begins in a back garden in Essex in the long, hot summer of '76. The summer you inherited a set of keys from an otherwise estranged great aunt, and we moved from a single bedroom in a South London squat to a ramshackle red-brick semi; if not in the country, at least in the leafier part of small-town Saffron Walden.

'Small town, small minds,' you say, as now-to-be neighbours watch us through twitching nets as we drag dustbin bags and old crisp boxes from the back of Maudsley Mick's Transit. I stare back defiantly and march up the path, ignoring the trail of tampons, tubes of paint, a potato masher that I leave in my wake. I am still, of course, happy to style myself as you – my swearing, cigarette-smoking slip of a mother. Because you – and Mick, and Toni, and the revolving cast of misfits, dropouts and almost-damned that bed down on borrowed floors – are all that I know.

But that is about to change.

Mick leaves as soon as the last suitcase is pulled down onto the pavement.

'I don't have to go,' he offers. 'I could stay to help. Unpack and stuff. I don't mind.'

But you do. 'We'll be fine,' you insist. 'Won't we, Di?' You look over at me, teetering along the neat flint of our new garden wall.

I nod, and hop down from my tightrope, insinuate myself around your legs, under one arm; a determined barrier between you and this man-boy who has shared your bed – our bedroom – for the last four months.

'If you're sure,' he says.

'Oh, we are,' you reply.

Mick shrugs and turns to go but you, feeling sorry for him, maybe – or yourself, more like – pull him back and into an embrace. I feel his leg nudge me aside, hear the wetness of his tongue against yours and think of the eels we saw once on the Old Kent Road. I shiver despite the heat.

The kiss lasts for two minutes and twenty-three seconds. Enough time for my right foot to go numb. Enough time for the peeping Toms and Tinas over the road to have raised their eyebrows and formed clear opinions of just who is moving into number twenty-seven.

'Something to remember me by,' you say as you gently push him away, then haul me up onto your hip in one practised movement.

'I'll see you again, won't I?'

Even I, aged six, can sense the desperation in his already speed-jangled nerves.

'Maybe,' you say. 'But this is a different world out here.'

And I watch triumphantly as Mick, defeated, retreats to

his van and reverses down the mews and out towards the A11.

'Just us now,' you say.

Just us. And at those words I feel the air crackle with possibility, with the attention I might now get, the adventures we might have. Overcome with this unnameable electricity, I hug you hard, my arms enclosing skinny ribs, my face buried in Mick's sweat and your patchouli that forms a damp patina on your neck.

'God, you're getting heavy,' you say, dropping me down onto tacky tarmac. 'I'll be inside.' And you walk, hips swinging, towards the house. 'Fuck it's hot,' you add under your breath. Then louder, for me, 'I wouldn't stay out too long. You'll burn.'

'Fuck,' I repeat when you have disappeared into the gloom. The word feels delicious in my mouth, and dangerous too. Like the liqueur chocolates that the skinny ginger-haired man let me have last Christmas, then laughed as I danced with him around the front room in my tinsel hat and boa. 'Not so funny now,' you said when I threw up on his shoes.

I swallow the word down, then check to see if our audience has heard me. But the curtains are pulled against the noonday sun now, and so, sighing dramatically, hips swinging in imitation, I take thirteen steps up the path and into our new life.


'It's smaller than I remember,' you say, your voice tinged with a disappointment that threatens to seep into me via a special osmosis, a gossamer thread of connection that, despite its apparent lightness and fragility, seems forged of an element so unbreachable it could form a wall to block munitions or stop mighty armies in their tracks; could fell, even, their monstrous number.

I feel my face fall, even though this is more house than I have ever had, or even imagined. Though in my conjurings, there was markedly less dust, fewer paintings of naked ladies, and more zoo animals. However, one of the ladies has no pubic hair, like me, and I am filled with a sudden hope that I will be spared this strange, animal fur.

'I like it,' I say, hoping words will make it so.

And, abracadabra, they do.

'Oh, so do I, Di,' you say. 'It's perfect. It always was. Though any place where my mother wasn't was bloody paradise back then.'

'Back when?'

'God, nineteen-fifty-something. Fifty-six? Fifty-seven? I don't remember. I was six.'

Six. My age. I feel a prickle of delight at the symmetry. A barley-sugar sweetness swallowed by wonder at what kind of paradise could be had without a mother.

'Christ, I'm starving,' you announce then, a change of subject swift and effective: a speciality of yours. You open the fridge, a hulking, humming behemoth of a thing that lights up like a stage as the door opens and closes, a feat of unfathomable magic that will continue to amaze me well into my tenth year. You, however, are less easily impressed, regarding the empty shelves with disappointment rather than disbelief. 'They could have at least left some bloody butter,' you opine.

'Maybe she ate it all before she died,' I suggest, trying to lighten your gloom myself. 'Or maybe she preferred margarine.'

'No one prefers margarine,' you say. 'No one worth knowing, anyway. And not the point. Someone's been in and had away with it, and the fucking Hockney.'

I have no idea what a Hockney is, but it cannot possibly be as delicious as the lunch you eventually assemble – crisps and a hunk of sweaty cheese from the corner shop.

'I'll get real food tomorrow,' you say.

But I'm not complaining. After a diet of sloppy stews and stir-fries cooked with stolen electricity, the tingle of salt and vinegar on my tongue is luxury, a feast fit for a princess. I flick the light switch next to the table on and off, on and off, my finger circling the smooth Bakelite.

'All right, Di, it's not a bloody disco.'

I pull my hand away, leaving us bathed in a sodium glow.

You sigh and snap the light off. 'Don't,' you say. 'That stuff costs money now. Besides, it's giving me a headache.'

Within half an hour the headache has forced you upstairs to 'lie down for a minute'.

'You must be tired too,' you insist when my face falls at this disappointing news.

I shake my head. I'm not tired at all, and besides your room smells of old person.

'Well, explore, then,' you say. 'But don't go too far.'

'How far?' I ask, wondering if this new house – this new life – comes with a frontier.

'Timbuctoo,' you reply.

'Where's that?'

'The end of the road.'

I listen to the tread of your bare feet on the narrow staircase, counting the steps as you turn left on the landing into the front bedroom. Seventeen. I hear you flop inelegantly onto the bare mattress of your bed; the sheets and duvet still stacked on shelves or wrapped in black plastic, where so many things will remain for weeks, months even, until you finally admit this is home. Then the house is silent but for the insistent buzz of the fridge and the flies that hover lazily over our leftovers.

I am alone.

The realization is both thrilling and terrifying, and the urge to race after you and cling to you like a raft from a sinking ship immense. But you are ill, or your version of it, and I can already imagine your groan as you push me off: 'Not *now*, Di.' So instead I sit on my hands and cross my legs until the need has passed. And then I hop down, pick up a crisp that has hidden itself under my chair and, with the sliver of potato dissolving on my tongue, explore the four rooms that make up our downstairs.

After five minutes the possibilities have been exhausted. There is no cellar, no secret passageway to France that wolves might slink through in the night, and, worst of all, no Narnia at the back of the larder, just two tins of pineapple, though admittedly these hold an exoticism all of their own.

The mantelpiece offers up no genie lamp, just a dust-dirty ashtray that fails to emit anything more than filth when I rub it. On the other hand I have found a glass marble that looks like an eye, two old pennies, and a dead beetle, all of which are now rattling satisfyingly in the pocket of my purple shorts.

Maybe there's something outside, I think to myself as I press my face to the downstairs lavatory window. But the glass is ridged, cobbled, and all I can make out are overgrown shrubs, a tangle of green repeated in fisheye circles. A forest, I decide with delight. Because a forest is where all the best stories begin: where Red Riding Hood meets the big bad wolf; where Hansel and Gretel find the gingerbread house; and where Max makes mischief of one kind and another and sets off to find the Wild Things. And so, out of the back door and into the woods I go, my flip-flops slapping against my heels, my tongue clacking out my horse's hooves, off to seek my fortune, rescue my damsel in distress, and meet my handsome prince.

And within minutes I manage all three.

The stretch of land nearest the house is clogged with slowly browning rose bushes and the desiccated heads of overgrown hydrangea. There are no wolves here, I think, no dragons. But at the end of the garden rise beanpoles and beyond them hang the low-slung branches of someone else's chestnut tree, the ground beneath brindled with light. This, this is my secret garden, I think, and, bold as Mary Lennox, though not half as belligerent, I head into the thicket to investigate.

11

I have never seen fruit on a tree before, understand even less about harvest times, though I know a plum when I see one. I reach up and pull one from a branch, bite into it and, gagging, quickly spit out the shrivelled, bitter flesh. Then I watch, fascinated, as ants swiftly colonize the bolus, swarming over it as if it were a careless drip of jam.

I look up. The garden is darker here, cooler, overshadowed by the houses behind the wall. Show-off houses, Mick called them when we drove past earlier; fat mansions with their own serried ranks of look-at-me leylandii standing sentinel over their wide, well-stocked land. 'Still got burnt lawns same as everyone,' he said. You ignored him, so I did too, and instead stared, mesmerized by their smart red brick, their singularity. Now I am staring again, and want to see closer. There is a wall between us and, astonishingly, thrillingly, a gate. But when I rattle the rusted handle I find it locked. I make a mental note to hunt for the key in the house, buried as it might be beneath floorboards, or guarded by a troll.

But, for now, there is another way in. From where I stand I can climb, nimble as a monkey, into our apple tree, then haul myself higher into their horse chestnut until I am peering out through a crackle of papery leaves onto enemy territory. And that is when I spy them, from my crow's nest aboard the *Hispaniola*. Not pirates though, or Indians, or any foe I have come across, but a boy and a girl, completely naked, their sunlit skin tanned and shiny, their hair spun from straw into pure gold as if by a miller's daughter. This in itself is treasure enough, but the real diamond in my discovery is that they are sitting in the makeshift blue lagoon of a plastic paddling pool: a thing even I know is contraband in this drought.

She, my age or thereabouts, is sitting sideways, one hand on her hip in the manner of a diffident mermaid; he, older, unimpressed, is idly kicking a plastic boat towards her. And in that instant I fall in love. Not just with him, though he is the better part of it, but with them both, with the whole scene: the house, the garden, the magazine perfection of it. And I want very badly to be in this picture. So badly that the want is a physical thing, a hard ball of need that sits and swells in my stomach with the crisps and cheese. So badly that I, in my only act of daring to date, dangle myself from my vantage point, then drop down onto their lawn, flip-flops, dead beetle and all.

Their heads turn and mouths gape in perfect synchrony.

'Who are you?' the girl asks first.

'I—' But my bravery is used up now and I can barely stammer out a 'D-Dido.'

'That's not a name,' she says, matter-of-factly. To which I have no answer. 'Anyway, what are you doing here?' she asks. 'This is *our* garden.'

I look sideways at the boy, whose eyes are wide but his mouth closed now, holding in a smile.

'I asked you a question, young lady,' the girl demands. She is standing now, both hands on her hips, a perfect miniature mother, or the ones I have read about.

'It's hot,' I say, pointlessly, face reddening as soon as I've said it.

'You can sit in our pool if you like,' the boy says. 'There's room.'

I feel the ball of want, of hope, fragment and scatter; butterflies soaring into my throat and down into my very toes. 'Thank you,' I manage to whisper. And without another word, I kick off my flip-flops, pull down my purple shorts and Wednesday knickers, slip off my vest top and climb in.

The water is warm and milky.

'It's from the bath,' the boy says. 'The news said you could use that.'

I wonder whose water it is, or was, as I raise and lower my legs, watching my pale thighs shrink and grow in the deceptive opacity.

'You're fat,' the girl observes.

'Shut up, Harry,' the boy urges. 'You're not allowed to say that.'

'Well, she is,' the girl – Harry – replies. 'You can buy slimming drinks. It's in my mummy's magazine.'

I am too busy marvelling at the name Harry – Ha-rreeee – seeing how it feels on my tongue, to realize she is addressing me.

'Are you talking to yourself?'

'No,' I lie. 'And anyway fat is a feminist issue.' I repeat the words you spelled out for me from the torn piece of paper Toni had pinned to the bathroom door.

'What does that mean?' Harry asks.

I shrug. 'I don't know. It was in my mummy's magazine.'

She smiles then, and, encouraged, I kick a tidal wave across the bathwater and sink the boy's boat.

'Oi,' he says. But he's smiling widely now, too, and sends an arc of water soaring over us.

'To-om!' Harry complains, and kicks both feet furiously.

'Tom,' I say to myself, feeling the shape of the word, hard and round like a pebble, as I do the same.

Soon all three of us have turned the peace of the Fenjal lagoon into a raging sea that slip-slops out and soaks into the hard earth beneath, our legs tangled and toes pushing into who knows what.

'Harriet?' comes a voice.

I look up to see a woman stalking across the lawn. She is a stretched, hardened version of the girl sitting next to me, wearing an immaculate white kaftan and straw hat, and carrying two plastic beakers, one blue, one pink.

She stops short of the paddling pool, staring first at me, then at the shipwreck we have created, then back at me again, unsure, I assume, which disaster to deal with first. She picks me.

'And who might you be?'

Where your voice is low and rounded, like the smoke ring from a cigarette, hers is precise, sharp, like glass. But fragile, as if it, too, is ready to snap.

'Dido,' says Harry.

'Die-doe?' She repeats the name as if it's a dirty word, or a lie.

'Dido Sylvia Jones,' I say quickly, as if the rest will balance it out; make it a real name after all. 'The Sylvia is after a woman who wrote poems and put her head in an oven.'

'Really.' Her face is taut and unimpressed. 'And where exactly did you spring from, then, Dido?'

Harry looks blankly back and I realize I never told them, because no one asked. Maybe they think I am a fairy child fallen to earth. Or an orphan. It is on the tip of my tongue to say the last one, to see if she'll adopt me, so I can live forever in the big house with the paddling pool and beakers of orange squash. But Tom pipes up, 'She's moved to the house over the back, haven't you?'

Astonished at his soothsaying, I am only able to nod.

'Really,' the woman repeats. 'And where is your mother?'

I look at Tom to see if he knows that too, but it seems his psychic ability has dried up for the day.

'Lying down,' I say. 'She said she's buggered from the move.'

I feel the minute change of air pressure as clearly as if it were the clang of a bell. And I realize in that instant the potency of words, their inherent magic to disarm and disturb, and realize too that this one – buggered, I assume – has damaged only me, marked me out. And I vow to try to mind my language. Once I know what is and isn't permitted.

It is Tom who breaks the tension as he lets out a snigger.

'That's enough, Thomas,' his mother snaps, her voice rising. 'And close your mouth, Harriet, you'll swallow a fly.'

The pair do as they are told, clamping their lips between their teeth to stifle the thrill, and are handed their beakers as reward. I look hopefully at the kitchen, but there is no squash for swearers.

The woman turns to me again. 'Does she know you're here?'

'Sort of,' I say.

'What does that mean?'

'She said to explore, but only as far as Timbuctoo.'

The woman raises an eyebrow in disbelief and I wonder if Timbuctoo is a bad swear too.

'It's true,' I insist. 'She doesn't mind, as long as I don't talk to strange men or try to bring home dogs.'

'What about your father?'

'I don't have one.' It is my turn to be matter-of-fact. This is the most questions anyone has ever asked me in a row and I am quite pleased with myself for getting most of them right, even with the 'bugger' thing.

'Everyone has a dad,' says Harry.

'Well, I don't,' I declare. 'I thought it was Denzil, but Edie said don't be daft because he's black.'

'Good lord.' The woman touches the palm of her hand to her hair, which is held up with an invisible force, folding in on itself at the back. Neat, coiled, like her. 'How old *are* you?'

'Six years and seven days,' I say, still truthfully.

'You'll be in Harry's class, then,' says Tom. 'She's seven in September.'

'Well, only if she's at the same school,' his mother corrects. Then turns to me, concern edging her voice now. 'Where *do* you go to school?'

'I don't,' I reply. 'Toni teaches me at home, and sometimes Chinese Clive who isn't from China at all, he's from Jamaica, but he loves pork balls with sweet and sour. But that was in London. Edie says now we're in the wretched provinces I can go to an actual school, so I'm starting at St Mary's in three weeks and two days.'

'We've got Mrs Maxwell this year,' Harry says. 'She's fat and old and Karen Kerr said she once hit Brian Banner with a board rubber just for coughing too loud.'

'She didn't,' Tom retorts.

'Did too. You're just cross because you haven't got Miss Wicks any more.' She turns to me conspiratorially. 'He loves Miss Wicks.'

She draws out the vowel to a long 'urrr' and with it I feel a strange sting, the first, it will transpire, of many. Confused, I quickly offer up the only school story I know. 'Edie says in her old school in Cambridge, which was all girls and you had to wear hats, one girl nearly got expelled for kissing the music teacher.'

I do not tell them the one girl was Edie – you – but the woman's lips thin anyway.

'And just who is this Edie person?'

It is my turn to look incredulous. 'My mum, of course. She's really called Edith but she hates that and our surname because of the pay-tri— pay-tri something. She says for her thirtieth birthday which is in four years eight months and . . . seventeen days she's going to change it.'

'What to?' Harry asks.

'She said Moon or maybe Nefertiti. But Toni – she loves women – told her to stop being mental.'

'That's enough.' The woman ponders this latest atrocity.

'Well, this isn't Timbuctoo,' she says finally. 'This is the Lodge. And it's high time you two came in before you get sunstroke.'

Tom stands up, obediently, and for the first time I see him in all his naked glory.

And so does she.

'Oh, for heaven's sake, Thomas, sit down,' she says. 'Or put some clothes on.'

'It's all right,' I say. 'I've seen loads.' And I have – Maudsley Mick's, Chinese Clive's, and all the others who think I'm still asleep when they creep out for a pee in the middle of the night. 'It's only a penis,' you said then, and I repeat it now.

But the words fail to have the calming effect I was aiming for.

'Inside, both of you,' she says, then turns to me. 'And you'd better run along, too.'

'I can't,' I say.

'Why ever not?'

I point at the tree. 'The branch is too high on this side.'

'Oh, for heaven's sake.'

I am expecting to be led solemnly round to the front of the house, all the while hoping for a reprieve, a stay of execution, to be invited into the fairy-tale castle, even if it is by the ice queen. Incredibly, inconceivably, I am offered the next best thing: a gleaming talisman in the shape of an old iron key, a key that wasn't in a drawer or a magic lamp but in the gate itself, on this side of the wall. She turns it and it sounds a delicious clunk like a full stop.

'Bye, Dido,' Tom says.

'Ciao,' I say. 'It means hello and goodbye.'

'Chow,' mimics Harry.

'Oh, do come along,' her mother pleads. And this time both children obey, their glimmering bodies galloping ahead of her across scorched lawn.

You forgot to lock it, I think. But I do not say it. Instead I slip my feet into my flip-flops, pick up my pants and vest from the lawn and slide the key quietly, carefully out of its lock. And, as I feel its weight, its power, its importance, I realize that I have found exactly what I've been looking for after all. I've found my Narnia, my Neverland. And in it are no fauns or crocodiles or talking beavers, but a would-be Wendy and a not-at-all-Lost Boy, and a world of what I will later find out is called normal.

But for now, to me, is pure enchantment.

And with the key to this Wonderland clasped tightly in my hot, damp hand, I dance up the path to tell you all about it.

# Hansel and Gretel

## August 1976

There's a Polaroid in my purse – it used to be stuck to our fridge with a Busby magnet, do you remember? A blurry snapshot of a boy and a girl – Tom and me – in ersatz German costume squinting at the camera, hand in sweaty hand, faces red from the polyester heat. Do you remember that day?

That was the day you met *him*.

It was almost September, a Saturday tagged onto a summer that was turning Indian in its persistence. The garden matched our carpets in swirls of brown and burnt umbers, and any fruit that had managed to claim enough water to swell beyond a pip had long since dried to raisins or been reduced to a wasp-blown corpse. I'd grown an inch in height – tall enough to reach the cupboard in the bathroom where the tablets were kept. Yet time refused to obey similar rules, elongating hours into what felt like days, or standing still entirely.

Because *they* were gone.

Every day, since our paddling pool meeting, I'd slipped through the gate in the wall; every day I'd found the garden

21

deserted, the house locked, the curtains drawn. I worried they'd all died in the drought. Or moved away, horrified at the arrival of a girl with a strange name who said 'bugger' and thought nothing of a penis. It wasn't until the eighth afternoon, when I came across a fat grey woman who was in the kitchen feeding a thin grey cat, that I found out they'd gone on holiday.

'Cornwall,' she says, her cheeks wobbling like pink blancmange. 'Three weeks, same every year. Didn't they tell you?'

I shake my head.

'You're in the old Henderson house, aren't you?'

'Henderson-Jones actually,' I say. 'We're just Jones because of – ' I try to remember if this is about men or racists or poor people – 'something bad,' I offer.

The cat woman frowns, her forehead creasing easily like a thin sheet.

'You're related?'

I nod. 'Only no one told us she was dead for ages so we didn't even go to the bloody funeral.'

The woman's cheeks deepen to a ruddy scarlet. 'Right, well, shoo now, I'm locking up.'

So I shoo, and come running home with my news.

'They're not dead!' I announce. 'They're just in Cornwall.'

'Good as, then,' you sigh from the sagging velvet of the chaise longue. You spend a lot of time on this piece of furniture, claiming it for yourself, nesting on your back in the cushions with a novel and a jar of nuts.

'Three weeks, she said, so that's . . . thirteen days to go.'

'Who's she?' You open one eye, look hard at me. 'The cat's mother?'

'No, the cat *feeder*. She had a moustache.'

Other mothers, older mothers, would have pointed out it's rude to stare, rude to even see these things. But you just snort out a 'Ha!' and close your eye again.

'Why are we just Jones?' I ask then. 'I couldn't remember.'

The smile that had lingered on your lips at the thought of the cat lady slips quickly and you stand and push past me into the kitchen. 'Who's asking?'

'The cat feeder,' I reply, following you. 'And me.'

'Because . . .' you begin. Then change your mind. 'God, Dido, will you just stop with the Spanish bloody Inquisition?' You pull a pink cocktail cigarette from the packet, your seventh of the day so far, and light it leaning over the gas cooker. I hold my breath as I wait for your hair to catch fire. It doesn't, and I am almost disappointed.

'Go, go and read a book or something,' you say, flapping your left hand.

And the conversation is over.

I stamp up to my room, lie down on my bed – a narrow, rigid thing that, unlike yours, and to my continual chagrin, holds no princess-and-pea potential, though at least, you tell me, no one died in it – and, huffing audibly, calculatedly, take a foxed and faded copy of *The Velveteen Rabbit* from my bedside table and turn to page one.

I am a precocious reader, taught by Toni who labelled the squat with zeal and a Dymo printer for the benefit of both me and a brown-toothed Frenchman. *Toilet, table, tangerine,* we learned. *Bathroom, bastard mice, bong.* There, though, the books had dull covers and duller contents, and, worse, were borrowed from the library so that by the time I was half a chapter in, we had to return them to Mr Higgins with his sallow skin and sour-milk smell.

Here, there are books galore and all of them mine: Woolf and Wilde, Waugh and Wharton, alphabetized and coded by size and colour. I have built myself a reading fort, watched over by a stuffed raven in a glass dome, a creature I found in the attic and you deigned to keep, despite your tangible disgust. You have your own treasures, anyway – a wardrobe of shot silk and black taffeta and furs that promises adventures but, when I climb inside, offers up only mothballs and worm-chewed wood that cracks underneath me, an accident that sends you into fits of laughter, hurting my pride, if not my bare behind. And so as you retreat, revel in costume changes, I strike out into my own make-believe, a world populated by rabbits that come alive, by boys that can fly, by mothers who make picnics, plait hair, and wait patiently for their husbands to come home.

Later you climb into bed with me, whisper a smoky 'Sorry' into my neck, and then haul me up so we can dress as 'ladies', sticking feathers in our hair in the flyblown mirror; dabbing our necks, our wrists and, to my fascination, the hard bone between my nipples, with a deep-amber liquid from a label-faded bottle; painting our lips with a coral stick as thick as clay. The day after that, still in our finery, we go to town and buy scratchy school shirts and checked dresses and, to my delight, red T-bar sandals. And the day after that we get rocket lollies in Glover's and eat them in the market square watching the fruit and veg men whirling closed paper bags of hard potatoes and fat Cape apples, copying the egg man calling out his price for a dozen. But really, this is white noise, set-dressing. Because what I am really doing all this time is counting down the days until Harry and Tom come home.

I awake on the twenty-eighth of September – D-Day – to a hammering sound outside my window. On the other side of the curtain is our garden, then their garden. And in their garden is a man in shorts with a moustache, only a proper one this time, and he's up in the tree doing something with wood.

'Edie!' I yell. 'Trespass!'

'Jesus, fuck,' comes your voice from the other side of the landing. 'What time is it?' There's a pause. Then, 'Not even ten, yet.'

'But there's a man,' I insist. 'In the garden.'

'What?'

The threat – or maybe prospect – of a man, even a trespassing one, lures you out of bed, and you appear at my side naked but for a string of beads and a pair of black knickers. Then sigh heavily. 'He's not in *our* garden,' you say. 'He's over the back.'

'What if he's a burglar?' I suggest.

'Hardly,' you say. 'He's got loafers on.'

We watch him for a minute, see him swap the hammer for a saw, see him flex it professionally, like the magician from the Palladium about to slice a lady in half.

'What the . . . He'd better not be bloody chopping down that tree.' You bang viciously on the window.

He glances over, sees us, and waves. Then cups one hand to his ear as if he has misheard.

You open the window to point out his folly. 'You'd better not be chopping that down, I said.'

'I . . . er, Mrs Jones?' He points at you, confused.

'What?' You look down. 'Oh. Fine. Hang on.'

You stalk back to your room, then return pulling on Maudsley Mick's Grateful Dead T-shirt. 'I said you'd better not be chopping that down,' you yell. 'And it's not Mrs anything.' You pause. 'It's Edie.'

'Call me David,' he yells back. 'Hang on. Do you want to come down? Be easier to talk then.'

'Fine,' you hiss, and, leaving the window wide open to the world, you march downstairs in your cigarette-burned top and knickers with me in my apple-print nylon nightie hurrying behind.

Call-Me-David is also called Mr Trevelyan, which gives me another fat fact to keep safe in my pocket: 'Tom Trevelyan,' I say to myself while you discuss the wood and the weather and when we got here and why. 'Harriet Trevelyan.'

'It's her birthday party today,' a sentence finishes, and my ears prick up. 'That's what this is for. Should have done it weeks ago but we were waiting for the Wendy house to arrive. This is the platform, see.' He pats the wood that is already stretching across two branches as if it is a horse or a hound. 'Then the house will sit on top. Won't be done before the party, though.'

'What a shame,' you say, with no hint of irony, which, for you, is astounding.

'Apparently so,' he says, his voice tinged with regret, and inevitability. 'It'll be me shut in there later. In the doghouse.'

You laugh loudly, affectedly, so that he smiles.

'You should come,' he says. 'Both of you.' He looks down at me, finally. 'You must be Dido,' he says.

I nod eagerly, thrilled that they have told him my name, bestowing me with importance.

'It's fancy dress,' he warns. 'I said we shouldn't bother, just let everyone wear swimming costumes, but it's all planned, see, on the invites.'

'Oh, we can manage fancy dress, can't we, Di?' You don't even look at me when I offer an emphatic *yes*.

'Three o'clock, then. And sorry about the noise.'

'*De nada*.' You dismiss the inconvenience as if you are waving off a fly.

'I'm sorry?'

You smile again. 'Spanish. It means "any time".'

By three o'clock I am dressed in a hastily assembled hotchpotch of your old yoga leotard stapled with crêpe paper leaves then safety-pinned to size, topped with a tiara plucked from a silk-lined case. And I am delighted, though unsure as to who or what I am supposed to be.

'Gaia,' you explain for at least the third time. 'Mother Earth. The queen of bloody everything.'

I like being the Queen of Bloody Everything, even in an itchy leotard and a crown that pokes my left ear uncomfortably, and I march regally around the downstairs and then along the path to the door where, behind the wall, things are happening.

From my bedroom observatory, I've already watched a trestle table being laid with a red paper tablecloth and white paper plates, seen the quoits and beanbags set out, noticed the hired-in umbrellas raised for shade. But there has been no sign of Tom or Harry, only their nameless mother and David arguing over the Wendy house, which is, apparently, the wrong sort of pink. But now I can hear squeals and scattergun laughter, the slaps and monotone of a clapping game: *I went to a Chinese restaurant to buy a loaf of bread-bread-bread, he wrapped it up in a five-pound note and this is what he said-said-said.*

'Come on,' I plead, my legs jiggling with want.

'Coming,' you claim. But it will be another four minutes and ten interminable seconds before you appear at the back door in your bikini and a black wig from Great-Aunt Nina's costume box.

'Who are you?'

'Cleopatra,' you say, lighting a cigarette from the packet stuck into your bottoms. 'On holiday.' You slip the lighter back into your bra top, and turn the handle of the now permanently unlocked gate.

'Shall we?'

I have seen moments in films, on television, where a person walks into a room and everything goes pin-drop quiet, either because their beauty requires that degree of reverence, or their dastardly deed silent fury. This moment, I think, falls into the latter category.

I close the gate behind us, thinking that's what they're all waiting for – the children with quoits poised in their hands, the mothers by the trestle table with cups of tea. It takes me a moment, after I've spotted an Indian, two cowboys, and four princesses, to notice that not one of the grown-ups is in a bikini. Not one of them is in fancy dress at all.

'Bollocks,' you hiss under your breath and give my hand a squeeze. But I, in my first act of defiance – and disloyalty – do not squeeze back. Instead, sensing the enormity of your mistake, I let go.

'Edie,' a voice says eventually. 'And Dido. Glad you could make it.'

It's David – Mr Trevelyan – emerging from the kitchen with a plate of sausages on sticks.

'Interesting outfit,' he says, raising his eyebrows and pulling his lips in to stifle amusement. And in that instant I have a vision of Tom: the same eyes, the same smile, and search frantically and fruitlessly for him in the crowd.

'Sorry,' he adds, 'I should have said it was just the kids. But you look great, really.' He looks at the mother. 'Doesn't she, Angela?'

'Angela,' I say to myself. The word is golden, a precious treasure in my mouth. Because she is – an angel.

Angela – Mrs Trevelyan – doesn't answer, just makes the thin-lipped face again. So you, of course you, stride up to her and offer her your hand.

'Edie,' you say. 'I think you've met my daughter.'

She takes your hand briefly before dropping it as if it is hot, or dirty. 'Yes,' she says. Then, 'She has my key still. Clearly.'

'She tried to give it back,' you say. 'But you were away.' You take a drag on the cigarette, blow out a lungful of smoke. 'So where is the birthday girl, anyway?'

'Oh.' She shakes her head, irritably. 'In the Wendy house with Tom. She doesn't like her costume. Says it's too hot.'

'It's Gretel,' David says. 'You know, German thing. Pinafore.'

'Tom is perfectly fine as Hansel,' Angela continues, 'so why she's making such a fuss about it I don't know.'

'Tea?' offers David. 'Or something stronger?'

The voices have recovered from the shock of us and rebuilt to a steady hum and tinkle, and I have no idea what you say in reply, or even if you do, because all I can focus on now is the wooden house. I very badly want to see inside, see them. And I, I think to myself, am the Queen of Bloody Everything, so I can do what I bloody well like. And I slip quickly across the neat, beige grass to do just that.

The house has a real plastic window with red gingham curtains, and smells of paint and newness. Inside I can see Harry sitting cross-legged and crossly on the floor, and can see, too, the end of Tom's legs sitting opposite her.

'Hello,' I say, stepping inside. Then add, pointlessly, 'It's me.'

'Hello, Dido,' Tom says.

Harry says nothing and I notice her face is red and puffed from crying.

'What's the matter?' I say. 'If it's too hot you could take off your knickers. Edie always says that helps.'

'It's not because it's hot,' Tom says knowledgeably. 'It's because of it being Gretel and I'm Hansel and it's *her* birthday party not *ours*.'

'Well, it is,' says Harry. 'And I never picked the costumes, she just went to the shop and got them.'

'They cost five pounds for three days,' Tom says. 'Which is a lot. That's why Mummy's cross. And anyway there isn't a choice because she hasn't got another.'

And then I have an idea so brilliant in its simplicity that for a second I really do feel invincible and all-knowing.

'We could swap,' I say. 'Me and you.'

Harry stops sniffing and looks harshly at me, and, like Tom with his father, I see her mother's thin lips in hers. 'Who are you even meant to be?' she says.

'Gaia,' I say. 'She's a queen. Of everything.' I do not say *bloody* because I know now from saying it to the man in the corner shop who smells of dog that this is a mind-your-language word and for in-my-head-only.

'You look weird,' she says eventually.

'But it's not hot,' I say. 'And the leaves rustle.' I wiggle my hips to prove it.

And that, plus the crown and the title, are enough, it seems. Because within less than a minute, Harry and I have wriggled out of our outfits, exchanged them, and emerged from the Wendy house, thrilled with our new incarnations, however ill-fitting.

You are at the trestle table still, but with a glass in your hand now with what could be wine in it, or wee. I have seen both before, from when our water got cut off and the toilet blocked, but, as you are drinking this, not pouring it down the sink, I assume it is wine.

'Oh!' you exclaim. 'You've swapped. How clever.'

But not everyone sees the genius in this plan.

'Oh, for heaven's sake, Harriet,' Angela snaps. 'That's not yours.'

'It's Dido's,' she says. 'I liked it more.'

'I don't even know what you're supposed to be.'

'Mother Earth,' you say, one eyebrow arched in daring.

'Of course,' Angela says. 'Who else? Honestly, Harriet. I've got the camera ready so we can have you and Tom and the playhouse. It was all planned.'

'So Dido can be me,' says Harry, still sing-song happy with her paper leaves and paste diamonds. 'I don't care.'

And that is how the six-year-old me comes to be stuck to our fridge, standing proudly in front of a flamingo-pink Wendy house and flanked by two prouder red-faced parents, not even my own. But do I care that I'm just a stand-in for another girl? A surrogate for Harry? No, I do not. Because now my hand is in Tom's; now, you see, I am in the picture, their picture. And you? You are nowhere.

I will spend the next twenty-seven years trying to recreate the perfection of that Kodak moment, that camera-ready version of my vision of family. I will squander days, weeks, months trying to pull it, rabbit-like, out of a hat; tracking it, trying to follow the trail of breadcrumbs I believe must have been laid for me, if only I look hard enough.

God, what must you have thought, Edie?

And yet now, here we are.

# The Princess
# and the Pea

## June 1977

It's June 1977, and the Jubilee. We're not celebrating because you don't believe in the Queen or any of the royal family. 'She's a bloody sponger,' you tell me, 'a drain on society, her and all her inbred offspring.' And so I slip the sheaf of red-white-and-blue-themed drawings I have painstakingly traced out into the wastepaper basket. But the commemorative coin I queued for – holding out my clammy hand for Mrs Bonnett, and expressing my awe in solemn turn – this I pluck from its plastic case and drop into the dark-glassed Marmite jar with my marble and the various buttons and bits of broken china I have dug up in the hard mud of our now-wilderness.

I still have these treasures, and more. All squirrelled away in a suitcase under my bed. Found objects, and kept objects; postcards from far-flung places and notes passed under desks in the tick-tock tedium of double physics. And evidence, always evidence. A box of delights, and of danger too, like the Ark of the Covenant it sits, two rusted clasps all there are to keep it from releasing its unfathomable power. But we know where I learned that trick, don't we? Though your secrets were less conveniently corralled. Instead you scattered them about like so much ephemera, pushed them into crevices, between cracks in the floorboards, or locked them, skeleton-like, in your cupboard.

But I've lost the thread again, strayed from the path, and there was a point to this story.

The Jubilee summer. Do you remember?

By June I have never been more in love with the world – with our world. Of course, there is a list of things I would alter, were I in charge: the dust that clings to curtains and coats every flat surface, choking me when it billows from pillows, gathering in a clod on my finger when I draw a ladybird on the mantelpiece; the dirty laundry that piles inelegantly in the corners of our bedrooms, until, exasperated, you finally pull out the terrifying twin tub and spend a day sweating over suds with a pair of wooden tongs as long as my arm; the persistence with which you demolish my book fort and filing system, knocking over ramparts, dropping unread copies of Crompton carelessly on my 'finished' pile, pushing Blyton back on a shelf between Dahl and Dickens.

But, while I covet the Lodge, with its sharp lines and neat piles and air fresheners in every room, where the beds are always made, the toilet always lemon-clean, and the overall effect one of walking onto the set of a television sitcom, I am happy with our house. Because it is just that: ours. There are no strangers asleep on sofas or, worse, in our bed when I wake up; no kitchen thieves to 'borrow' my bananas, or make my Milky Bar disappear in a foolish lapse of concentration.

We are lords of all we survey, Queens of Bloody Everything, and my future, it feels, is assured.

Until one Saturday in Jubilee June.

Because while I revel in the peace, you have been going quietly spare. You wander restlessly, an unsettled cat, so that I am almost scared to let you out in case you don't come home; I remember a story in a comic about buttered paws, and wonder idly if it might work on you.

'I miss London,' you announce at breakfast.

'I don't,' I say quickly. 'It smelled weird and I saw a man do a poo in the road.'

To my relief you laugh. 'Oh God, I'd forgotten that,' you say. 'But still, you'll be the one begging to go back when you're sixteen and climbing the walls.'

The image is compelling as I see a supersized sixteen-year-old me scaling the ceiling like a spider girl. 'No, I won't,' I snap. 'And anyway we're not going because we live here now, so there.'

'Christ, Dido, I only said I missed it, not that we're getting the next bloody train.'

But despite your reassurance, so scared am I of losing it all – the house, the Lodge, this life – that I lock myself in the bathroom and refuse to come out until you agree to my demands.

'What are they?' you ask, half amused, half weary.

'To always live here forever,' I say. 'Unless we move into the Lodge.'

'Well, that's never going to happen,' you tell me. 'And I

can't promise we'll always live here either. Not forever. What about when you go to university?'

'I shan't go,' I reply.

'Your call,' you say, a frequent mantra and one that Harry revels in with its offer of free choice, but one I secretly resent, preferring rules and boundaries so that I know where I stand.

'Then I'm not coming out.'

'You'll starve,' you try.

'I've got garibaldi biscuits,' I snap. 'And I can drink water from the tap so I won't die of thirst either, if that's what you're hoping.'

'I'm really not, Di,' you say. 'In fact, I think this is marvellous. Your first protest. Wait until I tell Toni.'

At these words, I know I have lost. But I still manage an entire morning until the pull of the *Pipkins* theme tune being played loudly from the living room becomes too much to bear and I unlatch the door and stomp down to the sofa, refusing your arm around me, but accepting the cheese on toast you offer as a peace treaty of sorts.

'What if I asked them here instead?' you ask after a while. 'Toni and . . . the others.'

I try to focus on Hartley and Topov, try not to let the butterflies in my stomach flap their frantic wings again. 'What others?' I say.

'I don't know, Denzil? Chinese Clive maybe?'

'He won't want to come,' I say. 'There's no pork balls.'

'Probably not,' you assure me. 'But I'll ask anyway.'

So it is in this precarious landscape that I find myself in

Jubilee week: a world and future I had assumed was assured now ever so slightly in the balance. Because, despite the lack of readily available takeaway, Chinese Clive has agreed to come, and so have Toni and Denzil and, to my serious concern, Maudsley Mick.

'We can have an alternative Jubilee,' you say. 'Without the Queen.'

I sigh in exaggerated disappointment, because what, I think, is the point of a Queenless Jubilee? But by Saturday afternoon, my sulking has slipped into a frenzy of anticipation. Not for our party, which I am still studiously ignoring, but because they are late, and you are weakening.

While you skulk inside in the half-cool of the house, I hang over the gate, mouth gaping at our neighbours as they troop round the corner in their paper crowns and fake ermine, waving plastic flags and bearing paper plates of fresh-from-the-oven sausage rolls and neat, shiny halves of devilled eggs. It is not so much the festival I feel I am missing out on, as the food. At home you are in a determined grow-your-own phase and every meal is accompanied by a mound of bitter, stringy mung beans from the cultivator on the counter, and a dollop of home-made hummus. But out there are Wagon Wheels and Majestic wafers, packets of Salt 'n' Shake crisps, and bottles of Corona cream soda or, even better, Sodastream. Harry's father brought one home and let us all have a go, making cola and Irn-Bru and cherry-ade until the six ridged bottles were filled and capped and lined up in the door of their enormous fridge. In ours sits a pint of silver top, a carton of orange juice and a half-empty bottle of vodka, the last of which you are drinking right now.

'I wish they'd all bloody shut up,' you snap from the sofa. 'God, I can hear Mrs Lovejoy from a mile off, she's like Foghorn flaming Leghorn.'

But I ignore you, as well as your demands to *stop staring* and *come inside*, and *shut the bloody door at least*, and carry on swinging backwards and forwards, feet firmly wedged between the wooden struts as I watch the world go by without me.

By three o'clock you can bear it no more and tell me to 'Just bugger off there, then, but don't expect me to join in. If anyone needs me, I'll be here. Plotting a bloody republic.'

And bugger off I do.

The seats at the tables are all taken so I squeeze between Harry and Tom, nudging my bum onto a quarter of her wooden chair, a sum that does not quite add up, however hard I try.

'I thought you couldn't come,' says Tom.

'Edie said,' affirms Harry. 'Because of the Queen being horrible.'

Two seats down, Mrs Payne, mother of Brian and owner of a gravity-defying hairdo, glares pointedly at me. I didn't say it, I think. Harry did. But it is never Harry's fault, I am beginning to discover.

'She's not horrible,' I say quietly. 'Just why should she be in charge and have loads of money instead of me or you?'

'We do have quite a lot of money,' says Harry. 'Daddy said we're getting a new car next month. A Cortina.'

'What about the Capri?' I ask, thinking of its sleek pleather seats and the satisfying clunk-click of seat belts into slots; its smell of tobacco and newness and success.

'Someone poorer will get it,' says Harry matter-of-factly. 'Maybe you could have it?'

'Harry!' protests Tom.

'What?' she asks, genuinely baffled.

'I'll ask Edie,' I say. 'When I get back. She can't come because she's waiting for Toni.'

'Who's Toni?' Tom asks.

'Duh. Her mum's best friend,' answers Harry. 'The lesbian.'

Mrs Payne's face flushes from pale blancmange to raspberry jelly and she casts a glance for Mrs Trevelyan to intervene. But Angela is conveniently serving pineapple on sticks to the Lawson twins and is blissfully unaware of the X-rated conversation at our end of the trestle table.

'What's a lesbian?' asks Tom.

'They kiss other women,' I say. 'But they can't marry them or have babies.'

'Because no sperm,' hisses Harry.

'Is your mum a lesbian?' asks Tom.

Harry pulls a face. 'No, silly, or how did she have Dido?'

'But she did kiss Toni once,' I whisper.

Mrs Payne slips out of her seat. But I am enjoying commanding an audience for once, Brian and two of the Gibbs girls now rapt as well.

'It was in bed. They weren't wearing anything. I think they rubbed each other, too.'

I made that bit up. I don't know what you did, or for how long. All I know is that I woke alone, and when I padded down the landing and checked, Scooby-Doo-like, behind all the closed doors, it was Toni's room I found you in, wrapped around her naked body, your hand between her legs, your lips against her neck.

'Edie?' I asked quietly. Then louder, because I needed a wee and the toilet was blocked, again. 'Edie!'

You shifted, and as you did, Toni kissed your hair and you moaned. Then you lazily opened your eyes and brought them into focus. And saw me.

'Di?'

Toni sat up and I saw her breasts, white and veined and pendulous. I was fascinated by breasts at that age; had seen at least five pairs, but yours were my favourite. I preferred them small and stiff, not these hanging mammaries that seemed so cow-like in their swaying.

You pulled a T-shirt on, one of Chinese Clive's, and pushed yourself up from the futon. 'Do you want some breakfast?'

I nodded solemnly and, still staring over my shoulder, allowed myself to be led from the room.

That was six months before we left the squat. And a life-time ago it seems now, yet still its ripples are felt in every corner of the pond. The beginnings of them fanning out that hot afternoon in June.

'Are you a lesbian?' asks Brian Payne.

'No,' I say decisively, and focus entirely on Tom. 'And nor is Harry.'

I feel a Clarks' heel kick sharply at my shin.

'What?' I complain. 'You're not.'

But I know what Harry's protesting against. Not the declaration, but about letting slip that we're so sure.

And why are we so sure? Because, like a costume, like another character in the line of Cinderellas and Rapunzels we try out for size, we have played at being lesbian for an afternoon. We kissed, or rather Harry kissed me, in the bathroom at her house one Sunday after I first told her about Toni.

'What do they do?' she asked.

'The same as with men,' I said. 'They put their tongues in each other's mouths and wiggle them.'

'Like this?' asked Harry.

I smelled the Rowntree's Fruit Pastille she had lodged between her gums and upper lip as her face loomed towards mine, tasted blackcurrant on her tongue as it pushed fatly against my own. I listened for a few seconds to the wet, smacking sound, and pulled away.

'Like that,' I said quietly, wiping my mouth on the sleeve of one of her cardigans.

'I don't see why they'd do that,' said Harry archly. 'That was . . . boring.'

And though I felt nothing move, heard no violins, I, aged six, was still wounded by the disappointment that I did not make a good lesbian lover.

'Mrs Beecham from Pennings is a lesbian,' declares Nicola Gibbs, knowledgeably. 'Jason Stint says so.'

'And she has hairy legs,' adds her sister Donna, as if this is the trump card, the silver bullet.

But Brian dismisses it as peripheral at best. 'She's married to Mr Beecham,' he says. 'So she can't be one.'

'Toni did sex with a man once too,' I say. 'So there. Also my Great-Aunt Nina was a lesbian and she had a child but it was already dead when it came out of her vagina.'

I am triumphant for all of a single second, before the real queen appears, and lays down the law.

'Dido Jones, that is enough.'

I look up to see Angela in a tiara and gold maxi-dress, her jaw so set the muscles in her neck protrude bone-like and threatening.

If it were anyone else I would argue my case – that it's true, Toni did do sex with a man, and Great-Aunt Nina did have a dead baby and also a lesbian lover – but this is Angela, Mrs Trevelyan, the sort-of-stepmother I aim to please. And so I mumble a 'Sorry' and stare hard at my lap, and the cache of biscuits I have managed to purloin.

'I thought you couldn't come,' she continues. 'Your mother – ' she spits the word out as if it is a pip – 'said you don't do this sort of thing.'

'*She* would,' adds Mrs Payne, and, though it is unclear to whom or what she is referring, Angela nods vehemently.

'Does she even know you're here?'

'Yes,' I insist.

But Angela looks doubtful, and again I decide to allow truth to slide in favour of fitting in.

'I'd better go,' I say.

'Yes,' says Angela. 'You had better.'

But as I slip off my small portion of chair, I hear the sound of my name being called, and not by you.

As I turn unsteadily to its source, I hear the squeak of wooden chairs as twenty children do the same.

'Is that her?' asks Harry, barely disguising her delight. 'Is that . . . Toni?' Her name is uttered with hushed reverence, a detail that does not go unnoticed by Angela, who hisses a *for heaven's sake* in a bid to defuse it.

But there is no dampening the crowd's delight, or parents' disgust, as Toni, dressed in a 'Fuck the Queen' T-shirt and fishnets, appears before them, accompanied by two enormous black men, one also in fishnets, and a ponytailed would-be prince.

'Hey, girlee,' says one of the black men and grins, a smile that banishes my fear and guile with each bright white tooth.

'Denzil!' I say, and let myself be pulled up into his enormous arms and sweat-smell, before he drops me neatly down again. 'This is Denzil,' I say to no one in particular. 'He's not my dad after all. And this is Chinese Clive, because of the balls. And Maudsley Mick. Because of the mental hospital where he lived once.'

Mick shrugs in vague affirmation.

Angela's mouth hangs open. Brian Payne's mother's

clamps shut and she puts her arms around her son as if to protect him.

'Come on then, Di.' Toni smiles and takes my hand. 'I thought we were going to have a party.'

'Yeah, girlee, where's the music?' booms Denzil.

'I'll show you,' I say, taking Toni in one hand, and Denzil in the other.

'Can I come?' Harry asks me desperately, then turns to her mother. 'Can I?'

'Absolutely not,' snaps Angela, then blanches. 'It's . . . this party isn't done yet, there's the costume prize and pass the parcel, and by then it will be time for a bath.'

'But—'

'No buts.'

'Butts are for sitting on,' Mick offers.

I laugh. 'That's American,' I say. 'Butt means bottom there.'

Angela bristles. 'I think we all know what it means, thank you.'

'I didn't,' says Tom.

'Nor did I,' pipes up one of the Lawson twins.

'Well, happy to be of service,' Mick says.

I flinch at that, a sentence I've heard him say before, and not in this context. I wonder if he's going to try that later, in your dead-lady bed.

Well, I'll just have to stop him, I say to myself. Because I am the Queen of Bloody Everything.

'Come on,' I say, with renewed urgency – motivated both by Angela's complete enragement and my own part-embarrassment, part-delight – and pull at Toni and Denzil. 'I'll show you where to go.'

We must make a motley group, a circus almost, in this small, white town – a not-yet seven-year-old, a lesbian, two West Indians and a certified mental patient – and even then I sense it. But when I walk in the front door and see your worry and weariness lighten and lift, when later I watch you dance with Clive, and then Toni, whirling around the kitchen in each other's arms like an unanchored carousel, when dark falls and I smell the sweetness of a fat cigarette, listen to you all singing along to Toots and the Maytals, I feel a sudden rush of homesickness so acute I almost throw up the mint YoYo and raisin Club I hocked from the trestle table before I left.

'Bed,' you say, seeing my greenness even in the half-light.

'I'm not tired,' I lie.

'She's not tired,' insists Toni. 'Let her stay.'

'She is tired,' you counter. 'And it's grown-up time, now.' And with that as your final word, you let Denzil pick me up and carry me up the seventeen stairs to bed, where, still fully clothed and with teeth unbrushed, I fall instantly and heavily asleep.

I wake in the early hours of the morning, to the first sliver of sun seeping through unclosed curtains and the murmur of voices from below.

I slip out of bed and across the landing, sit on the top step, legs dangling through the banisters. From here, though I cannot see what is going on, I can hear what is being said, and by whom.

'This *is* home,' I hear you tell someone.

'I'm only saying it because I care about you.' Toni, I think. Of course, Toni.

'Well, stop,' you spit.

'Stop caring?'

'No. Just . . . We'll be fine. We always have been.'

'I know, I know. I just wish . . . I wish you weren't so far away.'

'Is that all you wish?' you ask.

'Don't. That's not fair and you know it.'

You change the subject, or slant it, anyway. 'Are you with anyone?'

I don't know what Toni answers – a nod or a shake of the head. But when she asks you the same you say, 'Sometimes.'

'Sometimes you're with someone?'

'Sometimes I think he wants to be with me.'

'Who?' Toni asks.

Who? I think. Because this is the first time I have heard of a fancy man, a handsome prince, since Maudsley Mick drove off in his white van. I hope it's not him again, hope he hasn't been sneaking here while I am at school.

'Doesn't matter. No one important.'

The voices stop then, leave a gap, a wide chasm into which I pitch a cough that I have struggled and failed to keep down. The soft hum from the front room solidifies into a tense silence.

'Dido?'

'I'm *going*,' I say. And thump back to bed.

The next time I wake it is late, and I slope downstairs still sleep-heavy and damp with sweat to steal into your sofa bed. But the cushions are bare, the only trace of a body the well-worn hollow left by your foetal curl and a wine stain on the arm. Panicked, I double back and clatter up the stairs, not caring who hears me now, prise open your door, praying there won't be a replay of the scene in the squat – of any scene at the squat – Toni, or Mick or any of them. But you are face down, one arm flung out of the bed and dangling so that your chewed nails brush the floorboards. And you are alone.

The attic is empty too, the van and its occupants long gone down the M11, the only sign that we were ever more than two a binful of empty Guinness cans, a belated birthday card for you on the mantelpiece, and a toilet seat left up. And all the relief and disappointment of the Day After – after a birthday, after Christmas, after a one-night stand – washes over me like so much thin, cold soup.

I won't see Toni again for seven years, Mick and the others for more than twenty. But I know now, of course, who you were talking about that night, and why.

Why didn't you tell me, Edie? Why did you let me wonder for so long, lost in an imagination you knew was both vivid and desperate? The mind is a dangerous thing, Edie. Because we can conjure up demons and dragons and devils in disguise. But worse than that, we can imagine angels. And God,

Edie, I conjured such a creature for your suitor. So gilded and beautiful, so perfectly cut to slot into our strange lives and make them fit, make us family.

No wonder I didn't see him for who he was.

But then, I suppose, no wonder you hoped to hide him.

# Heidi

## March 1978

Toni's here now. All pink hair and patchouli, still, at sixty-five. She arrived at stupid o'clock this morning, alone. Left Susie without even a note. But then, you knew she would, didn't you? You knew she'd drop everything and come running like she always does when she's called – like a dog or a half-witted child. I see it in her because I see it in me; in the way I answer Harry's cries for help, crisis after crisis. The time she got her thumb stuck in her mother's en suite tap, despite being banned from the bathroom; the time she woke up still drunk in Denny Stevens' bed in a village in the middle of nowhere and I, the white knight, the fool, had to wake you so we could gallop into the night to rescue her; the time she . . . no, that one I'll save for later.

And why do we come running? Because you, you are the bright stars, of course, and our worlds turn for you.

Within months of our arrival I have beaten off Tina Fraser with her Girls' World head and eight Barbie dolls, and Melanie Best who has a parakeet and hair that skirts her buttocks, to secure my place as Harry's chief sidekick. My tactics are nothing more complicated than proximity and persistence, whereas the reasons for my pursuit are both manifold and eclectic: her perpetual scrubbed shininess, like a Coke-dipped penny or a polished silver spoon; her confidence in all subjects, from Olympic gymnastic placings, to whose daddy earns the most; her wardrobe of cellophane-new skirts and blouses, bought straight from the Ladybird shop rather than second- or third-hand from Roundabout next door; and, of course, Tom. By now Harry has tired of his being older and therefore better, which plays to my advantage in securing her precious attention and time. But where I try to lure him into our games, she slams doors in his face and tells him to bugger off round Michael Nelson's, which he does eventually, gliding down the road on his Chopper like a skinny-limbed, shrunken version of *CHiPs*, leaving Harry and me to our childish games.

And the reasons she lets me win?

There is only one.

You.

In my head, in the idle afternoons spent lolling on the squat sofa watching blurry films on Toni's black-and-white portable, I'd conjured for myself a long-lost twin sister, a straight-out-of-*Parent-Trap* double who would mirror me in looks and deeds. And then my mother and her father would meet again and fall as desperately in love as they'd been when they made us.

It sounds pathetic as I say it out loud, in the truest sense of that word. And ironic, given all that has happened. But back then my hope was unbounded, my imagination wild, and I pictured the two of us duetting on Stevie Wonder songs, me on my recorder, she on guitar. Maybe, better, she'd be blind, too, and I could be her guide, her eyes, her link to the world: essential; indispensable.

But I have to stop fooling myself when I find Harry. I know full well that I am as far from the Hayley Mills mould as she is thrown straight from it. She is skinnymalink thin and graceful with it, where I am puppy-fat and fumbling; pitch-perfect where I am always half a tone and several beats out; ruthlessly ambitious where I am willing, always willing, to follow.

We are as unlike as a pea and a peppercorn. But we have two things in common: an unwavering belief that we are destined for a world with flares and flashbulbs, and a profound disappointment in our own mothers. For, just as I covet Angela, her precision, her rules, her glorious, tedious normality, Harry wants you. She wants to eat olives for breakfast, because *why not?* you say. She wants to paint henna on her hands and feet and kohl her eyes to look like Mata Hari, even on a school day. She wants a mother who collects her in the playground dressed in a silk slip and Afghan coat and carrying a handful of sweet and sticky halva she's been handed under the counter by Mr Morris in the wholefoods shop. Not the mother I am eyeing with the frown and a sliced-up apple.

And so we are bound together, not so much by our past or our present, but by our dreamed-of future, by desire.

Our Top Five Favourite Things to Do, in ascending order, are:

1. **Running a shop.** With Harry's cash register and Post Office play money, we set up a stall at our front gate, selling everything from windfall apples to single playing cards. Once, we rig up a makeshift tent – pegging a ticking-striped bed sheet to the boughs of the cherry tree – and hang a sign declaring that fortunes will be told for ten pence. But our only visitors are the cat feeder lady – Mrs Lovejoy – who buys a bag of bruised apples for five pence, and Mr Messenger's dog Titus, who runs into the tent and pees on the sheet enthusiastically and copiously.

2. **Making potions.** This is an activity barred from Harry's house for a list of reasons so long and complicated that we barely bother to register a single one, instead running into your kitchen, where no cupboard is out of bounds, no bottle too precious or its contents too toxic. There, in an orange washing-up bowl that also doubles for foot baths, pet frogs and vomit, we concoct a groundbreaking amalgam of Jif, ketchup and the winey dregs of all the glasses that we find on shelves and bedside tables, imagining it will either dissolve a witch, or at the very least make stains disappear as effectively as Persil, thus winning us a slot on a TV commercial, which we have also written and practised until we are word-perfect and camera-ready.

3. **Roller-skating.** Ideally, we would be wearing ice skates and sequinned leotards and performing double axels and spirals like John Curry or Dorothy Hamill. But the closest rink is forty miles away and in a town that Harry's mother, for some reason, refuses even to name. So instead we substitute wheels for blades and take turns clattering up and down the bumpy tarmac, all the while imagining the roar of the crowd as we each score perfect sixes. Sometimes we sneak flowers from the gardens – ours is easier, as the likelihood of you noticing anything missing or misplaced is minimal – then stand on a bucket podium making our thank yous and taking our bows.

4. **Playing *Cinderella*.** We have tried *Heidi*, *Sleeping Beauty* and even, in a rare moment of anthropomorphism, *The Wind in the Willows*, but neither of us wanted to play Toad, and so again and again we return to this classic, dressing up in Great-Aunt Nina's cast-offs, and your clung-onto costumes, complete with feather boas and, once, a coconut bra. It is not hard to guess who takes the title role. But I am content to play the Prince. After all, it is me who does the rescuing, and I get to wear a fez, which has an allure of its own. Sometimes we persuade Tom to play, and so he takes my part, relegating me to the Ugly Sisters, and forcing a pair of Tiny Tears dolls into redundancy. None of us see the inherent

impossibility of their union. After all, who wouldn't want to marry Harry?

5. **Digging for diamonds in the pavement on Pleasant Valley.** In the heat of summer, they slip out as easily as a hard, ripe pea from the soft fur of its pod. So far we have mined three hundred and seventy-four, though that barely covers the bottom of our Golden Shred jar. When we've filled it, we're going to sell them to the jewellers on King Street and use our fortune to buy a mansion in Kensington and attend the Royal Ballet (we are in a Noel Streatfeild phase). Tom says we're being mad, that it's just mica, no more precious than a chip of broken glass. Now I know him to be right, of course. But back then our dreams were achievable things. Because we had the folly of youth and all its endless promise on our side.

It would be almost Disney-perfect if you and Mrs Trevelyan – Angela – were similarly inseparable; shared glasses of lemonade over the fence the way I see Tina Fraser's and Melanie Best's mums doing; went to Hair By Us to get matching perms and manicures, or just filter coffee and lemon gateau in the Corner Tearooms. But I see the way she looks at you; see you and me and our strange, messy house and strange, messy lives through her narrowed eyes. And I see that we are the Gollums to her perfect Galadriel, and so I take another step away from you, desperate to distinguish myself in

Angela's picture. While you are merrily oblivious, because you've never been desperate for a friend, have you? You've always had the luxury of assumption, because they've always been there, always done your bidding, danced in your wake, handed you what you asked for on a plate. Whereas people like me, we have to fight to find and keep our place. And fight I do.

By the spring of 1978, my friendship with Harry had endured faultlessly for eighteen months and twenty-seven days, our only cross words a disagreement over who was better, Sindy or Pippa, and who had to have the green Opal Fruit and who got the red one. I lost both, or rather I backed down, calculatedly, given that neither the dolls nor the sweets in question belonged to me. But this time there has been no argument, no imagined slight, we have just slipped into silence and, on my part, feigned indifference. Because, while all the time I am playing patience and solitary hop-scotch and one-hand-clapping games, Harry has been walk-ing arm in tweed-coated arm with my replacement: Heidi Fulton-Hicks.

This is not the last time this will happen. But the first cut, as they say, is the deepest, and this wound bleeds.

Heidi is an affront to me on several grounds. Firstly, she has the name of my goat-herding heroine, the girl I – at least this month – would most like to be. Secondly, she doesn't even know which wives Henry VIII beheaded and which ones he divorced, or how to do cat's cradle, or more impor-tantly, which china Whimsy animal is Harry's favourite. But thirdly, and most injurious of all, she has clearly stolen this coveted position from me purely by dint of having two surnames.

'But I could have two,' I protest, dropping my satchel on the floor to indicate the level of my disappointment. 'Why didn't you keep Henderson?'

'Because names are a . . . a marker,' you say, gesturing wildly with your cigarette in your batwing dress so that the overall effect is of a smouldering curtain, 'a siren. They stop you being who you want to be.'

'But I want to be Dido Henderson-Jones,' I protest.

'Harry'll come to her senses soon.'

'But *when*? Heidi has a pony. *And* a Jacuzzi bath.'

'And I expect the taps are gold and she shits glitter too.'

I ignore this comment, though the prospect of shitting glitter is momentarily intriguing. 'Why can't we have a pony?' I moan. 'Or another pet, like a cat. Or a . . . a fish?'

'Because I'm allergic. You know that.'

'To fish?'

'Fish give me the creeps. Dead eyes, Dido. It's not right.'

And so I am reduced to playing my only remaining card, the last resort of every wronged child. 'But, Edie,' I wail. 'It's not *fair*.'

'Life's not bloody fair,' you say as you tap ash into the crockery-piled sink. 'And if you think this is bad, wait until secondary. That, Di, is *Lord of the* bloody *Flies*.'

But I am only seven years and seven months, and can imagine nothing as bad as this, not even with flies in it.

And you, for once, can see my need. 'Oh, Di.' You drop

your cigarette butt into the sink where it fizzes in congealing porridge. 'Here.' You hold out a wing and beckon me under it. 'Just . . . don't let it show,' you say. 'Pretend you don't give two hoots and she'll start giving at least one.'

'Maybe,' I sob.

'Definitely maybe,' you say.

And so, my snot wiped off on your black satin, I shuffle upstairs to suffer nobly in silence, watching through the breath-misted window as the inseparable pair play Horse of the Year Show over milk crates and broom handles, on the course *I* designed. And I try, oh how I try, not to give a single hoot.

But, while Harry may not have seen, still less admired, my steely stoicism, my dignity in defeat does not go unnoticed. Because Tom, now aged ten and thus above any of Heidi's tricks and razzle-dazzle, appears to be affronted too.

'She's a cow,' he says knowledgeably as we sit on his front wall chewing Tooty Minties. 'She said I smelled of her grandma's toilet.'

'You don't,' I say, even though I have never smelt Heidi's grandma, let alone her toilet, I know that he smells of Fairy washing powder and sometimes Mr Trevelyan's Eau Sauvage that is kept on a doily on the mahogany dressing table. My loathing of her clicks up another notch.

'Do you want to watch *White Horses*?'

I shrug, which is itself an enormous effort given the size of the lie. I want to watch it more than anything. We don't have a telly at the moment, not since you threw a mug of coffee at the portable and cracked the screen, and just the thought of the theme tune elicits a pale breathlessness at the prospect of escape and adventure; the way, later, cocaine will cast its spell before the powder is even out of his pocket.

But for now my addiction is manageable, paling as it does beside my need to win Harry back. And my latest ploy, devised by you, is complete absence. 'That way she'll start missing you. You have to play hard to get,' you advise. 'Then they always come running.' I don't stop to wonder who you've tried this trick on and with how much success. I am just eager to test out anything that might return my small world to its status quo. And so, as Harry and Heidi return from the corner shop, giggling over their daring to eat Mivvis before May, I turn down my place on the Sanderson sofa, slip down from the wall, and march straight past without stopping.

'Not staying for tea then?' you ask as I stamp up the stairs.

'No,' I say, hands on hips on the very top tread. 'And I shan't until she bloody well changes her mind.' And I flounce into my room and slam the door, glowing with the sudden realization that I have never, ever seen you more proud of me than you are right now.

My resolve lasts two days into the Easter holidays, when the lure of Tom, and the bait of the television, grow too much to bear. And I clomp down the frost-crusted garden path and through the gate into a sparkling almost-Narnia, climb the fourteen rungs to the Wendy house, and wait.

He comes. Of course he comes. It may have been Harry's gift, her perfect version of her mother's world in miniature, but it is Tom who has taken over the space, at least for now. In here, in his blue duffel coat and red bobble hat, amongst the woodlice and spiders and, once, a curious wren (for not even Mrs Trevelyan's weekly Jif cloud can keep those at bay), he commands armies, ranks of green plastic privates and officers bought by the jar, fighting to the bitter end over a patch of mould-dusted Axminster; he explores underwater realms, his Jules Vernes stacked neatly on the shelf alongside a colander and a pepper pot; and twice he has put his hand under the waistband and snake belt of his corduroys and inside his pants, and delved into that unknown territory too, with me watching through the window, perched like a goggle-eyed pigeon on a branch outside.

Today, though, I am inside, squatting next to the stove, on which I am 'boiling' us breakfast: a can of Lilt emptied into the milk pan for porridge, and some Bourbon biscuits under the grill. In my imagination I am Susan in *Swallows and Amazons*, awaiting the return of the hero aboard his boat, or, better still, I am Mrs Herriot, from *All Creatures Great and Small*, another programme to which Harry and I have sworn our devotion. Or rather, we are sworn to its leading men; Harry to the impulsive and impossible Tristan, and I to the practical but still dashing James.

'James,' I say to myself, 'you must be exhausted from having your arm up a cow all night – ' an act I find unfathomable and unsavoury, yet somehow compelling – 'sit down and have some breakfast.'

And James kisses me on the nose, and insists there's no

time, because Mrs Pumphrey's Pekinese Tricki Woo has a dicky tummy again.

And at this I sigh, and place a hand on my heart as I watch him depart with his white coat and black bag, the very mark of a man, and give the porridge to the dog, again.

'Why are you pouring pop onto a plate?'

At the sound of his voice I drop the pan, sending a slop of fizzy pineapple and grapefruit across my wellies and seeping into the swirling shagpile.

'It's . . . it was a game,' I say.

'What game?'

But I am too embarrassed to admit my imaginings, and so I pretend it was a taste test, to see if he could guess what it was.

'OK,' he says.

And to my bewilderment and delight, he lets me blindfold him with my green scarf, and feed him the Bourbons and the plate of pop, both of which he guesses first time. And then, back inside the full-sized and centrally heated kitchen at the Lodge, we take turns and try out lime marmalade, salad cream and sweet piccalilli, only the last of which I can name, for the others are as alien to me as avocados once were.

'What are you two up to?'

I pull up one of my pirate eyepatches, though I would recognize her voice across fathoms and light years. She's wearing a dungaree dress and a striped polo neck, and on her arm is an identical Clothkits twin.

'We're taste-testing,' I say. 'Want to try?'

'No thanks,' says Heidi-the-twin, eyeing me, and clinging

to Harry. 'We're going to the roller disco, aren't we?' And she tugs at Harry's arm.

Harry nods – why wouldn't she? Even I would find it hard to turn down a trip to the rink in Mr Fulton-Hicks's Mercedes-Benz. But as she turns to go, her eyes linger on me for a second too long. And I feel a thrill of victory as I realize I have fired my first arrow straight and true.

And so I discover that all it takes – all it will ever take – to win Harry back is for me to take another lover. Because as Tom and I become the ones joined at the hip, as we huddle, tones hushed, heads touching over Lego, Meccano, his birthday Scalextric, the injustice of losing a friend *and* a brother becomes unbearable, and by the end of the week, with Heidi out of the picture on a package holiday to Portugal, I am back in my rightful place at Harry's side, if always playing catch-up.

Tom accepts this swapsies with markedly less complaint than when Colin O'Donnell persuaded him to exchange his brand-new boomerang for two broken Action Men. Instead, he smiles at me as I saunter in the back door, and saddles up his Chopper for solo adventures.

But one thing has changed.

Now, when we watch *White Horses*, it is I who gets the coveted middle seat, the pudge of my thighs pushed hard against Harry's slender ones, but my head tilted, ever so slightly, towards Tom. And his towards me.

It will last for a single week only, until school starts again, and our days are timetabled and our evenings scattered and taken up with chess club and swimming club and, in my case, book club (membership: one). But for those seven days, I am golden.

And for a minute, now, I feel pity for you, and for all the bright stars, the leading ladies; that you will never get to glory in such a small but hard-won victory. And would I swap my place with you, or Harry? I used to think so, used to believe I would slip off my skin and slide into yours or hers in a heartbeat, in a New York minute. But today – when I see you here, corroded by life, prone and diminished against starched sheets, your skin yellowed tracing paper, your eyes holes in the snow; when I look at her in the waiting room, child-tired, wearing a life she swore she was never meant for, like a four-year-old playing dress-up in her mother's furs – today the answer is no.

# A Christmas Carol

## December 1978

I still have my stuffed monkey; the velveteen of his fur worn almost bare now and his once-bright glass eyes milky with scratches. He arrived in a jewelled waistcoat, though that disappeared within weeks, left in the garden or a park, or lost to the mound of chiffon and lace that had outgrown your wardrobe and begun to breed on the bedroom floor. But this carelessness belies the truth, for how I loved that creature, my devotion so furious that wresting him from me for school or a bath became a complicated battle of bribery and threat – one you did not always win, for I remember at least one occasion when he shared my murky bathwater, despite your insistence he would go mouldy and bad.

Charles was his name. I shan't even ask you if you remember the day we got him, because of course you do. How could you not?

I had staked my future on the possibility of a life like the ones I read about in books and saw on television, and never more so than at Christmas. I wanted tinsel, turkey and, if not a flaming pudding, then a Wall's Viennetta for dessert. I wanted a jumbo tin of Quality Street, its foil-wrapped contents gleaming like a pirate's stolen treasure; I wanted the Ghost of Christmas Future to show me my glittering career; I wanted an angel to visit me and show me what a sad, broken world it would be if I were not in it. But more than anything, I wanted an invitation to the Trevelyans' annual Christmas Eve party.

After tea, I would watch from the window as Mr Trevelyan bundled Tom and Harry into the car for the Christmas tree service, where they would sing like angels, then nobly donate last year's worn-out presents to 'poor people'. Then, and I knew this only from Harry's retelling and my own vivid imagination, they would be ferried home, already dressed in their best party outfits underneath their brand-new coats, to await the arrival of the guests, including Mr Evans, who was the captain of the Golf Club; Mrs Baxter, who was the principal of the ballet school, to which I was not admitted; and a man who had written a book about bees and had once been on *Blue Peter*, although Tom said he dropped cigarette ash on the carpet so his mum might not invite him again. I also knew there would be Shloer, which Harry said was wine for children and thus the holy grail of soft drinks; two kinds of crisps – plain and prawn cocktail – and Twiglets, all served in cut-glass bowls; along with pastel-coloured sugared almonds, which were edible as long as you just sucked the sugar off and then spat the nut in the bin when no one was looking.

'I don't see what's so exciting about it,' you say from the sofa. 'There's some apple juice in the fridge and we can buy some crisps from the Co-op tomorrow if they're so bloody important.'

'The Co-op's shut tomorrow,' I say sullenly. 'It's Christmas Day. Everything shuts on Christmas Day.'

'Which is another reason why it's a load of buggery bollocks.' You smile, as if you have just potted black, or scored a hat trick.

'We could just go to the church bit,' I suggest, picturing a scene in which Mr Trevelyan insists we sit in their pew, and then chauffeurs us back to the Lodge in the Cortina and makes us the guests of honour.

'What for?' you ask.

I rack my brains. 'To give toys to a poor child.'

You snort. 'And who do you think this poor child is?'

I shrug, imagining it's Neville Watkins, who's adopted, or one of the Priestley boys who I've seen picking up cigarette butts outside the White Horse for their dad, and who smell of smoke and wee.

But you know better. 'Take a look in the mirror,' you say. 'I don't want their pity.'

This is the first I have heard about us being poor. I had assumed until then, going on my peers' pronouncements, that we were merely weird. But now there is another frontier to fight against in my battle to be normal, though I am still not swayed in my determination.

'If you pretended to believe in the Bible maybe they'd ask us,' I say, with astounding insight into the workings of Angela's head, but a complete lack of insight into yours.

'I doubt that woman believes in anything but bloody *Good*

*Housekeeping* magazine,' you snort. 'The difference is I don't lie about it. Besides, Jesus will know she's faking,' you add, placing a sour cherry on top of your cake of disappointment.

But I have noticed a chink in your armour. 'That means Jesus is real, then.'

You eye me, half irritated, half proud. 'No, it doesn't.'

'But you said—'

'I said nothing, clever clogs.'

And you win again. For now.

Because of course it isn't your lack of piety that's keeping us from the Trevelyans. It's the absence of breeding, along with an utter abundance of everything else, particularly wit, cleavage, and ability to drink.

But this year, the Winter of my Great Discontent, that is about to change.


The Daimler pulls up at eleven twenty-eight on Christmas Day. I know this because I have checked the precise arrival time on my Mickey Mouse Timex watch, which I unwrapped at eight forty-seven. I have also opened a box of pink Turkish delight which tastes deliciously of soap (Toni); a purple purse with beads sewn on it in the letter D (the Trevelyans); and a Terry's Chocolate Orange (Mrs Housden and Debbie the cat from next door). My stocking – an item you only allow by claiming it's filled by Pan and some unnamed 'goddesses of earthly abundance' – contained four walnuts, a satsuma, a rubber that allegedly smells of grape, a spy pen that writes in invisible ink, and a Slinky, which is already broken from where I tried to skip with it, which you said would happen but that it was my present so I could do what I liked, so I did. Sometimes I wish you'd tell me to stop instead.

But now I am chewing slowly on my third walnut – which I have cracked using a rolling pin, sending shards that will linger for years skittering under kitchen cupboards – and staring out of your bedroom window waiting for something to happen. And I feel a prickle of excitement when I realize that something is the car. Because not only has it stopped outside our house, but someone – a man – has got out and is walking up our path.

'Edie,' I stage-whisper, spitting nut onto the window, 'Edie, there's a man coming.'

'What sort of man?' you reply from the bed, from which you have not moved except to get the jar of peanuts and a vodka and orange.

The man is tall and thin, with the gaunt face of a cadaver. 'An old man. With a hat,' I manage.

'What colour hair?'

It's hard to tell but I manage, 'Darkish and greyish.' And that, it seems, is enough. Because when I turn to you for more guidance – on whether he might knock at the door and if he does should I let him in and do you think it's Father Christmas in a sort of normal suit – you have paled and shrunk somehow, an ink blot seemingly swallowed by pillows.

I look back out of the window. The man is on the doorstep now, his leather-gloved finger poised on the doorbell, a brass button that I love to push for its thrilling click. But it has long since lost its ring and it takes him a minute to realize this and try rapping sharply on the door instead.

'Shall I go?' I ask after the third round of rat-tat-tatting. You shake your head, put your finger to your lips.

But your shushing is in vain. Because the man looks up – by chance or design – and sees me. And I, the guileless child you have encouraged me to be, wave at him.

'Dido?' he shouts up, cupping one hand round his mouth like I've seen in films.

'Yes!' I cup my hand back, both terrified and charmed that this stranger knows me, as if I am a TV star, or, better, baby Jesus. I am so famous my notoriety has spread to towns far and wide.

'Christ, Di,' you say, breaking the bubble. For someone who does not believe in Christmas, I notice Jesus comes into your conversation on a regular basis.

'What?' I ask, turning to you, your practised belligerence now painted across my face, for what can I possibly have done now? This man knows my name so he's clearly not an axe murderer or rapist (the two *Daily Mail* demons who haunt Harry's and my daymares, and populate our games on an increasingly frequent basis). But when our eyes meet there is a moment of something strange, a crackle of meaning, and I feel a scattering of butterflies in my stomach as I realize the obvious.

I've been waiting for him after all. Wondering. Praying to the God you don't believe in and the goddesses you do to send him to me. Only it is fair to say I was expecting someone younger, with more of a beard and a T-shirt and flared jeans instead of a suit.

'It's him. It's—'

But I can't say it. Can't get the word out. Can only stammer a single letter 'D' and let you insinuate the rest.

'Oh, Dido, no.'

You are behind me now, a moth-eaten mohair jumper, maddening as itching powder, barely covering your man's pyjamas. You pull me into its tickling scarlet embrace as you look down at the visitor, and he up at you.

'It's not *your* daddy, Dido.' You pause while the significance of that stress on 'your' sinks in, and then clarify. 'It's mine.'

The day unfolds in such a dizzying cavalcade of new people and new places that I recall only snapshot moments now, and few of them feature you. Though you were there, I know you were – you wouldn't let me go alone, although that was suggested when you refused to get dressed, and then refused to get into the Daimler. But in the end you came, in your pyjamas and jumper with a tutu skirt pulled over the trousers. Though you spent most of the day lying on a bed, or smoking in the bitter cold of the garden in a coat reluctantly borrowed from your mother.

So these are the things you missed out on, and the few you might recall:

* The electric windows in the back of the Daimler that I was allowed to play with all the way from our road to the bottom of the High Street, when Grandpa said they might get stuck and if they were stuck on open we'd all die of exposure.

* The presents: wrapped not clumsily in brown paper
  but neatly, with bright forest scenes and pictures of
  kittens wearing red ribbon and bells, and topped,
  every one, with a nylon chrysanthemum bow. And,
  inside, new gloves, a hat, another recorder – but that
  one wasn't chipped and didn't have a plastic horse
  wedged inside it.

* Two dogs: a red setter called Sasha and a Scottie called
  Othello. Sasha I didn't mind but Othello's breath
  smelled and he rubbed his willy on the carpet, which I
  noted in my head to tell Harry later so we could gasp
  and secretly wonder what that would feel like.

* More food than I had ever seen on one table. And a
  confusing number of knives and forks and plates, all
  of which I used at the wrong time, because I was
  copying you, and you, Uncle Lawrence said, were
  being *deliberately obtuse.*

* The morning room, for its name only. Because until
  then I had assumed rooms were for all times of day
  and anyone. But there, there were rules over when and
  who, and it was usually not me. Which was a shame,
  because the potential for portals and secret passage-
  ways in a house like that was quite enormous.

* The chequered tiles that decorated the hallway floor,
  like a vast chessboard, forcing me to pick a colour and

tread only on that as I made my way to and from the downstairs toilet, which I did several times for the unique experience of weeing in what I now know is a bidet, but which I then assumed was a toilet made especially for children.

* Rotund twin cousins – Hugo and Giles – dressed in matching red-velvet trousers and yellow cable jumpers, so that the overall impression was of four-year-old versions of Tweedledum and Tweedledee. They followed me round the house while I blew tunelessly on my new descant, and I felt for all the world like the Pied Piper, and the power, while it lasted, was intoxicating.

* The curve of the wall in the drawing room, in which I stood, back snug against it, for nearly forty-four minutes, until I was forcibly removed.

* Your bedroom, in which you lay in for hours that day, but you were staring stubbornly at the ceiling through a fug of smoke and incense, and couldn't or wouldn't see what I did: the concert tickets drawing-pinned to a corkboard; the postcard from Manchester – a *wish you were here* from Toni, postmarked July 1970, the month of my birth; a threadbare rabbit; a porcelain doll; a crystal ball with a crack down the middle. And the whole effect I see now is of a shrine, or a room left exactly as it was abandoned, awaiting its occupant's return.

*

I am in there, sitting on the edge of the bed, when he comes – Grandpa. He crouches down so that he is almost as short as me, and hands me a package – beribboned like the others, but this time the paper is flecked with shining silver and I decide the contents must be the prize of all prizes: gold, frankincense and myrrh rolled into one. And when I open it, it is all that and more: a stuffed toy monkey, dressed as a prince.

'He's come all the way from India,' Grandpa tells me. 'To keep an eye on you.'

I look at the monkey. He looks blackly back, above his cold plastic nose and his sewn-on smile. And I decide Grandpa is not lying and this monkey may well have secret powers, ones that must never be questioned or tampered with, or, as with an ancient curse, a terrible fate may befall me.

'What's his name?' I ask.

'Whatever you want,' says Grandpa. 'What do you want to call him?'

I press my palm against the nap of his still-stiff fur, my head wheeling with the possibility, the responsibility of this task.

'What's your name?' I ask eventually.

He pauses. Then, 'Charles,' he says. 'But I'm sure you can do better.'

'What are you doing?'

I look up, startled, as if caught in some act of betrayal, only I have no idea who I am betraying or how. But Grandpa doesn't flinch.

'Giving my granddaughter a gift,' he says, and winks at me.

I wink back, eager in my complicity.

'She's already got the bloody recorder,' you say.

Grandpa's face lines with disapproval. 'There's no need to swear,' he says.

'I'll fucking swear if I fucking like,' you reply. 'I'm not a child any more.'

'Well, Dido is,' he says, nodding at me.

'It's all right,' I say. 'I've heard it all before.'

But these are not magic words, I realize. And this is not about a monkey in any case. This is about a list of things, a scrawled roll call of misdemeanours, minor and major; some I already know of, some I cannot begin to imagine, but the greatest of all right now is Great-Aunt Nina.

'I suppose it was you, wasn't it?' you spit. 'Took the Hockney?'

'Your brother, actually, not that that matters. It wasn't in the will so it seemed only fair.'

'Fair?' You snort with such incredulity it is as if he has just announced he is a wizard, or a woman. 'Fair would have been letting me know she was ill. Letting me know there was a funeral.'

He pauses, as if summoning patience. 'We didn't know where you were,' he says. 'Your mother had to write to the university to get an address for Antonia's parents. It was quite a merry dance letting you know at all. Perhaps if you'd kept in touch . . .'

'Perhaps if you'd given me reason.'

'Is it the money?' he says then. 'Is that what this is about? It's not worth that much, I can assure you. Lawrence had it valued.'

'Unbelievable,' you spit. 'It's not about bloody money. I don't give a shit about money. It's about her.'

Grandpa is fascinatingly silent at this, and I will him to make some enormous revelation – that she was a spy, a princess, a hobbit. But I am to be disappointed.

'You never could stand her, could you?' you continue. 'Embarrassing you. Shaming the family name. Is that why you hated me too? Did you think I'd end up like her? Well, I hope I do. Rather that than any of you bloody lot.'

'I think you've had too much to drink,' Grandpa says then.

I nod sagely at this. Because I've seen you drink a coffee, half of my orange squash, four sticky yellow things in round glasses, and two of something called Port, at which I wondered where Starboard had gone.

'Why did you even bring us here?' you ask. 'To torment me?'

He shakes his head. 'Because the child needs grandparents. She needs a father figure. Your mother thought that and I agreed.'

'She needs neither,' you snap. 'She's fine. We both are.'

'Do you even know where he is?'

'Her father? I'd need to know *who* he was for a start.'

'Good God!' His forehead is damp with sweat now, so that I can see the light bulb reflected in it. 'At least the child seems oblivious,' he adds.

'Oblivious,' I think to myself. 'I am oblivious.' It sounds like a good thing to be – expansive and important.

You grab my hand and pull me to my feet. 'Give it back,' you say. 'The monkey thing. Give it back to him.'

'No,' he says, standing now. 'Keep him, Dido. I insist.' And it is clear that those are his last words on the matter.

And so I do keep him, because I want to please all the new grown-ups today with my manners and obedience and ability to recite the kings and queens in order, which I have learned especially lest such an occasion as this should arise.

'I'll drive you back when you're ready,' he adds. And as he walks back down the landing, his shiny shoes making not a sound on the carpet, as if he is Jesus himself on the water, I clutch the monkey tight to my chest, and chant the names silently in my head, willing him to hear my telepathy.

'God, I can't stand this bloody place,' you say then. 'Wolves in the walls.'

At that my heart leaps and I glance longingly at the fireplace in case that is the passage to France and this Willoughby Chase.

But it isn't. It's not that special; just another old house with skeletons and sour memories.

Grandpa drives us home from Cambridge, the car heaving with his silence and your smoke, windows rolled tight because, as you sarcastically insist, 'God forbid we should die of exposure.' And as we pull into West Road, I know with unwavering conviction that this will be our one and only Henderson-Jones picture-perfect, plucked-from-the-catalogue Christmas. But strangely, I do not feel cheated.

Because someone is watching us from her front garden as she drops a picked-clean turkey carcass in the dustbin. The same someone who sees me wave with my new white gloves in my new red hat with my new fur monkey, face pressed against the glass. Someone who assumed, last night, that I was the poor child who should get the second-hand presents from the church service. Only in less than a day I have all the riches in the kingdom, or at least some new clothes and a recorder. And so as you turn away, lean your head against the window and sigh, I wave and wave and wave like the Queen of Bloody Everything until my hand hurts and we disappear from view and become a snapshot ourselves.

And that is the scene of my greatest victory. Even though I throw up pink sick three times that night from 'all that disgusting meat'; even though I don't get to lord it over my fat cousins ever again; even though we will spend the next Christ knows how many Christmas Days just you and me and my monkey, and a box of Toni's Turkish delight. Because on the following fourth of December, an invitation plops ripely onto our doormat, on cream Basildon Bond and written in blue ink, not biro.

We are cordially invited to spend Christmas Eve 1979 at the Trevelyans'.

Charles and I RSVP in less than two minutes, and in breathless, bright-eyed person.

Because that, I decide, with uncharacteristic clarity and conviction, is what I will name my monkey. A decision that you argue against for at least a week, coming up with an absurd roll call of your own possibilities – Toto, Mr Fidgett, Constantine – as bewilderingly desperate as Rumpelstiltskin. But none of them works, none of them feels right in my mouth, none of them has the precision and importance of 'Charles', and so the name sticks.

And so we slide from one decade to the next, still an awkward pair, an odd couple: the slip of a mother barely more than a teenager herself, and her oblivious child. But I have a monkey by my side and a best friend and a whole surrogate family on the other side of the garden wall, while the squat and its revolving cast, its chaos, its damp that crept into every crack and crevice, are fifty unbreachable miles down the M11. And, with that slip of cream paper, our place in neat, box-hedged, flint-walled Saffron Walden society is assured.

For now.

# Are You There, God?
## It's Me, Margaret

### April 1980

Your feelings on God were clear from our days in the squat; from the joy with which you slammed the door on Jehovah's Witnesses, and scoffed at the faithful in their hats and coats outside the gospel churches on a Sunday morning. 'It's oppression,' you would tell me. 'Opium for the masses.' And though I had little idea what oppression was, still less opium, I would nod, and scurry in your still-dressed-for-bed wake down to the corner shop to buy baked beans and biscuits and litre bottles of cheap wine.

Maybe that's why, later, I tried so hard to find Him. Because, if you won't tell me who my father is (and I have asked, on a regular basis), I will claim this other one whose exile you are so very keen on.

Besides, the Bible has all the best stories, and I write myself into them on a regular basis: brave Esther, bereaved Ruth, the blameless, nameless daughter brought back from the dead; casting you as Eve and Mary Magdalene in turn. But who was our Messiah? Our saviour?

You knew even then. And I, fool for fiction that I am, wrote the part for him.

\*

The Brethren chapel is Harry's idea. She's heard from Tina Fraser who heard from her brother Darren that there's a stereo, a pool table, and a tuck shop with flumps and flying saucers, and mostly it's playing shipwreck, making things with felt, and kumbaya. 'We have to go,' she informs me. 'Everyone else is.'

And so, the irony not lost on me even then, I tell a fat white lie in order to meet God.

'It's a youth club,' I tell you.

'In a church?'

I nod, praying to the God I am hoping to purloin that she will not see through my paper-thin ploy.

'On a Sunday morning?'

'They have a service after but you don't have to do that bit. And Harry's dad will take us and pick us up and I can stay for Sunday lunch. It's lamb.' Which is, of course, the crowning glory of this plan. Because you are back in a vegetarian phase, but, in your determination to allow me freedom over my body (though I note this does not extend to the ear-piercing I so desperately crave, or, in a few months' time, leg-shaving, which I have to do at Harry's house with a borrowed Bic), have told me I am allowed to eat meat at school and at other people's houses if I choose. And I do choose, with regular and wild abandon.

'Well, only if you go straight back to Harry's,' you concede. 'And if they start bloody yapping on about Jesus you can tell them you believe in Karl Marx. Or Sweet Fanny Adams.'

'OK,' I say, another fat fib falling from my lips. Because,

even if I'd known who Karl Marx and Fanny Adams were – definitely if I'd known who they were – I would have told them no such thing. Instead, when the oily-haired preacher, Mr Matlock, asks if I believe in *our Father*, I will nod vigorously, and without guile or guilt. Although this is, really, only a half-truth. Because, while I want so very badly to believe, I am unsure that there is enough evidence to warrant my faith.

'How do we know God exists,' asks Mr Matlock, 'if we can't see him?'

Cherry Palmer sticks her hand up so high and with such need that Harry nudges me and whispers *swot*. I nod, though in my head I'm just cursing her for having the right answer when I have none.

'Because we can *feel* him,' she announces, drawing out the 'e' deliciously, in what I see as a direct taunt at me.

'That's right, Cherry,' says Mr Matlock. 'We can feel him all around us.'

Darren Fraser and Neil Boutwood, who are fourteen, and thus ten per cent barely visible moustache to ninety per cent sex jokes, snicker. But June, Mr Matlock's Purdey-haired assistant, shushes them, and they, in hormonal thrall to her breasts, even encased in a pie-crust-collar shirt and tank top as they are, shush.

Harry, who is herself in thrall to Neil Boutwood, is nudging me again, but for once I am busy with a man of my own: I am trying, desperately, to feel God. But all I can make out is the hard wood of the chair, and the cold metal of its tubular legs, the paint scratched off by bored children and teenagers during decades' worth of amens. At home I try to feel him, too, but all I can sense there is the stiff brush of Charles's fur and crumbs on the carpet. Nor is God in the garden, or the mould-freckled bathroom, or under your bed – my latest hideaway, where I stay sometimes for hours, testing to see how long it takes you to find me, or even look for me. Your record is two hours twenty-two minutes, and that was only because I was jiggling because I needed a wee.

God, it seems, is similarly keen on staying hidden. But still I do not give up on the possibility of faith. I attend Sunday group, and chapel swimming trips and even holiday Bible camp – by which point you've decided God is welcome in the form of free babysitting – until, after three years and fourteen weeks of endeavour, Harry tells me that she's heard from Tina that under the floorboards at the chapel is a massive bath and that, when you're fourteen, they push you under the water in your actual clothes to baptize you. We leave that very day, claiming we have hockey fixtures for the foreseeable future.

But even without the chapel, it is hard to escape God in a small town. In our primary school He is around every linoed corner, stalking the corridors in the form of our Reverend head teacher, Mr Roe, who watches over us, nodding as we offer up our fruit and vegetables and – in my case – a small tin of mandarin segments and a slab of black cherry jelly at the Harvest Festival; and He seeps into lessons when Mrs Drewery tells us we all have two fathers.

'One who made you – your daddy at home – and one in heaven, who watches over you all.'

'Stacey's got three, then, Miss,' Trevor Pledger pipes up.

Mrs Drewery looks unconvinced.

'It's true,' Stacey confirms. 'My dad dad, God, and Barry Benson from the Co-op. He's my stepdad.'

Mrs Drewery's face falls and my stomach sinks as I cross my fingers in the hope that no one points out that I can barely muster one. Harry says nothing, for now. But at Sunday lunch the question she's kept bottled and stoppered finally slips out during dessert.

'Do you really not know?' she asks. 'Who your dad is, I mean.'

'Harriet!' Mrs Trevelyan barks. 'That's not polite at the table.'

I am unsure whether she means the daddy thing, or the fact that Harry is about to eat a spoonful of clotted cream straight from the pot, and I don't like to ignore Harry so I shake my head. 'No. Cross my heart and hope to die. And nor does Edie.' As if the addition of truth may make it more palatable.

It doesn't, and the subject is swiftly segued to the height of Mr Judd's fence (too high, apparently, and the excess shade may wither the floral border). But later, in the den, while Mrs Trevelyan has a lie-down, Harry reprises our curtailed discussion.

We are half watching the motor racing with Mr Trevelyan, but mostly engrossed in a plate of biscuits and glasses of cold milk with Crusha strawberry syrup.

I watch Harry carefully snap the top off a custard cream with her teeth, scrape the filling out, then, glancing at her father, who is usefully immersed in the angry-bee sound of Alain Prost's McLaren, push the biscuit pieces to the bottom of the bin.

'I'd have had them,' says Tom.

'That's dis*gust*ing.'

'Waste not, want not,' says Tom. 'What about the starving children in Cambodia?'

'Send it to them, then,' taunts Harry, picking up another biscuit, and turning to me. 'So who *might* it be, then?'

'Who?'

'Your dad, duh.'

I pretend to rack my brains, as if I am considering a range of possibilities. But really, it comes down to one person: a nameless man from Manchester. His face changes every time I conjure him, though he always has my Toffo hair and pale, paint-spattered skin. Someone from your art course, or the pub, or who shared your house, even.

'God, stop asking,' you beg me on the few occasions I have persisted. 'You don't need him. And he doesn't need you.' But this only makes sense when I change that second need to 'want', and give him a cartoon villain's moustache to twirl and an alter ego like my current favourite television nemesis, the Hooded Claw.

'Maybe it's Prince Charles,' says Harry, shooting, as ever, for the moon. 'Or the man from T. Rex. Or Bryan Ferry.'

'He's got curly hair,' Tom says. 'And anyway, he's dead.'

Harry pulls a face. 'Bryan Ferry is *not* dead.'

'Marc Bolan is, though, you moron.'

'I'm telling Mum you said that,' Harry protests.

'Then I'll show her the biscuits in the bin,' Tom taunts back.

'Would not.'

'Would too.'

'Would not.'

This stalemate – a frequent feature of our Sundays, which, now that Tom is at secondary school, are my only real chance to see him – continues for a few more choruses until Harry gets bored and has a better idea.

'You could get a new one, Di.'

'A new what?' Tom asks.

'Duh. A new dad.'

It's as if, then, the world has turned into one of those clever camera close-ups where the background rushes away, while the face itself appears to get bigger, and more significant. Because this is obvious, of course, yet has not once occurred to me. But now my head is whirling with the possibility of it, with the plethora of potential surrogates. Though not the same ones, it seems, as Harry.

'What about Mr Morris?' she suggests.

'From the healthfood shop?' Tom asks. 'Are you joking?'

'What?' demands Harry, butter not melting. 'Edie's always in there and he gives her free stuff all the time so he *obvi-ously* likes her.'

'But he's got a hunchback,' I say. 'And a wife.' (The order of these obstacles being significant, in my assessment.)

'Fine,' she concedes. 'What about Trudy Hewitt's dad, then? He's not married to Trudy's mum and he looks like Luke Duke.'

'He lives in Harlow,' Tom dismisses, as if it might as well be Mars.

'Well, you come up with someone, then.'

'Michael Nelson fancies her,' Tom admits with a snigger.

I am disgusted. Both by the idea, and at Tom thinking of it, though I try to overcome the latter by telling myself he is only being honest. 'He's twelve,' I say. 'And he still likes Bay City Rollers.'

'It's illegal,' says Harry knowledgeably. 'Not the Bay City Rollers. The being twelve. You both have to be sixteen.'

A fact I do not bother reminding her of in four years' time.

'Mr Hunt?' Tom tries.

'From the swimming pool? Are you mental?'

The list goes on, as they compete to come up with more and more preposterous father figures, from the black-faced coalman to Mr Ginster who has a squint and a spastic boot, until my presence is long forgotten, faded in the face of sibling rivalry.

I pick up my glass of pink milk and sigh.

'Ignore them, Dido,' says Mr Trevelyan.

I look up, startled, having forgotten he was there.

He smiles widely, benevolently. 'Not so bad being an only child after all, eh?'

And then it comes to me that I don't need to look as far as Harlow, nor even the end of the road and Mr Jennings with the bad breath and the Labrador. Because there, in front of me, is the perfect surrogate father.

He is nothing like I imagined, but everything I have ever hoped for: he lets us play on the furniture, and on him too, carting us around as if he is a lolloping shire horse, or a giant climbing his beanstalk, his kidnapped Jack on his back, as we take turns in screaming our way up the stairs. And he's tall, and handsome, of sorts – at least in a clean and tidy television way – and rich, too: he can afford for Mrs Trevelyan to buy Harry an actual snorkel jacket with real rabbit fur on the collar when I have to make do with an anorak off the Saturday market.

There is Angela to contend with, of course. But they argue a lot, I've noticed. And when Tom and Harry are fooling about and she's getting cross and threatening to send everyone upstairs with only cream crackers for tea, he sometimes looks at me and pulls a face. Maybe he's thinking he wishes he were at my house, instead. Even though cream crackers is quite a usual kind of dinner in our kitchen.

And then, in a sudden flush of inspiration and desperation, I do something terrible but which I know will render me the centre of his attention.

I bite hard on my glass. So hard that I break it.

This isn't entirely spontaneous. The urge has been with me ever since I first drank orange squash at their dinner table. Not through daring, but because I dislike intensely the circularity of the glass. The way it fails to lie flat against my teeth and tongue; the tinkle of it when it click-clacks against my incisors. At home we have thick-edged pint glasses hocked from pubs, chipped china mugs, and Tupperware beakers that taint their contents with an undertone of plastic.

But this glass is delicate, and when I rest the rim between

my teeth I press to test for give, checking just how much pressure it would take to crack its clean fragility.

'Don't you ever feel that?' I asked Harry once.

The look she gave me said *no, duh*, though I suspect now she was storing it as a possible habit to acquire, strange and dangerous in one.

In the past, when the urge was overwhelming I always put my glass down to avoid temptation. But today, this is not about my irritation at shape and sound. This is about keeping attention, eliciting love and pity. *His* love and pity. So that he can be my saviour. And instead of stopping myself at the tipping point, I push my teeth together.

In one swift snap the tumbler cracks, a seam opening down its length, a jagged shard breaking off and pushing into my lower palate. The glass still clutched in my hand, I watch as pink milk spills, forming a puddle on my skirt, then an inkblot test spreads out in deeper crimson, from the drip, drip, drip of blood from my mouth.

'Dido?'

I look up at Mr Trevelyan.

'Dido, what have you done?'

Harry and Tom stop their bickering to stare.

I open my mouth and let the glass fall into the lake on my lap, followed by a gob of blood.

At that, the chaos begins. 'Muuuuuum!' yells Harry. 'Come!'

Even in my pain, I am annoyed at her for taking this opportunity away from my possible parent. The man who, right now, is mopping me down with the sports section of his *Times*, whilst holding my head back. I assume, in my naivety, that this is to help me keep the blood in, to somehow slow circulation. But I now wonder if he was only trying to keep it off the carpet.

Mrs Trevelyan arrives, having woken to possibly her worst nightmare: stains on the Axminster; Tom swearing, 'Bloody hell, Dido'; and me at the centre of it all.

'Good God,' she exclaims. 'Why ever have you done that?'

I shrug, unable to speak.

'Harry? Harry!' she snaps at her daughter, now wide-eyed and mute with horror and, I suspect, respect. 'Oh, I give up. David, fetch a sodding cloth.'

I start at this – it is as if God himself has sworn in Jesus' name – and wonder how she even knew that word at all.

But clearly desperate times call for desperate measures, and *sodding* has its desired effect, sending David and his soaked-through newspaper scurrying into the kitchen for a cloth, the Jif and a bowl of warm water, while I am marched, head back, into the bathroom, the door shut and locked behind us to keep an audience out.

'Here.' She hands me a tooth mug full of tap water. 'Rinse your mouth out and spit. In the sink,' she adds, as if my feral tendencies might lead me to choose the floor.

I do as I'm told. I gargle and spit still-minty water until it runs from scarlet through squashed-berry juice to the pale translucence of home-made rosewater. Then, one hand clasped around my chin, one across my nose, she holds my mouth open and peers inside. I smell the citrus scent of hand cream, and feel an unexpected roughness. Not like the scars on yours, from knives carelessly wielded whilst chopping carrots and shouting at Toni, or whoever has slighted you this time, but a more profound ridging, as if her skin is literally thicker, has built layer upon layer to counteract a deeper fragility, forming a carapace that no balm can soften. Hands that are at odds with the life they are leading.

'I can see a cut. But not deep.'

She lets go and washes her hands fastidiously; coats them once again in Atrixo.

'Here.' She hands me another beaker now. This time the liquid is pale urine-yellow with the unmistakable antiseptic tang of TCP. 'Wash your mouth out.'

And I do. I wash my mouth out, but that is all; the bad thoughts I keep to myself.

'You'd better go now,' she says when we get back downstairs to a rapturous Harry and Tom. 'Tell your mother. She can decide if you need to go to the hospital.'

'You can't send her home like that,' Mr Trevelyan protests.

'I'll go!' volunteers Harry.

'Me too,' offers Tom. 'If you want.'

But for once I don't want. What I want is for Mr Trevelyan to pick me up and carry me down the garden, through the gate and over the threshold of our back door, like the knight in shining armour – or corduroy – that I have decided he must be. And to my utter astonishment, and arousing in me a temporary faith in prayer, he does exactly that.

Do you remember him coming in? You were on the chaise, as ever: the papers strewn on the floor, and dotted with the detritus of your Sunday – a wine glass, the ashtray, an empty packet of peanuts and a half-eaten orange.

'Edie?' he asks you.

You look up and see me in his arms, and smile. 'Dido,' you say, holding your arms out. Then, realizing the gravity of my return, 'Did something happen?'

To my delight, Mr Trevelyan keeps hold of me while he tells you. So I get to keep my face half-buried in his jumper; smell the washing powder and faint taint of Hamlet cigar, feel the way his heart beats strong and steady in his chest, a rhythm I repeat in my head until you tell me to stop it, and I realize I've sounded it aloud.

'It was an accident,' he says.

'God, I bloody well hope so,' you say.

'Of course it was,' he says. 'And she's fine, aren't you?'

I open my mouth as he lowers me down to your face for you to check.

'Just exhausted now,' he says, lifting me up again. 'Shall I take her upstairs?'

You nod, astonished, I think.

And so, for the first time in my life, a man carries me up the seventeen stairs and across the four steps of the landing to my bedroom. Though he, of course, being manly, does it in two. Then he lays me down on my bed, and tells me to take it easy, and I nod him a promise, and say another silent prayer.

For a long time I lie there, adrift in the comforting soup that I seem to be swimming in, tasting the faint metal tang on my tongue and listening to the hum of the radio left on in the bathroom, and the soft voices from the living room below.

He is still here.

I can't make out words. But I can hear that you are crying, and I realize that the red-rimmed eyes I saw when I came in must have been from the sting of tears. In my selfishness I imagined you'd been smoking funny cigarettes again, though I couldn't smell the fust of them this time.

I creep out of bed and, keeping to the left of the landing and missing the top step, sneak creakless to where I can spy on you.

Mr Trevelyan is on the sofa, and you – oh happy day! – are in his arms now, your face in the place on his shoulder where mine had lain, soaking salt water into pale-blue lambswool.

'Tell me,' he coaxes.

'I can't,' you say. 'I can't explain it.'

He tells you to try, but instead you get up and pour yourself another glass of wine.

'Want one?' you offer.

*Have one*, I will him.

But he shakes his head and stands. 'I should be getting back. She'll be wondering what's happened to me.'

'Thank you,' you say as you both walk to the door.

'Any time,' he says. 'Though try not to make a habit of crying. It doesn't suit you.'

'Does it anyone?'

He laughs. 'I suppose not, no.'

'I always thought I wore melancholy well.'

'You wear most things well.'

There is silence for a second.

'You should go,' you say.

'I'm going,' he says, his eyes still on you.

*Kiss her*, I say silently, my head filled with *Parent Trap* and too many matinees. *Kiss her!*

But eventually he turns and walks out of the back door, closing it softly behind him. And so my prayer goes unanswered, and my faith dissipates once more.

I wait for seven minutes exactly, then I tiptoe down the rest of the stairs and push in next to you on the sofa.

'He's a nice man,' I hint.

'He is,' you say.

'Like Jesus,' I say.

'Hardly,' you counter. 'For a start, David's real.'

'I wish he was my dad,' I add.

And though you say nothing, in my childish but fertile imagination I see you nod, make a mental note, and begin to plan a story of your own.

# Third Year at
# Malory Towers

## September 1983

Of all the hierarchies I have had to fathom, to find my place in, fumble my way slowly up, there is none so complicated, so all-consuming, as the one that dictates your rank at secondary school.

Forget primary. Primary is a game of kick-can in the park compared to this; its pigtail-pulling and name-calling rounds of *You smell, No, you smell* just line-writing practice for bigger and badder things. Secondary school is where it really starts. A battlefield in ballet flats; an Edith Wharton world in which conspicuousness passes for distinction, and the wrong shoes can buy you a ticket to seven years of, at best, obscurity, and, at worst, daily humiliation. A decision as seemingly simple as where you sit in the canteen can dictate your social ranking for your entire school life. Yes, your stock might rise if you get pixie boots from Chelsea Girl, or persuade your mother to let you get your hair cut into a rat's tail. Or fall if you let David Stainton put his fingers in your knickers at the lower-school disco. But, in short, you are the sum of your dumbest utterings and your most unflattering outfits.

You were right, Edie. It is *Lord of the* bloody *Flies*.

And me? I am Piggy.

Somehow I had managed to negotiate primary in spite of myself. Or maybe because of myself. There, my strangeness was alluring, my ability to swear held in the highest esteem, and my ready access to biscuits hard currency in the playground swapsies regime. For one single packet of pink wafers I managed to acquire a pair of Sindy shoes, seven Panini dinosaur stickers and a Matchbox digger. Besides, when you're eight, nine, ten, who cares where your clothes come from or where *you* come from when there's hopscotch to be played or handstands to be compared for straightness and duration?

But here, in the vast teenage wasteland of legs, lipstick, and Lady Di cuts, nothing about me fits. And while Harry slips seamlessly into her new position as third-prettiest girl in the year – beaten only by Dawn Heaton and Julie Gilhoolie, and only because both of them have older sisters and bigger bras – I am relegated to the bottom of the league. Admittedly, there are others worse off than me: Maria Costain who wears a head brace, Jeanette Pledger who has some kind of skin disorder, and the entire remedial class. But even with Harry to lift my stock, my place is set: I am an oddball, a weirdo, a girl least likely.

And you? You only conspire to make it worse.

I am thirteen and awkward; aware, suddenly, of every cell in my body, every ounce of flesh, every spot, every poorly executed hairdo, or poorly thought-out sock choice. I wear the same market-bought rah-rah skirts as the others, hock the same blue eyeliner from Woolworths on a Saturday, declare I am on the same diet of carrot sticks and orange juice that will not only shed half a stone but make my skin as tanned as George Michael's. Because where you strive to be different, beg the world to see you, acknowledge you, I wish for nothing more than to pass through life unnoticed, unremarked upon. To slip, golem-like, down corridors and into classrooms without comment, to be left alone in the sanctuary of the library so I can indulge my lingering addiction to Blyton's school stories, imagining a world with strict uniform, come-uppance, and, best of all, a swimming pool in the cliffs.

But I am foiled, damned from the start. Because, it seems, if I am not prepared to stand up and be counted, you will do it for me.

In later years I learned to lie, to hide the school's notes about uniform abuses, or class visits from our Conservative MP, or to a pet food factory. Or, better, to forge your spidery signature. But in the first week of my third year, I was still naive enough, green enough, optimistic enough to think you'd scrawl your name on the dotted line and be done. I even pick a moment when you are suitably distracted – a canvas propped on the stand at the attic window, the beginnings of a distorted figure beginning to take form. You are experimenting again, trying to find – or refind – your subject and your medium, but it appears to be neither still life nor oil.

'That's good,' I say, though I have no idea what is good about it, art not being one of my accomplishments, along with geography (for of what interest is an oxbow lake compared to the landscape of Middle Earth?) and netball.

'No, it isn't,' you reply. 'It's sixth-form bollocks. Bloody awful.'

I shrug, my current preferred means of communication. Besides, I am as clueless as ever. Sixth form, to me, is the pinnacle of achievement and kudos, promising a common room, coffee, and the right to call the drama teacher Dave, while demanding nothing in return but sneering condescension and a wardrobe of band T-shirts. I have never heard of it being used as an insult.

You drop your brush, disgusted with yourself, sending a spatter of crow-black across your own bare toes, then light a cigarette, eyeing my galumphing presence – all slumped shoulders and toes turned in – with suspicion. 'What's that you've got there, then?' you ask, nodding at my hands, which are contorted behind my back.

'Nothing,' I say. 'Doesn't matter.'

'Yes, it does.' You hold your hand out, expectant. 'Come on, dish.'

Reluctantly, I do, offering you a crumpled sheet, sticky with KitKat stains. 'It's for electives,' I explain. 'We get to choose two, instead of having just PE.'

You scan the list, looking for my 'X' marked neatly in the boxes.

'Drama.' You nod with approval, and I feel the spring coiled tight in my stomach relax an increment. But too soon. 'Book club? What's that?'

'We . . . read books?'

'But you do that anyway. That's all you bloody do. What about art? Or—' You scan the list again, grasp at something, anything. 'Woodwork. You could do woodwork.'

'No, I couldn't,' I say quietly.

'Why not? It'd be good for you. Create something. You could make a bloody bookcase. Ha!' You laugh at your ingenuity, at the perfection of your plan.

But there's a flaw.

'I'm . . . I'm not allowed,' I say, hoping this explanation will suffice.

You look blankly at me. 'And why might that be? Have you attempted blue murder on Mr Whateverhisnameis?'

I feel the spring tighten. 'No,' I say, stammer. 'It's— it's because— it's because it's for *boys*.'

I say the word with as much trepidation and reverence I would give to *fuck* or *fascist*. The response it elicits is proportionate, and terrifying.

'Well, we'll see about that, won't we?'

To your credit, your opening shot is measured, calm even, by your standards: a letter to Mr Collins, our dough-faced and entirely ineffectual headmaster, fat liver spots dotting his hands and forehead, and his sparse hair like persistent wisps of Caramac. On a single page of violet Basildon Bond, you demand to know why he is *operating a system of effective apartheid*, likening him to P. W. Botha and thus, by insinuation, yourself or me, maybe, to a beleaguered Mandela. You end with a demand that he immediately allow me to take both woodwork and metalwork, along with any other girls who desire it, while also questioning why they would even offer home economics and needlework, which only encourage drudgery and domesticity, two things I suspect Mr Collins lives for.

'But I don't want to do metalwork,' I protest. 'Or wood-work. They're boring. And hard.'

'Not the bloody point,' you reply. 'This isn't about lessons, this is about penises.' It is always about penises. 'Why should you be excluded from anything because you don't have one?'

'They're excluded from needlework,' I remind you.

'Everyone should be excluded from that,' you counter. 'Besides, half the world's haute couture is made by men. Givenchy. Dior . . .' You flap a hand, grasping for another name. 'That bald one. Penises don't stop them sewing. Penises—'

'All right!' I interrupt, desperate for you not to say the 'p' word a single time more. 'Here, I'll post it now.'

'I'm not wasting a stamp on him,' you reply. 'Besides.' You smile. 'You'll probably try to sabotage it.'

'I won't,' I lie.

But you clearly don't believe me, though I have no idea why, because sabotage is your field really, another one I've never shown any talent for.

'No.' Your mind is made up. 'I'll hand it over myself in the morning.'

And with a lick of glue, if not a loving kiss, my fate as lower-school laughing stock is sealed.

Harry, of course, is delighted, ambling easily by your side as she recounts what an 'utter fucker' each of the boys we pass is.

'Adrian Boyle. Utter fucker. He once unclipped my bra through my shirt in chemistry.'

'Utter fucker,' you agree.

Then, a minute later, 'Paul Mull. Utter fucker. He dumped Kirsty Coogan's tampons in the tadpole tank.'

'Utter fucker,' you agree. 'What about him?' You point to Lee Sweet, who is, that very moment, twisting Gary Bower's head in an armlock as he tries to push him into a pile of dog poo.

'Fucker,' Harry proclaims. 'Utter. He once tried to stick his hand up Dido's skirt in assembly.'

'You never told me that,' you complain.

'I forgot,' I lie. And I shoot Harry a look I hope would fell a colossus, but only succeed in making her eyes roll.

'You could report him,' you say. 'Maybe I'll report him.'

As I am about to plead mercy, or pray for the ground to swallow me, Harry finally comes to my rescue. 'You'd have to report the whole school,' she points out.

'True,' Edie says. 'Utter fuckers. I blame penises.'

And with that word ringing in my ears, and dancing on the tongues of several first years milling around the gates still unsure of their place, or route to it, you finally, mercifully, abandon us, abiding as I insist you do by the rule that dictates parents must use the upper staff entrance.

'God, bloody rules, Di,' you say. 'Don't step on the cracks, don't colour outside the lines. You sound like your grand-mother.'

I smart, knowing this is the worst kind of insult possible, but cling still to the idea of boundaries. Because I like rules.

Rules make sense of things. Rules make things safe. Harry's house is full of rules and I know them all, and stick to them, earning if not a gold star, then at least an appreciative smile from Angela.

'You just . . . can't come this way,' I insist.

'Fine,' you relent. 'I'll see you later.' To my joy you don't attempt to hug me, just stalk up the hill in an inky blue-black ballgown, a blot on the landscape, a thorn in my side.

I spend the day on tenterhooks, fidgeting at my desk, my stomach a restless, churning sea, half expecting to be hauled out of chemistry by the lemon-sharp school secretary Miss Loach and frogmarched to the office to explain myself, and you.

But the day passes in its habitual march of clock-tocking, desk-scrawling, toe-tapping tedium, the only nod to your presence on school property an assertion from a fourth year alleged to have a penis as thin as a Peperami, that he would *do you*. To which Harry trumps him with an *in your dreams, with what?*

But this is nothing, child's play, sticks and stones; the real humiliation is being saved for second course.

'What happened?' Harry calls into the kitchen, as we fling ourselves down in the front room, me on an uncomfortable, hair-ridden armchair clearly once reserved for a cat, she on the worn chaise longue – your spot.

'Collins?' You glide in, two glasses of Coke in your hand, complete with cocktail umbrellas. 'Oh, he said no.'

Relief washes through me, a cold shower on your towering inferno of intent. But it is brief, and ill-placed.

'So,' you continue, 'I wrote to the paper instead.'

That ghost of a cat takes hold of my tongue. I am unable to speak.

'Which one?' Harry demands.

'The *Walden Weekly*. Not that they'll publish it. Bunch of bloody fascists. But one has to fight the good fight, regardless. Next stop Fleet Street.'

'Cool,' drawls Harry.

The cat loosens its grip, or I become more determined. 'What, exactly, did you say?'

'Oh, you know.' You wave a hand dismissively. 'Sexist whatever. I can't remember the exact words.'

Please don't have used the 'p' word, I think. Please don't have mentioned me.

But you did, both. I know this because the 'bloody fascists' published the letter in full two days later, though at least with the 'p' word redacted. To protect the sensibilities of its small-minded readers, you say, who are in denial about the existence of many 'p' things, from penises to police brutality. Though perverts, they believe, are lurking around every corner.

'Exceptional,' you declare, dropping the copy amid the clutter of the kitchen table. 'They've even spelled our names right.'

'Exceptional,' I mutter, and stamp up to my bedroom to drown my defeat in Vimto and the vicarious thrill of Tolkien.

But not even Bilbo can protect me from the rounds of abuse and ridicule the orcs fling at me the following morning.

'Lezzer.'

'Commie.'

'I bet she's got a bloody penis.'

'Ignore them,' Harry says. 'They're only saying it because they've got minuscule ones. It's women's rights,' she shouts back at Lee Sweet.

'Since when have you cared about women's rights?' I ask.

'Since forever,' she insists. 'Edie says . . .' But I don't get to hear what you've said because it's blocked out by another shout of 'gayer' from Michael Marshall, a boy whose sole achievement, as far as I can tell, is to have a head the size of a motorbike helmet.

But worse is to come. A week later, after a record eighty-nine complaints, Mr Collins decides that the school must move with the times, nay, pioneer a new attitude, and possession of a penis is no longer allowed to be a deciding factor for participation in any lesson (bar netball, because there is no precedent, still less demand, and basketball is similar enough).

You are victorious, of course: you have stood up, been counted, and any pillorying, any name-calling has been worth it.

Me? I am forced to imagine what wonders will be discussed at book club, what worlds entered, what stories conjured, all the while watching Paul Mull weld his watch to the table, and listening to Adrian Boyle tell mildly racist jokes. That, Edie, is where breaking rules got me. The only girl in a sea of penises, because Harry of course failed to follow her ideals into practice, or failed to secure Angela's signature, and opted instead for home economics.

# What Katy Did

## December 1983

You were already a chameleon when we came to this town, or so the photos tell me, shifting allegiance as swiftly, expertly, and frequently as you changed your sleeping arrangements; sloughing off your self and slipping into a new one whenever you tired of the current incarnation, or when someone else tired of you. But Great-Aunt Nina's wardrobe extended your repertoire in both volume and eccentricity, so that I never knew which Edie was going to emerge each day: Monroe or Dietrich or Daisy Buchanan; happy-go-lucky Edie or the hard-done-by one; the Edie who threw tantrums and toys from her pram, or the one who thought to herself 'what a wonderful world'. But whichever version I got, you pulled it off with aplomb, word-perfect, the lines of fact and fiction blurring seamlessly on your spare frame. Though, disappointingly, you were never the mothers I plucked from the pages of Ransome or Nesbit – stoic, sensible, strict. The kind who never swear, who are always there, and who know what a nutritious meal comprises.

In my head I am other people too: I am all heroes and all villains; I am Dorothy in her red shoes and the Wicked Witch of the West as well; I am Sandra Fayne in *The Swish of the Curtain* and poor, poor Patsy from *Break in the Sun*. But these are flights of fancy, you understand, daydreams. I don't act them out, just mouth their words silently, and imagine having their bravery, their tragedy, their clothes.

Because I appear to lack your sleight of hand, your conjuring tricks, your daring; the real me seems stolid, inescapable, locked as it is in my still-awkward body and bound by my ever-awkward name.

What did you think was going to happen to me with a name like Dido? In Manchester, or in the squat, where everyone was foreshortened, or rechristened, or filthily nicknamed, the name was nothing, light as a puffball, just another off-beat moniker in a roll call that included a Juno, a Psychic Petra, and not one but two Govindas (one born Deborah Hastings, one born Steve).

But here, at an Essex high school in, at best, suburbia, there are four Sharons, five Tracys (and two Traceys and one Tracie), six Emmas, seven Karens and at least seventeen Sarahs.

But there is only one Dido.

Or, more commonly, Dodo. Or sometimes Doodoo, as in dog shit. And, increasingly, as us girls allegedly mature, and boys slip the other way, Dildo. And that is the name that takes, a gift of a shitty stick for our year's most talented bullies: Tracey One and Tracey Two.

'Oi, Dildo,' Tracey One shouts down B corridor at break. 'Up yourself much?'

'Dildo,' snickers Tracey Two. 'Closest you'll get to a cock looking like that.'

I feel humiliation wash through me, feel the prick of tears threatening to fall.

'Ignore them,' Harry says, pushing her arm through mine.

But it's all right for her. She's protected by the invisible force field afforded by thinness, a boob tube, and a 'wing attack' tabard. Plus, she's called Harry, which is not only vaguely normal, but has the added kudos of being unisex.

So is it any surprise that when you dangle the shiny golden bauble of becoming someone else by deed poll, I snatch it?

We're in our kitchen – you, me, and Harry. You, at the centre, holding court; Harry watching and learning, absorbing every inflection, every gesture for the time when she inherits that position, all eyes on her at the corner table in the Duke as she recounts her latest mishap or mistake, or someone else's.

But for now, it is you who are still the star. And you are revelling in it.

'I'm going to do it, girls,' you say.

'Do what?' asks Harry.

'Change my name,' you crow. 'I meant to do it years ago. But I forgot. Or I was broke. Whichever. Now is the time. I've got forms.' You wave a sheaf of official-looking paper at me, already decorated with a mug stain and something that may or may not be lipstick.

'There's one for you too, Di. Otherwise you'll be all alone as a Jones.'

'There are hundreds of Joneses,' I retort for the sake of it. But secretly I am thrilled. Because here it is, the secret potion, the magic key, the fairy godmother I have been waiting for to transform my appearance, my very existence, into something not exotic, not butterfly-like, but ploddingly, forgettably normal.

'Can I be anything?' I ask.

'Absolutely,' you say. 'Except for Jesus. Or Beelzebub, I think.'

'Who'd want to be Beelzebub anyway?' asks Harry.

'Or Jesus?' says Edie.

'The Spanish?' I suggest belligerently.

You roll your eyes and light a cigarette.

'So?' Harry demands. 'What are you going to be?'

You hold up a skinny, silver-ringed hand. 'Not what, who,' you say. 'And I'm still thinking.'

We wait in absurdly respectful silence for what feels like an eternity, at least at that age, until finally you pull a rabbit out of the hat.

'Paradise,' you say. 'Pearl Paradise.'

'Coo-ool. You sound like a stripper,' I hear Harry respond, in what I assume is awe and appreciation.

'Try it,' you say to me. 'Call me Pearl.'

I roll my eyes, practised, perfected. 'Why can't I just call you "Mum"?'

'Because I refuse to be defined by a single act,' you say. 'By one facet that is merely biology rather than achievement.'

As opposed to all your other achievements, I think, uncharitably.

'Though at nine pounds you were a bloody feat, I can tell you.'

'I was six pounds,' says Harry.

'I was premature,' you say. 'A slip of a thing.'

'I wish I could call my mum "Pearl",' Harry bemoans. 'Or even "Angela". "Mum" is so primary, you know?'

But I don't know. And I don't care. Instead I switch off and drift into my own imagination, my refuge, my preferred place to live.

Who do I want to be? I think.

The list of girls I would rather be is almost infinite in its length and impossibility. I have tried out so many, borrowed their outfits, their lines, already conveniently written out for me in black and white.

There was the tragically orphaned Heidi, of course, who got to sleep in a hayloft and spend all day with Peter the goatherd, my first and lasting crush. Then, over the years, and entirely through the pages of books, I worked my way steadily through Velvet Brown from *National Velvet*, who wins and then loses the Grand National disguised as a boy; Laura from *Little House in the Big Woods*, who may have to deal with bears and unbearable winters, but has a pa who can tap maple trees for syrup; George from the *Famous Five* who bests the boys at everything (Anne would seem a more obvious choice, but even aged eight I understood my own limitations); Jo from *Little Women*; any of the five Bastables, or indeed any child with a crowd of rowdy siblings. Given a real choice I might have plumped for the brightest girl with the most glittering future, but really any of them would have done. As long as there was a plentiful supply of lemonade and eggs, a clamour of brothers and sisters – preferably sharing bunk beds – and at least one normal parent, I would have been happy.

But now, for a change, I have set my mind on more tangible beings, made of flesh and blood rather than ink and imagination, but no less unachievable for it. First came Harry. Of course, Harry. Who could not want her legs, her hair, her popularity? But more than that: her house, with proper carpets and built-in everything; her parents (two of them! What luxury!) and her ability to slip into any scene, to play her part at a neighbour's cocktail party, a roller disco, a meeting of the cigarette select behind the bike sheds, as if she were to the manner born.

But then there is Tom.

If I am Harry, I am destined to sisterdom. Yes, I would get the strange balance of bitter brawls and then undying devotion that I watch on a weekly basis and so covet. But that is all I could ever hope for. And by now, I hope for so much more.

You must have known then. Before, even. Because I had hardly had the wit to know what to do with it, still less to hide it.

I love him.

I love his anger at the world and need to change it.

I love that he plays a stumbling, self-taught guitar with the same passion and belief.

I love that he only wears black.

I love that he has defied his mother's impenetrable list of rules and pinned a poster of Che Guevara to his bedroom door and stuck Siouxsie Sioux to his ceiling.

I love the way his school-rule-breaking hair hides his eyes, but if he likes you, he will flick it sideways and reward you with a wink.

I love the thinness of his hips and the fatness of his lips.

I love him so hard and so intensely that sometimes I am struck dumb for words when in his presence and am reduced to a pitiful stammer, or worse, staring.

And so no, I don't want to be Harry any more, I want to be someone who can love him the way I love him.

I want to be Katy Weller.

Katy Weller is fifteen and fit.

At least five foot nine, she is an inch taller than Tom and two more in her black suede stilettos. Her hair defies laws of physics with the aid of gel and spray starch, and she has her right ear pierced not once, not twice, but three times, the latter two both performed in the upper-school toilets with a safety pin, according to Harry. At the Christmas disco she put one hand down the back pocket of his jeans and the other up inside his grandad shirt. Though she has put them in several other places, according to Harry.

So yes, right now, I want to be Katy. Or a Katy at least.

'Katy?' Harry snorts. 'Don't be mental. You can't be Katy.'

'Why not?' I ask. 'It's a normal name.'

'Exactly,' you say. 'Why be Katy when you could be, I don't know, Delilah?'

'Well, if that's the only option I might as well stick to bloody Dido, then,' I snap.

'Don't be like that,' you say. Then, relenting, but not getting it, 'Fine, you can be Katy Paradise.'

'I don't want to be Paradise!' I insist. 'It's not even a name, it's a thing.'

'Well, what do you want to be?'

'What's wrong with Jones?'

'It's still half my father's surname,' you say.

'Fine,' I echo, seeing a glowing, if cruel, opportunity. 'What's *my* father's surname, then?'

You stub the half-smoked cigarette out, snort. 'You always have to bloody spoil things, don't you?'

'Sticks and stones,' I mutter. But you're not listening. Not any more. You are too busy being Pearl in your head. Wondering at how she will mend your messy life. The next day you come home with a new haircut. Pearl's haircut. It is pixie-short so that I can trace the shape of your ears and, under the glow of the Tiffany lamp, see the peach fuzz that coats them.

I love it, but I don't tell you that. I am still too busy hating you.

Harry tells Tom even though I beg her not to.

We're sitting slumped at the kitchen table after a trip to town; her laden with bags, me with a single eyeliner in my back pocket. Tom is leaning over the Dettol-fresh Formica listening to the radio and eating a sandwich, his jeans too low and his T-shirt too tight. I feel myself redden at thoughts I have barely had time to conjure.

And she sees it, and sees her chance. In her favour, she has managed to hold it in for two whole days – a new record – but this is too much to bear: the ridiculousness of it, the audacity.

'Dido's changing her name,' she blurts.

Tom looks up. 'Yeah? What to?'

Harry pauses for effect, assuming I am yet again allowing her the moment of glory, as opposed to being mute in the presence of beauty and humiliation. 'Katy,' she says. 'Can you believe it?'

I feel a rush of nausea and wish I hadn't eaten a Mars bar on the way up the hill. Oh God, I think. What if he works it out? He's bound to work it out. I am an idiot. I am a fucking dildo.

'From the book,' I say quickly, desperately trying to cover my clear-as-day tracks with the equivalent of a light dusting of sand.

But Tom barely looks up from his wodge of cheese and ham.

'What book?' says Harry.

'Duh, *What Katy Did*,' I say, adding a layer of insolence for better disguise.

'Yeah, right,' Harry says. 'Anyway, it's still bor-ing. If I could change my name I'd be Siobhán, or something exotic like that.'

'Siobhán's not exotic,' Tom says, still chewing. 'It's Irish for Joanna.'

113

'How do you even know?'

'I don't know.' He shrugs. 'I just do.'

'God, you always have to bloody argue,' says Harry. The wind knocked from her considerable sails, she snatches two cartons of juice from the fridge. 'Going upstairs,' she says to me. 'Coming?'

I stand, and begin to trudge obediently after her. But he calls out to me.

'Really? Katy?'

I turn back, see him looking up at me from under that fringe.

I nod.

He laughs, a single scoffing sound. 'You're not a Katy.'

My already flushed face burns now with indignation, and I find my faltering voice. 'Why?' I demand. 'Why can't I be Katy? Or . . . or anything I want to bloody be?'

'Hey, chill,' he says. 'I just think . . .' He pauses, trying to find the right words. But what he comes up with is, 'You're Dido. And you always will be.'

And it's as if he's spoken a fairy-tale curse, condemning me, not to sleep for a hundred years, but forever to be a fool. The one who will never quite fit. I feel the familiar prickle of salt water at the corners of my eyes and will my legs to start walking again.

But then he clarifies.

'Anyway, I like it. Dido, I mean. You shouldn't change because of those bitches. Who the fuck wants to be called Tracey?' And with that he takes another bite and turns back to the radio.

When I get home I tear up my application. And you kiss me on the forehead without saying a word.

I never knew what happened to yours. Did you forget to post it? Or lose it, perhaps? Whichever, you are still Edie Jones. And I am Dido.

And you know what? I am glad.

# The Holiday

## August 1984

There were always men.

I'd wake with the strangest sensation that the house was fuller, somehow. So cramped were the rooms, so pressurized the air space between the two of us, that the presence of another body seemed to send the atmosphere into a St Vitus's dance of potential. When I was smaller, I'd creep out of bed and pick my way across the few soundless floorboards, trying to snatch a look at whichever waif or stray you had collected in the Duke of York, or wherever it was that you went when I was safely in bed with a torch and a Judy Blume. I woke up once at half past ten to find the house empty – knew before I'd even sat up in bed that I was alone in the slackness and silence. I should have panicked, gone running to Harry's, or called the police as I'd been taught at school. But instead, ever practical in my over-imagination, I planned my campaign to persuade the Trevelyans to adopt me once your murdered corpse had been discovered down Battleditch Lane. It was to my severe disappointment the next morning to find you alive and well and in bed with a man who smelled of unwashed hair and went by the name of Milko. A year later I saw his face in the *Walden Weekly*, arrested after a drugs raid.

By the time I was thirteen, I just pulled on my clothes, ate cereal standing at the kitchen sink – the better to catch the slopped milk from mouthfuls too big and too rapid – then slunk over to Harry's and got into bed with her.

'Who is it this time?' she would ask, still sleep-drunk.

'Docs,' I would say. 'And a donkey jacket.'

'Miner?'

'Round here?'

'Social worker, then.'

'More likely.'

By the time I'd eaten lunch and watched a video on their newly acquired Betamax, the owner of the lost property would be gone and I would be safe to return without having to endure the undignified 'you could be sisters' routine. Which we both know was never close to being true.

But one or two stuck around longer than a night.

Noel, the self-declared therapist you acquired at a Labour party meeting, whose amateurish attempts to analyse our unfathomable relationship provided, if nothing else, something to laugh about when you had finally had enough of his weak chin, sobriety, and refusal to eat anything from a packet.

Mr Bruce, my barely-out-of-college chemistry teacher, whom you met, predictably, at the one parent–teacher evening we bothered to attend. My mortification was complete the morning I walked in on him masturbating in the shower. I gave up all three sciences as soon as I was allowed, along with any other subject that might take me to the far end of A corridor.

And Jermaine.

Jesus, Jermaine.

You brought him back from Somerset with you, do you remember? That summer. The summer you looked for your muse and found, instead, a man.

Toni rented a farm, or the runt version of one: a run-down, ramshackle long cottage at least four miles from the nearest village and connected neither to mains electricity nor sewerage. The back end of beyond, you call it. 'No hot water and you can't even flush the bloody toilet half the time.'

But you still insist we are going. 'It's going to be an arts commune,' you explain. 'I'll be able to find my mojo again. My muse.'

Back then I believed you. Believed that art, like literature, was channelled from a higher plane, from the gods, into the chosen ones, the golden children, the touched. Now I understand that it is as much craft as art; that the only gods ruling whether we succeed or fail are our own inner demons. There is no mysticism, no witchcraft. Just hard graft and the ability to ignore the devil who whispers in our ear, *you're not good enough*.

But still, I won't let you go.

'I don't *think* so,' I say, trying to affect Harry's sarcasm, which either fails, or falls on selectively deaf ears.

'For the whole of the summer,' you continue. 'There's a river and a goat, I think, or maybe a sheep, though I don't see what the difference is really, and an orchard and, God, Di, this is exactly what we need. To get away from it all, the bloody rat race.' Your words scattergun out and I should know from experience that you're spiralling and that you need this, or pills, perhaps. But I am almost fourteen and so the world revolves around selfish, awkward, desperate me.

'It's hardly Piccadilly Circus round here,' I reply. 'Besides, I need to be in Walden.'

'For what? Bible camp? I thought you'd knocked that bollocks on the head.'

'I have,' I snap. 'It's not that.'

And it's not for swimming club, or a Saturday job, or just to *hang around with bloody Harry* either.

It's for Tom.

But you knew that.


He's broken up with Katy. She let Julian Evans put his hand in her knickers down Bridge End Gardens two weeks ago when Tom was at band practice. Only Julian told Nicky Pakely who told Kerry Spackman who has a mouth bigger and dirtier than the murky Slade, and by last break half the new sixth-form intake know. Harry says she's going to kill her. Or at least write *slut* on her locker in lipstick. I nod, but it's not revenge I'm thinking about. I'm too busy working out how I can be his shoulder to cry on, so that then he can lift his tear-sodden eyes, look into mine, and realize I was The One all along.

By the time Harry's segued into whether or not Tom Cruise has had a nose job, I've planned everything from the soundtrack for our first kiss (The Cure, '10:15 Saturday Night') to his proposal in Paris on my eighteenth birthday. He is, I am convinced, my handsome prince, and this, finally, is his chance to rescue me. Only he hasn't been out of his room in two days, so a declaration of anything is proving hard to elicit. Plus he's playing Pink Floyd on repeat. Harry says if she hears 'Wish You Were Here' one more time she'll end up topping herself before she gets near bloody Katy. So being stuck in a lesbian commune a hundred and something miles away with no television, no radio, and no phone is not really an option. Only according to you I don't have a choice.

'Don't you want to do something . . . important with your life?' you demand.

'Like what?' I sulk. 'And anyway, what have you done?'

'Nothing.' You gesture wildly to indicate the nothingness of your life – our lives. 'That's the point. This is my chance to . . . to live differently.'

'What, like your life here is so normal?'

Then I replay her words, and feel my world tilt off-kilter. 'Hang on. What do you mean *live differently*? Are we moving?'

'No. Maybe. God, I don't know, Di. I just . . . I thought this would work, being here—'

'It *does* work,' I interrupt before she can tell me how bad our lives are. 'I don't want to move. And I don't . . . I don't want to go to bloody Dorset.' I am crying now, the words riding out on the back of fat sobs.

'Somerset. Di—'

'No. I won't go. I can stay with Harry.'

'They're going to Cornwall tomorrow,' you snap, as if that is the end of it. It isn't.

'So I'll go with them.'

You snort. 'You'd rather spend three weeks with Mrs bloody J-cloth-welded-to-her-right-hand?'

'Yes.'

'No,' you retort, a codicil to my full stop. 'You spend too much time with them as it is. It's unhealthy.'

'And you're what, exactly? The font of all things good?'

You pick up a pile of books, then slam them down again, unsure what they are or where they go. 'You're not going with them, and that's that.'

I almost want to cheer: after years of waiting, wanting, willing it, you sound like an actual mother. But that would be conceding at this point.

'I'll stay here, then. You're always saying women should be able to fend for themselves.' One point to me, I think, foolishly, as I fling feminism back in your face.

But I am new to mother–daughter brawling, and unaware that you will always, always wield the trump card.

'You're not a bloody woman,' you retort. 'You're a child.'

The word stings, as if you've slapped me hard across the face with it, for there is no worse insult, at least this year, other than being called a 'slag' or a 'lezzer'. 'Well, thank you for making that clear,' I hurl in desperation. And with my parting shot a pigeon pea to your silver bullet, I exit stage left, slamming the door like I've watched Harry do. But I forget it's on the latch so, instead of a satisfying crack, it just swings feebly back open letting in next door's cat, which I'm sure at the time I thought was a metaphor for my entire existence.

'We're back in three weeks,' Harry says. 'Then you can just come and stay with us.'

We're lying on sun loungers, dark glasses on, 'Shine On You Crazy Diamond' drifting into the garden from Tom's still-battened-down bedroom.

I attempt to feign nonchalance, and fail spectacularly. 'Is he . . . Tom, I mean, going with you?'

'He reckons not, but good luck with that.'

In the space of seconds I imagine an entire novella in which we both stay behind, write groundbreaking poetry, and then he invites me to the sixth-form disco.

'He's sixteen,' I contend. 'Legally he can do what he wants.'

'Have you met my mother? She'd have a total spaz-out.'

'God, I totally know how he feels.'

Harry sits up and lifts her Ray-Bans, all the better to throw me her 'Are you fucking kidding?' look. 'You have no idea.'

'I . . .' But I don't bother finishing that sentence, because I don't know where it's going and I'm pretty sure Harry's not listening any more, anyway.

If he doesn't go, I tell myself, then I won't.

The next morning I watch from my window as Mr Trevelyan loads the Volvo up with suitcases, a striped wind-break, and two members of his family. I hold my breath as Harry, Walkman already on, pulls her door shut.

'Drive,' I plead, 'drive.'

But as the car coughs thrillingly into life, threatening imminent exit, the front door opens and a scowling Tom slopes barefoot across the pea gravel and slumps in his place on the back seat.

Two days after that, we leave for Somerset.

The commune is, as predicted, purgatory, and the journey nothing less than a ferry ride across the Styx.

We have a car now: a juddering shell of a Citroën 2CV which you, in your ongoing quest to upset the neighbours, christen Elizabeth Taylor. When we venture into the Cromwell estate to collect it off a man called Dwayne, I am stunned. Not just at its awfulness, but at the very fact you can drive at all. There has been no evidence of this feat until now; you've always scrounged lifts from Toni, from Chinese Clive, increasingly from David. I had just assumed this was a necessity, not bloody-mindedness or poverty.

The car costs £200. It is barely worth it. Seemingly held together with nothing more than duct tape and faith, it stalls at every given opportunity, and smells faintly of cat pee and wet dog – an aroma that will only intensify as we add apple cores, chocolate wrappers, and the butts of your endless roll-ups to the already overflowing ashtray. Something rattles; no, *everything* rattles, and there is a Crystal Gayle tape jammed in the cassette player, so that every journey is accompanied by an ill-fitting easy-listening soundtrack. As if Elton John has been erroneously hired to score a Mike Leigh movie.

Years later, when I am clearing it out before it's towed to

its burial, I will find treasure: a spare key taped to the sun visor, four Murray Mints in the glove compartment, a man's grey leather glove pushed or kicked beneath the driver's seat. But for now it is the scene not of joy or discovery, but of resentment, regret and petty one-upmanship. And we've not even made it past Sawbridgeworth.

'Christ, Di. Anyone would think I was taking you to bloody borstal.'

'You might as well be.'

You push the heel of your hand into one eye, a gesture I'm unconvinced improves your already questionable concentration on the road. 'Fine. If you don't like it, we won't stay. Happy now?'

'I won't like it,' I say.

'You might. You don't know until you try. It's like blue cheese.'

It's not like blue cheese, I think, cursing myself for my U-turn from hatred to half a slab of Stilton in one afternoon. 'I won't,' I insist.

And for once, I am right.

I hate it.


It rains. God, how it rains. And so day after day, in my cold, dripping box of a bedroom, I pull down my hat and seethe into my WH Smith notebook, listing everything that is wrong with my life, which apparently runs to seventeen pages. In no particular order, these are the house's worst points:

1. There are three other women here not including us
   and Toni: Petra and Marta, who share the same lank
   hair, and bed, and who row frequently and violently,
   and Toni's girlfriend, Susan, an artist with a shaved
   head and a tobacco-furred tongue. At various points
   one or all of you will wander around naked in spite
   of the cold, and I find myself imagining glistening
   patches of secretion on the kitchen chairs, and take to
   wiping them down with toilet roll before I sit.

2. You told me the house was next to a wood and in my
   innocence and optimism, even in the face of potential
   devastation, I imagined bluebirds and green clearings,
   and myself an overgrown Little Red Riding Hood
   skipping through it all. But this is no enchanted forest.
   This is mud and nettles and the rotting corpse of that
   mythical sheep. Susan says it's art and takes photographs
   of its empty eye sockets and half-eaten lips while I
   retreat, gagging, to the house and vow to become
   vegetarian, a vow I keep for twenty-three days.

3. Nowhere amongst my fourteenth birthday gifts is the
   Walkman I requested to better lock myself in my
   melancholy. Instead I am given a ceramic pendant, a
   copy of *The Group*, and a rape alarm. The pendant
   was handmade by Marta and is shaped like a vulva.
   I know for a fact that it is a self-portrait, and redden
   with such intensity when I unwrap it you offer me a
   glass of water.

4. The nearest village is four miles away, the nearest shop and phone box another three beyond that. And the only way of getting to either of them is in the 2CV or Toni's van, both of which require an adult chauffeur and thus supervision. Twice I have braved it to call Harry's number in Cornwall, but the phone rings into empty rooms, and on the way home Toni tells me I should stop chasing *that boy* because I deserve better. I am mortified that she knows, and stick another invisible pin into my imaginary mannequin of you.

It is everything I remember about the squat, only with the volume amplified and in inglorious technicolor. Night after night of talk about taking a stand, changing the world, and yet you lie in bed, all of you, till gone midday, while I roam the house in two pairs of socks, picking up discarded mugs and cigarette ends.

But one vital ingredient is missing, one that you, I know, cannot do without: men.

Toni says you should stop disrespecting your vagina. You say it's your body and you can do with it what you bloody well want because it's the 1980s not the 1880s, but even so, it's a relief not to have them around because God knows they only ruin everything. And Marta, Petra and Susan nod sagely, like they've been there before. But Toni knows, and I know, and you know, that it is only a matter of time.

And three days later you prove us right.

*

It's my fault. Or so I thought back then. I am desperate to leave, but you are just finding yourself, you claim. Though where you are in the series of grim, outsized canvases, daubed in Rothko-esque gradations of red – for menstrual blood – I am yet to fathom.

'You can do this at home,' I point out. Then add belligerently, stupidly, 'It's not like you've got anything else to do.'

'I've got you, haven't I? What, you think that's not a full-time bloody occupation?'

'You don't even make my lunch.'

You flap a hand, dismiss it. 'Because you told me not to.'

'Because no one else has bloody hummus sandwiches. It's disgusting.'

'It's good for you.'

'What is, hummus?'

'This!'

You have handed victory to me on a plate, and I smile triumphantly before presenting my straight flush. 'If you cared about what's good for me you'd take me home.'

You pause, momentarily thrown but not fallen, then deliver an ace. 'If you gave a shit about me, you'd stay. It's your sodding fault I never finished art college in the first place.'

This is a slap, stunning me into a stomach-churning silence. Your fingers rest on your lips, as if checking that you really did let those words out. But you did, there is no taking them back, no swallowing them down along with your pride. No taking back the sucker punch I'm about to throw either.

'Well, I wish you'd never bloody had me.'

And, riotous applause ringing in my ears, I exit stage left, slam the door and lock myself in my room.

It's Toni who comes to me, an hour later.

'She didn't mean it,' she insists. 'You're the making of her. She knows that.'

I pull a face, an I-don't-believe-you.

'Look,' Toni continues, 'the only person stopping Edie paint is Edie. Self-sabotage, darling. She's too bloody scared to find out she's shit.'

'She isn't shit,' I retort, inexplicably, instinctively leaping to your defence.

'I know that.' Toni pushes strands of snot- and salt-soaked hair out of my eyes. 'But Edie doesn't.'

I consider this possibility. That you don't believe you're the gilded, glittered star you appear to be. It seems implausible, but Toni doesn't lie, never has.

'I don't wish she'd never had me.'

'Then tell her. Tell her that she's brilliant. And say you're sorry. And then let her say sorry as well. And if she doesn't, you send her to me.'

I half laugh, half sob.

'It's all right,' she says. 'It's going to be all right. Look, she's gone to the village for milk. She'll only be half an hour. Why don't you wait at the top of the lane for her?'

And so I do. I haul myself out of the damp, narrow bed, pull on a jumper and mud-clogged boots, and trudge up the lane to make it up with you, to tell you I'm sorry. To tell you you are beautiful, brilliant, born to be an artist.

To tell you I love you.

But these words will be left unspoken. Because seven hours later you come back milkless, car-less, drunk, and in the arms of a man called Jermaine. He is half limp, half swagger and he wears a hat with a pheasant's feather in the band. I hate him immediately.

'He saved me,' you slur as you stagger into the sitting room.

'From what?' demands Toni, prising you off his shoulder and onto hers. 'Dragons? Bloody hell, Edie. We were worried.'

'Did you send a search party?' you ask, hopeful.

Toni stays sullenly silent but the answer is yes. We all went out in the van to look for you. But there was no sign of the car, and the woman who runs the shop said she hadn't seen you since you bought a bottle of vodka, a lighter and a packet of French Fancies two days ago.

'I went on an adventure,' you continue. 'To find the big town. But Betty died.'

'Who's Betty?' Marta asks worriedly and in a thick accent.

You laugh, and manage to stumble even while standing still. Toni hauls you up, then lowers you onto the sofa. 'Elizabeth Taylor,' you giggle. 'The car!'

'Did he get you drunk?' Toni demands.

'No,' says the man, who is still, inevitably, here. 'She managed that herself. And it's Jermaine, thanks.'

'Yeah, well you can go now, Jermaine,' Toni tells him.

But Jermaine has other ideas. 'I'll see you, Edie. Bring back the car for you when it's fixed?'

'Thank you, Lancelot,' you say.

129

'Jermaine,' he says again. But he's smiling. And my stomach sinks because I know then that it is too late and he has already fallen down the rabbit hole of you.

I am right. The next day he turns up in a miraculously fixed Betty, with a four-pack on the front seat and a blanket in the back. You drive to the stone circle, to feel the spirits, you say. But when you get back your cardigan is covered in grass and your neck bruised, the same telltale purple oval I have seen Tina Fraser showing off in the lower-school toilets.

And it's not just me who sees it.

That night you and Toni row. I listen through the floorboards as she tells you the house is a safe space, and that men are barred, you know that. You say not every man is a rapist just because they own a dick. Toni says something after that and then there is a silence so thick and weighted I could spoon it like soup. Followed, a minute later, by the sound of a door slamming, then the reluctant choking and gagging of Betty being pressed into service, the slip of tyres on wet soil. And I pull the pillow over my head and beg for the ground to swallow me or the world to end.

Both fail to oblige, but I wake the next day to you flinging the few clothes I've bothered to remove back into my green suitcase.

'Edie?' I ask. 'What's the matter?'

'Di!'

You seem delighted, and, I assume, high.

'What's the matter?' I ask.

'Nothing,' you insist. 'Why should anything be the matter?'

'I . . . what are you doing?'

'What does it look like? Packing. You wanted to leave, we're leaving.'

I know then, even though we have lasted less than two weeks, that I haven't won. I know this is down to your desire, not my desperation, but I am too relieved to care, and I pull back the duvet, slide onto my knees and push my last remaining pairs of knickers into the peach satin pocket. In less than five minutes I am standing next to the car, waiting for you to say your goodbyes.

But you are sober, and stubborn, and so is Toni, and so it's me she turns to.

'Dido.' Toni puts a slender hand on my shoulder. 'Do you really want to go?'

At her concern, I feel myself tremble, feel tears begin their ascent. I am not used to being defiant; that is your role, Harry's role. On me it is a borrowed dress, one I can barely carry off. But I am tired, I am fourteen, and I am living in the middle of nowhere with four lesbians and a slut of a mother. 'Yes,' I say. 'Sorry.'

She hugs me then, and I stand, arms dangling awkwardly with my suitcase in one hand and my book in the other.

'Get in, then,' you say.

I put my suitcase in the boot, and climb wordlessly into the passenger seat.

You look at me as if I've sprouted horns or trodden in dog shit. 'What are you doing?'

'What?' I don't understand.

'In the back,' you say.

131

I look over my shoulder at the can-and-crisp-packet-littered rear seats.

'Go on,' you say. 'Unless you want to sit on Jermaine's lap.'

And then I realize that not only have I not won the battle, I have lost a war I didn't even know I was fighting.

As the three of us drive away from the house, and out of Toni's life for another three years, Crystal Gayle soundtracks our departure. 'Don't it make my brown eyes blue,' she laments.

Jermaine hits the cassette player and the tape flies out.

'See,' you say. 'I told you he'd be useful.'

I sigh, and slump back in my seat, then mentally click the heels of my red wellies three times, and say a silent 'There's no place like home.'

And when we finally get there, after two breakdowns, and an argument over a pasty at a service station that I still don't understand, I discover I am right.

He isn't broad, or even that tall, and yet he fills our house as if there are three of him. His shoes clutter floors and doorways so that I trip and stumble my way through the downstairs; he eats the bread, the cheese, my biscuits, a packet at a time, and forgets to buy more; he leaves long, curly pubic hairs lying on the tiles of the bathroom floor and stuck to the wall and, when he bothers to shave his beard, the sink is flecked and speckled with foam and clippings. And then there's the sex.

Oh, God, the sex.

He makes a grunting noise like a pig or a dog, and then, at the end, a howl, as if he is mortally wounded, and my imagination conjures up a Hieronymus Bosch scene of medieval torture crossed with the tattered copy of *Club* Harry and I once found in a hedge by the old railway track: all contorted faces and hairless, airbrushed parts.

I count down the days until Harry gets back so I can tell her how horrible it is.

But when, after eight days and four hours, they do pull up, I discover it's me who is out of touch.

Harry has met a boy – a waiter at the beach cafe in Rock – and is full of it. They kissed on the ferry back from Padstow, and promised to meet again next summer. But it's not the romance that's thrilling her, but what happened behind the bins when his shift finished.

'And then,' she says, eyes wide, 'he put his finger right inside me.'

I think of Jermaine's ridged knuckles and dirty fingernails and shudder. 'Did it hurt?'

'No. God, Di, why would it hurt?'

'I don't know.'

'It's like a tampon. Only nice. You should try it.'

And then it's not Jermaine I see but Tom. His hand sliding down under the once-white cotton of my knickers, his finger pushing through the hair (I was, thankfully I now decide, not spared this addition) and finding its target.

I feel myself contract down there, feel myself flush with embarrassment at what I want, despite my disgust.

But Harry hasn't noticed. She's got another secret to tell, and this one isn't about her. Hers, it seems, is just the appetizer.

'Tom did it.'

I feel my want slip-slide away as swiftly as it took hold, and fear take its place. 'Did what?' I ask, stupidly, pointlessly.

'Duh, *it*. You know. All the way. God, Di, you're so frigid.'

'I . . .' But there's no point defending myself. So instead I ask the one question I do not want an answer to. 'Who with?'

'Some girl called Marina,' Harry replies. 'Lives in Hampstead. Total rich bitch.'

'Oh,' I say, struck dumb with this information.

But really, what else is there to say? I missed my chance. If I'd been there, I could have stopped him. I might, just might, have made him fall for me instead. And now I will never be his first, and maybe not his anything. I forget the fact that I am far from being ready for sex, forget that his feelings for me are far from apparent, let alone confirmed. Instead I seethe. For days I suffer, nursing this betrayal – by you, not him – like a wound. But instead of letting it heal, I poke at it, pick at the edges whenever it begins to scab over. So that by the time you finally ask me what's wrong, my loathing is complete and my decrial Oscar-worthy. But do I voice a word of it?

'Nothing,' I yell. 'Just, God, shut up!'

'Hormones,' Jermaine says. 'Bloody mental, both of you.'

And God knows he was wrong about most things – that hair didn't need washing; that best-before dates were all a load of bollocks; that women were conditioned to clean things, it was scientifically proven (the final nail in his coffin, though it took more than two years to hammer that one in) – but about me and you, Edie?

I think he was probably right.

# The Outsiders

## July 1985

As we grow up and then older we each follow our own particular, meandering path. We can tell ourselves that we are all connected, from corner-huddled cliques to whole classrooms of kindred spirits, but the truth is we come together only briefly, then scatter like crows into our little lives again. But there are moments in time when our messy topography collapses in on itself, distance dissipates, and we all stand and face the same way, experiencing the same profound shock or joy or fear. So that later, when asked, every one of us will know where we were and what we were doing when Mandela was released, when John Peel died, when the Twin Towers came down.

The thirteenth of July 1985. That day is etched so clearly in my mind, in such minute detail, that I can pause and rewind the memory time after time and the tape will never stretch or snap; it will always show me the same perfect replay.

It was the day that rocked the world. Or so the tag line went. And, oh, how mine rocked.

*

I could have watched it at ours, should have done. Except that fate, in the shape of Jermaine, had decided two days before that TV was doing something strange to his brain – addling it, contorting it so that time and space refused to obey the laws of physics – and had unplugged it, along with the microwave and the lava lamp. We both knew it was the rank dope he smoked from the moment he stumbled out of bed to the point he fell asleep on the sofa. But you, two weeks into the latest in a string of part-time and half-hearted jobs, said nothing and I, disgusted by your weakness and the mere fact of his existence, just skulked in my room and turned up the radio, telling myself that books and music were all that mattered anyway.

'But what are you going to do on Saturday?' Harry asks.

We are walking up the hill from school, skirts rolled up, shirts untucked; perspiration glowing on her fake-bronzed forehead, sweat dripping unpleasantly down my pale neck, down the backs of my thighs, and pooling in the crevice between my too-heavy breasts.

'For what?'

She looks at me as if I am retarded, or deliberately obtuse, or both. 'Duh, Live Aid.'

I shrug. Her concern for me, though genuine, is edged with her own complicated reasoning. Because thanks to her recent but repeated fumblings with seventeen-year-old Don Juan Gary Bennett, Harry has been upgraded in the upper-school stock market from outer circle to inner-clique mafia, which comes not only with canteen seating privileges and entrance to the sixth-form common room, but also, it seems, a golden ticket to Wembley courtesy of Gary's dad who does something at Sony. He couldn't get me one, Harry said. I told her I didn't fancy it anyway. Which was as fat a lie as the nonchalance I'm currently trying to conjure.

'Listen on the radio, I suppose.'

But she's not letting that go. 'You could watch it at ours,' she offers. 'Mum wouldn't mind.'

I pretend to consider it. 'Maybe,' I say. 'But wouldn't that be weird?'

'Why? Tom's going to be there. I'm recording it and he's going to change tapes and stuff.'

It becomes clear. This offer is all about her need, not mine; I have to watch so I can look for her in the crowd because, in some future echo of iPhone Insta-culture, if no one sees her doing it, it might as well never have happened. But my tracing-paper-thin veil of couldn't-give-a is falling fast as I struggle against the heat and this new nugget of Tom-based knowledge. 'What about Caroline?' I ask.

'Athletics,' she says. 'Sheffield. Two-day thing.'

The relief that washes over me is followed by a more familiar surge of self-loathing. Caroline is the new Katy. But unlike her predecessor, whose tendency to allow unfettered access to her skimpy knickers rendered her ultimately disposable, Caroline is self-restraint and ambition personified: Deputy Head Girl, joint school Labour Society chair, and county long jump champion. Worse, she is five foot seven and weighs eight and a half stone, which is several inches more and several pounds fewer than me. But on the other hand she's at least two hundred miles away, all night, and, according to official records, she's never gone beyond third base. Not that I've even been to second, unless you count Ian Lambert pretending my left breast was a car horn and honking it twice during a lull in chemistry. And that was through three layers of clothing and more painful and embarrassing than thrilling. And not that Tom would even go to first with me. But I can wait, I tell myself. I am playing a long game.

'God, Di, come on. It's not like I've asked if you want to sit my maths O level for me, which I totally might, apparently Paul Burrell did it last year for Kev Thingy and no one even knew.'

'You know.'

'Not the point. Anyway, do you want to come over or not?'

I picture us then. Me and him in the den, lolling on beanbags, curtains drawn against the heat and light of the afternoon, our fingers brushing over a bowl of Twiglets.

'Yes, I . . .' The word escapes my lips before I have time to rein it in, to even pretend to consider my options.

'Cool. I'll say you'll be over by half eleven or something.'

'Half eleven?'

I get the idiot child look again. 'It starts at twelve. And you don't want to miss any of it, do you?'

Any of Tom, I think. The concert at Wembley goes on until ten at night; I know because Harry's not due back until one or two in the morning. And even after that there's Philadelphia. They're, what? Six hours behind? I am being offered more than twelve hours alone in a darkened room with Tom. No, I don't want to miss a single minute.

'Sure,' I say. 'Thanks.'

As we trudge our way up Borough Lane, my swollen feet begin to blister in my battered sandals, and the sun pinks the backs of my arms, as if letting out an I-told-you-so sigh that I will be sore and sorry tomorrow, but tomorrow doesn't matter. Right now my strange small world feels splendid in its perfection, and by Saturday my sunburn will be yesterday's news, faded into a fresh constellation of freckles, which I imagine him tracing with his fingertips, if not tongue.

But if life is never how it appears in books, it resembles still less the complicated scenarios I come up with in my vivid nearly-fifteen-year-old imagination. By Saturday, my arms and nose are still livid from the lack of sun cream and abundance of time spent trolling around the field while Harry watches Gary play cricket. ('If you got married, and had a kid, you could name it Barry,' I'd said. 'Or Larry.' 'Oh, fuck off,' she'd replied, unwrapping a stick of Doublemint to cover the cigarette she'd just bummed off Tina over at the far edge of the fencing. 'I'm not going to marry him. He wants to work in Harlow, for God's sake. I mean, I'd rather die.' And all the while I was trying to yank down my shirt sleeves to cover the ever-reddening skin, and avoid having 'Red Hot' added to the 'Dildo' that still echoed behind me down corridors.)

Now, in the dark of the den, the scarlet has softened, aided by a layer of hastily bought after-sun, but this has left a strange, silvery patina, so that my skin glows more ghost-like than ever. Over the top I am wearing Tom's cast-off Led Zeppelin T-shirt and a floor-length black skirt that Harry has assured me is flattering, but which contrives to give me the overall appearance of a half-hearted goth. But if I am failing to look the part, I am succeeding at least in the role of girl-who-knows-about-music, a part I have studied for at length, aided, incredibly, by Jermaine's eclectic vinyl collection and outlandish opinions. So that, instead of dismissing the Four Tops as irrelevant, or music for leftover casuals in their Kappa and Nike, I can confidently suggest that no other city has successfully crafted such a unique sound as Detroit.

'God, yeah.' Tom swigs from a bottle of by-now warm and flat Coke, that I am almost sure is a third spitback, but am totally sure I would swallow if given the chance. 'Although Nashville might argue.'

'Yeah, totally,' I agree, with no clue as to what I am agreeing to as, uselessly, Jermaine has not seen fit to include any country and western in his catalogue (because, as he will tell me later, it's music for *racist retards*, which even at the time I suspect of inaccuracy).

We agree too on the ubiquity of Sade and her easy-listening lounge sound, although her signature look we both admire for its simplicity and authenticity. Sting is dismissed as try-hard and his decision to disband the Police as premature; Bryan Ferry is slick, a dandy, a man ahead of his time, whose lyrics are nothing less than poetry, whose look exceeds Byron; Howard Jones a one-hit wonder whom no one will have heard of in five years' time.

And then there is U2.

It's not so much that I love U2 as that I want to be plucked from the crowd by Bono; pulled up on stage from the crush of bodies, rescued by the knight in shining black leather. I can barely breathe as I watch. There is not an atom of my body that doesn't wish that that girl from the front row were me; that doesn't understand how that must feel – the suburban nobody becoming not just somebody but world famous, beamed by satellite into thousands, no, millions of homes. That doesn't know how seething Harry will be right now: not only has she not featured on screen for a single second, but some dull brunette is up there, dancing, and she is lost in a sea of sweating faces. But that sea – that sea is the point. Because right now I feel part of something big. Bigger than this small town, this small life.

This is it. This is my Kennedy moment. Years later I will feel the same overwhelming optimism when, in February 1990, in the passenger seat of a clapped-out Nissan halfway up the A14, I hear that that bogeyman of our youth F. W. de Klerk is releasing all non-violent political prisoners, including Nelson Mandela. I will feel it again in November 1991 in a crowd of strangers on a southbound platform at Tottenham Court Road, when London Underground shares the news via the arrival boards that Terry Waite has been released. In May 1997, so full of belief will I be at the election of Labour's great hope Tony Blair that I will embrace, if not the devil himself, then his great pretender.

But this, this is my first. And in this moment I believe that anything is possible. So rose-tinted is my vision, so open my heart, that I turn to him, expectant, my face tilted up in readiness for the kiss that is coming.

He turns and looks at me long and hard.

'Bono's a dick,' he says and takes another handful of Wotsits.

It is late now, the curtain closed on Wembley, the crowd emptying out to Tube stations and waiting cars. The TV is still on, though, Duran Duran dancing on the screen down the feed from Philadelphia, but the atmosphere has changed, slipped from elation and expectation to, in Tom's case, disillusion, and in mine, the desperation that dull girls feel at the end of the disco when they are still, awkwardly, dancing alone. We are just inches away from each other, slumped on the beanbags, but almost flat now, as if we are in bed, a closeness so habitual when we were small that Mrs Trevelyan doesn't even bother to bestow a second glance on us when she comes in with ten o'clock hot chocolate. But we have not lain like this for years now, and never without Harry. And she is not due back for at least another hour; currently, I estimate, dawdling around the North Circular, snogging on the back seat of Mr Bennett's Audi, blissfully unaware that there has not been a single shot of her on screen all day.

'Do you want any more Twiglets?' I offer.

As pick-up lines go, it ranks amongst the worst. But, I reason, if he says yes, I can reach right over him to put the bowl down on his side of our makeshift make-out palace. And then, when he smells the Impulse I have sprayed liberally not just under my arms but over every inch of perspiring flesh, when he feels my not-insubstantial breasts brush his chest, he will be unable to resist me; will pull me into an embrace that will be at once tender and swollen with lust.

But my cue is not just rebuffed, but seemingly ignored entirely; met with silence broken only by his slow, heavy breathing and Simon Le Bon singing blue silver.

'Tom?'

He shifts his body, rolls a few inches onto his right-hand side, rolls towards me. My heartbeat speeds, racing ahead of me, of the music, to a near-vibration. Is he? Does he?

But as a sudden flash of stage lighting in Philly bathes le Bon in sodium glory, it reveals a less than potent scene in Essex. Tom hasn't turned to me for either a true love's kiss or Twiglets. Tom, it seems, has not even heard the question. Because Tom is fast asleep.

My stomach slops around, a soup of junk food and adren-aline, my heart still humming. I know what I should do, what good girls do, and I am a good girl, after all. I should get up now. I should turn off the television, tread softly along the cream carpet, then skip across the dew-damp lawn and through the gate back to my world.

Instead I have a reckless thought: a thrilling 'what if?'.

What if I were to kiss him? Right now, while he was asleep? What is the worst that could happen? He could wake and be horrified. But I could say I slipped trying to get the Tizer. On the other hand he could wake and, though momen-tarily surprised, be at the mercy of his own desire and pull me closer to him, on top of him, like Stewpot did to Claire in *Grange Hill* that time.

And so, in my second most daring act of bravery to date,

I lean towards him, until I can feel the rise and fall of his breath on my lips, smell the faint tang of artificial cheese powder, and I kiss him.

For a single exquisite second our lips touch, and then, panicked, I pull away, scared my prince will turn into a frog and lollop off.

But he doesn't. He doesn't recoil. He doesn't even open his eyes.

He is surrendered only to sleep.

Yet I am not disappointed. Because somehow, inexplicably, I have won. I have got away with a taste of ecstasy without being caught, humiliated, told I am not that sort of girl and he is not the sort of boy I will ever, ever have. That kiss, for me, is nothing less than a seal of possibility, a promise that one day, maybe, he will feel it lingering on his lips and will want to return it.

But for now, I can act as if nothing has happened. I can fall asleep next to this wondrous boy – a boy I have seen naked in a paddling pool, seen peeing in the woods, seen masturbating in the fading perfection of the Wendy house – without beating the butterfly wings that will skitter chaos across an invisible web, wrecking our fragile trinity of best friend, brother and me. And yet this day has still rocked my world.

I wake gone three to an empty room. But before I haul myself up I lean into the still-warm space his body has left, inhale the smell of him, put my arm across the Tom-shaped hole I still see etched in the air.

'Er, what are you doing?'

I start, my head shooting up, sending a spasm of pain down my right shoulder.

'Harry?'

'No, the fucking Dalai Lama.'

'I . . . when did you get back?' I ask, trying to calculate how much she can possibly have seen, or how much she will deduce. But the answer is little, and nothing. Because this is Harry. She has entered stage right, so whatever my intentions or whatever the directions, the scene is always only about her.

'An hour ago? But I totally can't sleep. I'm buzzing and I didn't even take anything. Apart from a whole beer. But I peed that out hours ago. Oh my God, it was amazing. Did you see? I mean, not the concert, did you see *me*?'

I raise myself up, turn so I am propped on my elbows, and take a big breath.

'Yeah, we did. We totally did.'

Later, I will brief Tom, and we will tell her that her five seconds of fame must have been during a cassette change, and she will curse Tom and sulk at me for at least a day. But right now Harry's elation is so complete, her conviction that the world turns solely for her so unwavering, that my lie is worth it. Because now, for the first time in a long time, and for a long time, we have both got exactly what we want. Our lives, little though they are, are perfect. This is that moment we will talk about in years to come, a moment we will be able to relay to strangers and it will still resonate.

So that when they ask, 'Where were you, when Live Aid

was on?' Harry will say, 'I was there. I mean, obviously. You can see me on TV. My first appearance.'

And me? I will say I was just at a friend's house in Essex, watching at home. Eating crisps, stealing kisses and planting a seed of hope for the future.

# Baby Blue

## April 1986

I have so many questions, Edie. Questions I should have asked you long ago when they burned so bright they turned my every thought to hot suspicion or vitriol and my hands into tightly balled fists. What happened with your mother and father that would make you refuse their love, and yet not Great-Aunt Nina's money? Why did you drop out of art school then barely pick up a brush for years? Why did we move here, to this place, when you professed to hate small towns so much? Questions I should have asked when you had the words to answer them. Except I was always scared the answer to one or all would be: 'you'.

Because I am the biggest question of all, aren't I: a walking punctuation mark trailing 'how's and 'why's and 'what if's in my next line. How did you conceive me? Why did you keep me? What if you hadn't?

But I never articulated any of them, preferring to piece together my own truth from your intermittent pronouncements on pregnancy, and abhorrence of other people's children. And the answer? I am lucky, I deduced, though luck was not the word I would have chosen for my life at the time.

But a miracle, maybe, that you decided to keep me. Because it wasn't love, was it, Edie; an instantaneous connection with this odd peanut of a creature growing inside you? How could it be, when I stretched your stomach and split your skin, leaving slivers of silver to mark my work? How could it be, when I made you sick not just in the mornings but every waking hour? How could it be, when you knew you would have to drop out of university for me, make sacrifices for me, lose friends for me? No, I decided, the only things that had prevented my termination were your morbid fear of hospitals and an equal determination to upset your parents.

I can't imagine how you must have felt when you first found out; knowing how it had happened, and what it meant. I can't imagine how discovering you are carrying a child, however it is conceived, and at whatever age, feels at all. But I know others who do.

Harry is pregnant, or so the pink lines claim.

'It could be a false positive,' I try, desperately scrabbling for a scrap of hope.

But Harry's rose-tinted glasses are shut away in the same drawer as the pills she forgot to take. 'That's three in a row,' she says. 'You can't get three false positives in a row.'

'Tina says her cousin's mate's girlfriend had four positives in a row once, plus the one they do at the doctor, and then it turned out she wasn't after all.'

But this she dismisses as bullshit.

'Is it . . . his?' I ask.

'Whose?'

'You know,' I almost whisper. 'Mr Macdonald.'

Mr Macdonald: the newly qualified and entirely useless music teacher who spends most of our pitiful lessons playing Ultravox samples on a Casio keyboard whilst eyeing Harry through a curtain of studiously messy hair. Yet so lacking is our school in dynamic father figures that he has already shot into second place of *teachers you totally would*, ranking behind only part-time PE teacher and full-time perv Mr Thomas who once came third in hurdles in a national athletics competition about a billion years ago.

I never understood the older guy thing. Couldn't see the attraction in a man with ten years on me or even twice my age: a man old enough to be my father. I know pop psychologists and tabloid tattlers would have me and others like me – the poor fatherless brats that we are – ruthlessly pursuing sugar daddies, subordinating ourselves to the rich but wrinkled in some kind of twisted compensation for all those lost years when we should have been sitting on their corduroy knee playing 'Grand Old Duke of York'. But the idea of it was beetles on my skin, so unthinkable I would shudder to brush them off my spine where they had begun their steady crawl.

Harry, however, had no such compunction.

'Oh God, Di. He's so bloody . . .' She trailed off in apparent reverie, before coming to make her final pronouncement on the subject. 'I think I might love him.'

'You said that about Gary,' I pointed out – and about five other boys before that, I thought, uncharitably.

'Yeah, well, I hadn't met Ewan then,' said Harry in her defence.

'Ewan? Seriously?'

'What? I like it. Better than Gary. God, he was such a . . . child.'

'So is it him?' I ask again now. 'Mr Macdonald – Ewan, I mean.' My imagination is already conjuring up a variety of school scandals, aided and abetted by the knowledge that Harry has been to his flat several times after school, on the pretence that he is teaching her piano.

'God, no!' she protests. 'I only let him use his fingers. Worse than that.'

'Worse than a teacher? So whose, then?'

She looks sheepish then, apologetic, though how any answer could possibly be worse than the music teacher is hard to fathom. 'Denny.'

'From the video shop?'

She nods. And I realize she is right. Somehow it is worse. I picture him – his white shirt undone to reveal a gold chain and carotene-tablet tan. His highlights. His insistence that George Michael is in no way homosexual. But he is three years older and drives a Datsun, which to Harry is better lubricant than KY.

'I thought he was going out with Suzanne Nichols?'

'He is.'

Bollocks, I think. But I am a faithful best friend, and it is not our job to agree with worst-case scenarios, so I grasp at straws again in a bid to make it better. 'Maybe . . . maybe this is just your body reacting in a panic to the possibility of it. You know, phantom pregnancy. I read . . . I read this thing where a horse thought it was—'

'A horse?' She is incredulous. 'I'm not a fucking horse. God, Di, you're such a bloody . . . you always look on the bright side. Only there isn't one. I'm pregnant. That's all there is to it.' She sounds almost defiant, her insistence that she is right outweighing her desperation to be wrong. But as she drops this third white stick into our bathroom bin, pushing it down under used cotton wool and tampon wrappers, her shoulders sag and she sits down abruptly on the edge of the bath next to me.

'Shit, Di. What am I going to do? What the fuck am I going to do?'

And then it comes to me. I know precisely who will have the answer. God knows she can't be bothered with homework, and she's not much help with stomach bugs because of the *horrible sick*, or the flu, because it's *so bloody boring*, but teen pregnancy, this is so her bag. And so, for the first time in an emergency, I actually do what the children in stories always did: I ask my mother.

I ask you.

Harry is nervous when she tells you. But not as nervous as she would be if it were Angela, and her apprehension is tinged with relief that you know about these things, and will not judge her. After all, you have let her smoke in the kitchen, given her condoms, taught her how to put them on with the aid of a banana. Maternal advice you've clearly not bothered to follow yourself, and the kind I would rather chew off my own arm than have to endure first-hand. I, however, am suddenly terrified. What if you tell her to keep it? You kept me, after all. What if she decides to go through with the whole thing and has a baby at the age of, what, eighteen, in the middle of her A levels, and it is all, all your fault?

But if I was hoping for a no, a 'don't even think about keeping it', when I get it I am thrown further than I thought possible.

'Not my decision, darling, but if you want my advice you'll get rid. Or you'll end up stuck in this shitty town and you'll turn into . . .' You trail off, knowing you are about to overstep a mark, which for you is self-restraint on an unprecedented scale. But then you go and ruin it.

'Just don't do what I did,' you say. Then turn to me: 'No offence.'

'None taken,' I lie.

'But will it hurt?' Harry asks.

'The abortion?' you ask. 'Yes. But only for a bit. It's like period pain, that's all.'

It takes me a few seconds, because at first I'm thinking about Harry having to have a knitting needle or whatever they use these days poked sharply into her womb. But then I understand what you're saying, and I feel the truth drip coldly down inside me. This isn't second-hand knowledge from Toni – of course not from Toni, because how would a child have even got in there in the first place, save for that one time she shagged a man?

You are talking about yourself. Not about me, not about

keeping me. But about getting rid of another child. A child that could have, would have, been my brother or sister.

'When did you have one?' I demand. 'An abortion, I mean.'

'Oh, ages ago.' You flap your hand dismissively.

But that doesn't answer the question. 'Before or after me?'

You purse your lips, a habit I have noticed you indulge in when you are about to actually tell the truth. 'After,' you say.

I feel my right leg begin to shake, and start to tap my foot in a bid to stop it, to fool it into believing I am fine. But I just succeed in looking strange and agitated, and you can see it.

'I know what you're thinking,' you say. 'But it wasn't a good time. And anyway, how could I love anyone as much as you?' You laugh, trying to lighten the leaden words, but it's strained, desperate. And when you try to touch my arm, I pull away.

But this drama is minor, it seems. My own fragile existence and the non-existence of my sibling a matter for another time, or not at all. Because you, you do not want to talk about it. And Harry? She is, inevitably, oblivious.

'So can we book it then?'

'Of course,' you say. 'Let's do it now. I'll come with you. We both will. It will be a day out!' You clap your hands as if you're promising a trip to the theatre or the zoo, with ice cream and balloons and a clown act if we're good. When even I, who know nothing about these things but the little that has been whispered around the upper-school toilets or gleaned from the *Dear Deidre* column, realize that the obstetric wards of Addenbrooke's are far from a tourist attraction and the procedure neither a party nor a picnic.

But Harry, it seems, is delighted with this solution, because when I look over to offer a raised eyebrow of apology, her face is painted with relief and the lip-biting tic of potential adventure.

In the end, I do not come. It's scheduled for a Friday and you think it will raise suspicion if we're both off school. The plan, instead, is that Harry will leave during free period and you will drive her to the hospital and then home again – home to ours – where she will stay the night – a sleepover already countenanced by Mrs Trevelyan, who thinks we're rehearsing for our roles in *Macbeth*: a bloody-handed murderess and one-third of a coven getting into character. (Roles we will eventually play with such authenticity and empathy that Harry will win the hearts of half the upper sixth, while I will court the attention of the unofficial goth society.)

For something you have cooked up, it surprises me by tick-tocking along like clockwork. When I burst through the door just fifteen minutes out of double English – my palms sweating, my heart marching with the fear of what might have happened, and the guilt of pretending to Tom that nothing is going on – you are both lying on your bed, with a blister packet of paracetamol on the bedside table and drinks in your hands.

'Gin,' you say. 'I thought it was appropriate. A kind of celebration present. And useful, too. Want one?'

I shake my head slowly, focusing now on Harry, who lies palely on your pillow, looking for all the world like she is trying to channel some consumptive Brontë heroine and yet still managing to exude glory.

'Are you . . . ?' I begin, then change my mind as to which question I will ask first, jostling as they are for attention. 'Did it hurt?'

Harry shakes her head, weakly, in contrast to the enthusiasm that decorates her voice. 'No. It does now a bit but the tablets are helping. And it wasn't gross or anything, was it?' She looks at you then, and I feel an unfamiliar prick of jealousy, a momentary desire to be the one who has been through this rite of passage, with you by her side.

Then I remember what you have done, and what you could have done to me.

'Good,' I say. 'Brilliant. That's . . . that's brilliant.'

If I sound like I'm struggling, it's because I am. I don't know what to do with the way I feel about you, about what is and might have been, about Harry being the girl I am not, about me being the girl I am. And so I do what I always do when confronted by this level of confusion.

I eat.

And I eat.

And I eat.

I sit at the kitchen table, working my way through two packets of Bourbons, seven custard creams, half a block of cheddar and then, at my lowest point, four unbuttered slices of white bread, which is so dry I can barely swallow.

Then, as Harry sleeps, and you drain the dregs of her gin,

I throw it all up at the bottom of the garden, heaving into a bush between sobs that rack through me like imagined contractions.

# A Little Love Song

## August 1986

Can you hear the music, Edie? Can you?

You loved this band, and, God, how I hated you for it. They belonged to me, I thought; I knew. Their sullen, sunken shoulders, the lyrics dripping with melancholy and the damp of bedsit walls, the jangle of guitars like a death rattle. Only they could possibly understand the misery I felt, the tragedy that tore through every day, every hour that I wasn't with him.

It's a cassette, one I made decades ago. You'd recognize the songs: God knows I played it enough times that the plastic is scratched and the tape held together in two places with Sellotape. You can still read the faded black biro on the title sticker though: *For Tom*, it says. *Goodbye, Essex*. This is just a copy, though, a simulacrum that meant we could lie on our beds, 156 miles apart (of course I checked, with two maps), both listening to Dylan and Waits and the syrup-sweet sound of Nina Simone lamenting that we don't know what it's like.

Or so I imagined. I'm not sure what happened to Tom's original; lent out, lost to travel, maybe, or left behind in a drawer in one of a string of raftered bedrooms, along with the flotsam and jetsam of youth: the gig tickets, the button badges, the hastily written confessions and promises on sheets of torn A4. But mine was as precious as Charles, as my absurd stuffed raven, and so it survived, stored in the suitcase of treasure, to be brought out when I needed to remember, or forget.

This next song – side two, track two – is the most worn of all. After each listen I would eject the cassette from my Walkman, and painstakingly rewind with a Bic Cristal biro (the orange ones weren't quite fat enough and slipped irritatingly, making an already tedious process unbearable) and listen again, and again, as 'Song to the Siren' called out to lost loves, or unrequited ones, and sent Elizabeth Fraser's voice soaring and tears cascading; thick, black Rimmel mascara running in rivulets down my cheeks.

It is the summer of 1986 and music is everywhere: waking us with the tinny pop of clock alarms set to Radio 1, sending us to sleep with the mellow melancholy of a copied Leonard Cohen cassette. And in between, soundtracking our every waking moment: our meals eaten standing staring into the open door of the fridge, our skulking in parks, our walks to work if we have to endure the inconvenient necessity of a holiday job. Then comes the torture of an eight-hour shift in silence or, worse, the indignity of the mum music of Radio 2 with its endless procession of Bonnie Tyler, Elton John, Rod Stewart; songs that have nothing to say, at least not to us, because we are young and gifted and, though we may be white, we wear our Anti-Apartheid badges with pride. It is a time when the land of comfortable slacks and slippers and staid Sunday lunches seems half a world away. Instead we spend our days off dressed in bikinis and band T-shirts, lying on the lawn of the Lodge with a stack of *Just Seventeen*s, a bottle of Hawaiian Tropic, and *Our Tune* on the radio, not for a minute recognizing our hypocrisy, not once realizing that our obsession with true love will likely lead us straight up the garden path to suburban mediocrity after all.

'Seriously? Spandau fucking Ballet? That is so third-year disco.' Harry rolls over onto her stomach in disgust and props herself up on her elbows. 'If it was me and Sean, it would be Chrissie Hynde, "3,000 Miles".'

'"2,000 Miles",' I say automatically.

Harry lifts her sunglasses and gives me the look. 'Fine. "2,000 Miles". It's the tragic story that matters, anyway.'

'What tragic story?' I'm not being devil's advocate, I'm honestly stumped, because as far as I know she's been with Sean Shattock for all of six weeks, and the only tragedy is that this is the song they first did it to, because the only cassettes he has in his mum's Mini Metro are a double edition of Fifty Festive Favourites.

'God, Di.' She sighs, as if I am something – a fool – to be tolerated. 'The tragedy that he's signing up as soon as he gets his results and I'm stuck here for another two years. They're bound to play it. They love a soldier.'

I think for a moment. 'Are they still called soldiers in the navy?'

'Jesus. Sea-whatever. I don't know.'

Sailor, I think. But I don't say it, because I am sidetracked into imagining a song for Tom and me and a story to go with it, one that will make Simon Bates's plastic DJ heart melt and guarantee an on-air dedication that Tom will hear in the warehouse up at the shuttlecock factory, put down his . . . whatever it is he does, and cycle the mile from the industrial estate to the back garden to declare his undying love for me.

Or not.

'This is such a load of bollocks.'

I start at the sound of his voice, spilling a glass of water over the soft folds of my stomach, and clutch a baggy black T-shirt to me, half mopping, half covering myself up.

Harry in contrast merely raises a practised eyebrow. 'Is not.'

Tom flops down on the towel in between us, picks up a magazine and drops it as quickly in seeming disgust. Most things disgust him right now for their latent racism, sexism or homophobia, or just their obvious middle-classness.

'It so is. I bet it's fake. I bet no one even writes in. Why would you? As if playing some bullshit ballad is going to fix anything, or make . . . any meaningful difference to the world. I mean, how bloody sad is that?'

'Totally sad,' I mumble, pushing down my idle thoughts of sending in a Smiths' song, and swallowing the *God, Tom, I love you* that seems to flirt on the tip of my tongue at any given moment.

Harry pulls a face. 'Can you just, like, shut up?'

'Me?' I ask.

I can tell by the pause that she's rolling her eyes, even behind the Ray-Bans. 'No, him. Mr Professional Fucking

Cynic. Just because you're off to sodding university doesn't mean you know *everything*.'

My stomach slides at the mention of this inevitability, this statement of a silent truth that we've been sitting on all summer, pretending the day will never come. Even Harry – who protests at his political zealotry, his new-found vegetarianism, his demands for a household ban on anything made by Nestlé and yes that includes Shreddies – can barely acknowledge that soon she will be living alone under the same roof as her increasingly neurotic mother and absent – at least mentally – father. 'Can't I just move in with you, Di?' she asked one afternoon. 'Sure,' I replied, the word slipping off my tongue as easily as *thanks* or *sorry* or *can I have a biscuit?*, but only because I know Angela would never let her.

'Here.' Harry holds out the suntan lotion, waggles it at Tom. 'Do something useful if you're determined to disturb us.'

He sighs, takes the bottle. 'Yes, Your Highness.' Then he smirks at me, marking me out as a co-conspirator, making Harry, for once, the odd one out.

I try to smirk back, but the unbearable situation of being half naked whilst watching the similarly undressed object of my affection rub coconut oil into his sister's back renders it more of a grimace.

'Want me to do you?' he asks when he's satisfied the few inches there are of her are sufficiently shiny.

'I . . .' Say something, I think. Say yes. Say anything. 'I'm fine. Thanks,' I manage.

'Don't be stupid,' Harry says, pulling herself up. 'You'll burn. You always do. Want a Mivvi?'

I nod without thinking. There is never a time I don't want a Mivvi, not even in the depths of December when everyone else is spooning custard over spotted dick or treacle tart.

'Tom?'

He shakes his head and Harry, taking this as a personal slight, huffs as she heads to the kitchen.

I look at Tom, then, who shrugs, as if defeated. 'You heard her.'

I did.

'Roll over, then, Dido.'

Oh God. I want this but I don't want this. But it might be my last chance. The results are out in two days and then . . . I don't even know what then. I close my eyes and turn onto my stomach, what little muscle I possess rigid with anticipation, my breasts spreading out under me like pooled blancmange. And I wish to every god and false idol that I was wearing a one-piece so that all he could access was the small patch of almost-firm flesh on my spine. But instead a wide, unflattering expanse of me is exposed, onto which Tom drips a slick of factor 15 and begins.

It is as if someone has stripped me and stood me under a spotlight. I am aware of every extra inch of me compared to her. What must it feel like to him, I wonder. Like kneading dough, maybe. Probably. And yet I don't stop him. I feel his hot hands slide across my back, pushing the puddle of oil outwards towards the seams of my bikini top. I hold my breath, willing him to stop at the same time as I'm praying that he'll slip one hand under a strap, or lower, skirt the top of my buttocks. But God, no, then he would know just how slack they are, how orange-peel dimpled. Panicked, I turn onto my side, out of reach. 'That's fine,' I say quickly. 'I'm all done.'

He looks at me, amused, bemused, for an appalling number of seconds. Then, with his eyes still focused on mine, he tosses me the bottle, which lands safely on the pillow of my stomach. 'Here,' he says. 'You can do me, then.'

Not a question. An instruction. Or, maybe, in my head, a desperate plea wrapped up in the cloak of cockiness?

Two can play at that, I tell myself, as if telling might make me believe it. 'Sure,' I say, echoing my earlier, affected ease.

But saying it is one thing; following through on the promise is another. Because if having him touch my own body was purgatory, this is a strange, exquisite hell.

His flesh is taut under my touch, tanned. I trace a line with my eyes joining the constellation of moles on his back that in my head form a perfect negative replica of Cassiopeia. I know the pattern by heart; know from memory the slope of his shoulders, the dimples on his spine, the dips just above his hip bones, above his . . . I remember the first time I saw him, here on this very patch of lawn. Naked in a plastic padding pool, his penis small, rigid. I find myself imagining it now, fleshing out the shape I have seen straining against the denim of his 501s. He is beautiful. How could I ever imagine I deserve this? But despite my awareness of my own limitations, of the absurdity of this situation, of its proximity to my best friend, his sister, I feel myself contract, shiver with it.

What if he can tell? I think. But his eyes are closed, his face turned away.

My fingers close in on the waistband of his shorts.

He lets out a sound, a half sigh, half groan. And I don't know if it's because of him being tired, because of last night – he was round Michael's until two, Harry says – or because of me, because of what I'm doing right now.

Because I could do it. I could slip my hand down, like Katherine does in *Forever*. I could touch . . . it. 'Ralph', the boy in the book calls it. I wonder if Tom's has a name. God, I hope not. Harry says Gary called his 'Little Gary' and it was more appropriate than he realized. I don't even know how big Tom's is. Is big even good? What if it's too big?

There are too many questions. Too many 'what if's. What if he likes it? What if he doesn't? What if Harry sees me and freaks out and tells her mother and I'm banned from the Lodge for ever and a day?

If I were anyone else, if he were anyone else, maybe I would.

But I'm not. And he's not.

And besides, we have company.

Harry is here, standing legs apart, armed with Mivvis. Half smiling, she holds one out, letting pink strawberry ice dribble slowly down the stick and drip onto the centre of Tom's back, just above my hand.

'What the fuck?' Tom slaps a hand round to wipe off whatever has hit him, holds it out, then licks it. 'Idiot.'

'Dick,' Harry replies. Then hands one to me. 'Here.'

I take it, and slide back to my side of the towel. Tom, I notice, does not move. And I wonder if it's because he won't. Or he can't.

'What are you doing, anyway? I thought you students all liked being pasty.'

'Like you'd know,' he replies as if butter wouldn't melt.

Maybe I'm wrong.

Harry, at least, is oblivious. 'You haven't even got in yet,' she retorts. 'I don't even know why you'd want to. I mean, seriously? Hull? Why not LSE, or King's at least?'

'London isn't the centre of the universe,' Tom says.

'Funny, because it was last time I looked.'

'Yeah, well, maybe I'm sick of that southern-centric view of the world.' He's pulled himself round now, and, I notice, draped my discarded T-shirt over his groin. 'All your bloody Waitrose shopping lists and days out to the Grafton Centre and nights in Cinderella Rockefellas.'

'I have *never* been to Cinderella's,' Harry points out.

'Whatever. It's a metaphor.'

'For what?'

He shakes his head. 'Give it three weeks and I'll be out of here. In the real world.' He lies back on his elbows, closes his eyes to the sun. 'And I can't bloody wait.'

Harry contemplates him, considering, I imagine, his optimism, his profundity. 'Tom,' she begins.

He opens an eye.

'Have you got a hard-on?'

'Jesus, Harry.' He stands up and, taking my T-shirt with

him, stalks back into the house. I hear a door slam, and then the dull, thudding bass of Zeppelin being played at a higher-than-allowed volume from his bedroom.

'Dirty fucker,' Harry says, then pushes the Mivvi halfway into her mouth, pulls it out again. 'Are you ill or something?'

'What?'

'Not like you to waste good ice cream.'

I look at my hand, see the sludge of vanilla seeping slowly out from its scarlet casing and down my fingers.

'Shit,' I say, and try to rescue it. But the sweetness is cloying now, the cream coagulating on my tongue, turning my stomach.

Harry shakes her head and sits back down. 'You and him are weird, you know that?'

I nod.

'Good thing he's going.'

I force a saccharine, strawberry-flavoured smile. 'Yeah. Totally.' Then cross my fingers on my still lotion-slick hand and make a wish that he will fail. Or change his mind. Or have some terrible accident that will require my undivided care and attention, and mine only. Then immediately hate myself and hope to die.

Stick a needle in my eye.

But it's a wasted hate. He gets three As, and accepts his place across the great, grey estuary of the Humber to study English and politics, as far away from small-town Essex, from small-town girls, as he can manage without crossing a border.

So that, one Saturday morning in late September, Harry

still in her baby-doll pyjamas, me in a knee-length T-shirt and faded leggings, we stand awkwardly, shoes and slippers scuffing the pea gravel, trying to say our goodbyes. In my right pocket is my breakfast – an already half-eaten Bounty bar. In my left, the mixtape I spent four evenings and three attempts making, two fingers hovering over the play and record buttons on my second-hand tape-to-tape deck.

The Volvo is packed so high the back window is blocked, the boot stacked with two blue suitcases, one just of books; striped raffia laundry bags sitting fatly full of fifteen-tog feather duvet, pillows, brand-new paisley bedding; a guitar, a set of bongos I've never even heard him play, a roll of posters – *Paris Texas*, *Betty Blue*, *The Wall*.

'Oh God, I suppose I should say it's like the end of an era or something,' Harry sighs.

'It *is* the end of an era,' Tom replies, dropping his rucksack on the ground. 'No more borrowing my Floyd CDs when you think I'm not about.'

'As bloody if.'

'Harriet, language.'

Mrs Trevelyan isn't going with them, claiming someone needs to keep an eye on Harry. But Harry is the queen of evading eyes, and besides, we all know it's only because otherwise she'll cry at the accommodation office and then all the way home. Or worse, take it out on David. That's what you say, anyway.

'Come on,' says a voice from inside the Volvo. 'I want to get there before lunch.'

Harry despairs. 'He's only saying that because there's a pub in Beverley he wants to try out.'

'It's in *The Good Food Guide*,' Mrs Trevelyan says quickly. 'Three-star rating. They do crab sandwiches and five kinds of ploughman's. Oh God, you will eat properly, won't you?'

'Yes, Mum,' Tom promises, smiling at me. I smile back. 'Bye, then.' He hugs her, making her squeal like a child, forcing her to laugh instead of cry. Then he grabs Harry and they stand, awkward at first, as if their connection is severed by age now, or needs to be. But after a second I see her relax into it, into him, and push her nose into the nape of his neck, where I know it smells of skin and sweat and the Kouros Harry gave him last Christmas. 'Go change the world,' she says quietly.

'I will,' he replies. 'You go . . . I don't know, talk about it on telly.'

She giggles, the laughs segueing into sobs, then pulls away, rubbing her face on her cardigan, last night's mascara staining the pale wool.

'I'm going in,' she says. 'Too cold out here.'

I nod. But as I turn back to say my own goodbye, he's edged round to the other side of the car, checking the guitar is secure and that it won't crack the window. 'How many times?' he's saying. 'We're going on a motorway, not bloody mud tracks.'

'Even so,' his mother says. 'You don't know what it's like up there. And lock the doors once you're in.'

I feel in my pocket, feel the hard shell of the cassette case, snap it open and shut to feel the scrape and hear the click. I can't give it to him. Not in front of them. Then I see my opportunity – the rucksack gaping open on the gravel, admissions papers poking out next to a copy of *On the Road*. And I know what I have to do. Heart marching, I pull my present out and push it down inside, until it is snug between the green canvas and the Kerouac.

'Stealing again, Di?' the voice says.

I swing round, panic and polyester combining to send a surge of sweat seeping from my armpits. 'I . . . I was just . . .' Think, Di, think. 'The wind was blowing the papers.'

Oh God. I am a moron.

There's no wind, not even a breath of anything but fading summer stillness.

And he knows it. But he says nothing. And I love him even more for it.

'Bye, then, Di.'

'Bye,' I say. 'Be weird not having you at the bottom of the garden.' I push my hands hard down in my pockets, scared he'll see they're shaking, scared I'll throw my arms round him.

'At least you've still got Harry, though.'

I nod. 'I . . . I have to go,' I say. I can't do this. I can't just stand by and watch him drive out of my life. And I can't hug him in case I never let him go.

I put my head down and start walking but he follows me, pulls my arm.

Then pulls me round.

It is brief. But long enough for him to whisper, 'I'll be back soon.'

There is only one answer to that. 'Like I care,' I say, sarcasm the better alternative to sobs.

'Yeah? Me neither.'

I laugh, let my face sink into that place.

'It isn't the end of anything,' he says then. His voice softer now, the edge gone, not playing for laughs any more. 'Nothing will change.'

I feel tears threaten and pull back, let my head drop, pretending I need to redo my hair.

'This place never changes,' I say.

He laughs. 'Now *that* is too fucking true.'

'For heaven's sake, language, Thomas!'

We both laugh then, and I am grateful for the interruption so I can wipe my eyes.

He picks up the bag and, without even looking, slings it into the back seat and slams the door. Then climbs into the front, rolls the window down.

'See you,' he yells to no one in particular.

'Not if I see you first,' I say.

He smiles. 'Right answer.'

Two weeks later, a brown Jiffy bag arrives, postmarked Kingston-upon-Hull. I snatch it from the pile of delivery leaflets and circulars and run clattering back up the stairs to my room, then sit cross-legged, reverent, as I peel open the envelope.

Inside is a tape. On the cover is a collage of magazine-cut

images – Bowie as Aladdin Sane; the Queen imagined by Warhol, with an anarchy symbol stamped on her head – and over them two words: *Thank You.*

And no, the first letter of each song does not spell out *I. L.O.V.E. Y.O.U.* – a realization that will strike me afresh on every play, disappointing me in his failure, and disgusting me at my own need. And no, there are no hidden tracks or confessions buried in the lyrics. But he has made me a tape, full of songs he loves and ones he knows that I do too.

And I play that tape until not even Sellotape can save it, all the while telling myself that nothing will change.

But it does. In the end, everything changes.

Because eight months later, I meet Jimmy.

# Seventeenth Summer

## June 1987

By the summer I turn seventeen I have kissed (and been kissed by) no fewer than five boys, a number and sorry line-up I justify as frogs in my bid to find my prince, though my prince, I am sure, is in mortal guise in Hull, and it will be only a matter of time until he rescues me from my red-brick and flint tower.

But until then I need practice, I tell myself, so that I do not disappoint. And besides, five isn't so many – it's still four fewer than Harry. Though none of them have made the earth move, violins sing, the way hers seem to.

Until Jimmy McGowan.

The first time I see him – I mean really see him – he is sitting on the back of a sofa in the sixth-form common room talking down Thatcher and bigging up the miners – a coal-faced race as far-fetched and alluring to my middle-class Essex existence as hobbits or hippogriffs. And there is something about the way he holds himself – half defiant, half defensive; the way he talks, walks through life, that resonates, sets my own strings humming in recognition.

I have noticed him before, of course – slinking forward in

the canteen queue, smoking behind the mobile classrooms, skulking in the corner at upper-school discos. But he is a year above me and, besides, my orbit has always been around Tom.

But Tom is gone, and at Christmas and Easter his talk is full of other places, other people, another girl – Della, whom he leaves to see long before the holiday is out. And those other boys were nothing: fumbles and stumbles and struggling with zips against the wall of the village hall. But Jimmy is different.

Everything about him is different.

He is half punk, half political geek. Part of the in-crowd but still the cat who walks by himself. Wanted, despite the blond curls, despite the lazy eye that marks him out, that you will later accuse me of fetishizing.

'You don't love him,' you say. 'You love that bloody eye.'

'What's wrong with the eye?' I demand. 'Are you saying he's a freak or something? God, you're such a . . .' I scrabble for a smart, startling insult. 'Eye racist.'

'That's not even a thing.' You sprinkle sick-smelling Parmesan over a plateful of overboiled pasta. 'All I'm saying is it's always the same with you. Your idea of love is a sort of warped pity.' You list the times I have brought home injured beetles in boxes, chosen a doll with a wonky smile over perfect painted plastic, a broken biscuit over an intact one. 'It's because you don't think you deserve better,' you finish, dropping the plate in front of me with a side-serving of pop psychology. 'I read about it,' you add, as if I need to be told. 'It's a form of self-harm.'

'What, as opposed to the beauty pageant that you parade in front of me?' I poke the penne around in the slop of oily sauce.

'That's not fair,' you protest. 'Jermaine was positively . . . normal.'

'He didn't believe in vegetables,' I remind you. 'And he had tattoos.'

'Tattoos are art,' you insist, pushing your plate away untouched. 'And anyway, he's long gone.'

I shrug, conceding the point. Because Jermaine is now no more than a forwarding address, a relationship that ended – disappointingly for the neighbours, who had at first complained vehemently but had later grown stoically accustomed to his late-night revving of engines and the smell of burning brake fluid – with a whimper rather than a bang. One morning you got up, packed his tools into a cardboard crisp box and his few clean clothes into the gym bag he'd swapped for a toaster down the Lizzie, gave him fifty pounds and a kiss and said it'd been an experience, but it was time, now. Since then, your bedroom has been empty; the only males to cross our threshold the reluctantly summoned fridge-repair man, and David, who fixes everything else. Though as far as I know, or want to consider, neither of them have been further than mild flirtation and the foot of the stairs.

But about Jimmy, you are wrong. It's not the eye, although I love it for its difference, for the story I weave about its occurrence – a beating from a policeman on a picket line, a blinding punch that leaves him disfigured but a hero – it's everything else. The wide smile that turns his face from glowering threat to easy Cheshire Cat; his absurd yet impeccable sense of dress that sees him defying the sixth-form uniform of Brideshead hair and Bono boots to come to school in a James Dean jacket and rockabilly quiff, a paisley waistcoat and pocket kerchief, a dead man's demob suit.

'He is so totally gay,' Harry informs me with authority as he walks into the common room with his eyes ringed in Rimmel kohl.

'He is so not,' I retort, watching him slide down into a stained armchair, my eyes taking in every inch of studied rebellion, my head playing out an elaborate fantasy in which he turns to me and winks, then later pulls me into a doorway behind the science block, pushes me against the cream-glossed wall and kisses me until I come – a reaction I have yet to discover is as improbable as the story itself.

'God, you are so bloody obvious. Anyway – ' Harry prepares to deliver the final damnation – 'Tom says he's a total twat.'

I bristle, feeling my first flush of ardour dampen, the cine-show of us in an orgasmic yet fully clothed clinch freeze-framed in my head. And then I glimpse something else – the chance to prove Harry wrong, to prove Tom wrong – and I vow to take it. But within weeks what begins as a fuck-off to my best friend and the boy I love grows into an obsession all of its own.

I dig around for details, carefully, casually, as if scuffing my shoes through stones. I find out from a girl called Amanda, otherwise known as Drip, that he once drank twenty-three glasses of water at his primary school dinner table for a bet, before he threw them back up into the copper jug they came from.

I find out from Julia Shelton, who is widely rumoured to have a third nipple, that he has snogged at least seven sixth-formers, and gone further with two, at the same scout-hut party, but that he is still, thrillingly, a virgin.

And I find out from his slack-jawed, pock-skinned side-kick Gary Reeves that he lives up the estate on Hunters Way, the youngest of five McGowans – three girls with shamrock-shaped names – Sinéad and Siobhán and Orla – and another boy – Brendan – with a dodgy Ford and an arrest record. In my head I imagine an Irish version of the von Trapps, all 'Danny Boy' and jigs and reels. Later I will find out that his mother died in childbirth to be replaced three months later by the grim-faced Deirdre, mother to the three girls, and bogey figure to everyone else: a fact – a tragic past – that only makes me want him more. But by June, the record of him not acknowledging my existence stands at an appalling two hundred and fifty-three days, and something, I decide, has to be done.

He drinks in the Duke, a free house favoured by sixth-formers, Peter Pans, and a mildly retarded man called Billy Bob who lets kids buy him half pints of brown ale in return for inept Fats Domino renditions and unconvincing card tricks. And you, of course, until I started going out, and you started staying in. It sits lumpenly at the top of the high street, all tarnished horse brasses, sticky carpet and as much mildew as graffiti in the toilets. And yet it still weaves a kind of magic, conjured from cheap spirits, cigarette smoke and desperation. Inside the Duke, anything might happen, and frequently does. The Duke is where Tina Fraser dumped a cheating Dean Auger, where Harry first kissed Lee Sweet while the jukebox played Steve Harley & Cockney Rebel, where Tom told us both about Della, and I had to close my mouth in case the vodka he'd bought me had loosened my tongue.

And so I set the Duke for the scene of my revenge and triumph. All I need to do is persuade Harry, for whom I have been perpetual wing-woman, to do a favour in return for me.

'Oh God, really?' She pulls a face. 'But Ricky wants to go to Stortford.'

Stortford is a gleaming Mecca of a town compared to Walden, a land of provincial promise with purpose-built pubs and a nightclub called Cats'. And though Ricky is, to my mind, a prick of a boy, he drives a Toyota, which is the Essex escape car equivalent of a limo or a Mustang, at least to Harry.

'Just for a bit,' I beg. 'If Tina's in there you don't even have to stay.'

'It's a waste of time,' she says. 'He fancies some girl from Friends' School. Daisy something.'

'Fairs,' I finish. 'And everyone fancies her.'

Harry's face tautens, a mirror of her mother. 'Ricky doesn't.'

He hasn't met her, I want to say. But I want this. I need this. And besides, she's probably right. 'Please?' I try.

She groans. 'Fine. But only for an hour. And you're paying.'

'Fine,' I say.

But it is so much more than fine. For with this deal I have struck a match, and I can hear the crackle and spit, smell the sulphur as I hold it out to the touchpaper of a small-town Saturday night.

It takes me two hours and eleven costume changes to get ready, and by the time I finish I have sweated off two attempts at Sixties eyeliner and driven Harry to new levels of boredom and derision.

'God, Di, he's not going to give a shit which bra you wear,' she moans. 'It's not like he's going to go near it anyway.'

'He might.'

'Well, if he does, he's hardly going to change his mind just because you picked black over navy. It's got tits in, end of.' She takes a drag on her Marlboro Light and blows the evidence out of the window, not that you'd care. 'Double Ds, too,' she adds. 'He'll think it's fucking Christmas.'

'What if he doesn't like big ones?'

'All men like big ones. As soon as I'm rich I'm getting mine done. So think of the fortune you've saved. And hurry up. I'm gasping for a gin.'

I stare at the me in the mirror. This is my Pygmalion moment, my ugly-duckling-turned-swan metamorphosis that I have longed for ever since I first opened that battered Ladybird *Cinderella* and saw her go from rags to riches in the wave of a wand and the turn of a single page. But transformation is not so slick in real life, not so easy to pull off. I am uneasy in this skin, it itches, and I find myself yanking at the skirt hem to cover up more thigh, hauling up my straps to hide my cleavage. I'm convincing no one, I think. Not even myself.

But I am wrong; have, not for the first time, done myself down. Because you, it seems, are mesmerized.

'About bloody time,' you crow as I descend the stairs and drift into your eyeline on the chaise longue. You wave a finger in a vague circle. 'Go on, then, give us a twirl.'

I shufflingly oblige, turning leadenly as you inspect the hair half up (bed hair, Harry said, so he thinks about sex), the top pulled down, the skirt short – too short, I think.

'Harry did it,' I say quickly, as if this will lessen the incongruity.

'Then Harry deserves a bloody medal,' you say. 'Or a double vodka, at least.' You fumble on the floor for your handbag, tipping over an almost empty glass of red and losing your place in a book on Man Ray. 'I thought you were welded into those shapeless fucking T-shirts,' you continue.

My armour, I think. To cover up the big girl that used to be under there. Because the puppy fat has finally slipped away – not down to time, as you claimed it would, but thanks to the pressure of A levels, and an F-plan guide pushed into my hands by Angela. 'I'm not saying you're big,' she said. 'But I know what it's like. That's all.'

So surprised was I at this admission of less-than-perfection, at this connection to me, that I felt I had to follow it to the letter, even when you complained about the smell of the lentils, the smell of me. And it worked, or almost. Because a ghost body still clings to me like a caul, hangs like an obese aura. So that when I picture myself in my head, even being generous, I am an ungainly hourglass, and am then surprised when the mirror tells me a different story. When you tell me a different story.

'You've got a lovely body,' you say. 'You should show it off more.'

'That's what I keep telling her,' Harry agrees. 'But she never listens.'

'You said I was Rubenesque,' I protest.

'That was Tom, not me, and anyway it was a fucking compliment.' Harry is still experimenting with swearing in front of you and I can feel her need for approval as keenly as my own.

'It is,' you say simply. 'Though you're more Rossetti now. All hair and tits and tragedy. Now go on. Bugger off.' You hand me a tenner and dismiss us with a wave.

'You could come,' Harry suggests then. 'Couldn't she?'

'I . . .' But I can't think of an excuse that won't insult you and so instead have to wait agonizingly while you weigh this offer up. For a terrible moment I think you're going to say yes. That you will march into the Duke, hold court, capture Jimmy's attention, and probably heart, while I shrink into the fading flock wallpaper.

But for once you read my mind, can see inside my head to the fear and self-loathing, and sheer need for this to work. 'No,' you say. 'You go. Go find whoever it is you're doing this for. Show him what he's been missing.'

I should tell you that I'm not doing it for a boy. I'm doing it for me.

But we all know that would be a lie. So instead I take the money and run.

The pub is heaving. Around the jukebox a cluster of upper-sixth boys try to outdo each other with their obscure musical taste, cueing up 'Crystal Chandeliers', 'Blueberry Hill', and Bananarama in a nod to irony that reveals a lack of understanding of the appeal of girl bands as well as of comedic convention. Behind the bar Bobby Norris pulls pints, passes over packets of peanuts, undercharges underage drinkers by a matter of pounds that will eventually see him sacked and working in the Waitrose warehouse for the next twenty years.

And there, sitting at the coveted window table, the still, shining centre of this whirligig ride, is Jimmy McGowan, brow furrowed, finger pointed accusingly at Gary Reeves as he extols the virtues of communism.

'What do you want?' Harry asks, shouting over Charley Pride and the high-spirited hubbub of who saw who do what and where.

'Huh?' I am still watching Jimmy.

'For fuck's sake, Di. Drink?'

'Uh. Coke?' I try.

'God,' she says. 'At least put a rum in it.'

'But . . .' I look over at Bobby behind the bar. 'Will you get served?'

'Jesus. He's been trying to get into my knickers for two years,' she sneers. 'He's hardly going to card me. Besides, I look at least twenty-one.'

I take her in. She's not exaggerating.

'OK,' I concede. 'But not rum. Vodka. And grapefruit,' I add. As if this added sophistication and contrariness will add years to me, gild me with magic that will trap Jimmy in its glow.

'Freak,' Harry mutters, but holds out her hand anyway. I hand over your tenner and watch as she heads to the bar, leaving me to squeeze into the old church pew that does for a seat at the top table.

'Do you mind?' I ask.

Gary glances over and shrugs a dismissive *whatever*, not even bothering to make eye contact. But Jimmy, Jimmy looks at me. I mean really looks: his gaze holding mine then lowering to assess all this work that was done for him, for this very moment.

He looks up again. 'Free country,' he says. 'Or so they claim.'

I see my opening. 'Fucking Thatcher,' I say as I drop into the seat, as I pray he takes the bait.

He nods. And bites. 'Too right,' he says.

By the time Harry gets back from the bar we have sacked the cabinet, staged a coup, and called a snap general election, a repeat of last week's that will see Kinnock sail to an easy victory this time.

'God, not politics,' she exclaims as she clatters the drinks down, budges me up. 'Aren't you bored of it by now?'

Her arrival brings with it a seed of doubt, the always-there fear that she will upstage me, outshine me, steal my thunder and thus this boy. But for Jimmy, Harry's political ambivalence far outweighs her skinny legs and social graces,

183

and he turns straight back to me and the problem of South Africa, so that after just two gin and slimlines, she says she has to go.

'Come on, drink up,' she instructs.

I feel disappointment wash through me, diluting the vodka and, with it, my conviction that this – me and Jimmy – will happen. 'I—'

'Is she your keeper?' Jimmy interrupts.

I start. 'No. But—'

'So stay.'

Harry is fuming. 'Di?' she snaps, stopping just short of stamping her feet.

I look at her, but all I can see, feel, is Jimmy's eyes on me. 'Go,' I say.

She stares back, daring me to repeat that. I dare. 'Go,' I say again.

'Fine,' she says finally. 'I'll call for you in the morning then, shall I?'

'If she makes it home,' Jimmy swaggers.

Harry shoots him a look.

He holds up his hands. 'Joke. We can walk her home.' He nudges Gary. 'Can't we?'

Gary shrugs again, indifferent. But I don't care what he thinks, anyway. And nor, it seems, does Jimmy.

Because three hours later he does walk me home. Alone.

He doesn't ask to come in and I don't offer.

He doesn't cup his hand around my face and lower his lips to mine.

He doesn't tell me he misses me already, the minute he has to go.

But three weeks later he pulls me into the bathroom at Fiona Lambert's eighteenth and pushes his tongue into my mouth and his hand into the wide cup of my bra. And as he groans at the feel of my nipple under his fingers, as I taste cigarettes and Doublemint and victory, I fall swiftly and stupidly in love.

And so engrossed am I, so joyous, that I fail to see that you have too.

# The Big House

## September 1987

Of course I can see them now – the telltale tropes and traits, the little giveaways. Maybe if I'd been less self-absorbed, or less absorbed in Jimmy, I would have wondered why you'd grown your hair into a neat Brooks bob, why you'd taken out the nose ring, why you'd taken to painting insipid watercolours standing at the attic window, hours idled away scanning the hawthorn-hedged landscape that I so adored, and you, for so long, railed against. Instead I put this down to timid settlement, cautious satisfaction. You'd grown up, I thought, grown out of childish things, those endless adolescent costume changes as you tried to find a life that might stick. More fool me for not seeing that this was just another turn on the carousel.

Maybe, though, I didn't want to see.

Because I am happy, in this humdrum town. Cannot imagine myself anywhere but these hugger-mugger streets of coloured cottages and clapboarding, clinging to the hills as stubborn and enduring as the amber-stamened crocuses that appear each spring: on the common, in the playing fields, in our own back garden, pale and etiolated underneath a canopy of dark browns and greens. After eleven years, the Narnia I had imagined over the wall has solidified into bricks and mortar that feel as much my home as our ginger-bread house, even with Hansel a hundred and more miles away. Harry and I leave the gate unlocked and largely ajar, slipping backwards and forwards seamlessly between two worlds, our lives tangled, melded. We take food from each other's fridges, sleep in each other's beds, swap clothes as easily as secrets. As easily as parents: Harry slipping into your bedroom to borrow ballgowns and cadge cigarettes; me making mental notes for my meticulously planned future as Angela shows me how to bake butterfly cakes and bottle fruit, how to sew on buttons, how best to prevent wrinkles by never smoking and smiling only when necessary – the only sliver of advice I fail to heed. And David? David we share, don't we? He traverses the portal as easily as us girls, playing father to all of us – taxi driver, rescuer from late-night parties, mender of broken things.

Life was sweet, or so we thought.

But we were fooling ourselves, weren't we, Edie? Nothing about our existence was fixed, dependable. It was a game: a domino run or a house of cards; everything balanced so precariously, so delicately. One flap of a butterfly's wings, one change in circumstance, one careless mistake and it would begin to topple. And who was it stacked it all?

You, of course, Edie.

I find out about the house by accident, sitting at the kit-chen table at the Lodge, making a shopping list for Harry's eighteenth – an official one, anyway, my looped handwriting listing crisps, Coke (the real kind, not own brand), cheese and biscuits – half child's tea party, half the cocktail sophistication we imagine we exude. The alcohol will come later, bought last-minute from Costcutter on the Cromwell estate, an entire square mile which has *Here be dragons* stamped over it on Angela's mental map, guaranteeing that none of her acquaintances will be lurking behind a stack of cat food eager to report back.

It's under the sports section of yesterday's *Times*, and it's mild curiosity rather than concern that makes me pull it out, because the last year has tick-tocked by so steadily and smoothly that I've forgotten Neverland ever came with a crocodile, or that wolves prowl my enchanted forest. But when I flick over the covering letter, see what's attached, I feel the hard walls of my world tremble as if they are no more than twigs. Because there, on official vellum, with a glossy photograph glued in the centre, is a picture of a house.

'What's this?' I ask.

Harry, who is busy being sexually enlightened by *Cosmopolitan*, looks up from the magazine and wrinkles her nose. 'That? New house.'

'What?' I giddy as the room spins, as the world stops turning. 'You're moving?'

Harry shrugs. 'Mad, huh? I mean, I've only got a year left and I'm not bloody coming back after that. Not except for Christmas. But Mum wants a waste-disposal unit or whatever and Dad doesn't really get a say, so . . . yeah.'

'Is it just . . . are they thinking about it?'

'Huh?' Harry looks up again. 'Oh. No, they've put a deposit down, I think. They're, like, buying it off-plan or something. You know, because it's not built yet. That's the show home.'

I feel a sudden sense of being unanchored, of drifting on open water, the swell of the water turning my insides. And I cling to those words – not built yet – like a life raft, like wreckage, all the while conjuring landslides, sinkholes, an ancient burial ground, that will foil their plan. But the truth is, I am lost. Tom is gone, Jimmy is leaving for London and university, and this – this has spun my safe, serried world so far off its axis that I am dazed, dizzy, desperate.

'Did you know?' I ask when I clatter in the back door.

'Know what?' you ask, fiddling with brushes and turpentine, the chemical taint catching my throat.

'That they're moving.'

You don't even ask who *they* are. You know exactly who I mean – because who else could I possibly care about? 'Bloody woman,' you say. 'It's all her idea. David's perfectly happy where he is. It's her childhood,' you add. 'Deprived. That's why she's always wanting new things. Bigger things. Why can't she see when she's already got it bloody made?'

This is the first I have heard of you coveting anything of Angela's. But even so, I don't think then to ask how you know this strange detail; I assume, I suppose, that it has wended its way over the wall or along the grapevine that clings to the brickwork of all small towns. The same way you knew that Tom had dropped out of joint English to swap to single-honours politics. That David had found condoms in

Harry's coat pocket when he was looking for a set of keys.
That Angela had agreed to her party. 'Of course, David had
to buy her off with a weekend at bloody Ragdale,' you added,
another detail I should have noted, that should have rung
alarm bells.

'What will we do?' I ask.

'When?'

'When they go?'

You shake the brushes, dump them on the draining board.
'Christ knows,' you say. 'Lock that bloody gate for a start, I
suppose.'

'But . . . it won't be the same.'

You open the fridge, then change your mind, grab instead
at the packet of Camels. 'So make the most of it,' you say.
'While it lasts.'

The house is teeming now, glitter-flecked bodies draped on
sofas, and against the staircase, ironic pop pumping from the
stereo and mixing with the two glasses of punch I've dared
to down so that my heart hammers and my head sings with
possibility.

This could be it, I think. This is West Egg and Harry is the
Great Gatsby, throwing the last hurrah. So I must make it
count. I have to seize the moment. '*Carpe diem!*' scream the
vodka and gin as they helter-skelter through my veins. And
I do, I seize the moment, or something anyway. So that just
an hour later, I am lying on my back, my skirt pushed up,
my top pulled down, under the naked weight of Jimmy.

He'd been begging for months. And it's not like we hadn't

done everything else. So why should this last step be any different, I asked myself. And though I failed to find an answer, failed to quell the nagging doubt, the wagging finger, the voice that said *Because it is*, I knew I would do it anyway. Because we fitted. We were one of the growing procession of the paired-up, the couples who slunk two by two into the Noah's ark of the common room, sitting on each other's laps on the sofas, slipping our hands into each other's pockets. In this louche world, we ruled, the Traceys and Michelles and Darrens long consigned to YTS schemes and army barracks. So that now, with Harry on one side and Jimmy the other, I was the Queen of, if not Bloody Everything, then Something at least.

And I'd already tried once. Or rather he had. In the back of his brother's Escort parked up Seven Devils' Lane on the night of my seventeenth birthday. Me drunk on B-52s, him pushing his luck. He got it in, only an inch, but it hurt, and I wasn't expecting it, and the shock made me yelp, then seconds later throw up a torrent of brown, Baileys-smelling vomit out of the car door.

But now I am here, my body alive with liquor and kisses, and I wonder why I've always thought my virginity was so precious anyway, something to be saved, protected. Now I want to get rid of it, in the same way as I've taken down my poster of Clare Grogan, packed my monkey away in a suitcase; just another marker of childhood, really, no more than that. I mean, Harry's already done it with four different boys, Tina Fraser with five, and they don't seem to be eternally damned, or only in a good way.

Jimmy pulls away, a string of saliva hanging between our lips like a silvery spit tightrope.

'What's the matter?' he asks. 'You're not, you know, that wet.'

'I'm fine,' I insist. 'Just. You know. There's people downstairs.'

'Hang on.'

He sits up in the single bed and reaches over to the stereo, presses play on whatever cassette is already in the tape deck. The sound of Pink Floyd floods out, almost drowning out the thump-thump from downstairs, and filling the room with Tom. Because, oh yeah, didn't I mention it? The scene for my impending deflowering is none other than Tom's bedroom.

I tell myself this is necessity – Harry's in hers with Ricky, the spare room is being used as some kind of dealers' den, and there's no way I'm risking getting anything on David and Angela's pristine sheets. But there's an element of deliberateness too, bravado born of alcohol and desperation: a need to show him who I am now, that I don't need him, that we are done. Though in truth I know we never really started.

'Better?' Jimmy asks.

I tug my knickers down, and pull him back on top of me. 'Yes,' I say. 'God, yes.'

And so, after a fumble with a condom and two false starts, I finally feel Jimmy push inside me, feel myself being slammed against a sticker-decorated headboard to the unwitting rhythm of Dave Gilmour singing 'Wish You Were Here'. An irony not lost at the time, nor when, three minutes later, the door bursts open and I see framed in a halo of landing light, not an angel, but the prodigal son.

Tom.

'Oh. Shit!' I push Jimmy off – who yelps in shock, or possibly even pain – and pull the covers up. 'I'm sorry . . . we . . . I—'

But I don't get to articulate any excuse I might be able to conjure in my drink-and-endorphin-addled mind, because Tom backs up and pulls the door closed again. I know he's seen me, though, and Jimmy. He couldn't miss us. And there is no shred of ambiguity as to what was going on.

'Fuck,' I say, and lean over the side of the bed, scrabble around for a top.

'What are you doing?' Jimmy demands, before pulling me back, pushing his still-wet, wide lips onto mine.

I turn my head so that his tongue slides, doglike, down my cheek. 'No, Jimmy.' I try to wrest myself out of his hands, but he grips my wrists, pins me down.

'Stop it,' he says as I wriggle, fight underneath him. 'Calm down. You're being ridiculous.'

But whatever I felt is gone now, adrenaline flooding it out along with the alcohol. 'Jimmy, please. I can't.'

'Because of Tom?'

I nod.

'Why the fuck do you care what he thinks? He clearly doesn't give a shit.'

I smart at that, a wince to go along with the pinch of his fingers on my pale skin.

'I just can't,' I plead. 'Not tonight.'

Jimmy stares at me, his face red, contorted. With desire? Or disdain, maybe. For several slow-ticking seconds I don't know what he's going to do, whether he might ignore me, do it anyway, finish what he started. But then he snorts, flings my arms away from him and climbs off me, the ride over.

'Call me when you've worked out what the fuck is going on in your head,' he says. He yanks a grandad shirt over his still-sweating body, pulls up boxers then black trousers – trousers I'd unbuttoned myself less than fifteen minutes ago, pushing my hand into his shorts to feel the hardness of him, to feel how much he wanted me, to show him I wanted him.

But I don't want him. Not now.

I want Tom.

But he is gone, and this night is over. And so, just seconds after Jimmy slams the door, I drag my top down and my tights up around my sweat-and-God-knows-what-else-sticky thighs, stumble along the landing, down the stairs and out of the back door, running shoeless across the wet grass, only remembering when I have slammed the gate behind me that I have left my Docs under Tom's bed.

I go to retrieve them the next morning, arriving scrub-faced, sour-breathed at the back door at the same time as David and Angela pull up at the front.

The kitchen is already wiped clean of evidence, bin bags rattling with cans already stacked at the dustbin; the acrid tang of Dettol almost managing to mask the faint aniseed whiff of Pernod vomit.

'Well, it barely looks as if you got up to anything at all.' David walks in, still in his driving coat.

'I . . . hi,' I blurt, managing to feel both outsized and gawky as I clutch the side of the kitchen counter to steady myself.

'So is Harry still asleep?'

I don't know what to say, whether to shrug or just guess at a 'yes' in the hope that she did at least spend the night here. 'I—'

'Yup. Obviously.'

I feel my painfully empty stomach contract as Tom walks in, piece of toast in one hand, J-cloth in the other.

'All right, Dad?'

David nods, wandering, almost out of place in his own home.

Tom finally turns to me. 'Soooo . . .' He lengthens the word out, takes a bite of toast, chews, still focused on my face. 'You disappeared pretty sharpish last night.'

I blurt out a jumble of words. 'Yeah . . . sorry . . . because this . . . and I . . . well . . . then . . .'

He raises an eyebrow, pulls his half-smile into a lazy smirk. 'Interesting, Jones. Very interesting.'

'Tom?' comes the shrill call of Angela who has finished her inspection of the hallway. 'Is that you?'

'Yup,' he says, then gives me one last smile before sloping off to greet the mother ship. I don't know whether to be relieved or disappointed.

'Shall I . . . ?' David is standing, baffled, in front of the toaster. 'Would you . . . like something?'

'No,' I say. Then change my mind. I need food. Food will make all of this all right again. 'Yes,' I say. 'Please. Two slices.'

'Jam?'

I nod and slide onto a bar stool, grateful for a tether, the way he is grateful for something useful to do with his hands.

I am cramming in a too-big bite from a slice of strawberry on white when David walks off, redundant again, and Tom wanders back in, with a bleary-eyed Harry in tow. I swallow, but my mouth is dry now and I feel the bolus of toast trap in my throat.

'All right?' She nods at me without really looking, then slumps on the nearest stool.

Tom grabs the stack of newspapers off the breakfast bar in front of her so she can slide forward, head resting delicately on folded arms.

'God, I feel like seven kinds of shit.'

'Heavy night, I take it?' Tom is still studiously rearranging scattered ornaments. I am still studiously avoiding eye contact.

'Something like that.' She turns her head so she can look sideways at me. 'Where did you get to?'

'Home,' I manage to cough out.

'Right. Why?'

Tom laughs then, opening the sluice-gate to a rush of adrenaline so fierce and full that I dare to look at him, dare him to say anything.

He holds his hands up. 'Whatever.'

'God, what are you two? Some fucking conspiracy? Jesus, I need coffee.' Harry gestures at the filter pot.

Tom pours her a cup, plonks it down between us on the counter. As he does so he leans over so I can feel his hair on my neck, his breath on my cheek. 'Your boots are in the hall, by the way.'

Whatever shred of doubt, of hope, I had clung on to dissipates, leaving me rudderless, dizzy. All these years I have depended on that one possibility – that Tom will be my first, my only. 'I didn't know you were coming back,' I say quietly.

'Nor did I,' he says. 'Until Della dumped me and I figured what better way to celebrate than with a houseful of fucked-up sixth-formers.'

I feel a surge of something as this sinks in – sorrow, maybe? Self-hatred?

'I— About last night . . .'

'What happened last night?' Harry asks. 'Did I miss something?'

Tom shakes his head. 'Nothing happened,' he says, as if it is no more than a matter of fact. Then he grasps the estate agent's details that are still stacked in with the newspapers, and wanders back to the table, breathing nonchalance. 'Fuck, that is one ugly house.'

'Language, Tom, please.' Angela clips neatly into the kitchen. 'David?' She looks around. Finds who she is looking for rooting in the utility room. 'David, there's vomit in the en suite. Can you . . .'

'Yes. Yes, of course.' He hurries off, head down.

'Well, that is the last time we let either of you have a party here,' she announces.

'What about at – ' Tom peers at the particulars – 'Nine The Beeches? Or will we ruin the generous through-lounge with south-facing French windows? Thatcherite wankers,' he adds under his breath.

'I heard that,' his mother snaps. 'And you're in enough trouble as it is. Do you know there's a pair of . . . of ladies' underwear in the office?'

'Well, they're hardly mine,' Tom protests. 'Ask Harry . . . or Dido.'

I flinch at the insinuation, and the daring look that accompanies it.

But Angela just shakes her head, as if exasperated at both his attitude and the fallacy that it could be me. 'Harry, can you sort them out, please?'

'Later,' Harry groans.

'The last time,' Angela hisses to herself as she pulls a pair of rubber gloves out from under the sink. 'David? David! Why aren't you wearing Marigolds?' And with the pink plastic fingers dangling like limp puppet hands, she stamps back up the stairs to supervise.

'I like the new house,' Harry says to no one in particular. 'I get a walk-in wardrobe.'

'Surprise, surprise,' Tom chants. 'So, what do *you* think, Di?'

'I . . .' I feel the toast flip-flop inside me, as if aware of the dilemma. But there have been enough lies, has been enough game-playing already. 'I hate it,' I tell him.

And he nods then, all the guile and sarcasm of the last few minutes gone, just like that. 'I knew you would,' he says.

I smile back then. 'I should go. It was . . . good to see you.'

He laughs, but a real one now. A tender one. Almost sorry. 'You too.'

'Harry?' I try. But her head is back down on the counter, and her breathing slowed to a steady semi-snore. 'Can you . . . ?'

'I'll tell her you'll see her tomorrow.'

'Thanks.'

I turn to go, heading for the back door.

'Di?'

'Yeah?' I turn back, expectant, hopeful.

'Your boots.' He nods towards the hallway.

I feel heat flood my cheeks again, chewed-up toast twitch and slop in my stomach. 'Oh, right. Course.' Then, to hide it, and in a last display of hope, I change tack, throw him a line. 'See you, then.'

But he doesn't say it then. Doesn't say anything at all.

Because maybe this time it's true. Maybe he won't see me.

And as I walk down the terracotta tiles of the Lodge's wide lobby, I count the ways in which I love this house, and hate the one in the picture. I hate its mock-Tudor gable, as if it's trying to be something it's not whilst laughing at those who fall for it too; I hate the shining surfaces, the shining family posed ridiculously next to a pristine three-piece suite. But most of all I hate it because it means the gate to Wonderland will be closed now. I hate it because it means he will never be waiting on the other side of the wall. I hate it because it means this is the end. Because I won't have a chance to rescue this paradise lost. Unless . . . unless . . .

That afternoon Tom heads back to Hull. Two weeks after that the prospectus for their English department drops heavily, pointedly, on our doormat.

Harry raises her eyes to the nicotine-stained ceiling of our kitchen, takes another Silk Cut drag. 'Could you be any more obvious?'

'What?'

'Oh, come on.' She taps ash into a saucer, looks me in the eye. 'He is never going to fuck you.'

'Who?' I say, I lie.

'Duh. Tom.'

'Who said I want to fuck him?' I mumble.

'What, like that isn't why Jimmy dumped you?'

'What? Who told you that?'

'Jimmy,' she says. Like it's obvious. Which I guess it is.

I should be glad he didn't tell her the whole sorry story, I suppose, though I know he's spilled a whole jarful of other secrets and lies to whoever would listen – that I'm a prude, that I'm a prick-tease, that I'm probably a lesbian anyway.

I pleaded with him to change his mind. Promised I would make it up to him. And for fifteen fuck-filled, wordless minutes he let me believe he'd forgiven me. Then he washed his cock in the bathroom sink and told me he never wanted to keep seeing me once he went to uni anyway. That Tom was welcome to me.

'Never going to happen.' Harry dismisses the thought. 'You are literally the girl next door. Besides, it's too weird for words.'

'I won't be for long,' I say in my pathetic defence.

Harry takes another drag, squints. 'Won't be what?'

'The girl next door. You're moving.'

She snorts. 'Oh, babe. Don't kid yourself. You will *always* be the girl next door.'

And I will.

Because three weeks and two days later, on Monday, 19 October – Black Monday – something called the stock market crashes, which is meaningless to me in our ginger-bread house. But not to those in the castle on the other side of the wall. Because, along with dozens of others who crowd the platform of Audley End for the early-morning clickety-clack commute to the city, David loses his job. And along with it, the new house.

'Seriously?' I say when you tell me. 'They're not moving?'

'Not any time soon,' you reply.

And I know I should feel bad for David, should worry at what this means for his future, should realize that they may have to move after all, downsize, head to Harlow even, where the houses are smaller and cheaper and the commute shorter. But instead I can only smile.

And, as you let smoke trail from your painted lips and out of the attic window, let your kohl-rimmed eyes fall on the wall between us and the Lodge, so, it seems, can you.

*

Not once have I asked you why, not once have I seen even a snapshot of what might have been going on in your head all that time, all those times.

I have so many whys, Edie, so many questions. I should have asked them back then, should have forced you to talk to me, or at least to a paid professional. I regret it now, regret all those missed chances, opportunities that offered themselves up even last week.

But here we are. Me so full of words now and you silent, not even managing to swear. The times I wished you'd shut up, stop saying *shit* and *bloody*, at least in front of teachers or friends or their parents; would feel the stab of the word as I watched the flicker of disbelief, and then the disgust in their eyes.

But now, Edie, I would give my arm to hear you tell someone to fuck off.

Even me.

# The Swish of the Curtain

## November 1987

The envelope is half sodden by the time I manage to prise it from our temperamental letter box, a creature that snaps angrily down on my fingers, adding a smear of blood to the wetness.

You glance up from your second cup of black coffee at my yelp.

'I'll fix that,' you say.

Which means you'll get David to fix it.

A month has passed since Black Monday, and he is redundant now in every sense, it seems. Angela has got herself a job as a receptionist at a new beauty salon – 'Just pin money,' she says, though we all know it is the only money, for now at least. But she has appearances to keep up, and so David, she tells people, is consulting now. Though the only consulting I have seen him do is to ask you whether you take sugar in black coffee.

That was why I wrote to Tom – or at least why I told him I was writing. To describe the acute change in atmosphere, the way our world seems off-kilter now, with David home all the time, with Angela out. I told him about Jimmy, too.

Told him I was glad of it, that I'd been planning on ending it anyway, a detail I justify by the momentary urge I had for him to disappear that night, for him never to have existed at all. I leave out the times I cried, that I told Harry I'd fucked up, begged her to call him for me, to ask him to take me back.

Because they weren't real, I tell myself. They were just a reaction to the threat of change, of loss, panic at the thought of having no one at all.

Besides, I have to be light, breezy, even. 'Tell me about Hull,' I write. 'Should I apply? The English department's supposed to be brilliant. Imagine – three years just reading books. What larks, Pip! Larkin was the librarian, so it should be good. I can't believe you missed him by a year. You could have told him it was true. "This Be The Verse", I mean. *They fuck you up*, and all that . . . Anyway, maybe you could show me around sometime. Only if you have the time, of course.'

And, it seems, he does.

*Dido Sylvia Jones*
*The Gingerbread House*

I recognize the handwriting – the looping, even slope – and the address too, because no one else would use my middle name, no one else remember my fairy-tale obsession. And my heart stag-leaps in dread and delight.

You look up from the chaise longue. 'What is it, anyway?'

'Nothing,' I lie. 'Junk.'

Then, dropping my bag on the floor, I clomp up the stairs

as if what I am holding is mere ephemera, of no more import than a churlish chain letter, or a Hallmark card from an erstwhile aunt, fifty pence Sellotaped to the inside. When all the time I am aware that this wet, brown oblong is hotter than a coal.

I sit on my bed and slip my finger under the flap of the envelope. There is no *SWALK* on the back, no red seal, and the thin paper almost disintegrates as I pull against the cheap glue. And though his reply is one side to my five, and wide-ruled to my narrow, it says all I need, all I want. That he hadn't read Larkin before but he has now and, God, I am so right about that poem, right about parents. That yes, Hull is brilliant for English. That yes, I should come up and *hang for a bit*. And though he doesn't say what, exactly, hang means in these circumstances, or how long a bit constitutes, I dismiss these as minor details, questions to be dealt with later, in person. Because all that matters, all I can focus on, is that I am going to see Tom again. And this time I will do everything right.

The phone rings seventeen times before it's answered. And then it's by a woman, who I know could be anyone – a housemate, a friend – but still I start when I hear her voice, thick with Northern vowels and a nonchalance I will never manage to attain. 'One-one-four. Who is it?'

'It's . . . can I speak to Tom?'

I hear the phone clatter – against a table, or the wall – and a muffled shout into a void that I try to furnish with mismatched chairs, paint-peeling banisters, his posters Blu-Tacked to flock wallpaper.

A minute passes as I listen in on the everyday sounds of student life, on muffled drumbeats, a shriek of laughter, the metallic ring of a pan falling; then footsteps, and the fumbling of a receiver being picked up, and, at last, his voice.

'Yello.'

'Hi,' I manage, a strangled whisper, half menacing, half sexual. Shit. 'It's me. Dido.'

'Hello, Me-Dido.' I hear the smile that stretches his words sideways, and almost sigh in relief. 'How's tricks?'

'Tricks is, yeah, good.' I pause, waiting for him to take his turn. But I've misunderstood. It's still my go. I take a breath. 'So, I was wondering if it was still OK to come up?'

There is silence. Then interference, crackling, and the sound of someone – her – in the background. 'You coming, Tom?'

A hand muffles the receiver. 'Yeah, give me a minute.' Then he is back with me, but already halfway out of the door. 'Listen, I have to go. Demo, you know.'

'Sure,' I say, like my life is just so full of moments like this. Like I'm not disappointed.

But he knows me better than that. 'I meant it,' he said. 'Come whenever. I'll be here.'

'This weekend?' I say quickly. Before either of us can change our minds.

'Sure,' he echoes.

'Cool,' I reply, my verbal shrug word-perfect for once.

'See you then, then.'

'Not if I see you first.'

If he replies, I don't hear it, just the clack of the phone into its holder, leaving me hanging, bathed in the buzz of dialling tone, and the hum of potential. And then, cartoon-like in my head, all around me questions soar, borne on the backs of bluebirds and butterflies, asking, *Where will I sleep? Will it be in his room? Should I take condoms?*

*Who is she?*

Harry is scornful, scathing even. 'That is beyond stupid,' she says as we trudge down Borough Lane, coatless despite the cold, and David's pleas. 'He's probably back with Della and you'll end up looking like a right twat.'

'I don't care about Della,' I lie. 'It's not about that. It's so I can see the English department.'

'Bullshit.' She dismisses my claim as if wafting away a fly.

'Bull true,' I counter. 'Besides, you're the one who told me to do English. You're the one who said I could be a writer.'

Harry was obsessed with growing up, with what – or who – she would become. 'Princess,' she declared at first. Then, when it was made clear that that would entail either a change in the law or marriage to the ageing and abominable Edward or Andrew, she set her sights on more achievable aims, working her way through the roll call of prima ballerina, pop star, prime minister – the most unlikely of all for a girl like Harry – before settling on the simple, but probable, 'famous'.

But me? I struggled even to think of an answer.

'God, it's not like I'm asking you the valency of boron or something,' Harry complained that time. 'Just pick a job.'

But it's not as easy as that. It's not just a case of plucking a career from the handbook.

'Teacher?' she offered.

I fake-shuddered. 'I'd rather stick needles in my eyes,' I insisted. 'I'd have to grow a moustache.'

'And never wash,' Harry added.

'And wear slacks. Slacks!' I wailed.

'Even the word gives me hives,' said Harry, having moved on from sarcasm to laconic exaggeration somewhere around the O-level mark. 'Inventor?'

'Of what?'

'I don't know. That's your problem.' She fumbled in her bag for a packet of Marlboro, lit one up with a flick of a Zippo, a trick she learned from you. 'How about artist, then? Like Edie.'

'She's not an artist,' I said. 'Besides, I'd rather be dead than be like my mother.'

Harry snorted. 'I'd rather be like yours than mine.'

'You don't have to live with her,' I pointed out.

'More's the pity.' She blew a smoke ring from Rimmel-coated lips. 'Oh, wait. I've got it. You can be that writer girl. You know, the one in the kitchen sink.'

'Cassandra Mortmain?' I'd asked, knowing perfectly well the answer was yes.

'Probably. Anyway, not her exactly. But a writer.'

'She doesn't even have a mother,' I observed. 'Just that Topaz woman.'

'The one who wanders around half-naked being weird?'

She passed me the cigarette, and I vaguely inhaled. 'Fair point,' I conceded. 'That is sort of Edie.'

'It's totally Edie.'

I sighed, deliberate, dramatic. 'Anyway, what would I write about?'

'Us,' she said, a silent 'duh' tagged on, as if it was obvious.

'We haven't done anything,' I said.

'Not yet,' Harry admitted. 'But we will. *I* will, anyway. I'm going to be on television one day. On *Parkinson*.'

'More like *Pebble Mill*.'

'Fuck off. Anyway, that's what you'll do. I bet you my entire Madonna back catalogue *and* my patent pixie boots you write a book. A heap of them, in fact.'

What I didn't tell her, what I don't tell her, is that it's not a writer I want to be, but the girl *in* the book. That the real reason I read – the only reason I read – is because I am imagining myself on the pages, trying to narrate a life for myself more ordered and more accomplished than the one I'm living. It will take me decades to discover that that is what writing really is – a giant game of make-believe. But for now, all I know is that I want to wrap myself in books.

And Tom.

She sticks her hands in her back pockets. 'Just don't come running to me when it all goes tits up.'

'I won't,' I say. 'Because it won't, because there are no tits involved.'

There is silence for a few seconds, while Harry thinks. 'Do you think mine are too small?' she asks finally, pulling her

Henley top out and peering down. 'Ricky says anything more than a handful's a waste, but he's got massive fucking fingers.'

'No,' I say. 'They're perfect. You're perfect.'

'*Pff*,' she dismisses. And the conversation is over.


If you are suspicious, though, you don't let on. At least not at first.

'Well, the car's buggered,' you declare, with less dismay than I would have hoped for. 'So I hope you weren't expecting me to drop you at the station.'

'I wasn't,' I say quickly. 'I'll get a bus or something.'

'Oh, God.' You shudder at the horror of the vomit-smelling Viceroy coach. 'David will probably run you if you ask.'

'Thanks,' I mumble.

That morning, though, you walk in on me in the shower – the bathroom lock broken (I suspect deliberately so, an excuse for Mr Fix-It to visit) – and catch me shaving. And not just my legs.

'David called,' you announce. 'You need to leave in half an hour.'

'Jesus, Edie,' I snap. 'I could have cut myself.'

You stare at my pudenda, at the hair-clogged razor, put two and two together.

'He won't care,' you say. 'Not if he's worth anything.'

'It's not . . .' But I don't bother to finish that sentence, don't bother to lie, because we both know who it's for.

'Well, you'd better at least do the other side, I suppose,' you say eventually. 'Otherwise you're going to look awfully skew-whiff.'

'God, Edie. Can you just . . . go?'

'I'm gone,' you say, turning, your hand waving a goodbye. 'Just, whatever happens, promise me you'll use a condom.'

Why? I say in my head. Worried I'll end up ruining my life by getting pregnant?

'Two,' I say out loud. 'At once.'

I barely eat on the four-hour train journey, barely breathe, it seems, so that by the time I step onto the wide, pitted platform at Hull Paragon, I am both faint with hunger and shaking from the adrenaline that seems to have replaced my blood pint for pint. All around me vowels are elongated and words stretched and strangled into almost undecipherable sentences by strangers dressed in clothes too tight, too short, too thin, so that I might as well be in the Gare du Nord, not the grim North, so foreign is this land to me.

Though you have found me five pounds for a taxi, I decide to save it for an emergency, or dinner, and walk to Tom's instead; walk off the dizzy, I tell myself.

I should have got the cab, I think.

I have wended my way slowly past the run-down red-brick two-up two-downs that crowd the station and into the pale stock of the avenues that surround Pearson Park. But despite my lack of speed, despite the season, I am sweating into my specially chosen 'student' clothes, my cheap leggings chafing my clean-shaven thighs and riding high into cracks and crevices.

I'll ask for a shower, I think, as I check my pocket-creased, library-photocopied street map and turn onto Park Grove.

Or he'll offer me one. And that tiny seed, no more than an accident of circumstance, is all it takes for the fiction to flow. Within seconds I have conjured a scene in which he walks in on me naked in the steam. In the first version he backs away, reddened, flustered, but I, the siren that I am, call him to accompany me, and he strips slowly, tantalizingly, before slipping into the hotel-impeccable bathroom of my mind. In the second version he needs no beckoning at all, but is so overcome at the sight of my voluptuousness, he is hard before he even climbs out of his Calvins.

'Watch it,' a passer-by warns, pushed off the pavement by my bulky presence and mental absence.

I come to, mutter a sorry, add a flush of pink to the patina of sweat that clings to my cheeks. In my imagination I briefly paint this as post-coital glow. In reality I know I appear nothing more than unfit and feverish, a look I am not sure has ever won hearts or minds. Then, checking house numbers, I wince and double back on myself, wiping my face on my coat sleeve before I turn up the cracked and weed-clogged path to 114.

There's no bell. Of course not. Instead a felt-tipped sign proclaims in psychedelic lettering that visitors should 'knock loudly or try round the back', under which someone has biroed 'fnarr'.

I peer down the passageway, a route I will later name in my newly acquired accent as the 'ginnel'. But for now it's just a bicycle-strewn side return, layered with a smattering of litter and cat shit. Taking my chances, I hammer on the front door. Once. Then again.

'All *right*,' comes a call down a corridor. I see a blurred figure, then a face form behind the stained-glass panels, giving body to a voice I recognize from the phone.

The door opens, and I see at once that this is her, but also not her – not the her of my imaginings, anyway. This girl is spiked, shaven, short. In one ear she has five piercings; on her T-shirt Tom Robinson lyrics confirm she is glad to be gay.

So relieved am I that I laugh, a short, sputtering thing, but a laugh nonetheless.

'What's so fucking funny?' She pronounces the words like foot. Fooking foony. I echo her, sounding them out in my head. Then remember her question.

'Nothing,' I say. 'I . . . it's been a long journey.'

She nods, peers. 'Dido?'

And my embarrassment is chased away by smug vanity – the knowledge that I am known, that he has told people about me.

But what has he told them?

'Attic.' She gestures behind and up with her head. Then, in case I am as dumb as I look, 'Top of the stairs.'

'Right, thanks.' And heaving my heavy rucksack higher on my heavier body, I climb up forty-eight bare-boarded treads to his bedroom.

The door is closed, and this one – though covered in post-cards and photographs and an old Polaroid of its occupant aged seven and naked – bears no instructions as to how to behave in this situation. Do I knock? Or just turn the handle and hope? What if there's a girl after all – a not-gay one this time – in there with him?

213

I listen for signs of sex, then, when there is no telltale groan, or rhythmic grunt, merely of life. But there is nothing. Just the traffic from Princes Avenue filtering in through thin glass and the warped, cracked wood of a dormer. 'Tom?' I try.

I hear the roll of a body on a creaking mattress. A low moan.

'Mmmm.'

'I – it's me . . . Dido,' I add to my stammer, in case I am unmemorable after all.

'Shit. Shit.' I hear the rustle of sheets, the thud of feet onto more bare boards. 'Come in.'

Pride pricked into a deflated balloon with the realization he has forgotten after all, I turn the plastic handle that is already hot in my hand, push the door ajar.

The room is wide, and long. A desk and chair and armchair under one eave, an unusually wide double bed – two singles put together, I think – under the other, on which he now sits, in creased T-shirt and boxers and a rumpled apology of a smile.

'I didn't forget,' he says before I can say my own sorry. 'Late one last night. I was just catching up.'

I nod as if I've been there, am always there, as if it's nothing. 'I can go,' I offer. 'If you're tired.'

'No,' he insists, shaking his head slowly. 'Christ. Come in, come in.' He pats the bed next to him and I walk over, sit down, feel the weight of my bag pull me backwards and have to hold onto the edge of the bed to keep steady.

'What's in there? A dead body?'

'Something like that,' I say, thinking of the five changes of outfit, second pair of Docs, hairdryer, make-up bag, and two books – one Stendhal, one Salinger – that I have packed in the pathetic hope of creating the perfect impression of the lit-student-to-be.

'Here.' He reaches to wrest it off my back, then drops it next to the bed, a bed I wonder immediately if I am to sleep in, if I am allowed to sleep in. 'That can wait. Tell me everything.'

'Everything?'

'Everything,' he confirms. 'Starting with that excuse for a sister of mine.'

So I do. I tell him everything. Starting with Harry's latest object of desire – some private-school kid with a scowl and a dick the size of a salami, she claims, along with him being The One (honestly, Dido, I really think he is this time) – and ending on the stagnant state of Saffron Walden, because even though I've only been in the big city for an hour, I can see the small town for what it is.

And in between we riff on the Smiths' split, Clause 28, the disappearance of Bovril crisps; we eat cheese on toast and drink flat Coke and the vinegary dregs of a wine bottle; and he puts on some trousers and I take off my boots, and we lie back on the bed and watch the sun set in the corner of the dormer through the haze of dope smoke and the pleasant fug of alcohol.

We don't talk about his parents, and the silence that clots the house, clings to the curtains and carpet with every sigh of disappointment, every look that says *You have failed*. We

215

don't talk about you, either, though there is plenty to say: the way you've taken to slinking into your bedroom with the telephone, trailing its extension cord down the stairs like a begging-to-be-lit dynamo fuse, slipping out at odd times *just for five minutes*, then an hour later returning, breathless and ruddy, from God knows where. I should demand an explanation, play mother to the persistent teenager you insist on being. But I don't think I want your truth, just as Tom avoids theirs.

The room is dark now, the street lights only managing to sneak in far enough to bathe a patch of floor in their orange glow.

'Pub?' he asks.

I don't bother with my *yes*. Just heave myself up and pull on a Doc, my sock sending a puff of stale feet into the already musty air. I must smell, I think. Unwashed since this morning, my floor-hung clothes are now infused with sweat and smoke and other people's fast-food lunches. But Tom still smells of last night, and clearly doesn't care, and I am drunk and drugged enough to join him.

And so the pub it is.

It's called the Queens and squats at the top of the park, straddling the back-to-backs off Beverley Road and the bedsit-divided mansions off Newland and Princes. Inside it could be any pub – could be the Duke on the High Street on a Saturday night: all brass and bad carpet and worse hair. Except that this is flushed with the exoticism of unfamiliar accents, music, clothes – Manchester baggy carried over the

Pennines on the cross-country train, at least a year before it will find its way to Essex – all sprinkled liberally like fairy dust, dust that rubs off on me and makes me glow in achievement and anticipation.

I can't remember the names and faces of the parade of people I am introduced to that night; I don't need to, because I don't leave Tom's side for any longer than it takes to queue and then pee in the peach-painted toilets. Then, five double vodkas and three hours later, laughing, clinging to each other as if the world might spin too fast and send us tumbling, we stumble back through the park, along paths, past statues that we salute and serenade, across flower beds we tiptoe through, avoiding daffodils and dog shit, then along the yellow-brick road, through the door of 114 and up the forty-eight stairs to bed.

Yes, to bed.

Did you know that, Edie? That that's when it happened; when he finally gave in to my puppy-dog pleading eyes and raging hormones and shagged me?

If I make it sound empty, meaningless, then I'm misleading you. Because it is everything but.

It is everything that my first time with Jimmy should have been, and nothing like it was.

It is slow, and breathtakingly rapid.

It is tender, and brutal.

It is never-ending, and over too soon.

Do I tell him I love him? God, no. I am not that brave, or foolish. But in the weak shafts of half-light as night turns to morning, I muster the courage for a question, ask, 'Is this . . . Are we . . . ?'

He smiles, a flash of white in the blur. '. . . A thing?'

I nod.

'Yes,' he says. 'Dido Sylvia Jones, I think we are a thing.'

She's sitting in the armchair when I open my eyes. Has been there a while, I guess from the almost empty mug of tea that sits on the floor beside her. She has a mass of blonde hair and an upturned button of a nose that belongs on screen or in a story. I know without asking who she is. I, on the other hand, it seems, am somewhat of a mystery.

'Hello,' she says, curiously.

I sit up, clutching sheets to me, though I'm still wearing a T-shirt – mine, not his.

'Tom?' I say.

He groans and rolls over, reaching across the expanse of sheet and the crack between beds that has, I notice with both sadness and relief, widened to a gulf in the night.

'Oh, you *are* in there, then,' she says.

It's Tom's turn to sit up. He's not so suitably attired, his back a patchy red and marked with lines that I tell myself, tell her telepathically, are just indentations from the creased sheets.

'Della,' he says. 'What the fuck?'

But his face is pale, and I feel his panic – that he has been caught out, can see who I am in the cold light of the freezing morning: a cuckoo, no more than that. Just Dido. His sister's friend. The girl next door.

'I should go,' I say.

'No, no,' Della says. 'You enjoy it. While it lasts. I'm off anyway. Places to go, people to see.'

She stands, knocking over the tea. 'Oops,' she deadpans.

'Fuck's sake,' Tom says.

'Fuck you,' Della replies, her acting skills wearing thin.

I shrink back, though I am invisible already, it seems, replaced by the drama, the backstory of these two. This girl who flings herself at the door, this fool boy who follows her, a snatched towel wrapped around his waist.

I am alone then, naked and goose-pimpled, the electric heater failing to warm the air above breath-misting levels; last night's promise, its platitudes, failing to steady the too-fast thrum of my heart. He didn't mean any of it, I realize now. It was a lie, though he needn't have bothered; he was already inside me.

I push that image out, picture them downstairs instead, him pleading, her pouting, eyes wet with the threat of tears. I feel my own well up, feel the prickle of salt and the run of snot as I gasp out a sob.

I will not do this.

I will not be made a fool of.

I will go. Now. Before he gets back. So that he can't see me, see that I care.

I don't care.

I don't care.

I—

'Di?'

I look up from my rucksack, yesterday's stained knickers in my hand.

'Di, what are you doing?'

I look away again. 'Going,' I manage. I push my pants down inside the canvas, grab at clean ones. 'I'll change my train. Or something.' Or sleep at the station. Or call David. He'll come, I know he will.

'But . . . I don't want you to go.'

I pause, hear the shudder of my breath, the soft buzz of the bar heater.

'Della – she's a drama queen,' he says. 'This was . . . a stunt. That's all. We're not . . . we haven't for a while now.'

I want to believe him, want to hold on to this sliver of hope so hard it will crystallize into a diamond.

'I told her about you,' he says then.

'Told her what?'

He crouches down, reaches for my hand.

I let him take it.

'That we're . . . that we're a thing.'

I sniff.

'Do you still want to be a thing?' he asks.

I laugh then, wipe my eyes, my nose on my already damp shoulder. 'Yes,' I nod. 'I want to be a thing.'

And so despite our stale morning breath, despite Della, despite what Harry might think, and Angela might say, despite Jimmy, despite my lopsided, cack-handed pubic hair, a thing we become.

We are a thing that night on the doorstep as we get in

from the pub; we are a thing the next morning, sheets pulled high over our heads as we stare at each other in wonder in the warmth of our makeshift tent; we are a thing on the damp platform of Paragon station as we say our goodbyes. Not a fumbling, forgettable one-night stand, but a thing. *Something*. Something bigger, better, with a shared life, a history – a glorious, brilliant one. And a shining future too.

The train gets in at ten and I call you from the station, bursting with it, so oblivious to anything but my own happiness I can't hear the slur of your words, though they drag like fingers through treacle.

'Edie!' I babble. 'Is the car fixed? Can you get me?'

'Can't you get a taxi?' you ask. 'I gave you money.'

'I lost it,' I lie, even though telling you I turned it into a round of vodka and tonics would probably elicit if not a yelp of delight then a quiet satisfaction.

'Fine,' you sigh before hanging up.

I call Tom then, tell him I'm nearly home, promise again to wait until Christmas to tell anybody, until we can do it together, promise to call him tomorrow, promise that I miss him. Then, my addiction sated for a few moments, I hang up and wait in the safety of the phone box for the chug-chug of the 2CV. But when a car finally pulls up, it's with the slow, satisfied purr of a Volvo.

It's David.

'Your mother couldn't come,' he says, holding open the passenger door as if he is no more than a taxi.

'I thought the car was fixed?' I ask.

221

'Yes. It's more—'

'Is she . . . is she ill?'

'Not exactly.'

When I get back you are clearly drunk. 'So how was it?' you ask. 'How did the haircut go down?'

I glance at David, grit my teeth. 'Edie,' I plead.

'We must celebrate!' you insist. You grab at the drinks cabinet, snatch a bottle of something brown.

'I think you've had enough,' David says.

'Oh, for Christ's sake,' you protest. 'You're just like her.'

'Edie,' he says, grabbing hold of your arm to steady you as you threaten to pitch into the fridge.

I don't know what's going on. Or rather, I do. But I don't want to see it, still less talk about it. I just want to be back in that attic room, on that avenue, listening to REM and planning our brilliant book-worthy tomorrow.

Because those few nights have allowed me to fashion a future for us, a filigree structure so splendid, so tangible, that I can forget that I am viewing it through the beautiful skew of rose-tinted glasses and punch-drunk love. I can forget that its foundations are nothing more than youthful folly, his stilted words and my blind faith; that its walls are as weak as Jericho's.

I should have said something. Should have stopped it when I had the chance. Then maybe I could have stopped it all coming tumbling down.

But instead I run up the stairs, slam my door, and flop onto my bed. Then, without even having to look, knowing what is cued up, I press play on the tape recorder, turn up the volume and let the Cocteau Twins carry me, let their Pearly Dewdrops drop and let myself swim back up the muddy Humber and into the sanctuary of his arms.

# The End of
# the Affair

## December 1987

We were marked out. Had been since that hot August morning we moved here; not for being outsiders, incomers, because the town bustled with new lives, imported from Cambridge, Stansted, even London – at least the better parts – but for being the wrong sort of settler. But as I shrank from the stares, hid behind your legs, did my best to camouflage myself in clothes that could be considered almost normal, you courted controversy. You waltzed down George Street in whatever had tumbled from your dressing-up box of a wardrobe that morning. You revelled in the attention, the disapproval, snorting with laughter and sticking your tongue out, with me scurrying red-faced in your wake, all too aware of the invisible leper bell that jangled with each step by dint of association.

'What's a pariah?' I asked, fathoming my way through the Bible stories Mrs Bonnett had set us as summer reading.

You looked up from a battered Plath, took a thoughtful drag on your cigarette, before replying, '*I* am, Dido. *I* am.'

But over the years the town had become inured to your more outlandish leanings, and we were tarred, in your eyes, with the tired brush of acceptance, if not absolute assimilation, replaced in their tattle-tales by a transvestite fishmonger called George and a woman with seven children of varying hues. I was relieved, delighted, at this change of affairs. But you, you bristled with unease. I should have known then you would find a way back to purdah.

It is Christmas Eve. The night of the Trevelyans' party – going ahead despite the change in circumstances, because Angela has new friends to flourish, the pampered and the preened to impress – and the night Tom and I have chosen to announce, or admit, our affair, on the grounds that, if Angela is pissed off, she's less likely to say so in public.

Harry knows something is going on, has asked me countless times what happened in Hull. Did we? Am I? But I brush her off, tell her it's complicated, that she should talk to Tom, until, exasperated, she stamps off to see Simon, the Perse boy with the penis.

If you know about Tom and me, if you believe what you blurted out, Bordeaux-drunk, the night I came home, you don't let on, or don't care. Your own life is drama enough, it seems, corralling you in the attic with your charcoals and paint, though on the few occasions I have bothered to venture up – to offer tea, toast, television specials – I can see little evidence of art, just a muddle of half-finished sketches and abandoned gouache, and you on your back on the day bed, staring blankly at the ceiling, waiting, you say, for inspiration to strike.

Or the phone to ring.

I should talk to you. Or at least call Toni. But I am seventeen and in love and so the world turns for me now. Wherever I walk is centre stage, the spotlight tracking me and a glitterball dappling me with diamonds. This is so much more than I felt with Jimmy, so much more even than I imagined from the brash Danielle Steels I have hocked from Harry or the dusty du Mauriers that line my own ever-expanding shelves. As I look at myself in the mirror, a debutante flushed with anticipation and advocaat, I see, finally, a story-worthy heroine staring back: a Bennet girl, a Becky Sharp, a Bright Young Thing.

You are sitting at the kitchen table with a packet of cigarettes, a book you are pretending to care about, and an almost empty bottle of red; a disappearing act I suspect is all your own work, and all tonight.

I fidget in the doorway, high on stolen Chanel and my own impatience. 'Are you coming?' I ask, more as a cursory attempt at politeness than an actual invitation.

You look up from the same page you were on when I went to change two hours ago. 'I don't think so,' you say.

This is before the age of the two-a-penny *whatever*, but the noise I make in reply carries the same contemptuous dismissal, and hits just as hard. Something – pain, pride, even – flickers across your face and I feel a rush of guilt as sobering as caffeine. 'See you later, then,' I add, my voice tinged with what I hope is hope.

You nod. 'Later, yes.' Then add, 'Have fun.'

I wait for the *Don't do anything I wouldn't do* that has always followed, to which my reply, albeit silent, has always been, could only be: 'Well, all that leaves is murder.' But instead what I get is the click, suck sound of another cigarette being lit, and the glug of Malbec into a greasy tumbler.

I write a mental note to make it up to you tomorrow, because I am already sure you will be long asleep by the time I stagger back. Then I close the door on your weird little world, and dance down the brambled garden path and through the wooden gate to Wonderland.

The house is full, fuller than I had imagined; the dining room and lounge a who's who of the self-appointed great and good of this parochial paradise, and around them a pecking flock in peacock colours. All hairbands and shoulder pads and sugar-free smiles; able to recite the calorie content of Waitrose ready meals as well as they can the Lord's Prayer. I search among them for a mop of hair that grows below a collar line, for a shirt that isn't button-down or pinstriped, but come up empty-handed.

'Di?' The question is soft but resonant, a tone that carries with it corduroy and the faint stain of cigars.

'Mr Trevelyan.' I turn and receive a kiss on my cheek: a greeting that is new to me, too continental for this man, this town, and I wonder where he has picked it up.

'Oh Lord. David,' he laughs. 'You need to call me David. Now that . . .' He trails off and I am wondering what the missing words are, worrying what they are, when another voice cuts through the crowd, this one cold and crystal.

'Dido.'

'Angela,' I say, trying the word out for size.

But her face, strained to start with, contracts further and I see that my privilege does not apply here.

'Where's your mother?' she asks eventually. There is calculation in her voice now, and so I try to work out the right answer.

'She's not feeling great,' I say eventually – a catch-all for any confession she later comes up with.

'Oh,' David almost blurts, his concern uncontained, and alarmingly real. 'Should I go and see if there's anything—'

'Oh, for heaven's sake, David,' Angela snaps. 'Not tonight.'

'She's fine,' I say quickly, then tangle myself into your web by adding, 'Just a headache. She'll be fine by the morning.'

'Well, if not, if she's not up to . . . cooking and whatnot, you're always welcome here,' David offers. 'Isn't she, Angela?'

It's a question, not a statement, and the look that clouds Angela's face tells me that welcome might not be quite the word, but, the queen of keeping up appearances, she forces out a clipped, 'Of course.'

'Can't have you going hungry at Christmas,' David adds.

'Thanks,' I mumble, wondering if the offer will still be open once they know what I've been doing. What Tom has been doing.

The thought of him, then, sends my stomach skittering, my heart soaring. He's been back a week but we've barely seen each other, barely been able to kiss, touch, talk even. At the Lodge there is a roll call of relatives to receive or visit, to recite his grades to, his postgrad plans. In the Duke he is cornered, claimed by his old tribe – Michael Nelson, at Imperial now, learning how to design Choppers, rather than ride them; Nicky Pakely, still gigging, still serving up burgers at ABC Barbecue until the Big Time comes calling; Katy Weller even, still lissom and at Loughborough now, training for the national squad, or the office of a suburban PE department. I scowl at her, silently, invisibly, but though Tom nods along, it is me whose fingers he feels for in the crush at the bar; me who he comes back to kiss in the shadow of the tree house where we used to play at mummies and daddies, where he used to stammer out an *I love you, Mrs Herriot*; me who he blows kisses to now as he walks backwards across the lawn and to bed.

He has not said the words. Not yet. But oh, God, the times I have mouthed them silently down the phone to him, or out loud at the photo Blu-Tacked to my mirror, in the elaborate stories I weave in my head, plotting out our lives as if they were as easily malleable as narrative on a page.

I love him, Edie.

I love him with a feeling I can only describe as a fever.

I love him so hard and so intensely that I cannot hold it in any longer, am going to tell him, tonight. Once we have told the others.

'She's upstairs.'

Angela's voice wakes me from my reverie. 'Tom?' I blurt.

'Harry,' she replies, her brow furrowed with confusion, or annoyance, maybe. 'But yes, him too.'

I climb the stairs to the den, each step shortening my breath, quickening my heartbeat. The door is ajar enough for me to see him lying back on a beanbag, letting the sound of something I cannot name or even place wash over him, albeit with the volume at a monitored no-more-than-seven. And as I watch his chest rise and fall, his hands trace time to the music, I cannot still my beating heart, much less the surge of need.

'Tom?'

He opens his eyes, and the trance lifts, his face creasing into a smile. 'Di.' He crooks a finger and I follow it, pushing the door closed behind me with a foot before falling, crawling, into his arms.

'Where's Harry?' I say when we finally pull apart, though it is a matter of inches, his breath still heavy on my face, my hair in hanks on his shoulders.

'Simon,' he says, as if that explains everything. It does explain everything.

'How is he allowed in her room with her?' I ask. 'Ricky wasn't.' Or any of the others boys Angela has treated like dogs, keeping them downstairs and off the sofas, corralling them in the kitchen if at all possible.

'Ricky didn't have a daddy with a yacht or a mummy with a minor title.'

I laugh, let my head fall back, let him run his fingers down my neck, trace the shape of my breasts, then track lower, a hand pushing under my skirt, pulling at the top of my tights.

I hear my breath catch, feel myself wanting him. But it's too soon.

'Tom, not here,' I say.

'Spoilsport,' he says, but pulls his hand away anyway, and

I roll off, slump against the edge of the sofa, pull an album from the stack.

'Play me this,' I tell him.

And he does. He opens the lid of the turntable, lowers the vinyl, drops the needle on the record, and then lies back next to me as we let Dylan soak us, cloak us in his voice of sand and glue, while Harry traipses in for a lighter, trails out again, and we steady ourselves, ready ourselves to tell the world, or at least this small town, that I am not just Dido, not just the girl next door, but permanent, perennial, here for fucking ever.

But, like Cinderella lost in rapture at her prince, I forget who I also am.

I forget that, a few yards away, you are sitting alone, drinking – a combination that never ends well. I forget that you cannot stand to see the world turn without you at its centre, can't bear to watch guests arrive at the ball while you – the real Belle – skulk alone in the kitchen.

And so, like the thirteenth fairy, at the stroke of not-even-nine, you trace my footsteps, let yourself in the back door, and utter a curse that will break this kingdom. A curse that will see the gate locked and the castle shuttered, see a wall of thorns grow, see a would-be queen cast into the wilderness for what will feel like a hundred years.

I wonder, now, what would have happened if you hadn't come; if you'd fallen asleep or thought 'fuck it' instead. Or if you'd lied, smiled through gritted teeth and said nothing more than 'Merry Christmas'. Would we be here now?

Would he?

I don't suppose you even remember it, though, do you?

I will tell you, then. Because, painful though it is in all its TV-drama glory, it is impossible to leave out of this story. It *is* this story, Edie. It is the breaking and making of me and you.

Tom and I are standing on the landing when we hear it, fingers entwined, poised at the top of the stairs for our debut, our Hollywood close-up. But then it comes, a screech, like a creature – a cat – being tormented, or worse.

Tom drops my hand.

Harry flings opens the door to her bedroom. 'What the fuck was that?'

The noise comes again, the squawl, then your voice above it, crowing, arrogant. And in the silence – because it is silent now, the crowd quieted by whatever spectacle they are witnessing in the unlikely Big Top – David apologizing, though it is unclear for what and to whom.

'Fuck,' Tom says. Then he is flying, Harry at his heels, into the crowd.

Simon and I look at each other, the left-behinds. And maybe I know then what is happening, or is about to, because I look back at the den as if to imprint it on my memory. Then, my heart offbeat, my stomach sliding, I say an inexplicable *sorry*, and stumble down the stairs.

It is worse than I could have imagined – and I can imagine widely and wildly. Angela is drunk, a state I have never witnessed, and one that she does not wear well. Her words slur and her accent slips. Aitches are dropped and vowels elongated. Her face is red and contorted and I see how truly ugly she can be.

'Creeping into our lives,' she says. 'First Dido's round here every hour of the day. And then you start on David.'

At my name I feel a slap of shame. At his, the first wave of nausea. Because I know what this is about. Have known for months, although you, for once, have done your best to hide it, and I have tried to deny it.

But it seems I am the only one who has guessed.

'What's she talking about?' Harry demands. 'Mum, what are you talking about?'

Angela doesn't hear her. Or ignores her. 'Like a bloody cuckoo,' she continues. 'No family of your own, so you try to snatch mine.'

'Not now,' David tries.

'Yes, now,' Angela insists. 'Because this time it's . . . she's gone too far. It's Christmas Eve. Christmas Eve, for heaven's sake! You should be with your family. *Your* family. Dido should be with *her* father. Whoever *he* is.'

This, it seems, is the tipping point. Because while Angela is drunk, anything she can do, you can do better. 'You know fuck all about my family,' you spit. 'And fuck all about your own.'

Don't do it, I plead. Don't say it.

But you do.

'You care so much about your family? Who cared about David when he lost his job? Me. Not you. You don't give a shit about him, as long as he can sign cheques.' I close my eyes, as I sense it coming, because I know you, Edie. I know

233

you play dirty. 'And who was it took your daughter to hospital that time?'

There's a pause. Then, 'What time? What are you talking about?'

'Nothing.' Harry snaps. 'Dad, take her home. Make her go home.'

But torn between two scorned women, David does not, cannot move. And you don't take Harry's hint.

'She was pregnant,' you say. 'Didn't know that, did you? But I did. Because who did she come to? Me. That's who.'

'Harry?'

My eyes are wide now, watching as Harry's face pales.

Please stop, I say in my head, beg in my head. Drop it now.

But you haven't played your final card, have you? And you're not leaving without laying that on the table for Angela to see.

'And your precious Tom?'

'Stop it, Edie,' I beg. Out loud this time.

But you don't stop. Don't even register my presence. 'You know he and Dido are fucking about behind your back. Literally.'

I feel my legs threaten to give way. 'Oh God . . .' I mumble.

'You stupid bitch.'

I swing around and Harry's face, once ashen, is rage-red.

'God, you're both the same,' she continues. 'As bad as each other.'

'No!' I protest, then plead, 'Harry, you have to believe me. I wanted to tell you. We were about to say something. We were just waiting for . . .' But before I can finish she has fled, Simon hurrying behind her.

I turn back to Angela, who has pulled her gaping face in, tightened it. 'Get out,' she says then, calm, cold Angela once more. 'Get out and don't come back. Both of you.'

'Angela,' David pleads.

'You too,' she says. Then she turns and leaves the stage, the audience gawping, the rest of the players standing awkwardly in the absence of applause, including—

'Tom,' I blurt. And I look at him, begging him to do something, say something, pull a rabbit out of the hat. 'No,' he mouths, shaking his head. Then he turns and walks down the hall. Seconds later I hear the front door slam.

'Edie, I . . .' David begins.

But as he trails off you swear again, then stalk out of the back door.

I am stranded then; caught, torn between two worlds – the one that contains my wardrobe, and this Narnia I have insinuated myself into. But it isn't Narnia, is it? It never was. And now Tom has left for God knows where and Harry – Harry won't talk to me tonight. So, scarlet-faced, wounded, I slink back across the frost-hardened grass like the thief's dog that I am.

You are in the kitchen, bottle in hand, when I come through the door – of course bottle in hand: you are a drunk, I see that then for the first time. Not Bohemian, not decadent, just a common alcoholic, no different from Billy Bob or the other sad cases and lost causes that line the bar of the Duke on a Monday night.

You look up and I see the truth etched in your sodden, sorry eyes, see clearly the lies you must have told, the lines you have spun. You stare at me, dare me to do something, and for a moment I think I am going to chicken out, do what I always do and stamp to my room to bury myself, my fears, my bristling anger, in a book, in words, wonderful words; words that can be controlled, can let me take the leading role I always seemed to shrink from in real life.

Until Tom.

But you couldn't stand it, could you? Couldn't stand to see me with the hero at my side, couldn't watch me welcomed, the improbable princess, into court while you were kept shut in the attic, going quietly mad.

And, emboldened by alcohol and blinkered by youth, so convinced am I that this is your entire motivation, that you have created this scene solely in order to push me into the wings, to put me in my place, that for once I defy your expectations and mine and tell you exactly what I think.

'I hate you,' I spit. 'I hate you so much right now.'

Your jaw sets, you swig, then swallow. 'I suppose you're going to tell me I've ruined your life.'

I feel my fingers ball into fists at the mockery. 'You have no idea.'

'Me? Ha!' you scoff. '*You* have no fucking idea. Do you know what it's been like? Do you know how hard it's been?'

I am raging now, heart hammering, words scattergunning out. 'What, shagging your neighbour's husband? Or hiding it? Yeah, that must have been really hard. Poor Edie.'

'It *was* hard.'

'Oh, cry me a river.'

You pull a face. 'Did you get that from a book?' you sneer. 'Word-perfect, aren't you? Always so fucking perfect, can't-do-any-wrong Dido.'

I baulk at that, feel myself falter, because perfect is so not what I am, what I have ever been in your eyes. But I am not letting you win, not tonight. 'You're supposed to be the grown-up,' I yell. 'You're supposed to . . . set an example. This isn't normal. Don't you see? The drink and – and the men and now . . . now *this*. It's wrong.'

'Why? Because it's not all Swiss Family Robinson? Well, life isn't like that. It isn't like it is in fucking fairy tales. It's messy and . . . disappointing and most of us are just lucky to get through it at all, let alone with a happy-ever-after.'

I pause. Then, 'You don't deserve one,' I tell you.

'Well, you should be thrilled then. Because I am so far from happy right now. And anyway, I thought you bloody loved David. You were always clinging to him, getting him to carry you around. I thought you'd be pleased.'

'What, so you did this for me?'

You flap a hand, scrabble for your cigarettes.

That was my chance. That was my cue to be the better person. To be brave. To be a grown-up.

But we are children, the pair of us, and we are too stubborn, too self-assured, too far gone now to stop. And so I let you have them, my three wishes, the ones that have pricked me, plucked my sleeve, burned a hole in my pocket; I fling them out like fire-tipped arrows, designed to hurt. 'Yes, I wish David was my father,' I say. 'And I wish Angela was my mother.' Then, the final aim, straight and true. 'Or I wish you'd never had me,' I say. 'Then we'd both be better off.'

You are still, the hand that had been reaching for your lighter suspended mid-grasp, the voice that had been banshee-loud now a thin, reedy whisper. 'You don't mean that,' you say.

I wait, hear the blood rush in my ears, the clock tick-tock twice. 'Yes, I do,' I say.

The words hum with meaning and malice, and I am as shocked by them as you. But they are neon-lit, suspended in the fog-thick air between us, and I cannot take them back.

So instead I walk slowly, steadily, stupidly up to my room, close the door, and count the ways in which I wish you were dead.

# Lessons for Children

## December 1987

We talked about it, me and Harry. Lay back on her bed with a shared bowl of crisps and cans of Fanta and decided how we'd do it, if we were going to kill ourselves. We treated it like some parlour game – *eeny, meeny, miny, moe* between overdose, drowning, gunshot or kitchen knife. Or an exercise in art history, the results strictly Gothic fantasy – all eloquent suicide notes and pale limbs draped delicately, or drifting Ophelia-like across a lily pond, our bodies somehow forgiven the blue lips and bloating.

The reality is so far from my imaginings.

I wake late to the stillness of Christmas morning. Gone is the thrum of traffic, the hammer of roadworks or refurbs; now there is muffled nothingness, a fug that clings to me, cloaks my room, our house; a heaving silence that cleaves a chasm where once sat a wall.

It hits me, heavy and sudden as a train door slam, and I sit bolt upright. I have to talk to Tom. I have to explain – something, anything, everything – and, panicking, I pluck at possibilities and half-truths: that you were drunk, that you were lying, that I hate you, and will forsake you. I pull on boots, a jumper over last night's party clothes, ignore the make-up that has been tear-smeared across my cheeks, the dark rings under my eyes. Tom won't care; we are a thing, a tangible thing. And clutching that knowledge as if it were diamond-precious and iron-solid, as if it were Frodo's own ring, I thud down the stairs, out of the back door and through the brambles to the portal in the wall.

The latch is stiff with age and cold, and rust coats my fingers, the catch snagging my skin as I struggle to lift it. But at last it clanks up and out of its guard and I push hard at the handle, poised to propel myself through the wardrobe. But instead, I feel a sharp pain as my fist gives instead of the door. I push again, cursing the endless wet that has swollen the wood against its jamb, cursing you for not letting David paint it when he offered, then, remembering, cursing him for offering. The door does not move. I rattle it, but it gives no more than a millimetre, still stands solid, unyielding. Then, in a fit of fury and desperation, I kick at it, hard and boot-heavy.

And then I hear it, the soft thunk of metal falling on lawn. A key.

The door has been locked, on their side.

The enormity of it swamps me. I have been exiled from the kingdom. My world has been sectioned off, shrivelled, flung away like a dried-up plum.

This is your doing, I tell myself. You have turned the key with your neuroses, your narcissism, your need to be different, special, the centre of attention.

Then you, I decide, will have to fix it.

I stamp back to the house, slam the door behind me, say your name.

Nothing. Not the whine of a *what?*, nor a groan to leave you alone or fetch you coffee and cigarettes. I walk to the foot of the stairs, wait, rigid, my hand poised on the banister. 'Edie?' I call again, louder this time. Still nothing but the soft whir of the boiler and the drip-drip of a tap into bathwater. The house sits, as zip-lipped as you.

And then I sense it, not just in the quiet but in a weakening of air pressure: there is something missing. Someone.

I feel light-headed, grasp the rail now, try to remember when I last ate – crisps maybe, in the den? But it's not that. Since when have you taken baths in the morning? Baths are an afternoon affair, or a late-night luxury. For reading Nin and drinking gin and sharing with whoever happens to be in the house and willing to swill in a soup of salts and skin.

I will not run, I tell myself, as I take each tread slowly, steadily. I am overreacting. There is nothing bad happening. You are confused, or this is a ritual – yes, a ritual! You are washing yourself clean of it, the mess of yesterday. That is all. I will walk across the landing, open the door and find you shoulder-deep in Badedas-green bubbles or blue food colouring, like you would do for Harry and me, letting us dye ourselves for the hell of it, because *why not?* Never mind that our skin would be tinged for days afterwards, that we would walk to school like washed-out Smurfs.

But for all my bravado, I do not say your name again. And when I push the door open and see that the water is not green or blue but a deep, dirty red – crimson whirls of it spiralling out from each side of you – I know that you have done what you always told Harry and me was the only way to go, pooh-poohing our imaginary arrangements with sleeping pills and suffocation.

You have slit your wrists. The blade of a string-handled paring knife that now lies on the lino dragged through your flesh.

Up. Not across.

You knew what you were doing. You have always known. This isn't a cry for help. This is deliberate, determined. This is suicide, and there is not one rock and roll thing about it.

The next few minutes – I think it is minutes – are played out as if I am wading through sand or am underwater too. I pull the plug, then panic that I have done the wrong thing and push it back, pulling your arms up instead as if the air will stem the flow. But blood pulses out and so appalled am I that I drop them again, sending a wave of bloody water over the side of the bath and onto my feet and a wave of nausea through me that has me hunched over the toilet, seconds wasted while I hurl up what little there is in my stomach – a pale plume of alcohol and bile. Then, somehow sobered, I pull the plug again and haul you out, a harder and heavier task than your still-whip-skinny body should make it; find tea towels to tourniquet, thanking Enid Blyton for filling in what the Brownies could not. And all the time invoking the God you have never believed in, saying, 'Jesus, Edie,' and, 'Oh Christ, Edie, please don't do this.'

But you say nothing. You cannot say anything. Your lungs are clear of water, but your pulse – because, thank that God or whatever woke me, there is a pulse – is too weak. Then I do what I should have done the moment I felt unsettled, felt the strangeness.

I call 999, answer no, yes, give them an address, take instructions and promise to follow them.

But instead, when they've rung off, I do something better. I call for a hero, a saviour who will sweep you up in his arms and carry you as he did me, who will mop your brow and bandage your wounds and make it better.

I call David.

The phone rings, once, twice, three times before I hear the clatter of a receiver picked up, the cut-glass pronunciation of 'two-two-three-one-nine'.

'Angela?' My voice is pleading, desperate.

She says one word before hanging up.

'No.'

I punch the numbers in again, and again, and again, even blurting out a, 'But Edie—' And each time she says the same word, and each time she hangs up, until eventually, exasperated, she takes the phone off the hook so that all I get is the insistent mocking of an engaged tone.

And then it goes dead.


'Has she done this before?'

'No,' I say.

This one is a psychiatrist: Dr Calvert – wearing a pearl choker and pursed lips. Before that there was the accident and emergency doctor, before that the admissions nurse, before that the paramedics. Each one calmly reeling off the same list of queries I should know the answers to, but instead have to pluck *maybe*s and *I don't know*s from the air, offering apologies for not knowing your blood type, for not knowing what you have swallowed besides bathwater, for not knowing you might do this at all.

But now, it seems, I have got one wrong.

'Yes,' Toni says. 'Well, threatened to.'

'What?' I turn to her. 'When?'

Toni tries to smile, but the five-hour drive on a hangover is taking its toll and her attempt is wan, weak, fake. 'Before you were born,' she says.

I do not ask how long before I was born, but I can guess. Eight, nine months, perhaps? When you knew about me. When you knew what you'd done and guessed what I would do.

But this isn't about me, is it? Not really. It never is. This is all about you. You have made it so I cannot hate you, cannot resent you, can only feel pity.

'I thought she was being dramatic,' Toni continues. 'She can be quite dramatic, you know. But I stayed with her that night.' She reddens at this, a bloom of scarlet spreading up her throat and across her cheeks. 'And the next day she said she was fine. That it was all nonsense. Drunk nonsense.'

I watch, stunned and sullen in the corner, as she plucks up your pale, fragile fingers, closes her tanned hand around them.

Without moving your eyes from the wall, you open your mouth to speak. 'I'm sorry,' you say at last.

But it is unclear who you are saying sorry to, or for what. And though Toni will try, these are the last words you will say to either of us on the subject.

Toni drives me home.

'Is there someone you can stay with?' she asks. 'Or who can come and stay?'

I shake my head. 'I'll be fine.'

'I'm just going to drop some things for her, then I'll come back. Make you tea.'

'You don't have to,' I say. 'I can do it.' Have been doing it for years now.

Toni nods, knowing. Then, 'Oh, Di,' she gasps, and grasps me, pulling me tight to her, so I can feel the bobbled wool of her hand-knitted cardigan, smell fusty patchouli and fried garlic. But I do not give in; instead I stand stiff-limbed like a furious child, refusing to cry.

Toni promises she won't be long, that she'll return – a promise she will keep for weeks to come. I mumble thanks and another apology, one that she wafts away with a flap of her hand, a flippant gesture – stolen from you, or bequeathed – that forces me to clamp my mouth shut, push my tears down anew.

I wait for the car to start, then, reaching for a sliver of hope as thin and slippery as worn soap, I slip out the back, run to the bottom of the garden, and try the gate one last time.

It does not move.

It will be more than a decade before anyone opens it again, and by then the landscape will be changed forever – no ice queen, no Aslan, and the children long since grown.

And so, my status as outcast certain now, I walk slowly back to the house, close the door, and lie, face down, on the chaise longue. Then, in the insufferable emptiness of this room – of my life – I finally begin to cry.

# The Bell Jar

## September 1990

I am not allowed to hate you, you have seen to that. But I cannot love you either. Because while you nearly died, it is me who is now in purgatory. You have prescription pills, some brand of mother's little helper to carry you through each day in a fug of comfortable numbness. But me? I have nothing to nudge me through this strange hinterland I am forced to inhabit, no one to hold my hand. I am lost, alone. And I feel everything.

While David and Angela manage to sweep us under the carpet like so much dust, word spreads on small-town tongues and our banishment beyond our back garden is far more brutal. In the supermarket we are stared at, sniggered about, a fact that incenses you so much that you encourage erstwhile strangers to fuck off; curse cashiers who stiffen, or try to catch the eye of colleagues when they see us approaching their till.

I am less brave.

At school my stock falls to an all-time low, my choice of canteen seat, of classroom clique, confined to an obese boy whose hunger extends to his nose pickings, and the four months pregnant Susan Roots. So, appalled, adrift, I give up study and take up chain-smoking. When I bother to eat lunch, it is fridge pickings and corner shop junk, crammed down in the stacks of the library. When I bother to turn up to school at all. Because on several days a week – on the days when the whispers, or, worse, silence, threaten to deafen me, I skip class and slip into the park, huddle in the folly and get high, lose myself in my drug of choice, party with my new friends: Cathy, Rebecca, Jane Eyre. Tragic women trapped in bleak landscapes and little lives. These are the girls I will become – am already; not a Bennet, not Becky and definitely not Cassandra.

I become a cause for concern for staff and the school board, who send letters home worrying about my sudden lack of focus, my loss of interest in sixth-form life, and beyond – letters that I lose, or hide, or reply to in your crabbed hand, claiming constant colds, and a persistent fever, possibly glandular. And so you seem surprised when I fail one A level, barely scrape two Cs in the others; rage at the school for letting me down, then, later, when they have asked why you ignored the warnings, why you assured them I was fine, rage angrily at me.

'Why would you do that?' you demand. 'And how? How do you go from being bookworm of the bloody century to an F? An F, for fuck's sake. That's not even just . . . just getting something wrong, that must have taken effort to screw up on that scale.'

I shrug but say nothing. Because we both know the answer to that. 'I can retake,' I say. Though I don't even mean it. Because the school is right, I have no interest in life beyond sixth form, beyond this town, this house. But I do not lack focus. My concentration is pin sharp and poker straight, and directed entirely at the Lodge.

I have called – of course I have called, on a daily basis at first, then at odd times of the day and night, trying to catch them out, trick them into talking. But at the sound of my voice, the phone is slammed wordlessly down. I try letters – sheets of painstakingly inked-out Basildon Bond pushed through the letter box. The first few are returned unopened; the rest are, I assume, dropped into the dustbin or perhaps pored over in the corner of the common room for kicks, pathetic evidence of how freakish and fucked-up we are, me and you.

Toni says I need to stop loving them, that it's not healthy, that I don't need them; life moves on. But she hasn't moved on, I tell myself, she is still here every weekend, cooking for you, cleaning for you, bringing you make-up and Merlot and magazines. So while you fix yourself with pills and soap and salacious gossip, I slink upstairs, sit on my bedroom window-sill, tapping ash onto the tops of bare-branched trees, or skulk past, hood up, head down, and I watch them.

This is what they – you – have reduced me to. I am a stalker, a peeping Tom – a name whose irony is not lost on me.

I watch David wear a suit again, watch him join the brief-case rank and file of the morning commute to Liverpool Street. I watch Angela, watch her alter her haircut, her wardrobe, her weight, all of them rigidly monitored, as if this control will afford her some small victory. I watch Harry most of all. Watch her slam the door of Simon's Golf, storming into the house as its wheels spin, churning pea gravel for David to rake later. Watch her lying out on the lawn, her slender limbs amphetamine-skinny now, her eyes shaded – always shaded – by outsized glasses, giving her the fragile appearance of a starving fly. Watch her stack the back of the Volvo with boxes and bags and a rabbit called Pig; the last remnants of her wardrobe, her childhood – our childhood – being exported to a new world.

It is a kind of exquisite torture, a persistent digging at a self-inflicted wound, like the peeling off of a ripe scab to find the flesh beneath still raw and bloody. And the deepest cut of all, the hardest to heal?

Tom.

I have sent letters to Hull too, called the house on Park Grove countless times, heard him *yello* cheerfully down the line before hearing my voice, my stuttered plea. Then he mutters back, 'I can't,' 'Don't,' or, once, a moment of hesitation so ripe with possibility that I sob, and then hear a hurried, 'I'm sorry,' and the clatter of the receiver being replaced. Those three syllables are as much as I get and eventually I swallow Toni's bitter pill, and try to stop loving him.

This, I discover, is a full-time job, requiring both rigid discipline and total abandon.

I take down photos and file away notes. I stop wearing the perfume he so adored and buy own-brand body spray from

Boots instead. I make New Year's resolutions on a monthly basis. Lists of things I will and will not do.

I will not call him.

I will not write to him.

I will not write his name on my arm in blue ink.

I will not write stories in which he repents and returns to me, and we elope to America.

I will stop reading stories while imagining he is the hero.

I will find someone else – anyone else – to play that part.

And I try. Because though friends are few, and female friends non-existent, there is always an unwitting but willing boy to fill the void.

I let Bruce Cooper push me over the photocopier in the solicitor's office he cleans on a Saturday.

I let a skinhead called Colin pull me into the field behind our primary school, counting his grunts as I count the coloured globes that decorate each classroom window.

I let Carl Jennings drag me onto the back seat of his Beetle in a pub car park in Harlow.

I screw and I get screwed over, again and again, and though each time I am further away from that bedroom in Hull, I cannot push him, wash him, out of me.

I try employment instead and acquire a pointless, thankless job stacking shelves and restocking pick-and-mix peppermint creams in Woolworths. It is a level of drudgery and servitude only accentuated by the navy nylon of my knee-length uniform, an outfit that disgusts you and delights me with its shapelessness.

'Do they think dressing you like a blind bloody nun boosts

sales?' you ask when I clump in one evening, sweat-smelling and foul-tempered from a ten-hour stocktake.

'Nuns don't wear American tan tights,' I bat back.

'No,' you concede. 'Even they draw the line somewhere.'

'At least someone does.'

'You're being deliberately difficult again,' you accuse.

'Did Dr Phil tell you that?' I ask, nodding at the stack of self-help books Toni has been adding to on an alarmingly regular basis. 'Or is that one all your own work?'

'God, Di,' you snap. 'At least I'm trying.'

'And I'm what, exactly?'

'You tell me. You're wearing a pinafore and lace-ups like some outsized primary school pupil and spending five days a week fucking about with fruit sherbets and Tupperware.'

Two can play at this game, I think. 'At least I have a job.'

But I am wrong. Always wrong. 'Better unemployed than . . . this . . . whatever it is.'

'Because I'm stacking shelves and that's beneath me? Or because I'm working for the Man. Is that it?'

You roll your eyes. I pull a face back.

'You know there is no Man,' I say then. 'There's just jobs and everyone has one.'

'They're all men,' you say. 'And if you're determined to work then at least find something you're good at.'

'I *am* good at it,' I yell. 'I bloody excel at restocking cotton reels and – and coat hangers.'

'And I suppose no one is quicker with a price-tagging gun.'

'No,' I retort. 'I am fucking supreme.' The Queen of Bloody Everything. I sound ridiculous and we both know it.

But though we cannot cry, we cannot laugh at each other either. Not yet.

'I just want you to *find* yourself,' you say eventually.

'Maybe I don't want to be found,' I say, at once desperately, self-consciously profound and pathetic.

'No, you just want to bury yourself in books,' you say.

'I wonder why,' I say.

For once you let me get the final word, though I hardly feel I can claim victory. And anyway, it's a lie. I do want to find me. That's *why* I read. Because in books I can be better, bolder, braver. I can have a bigger life, and a happy ending.

Whereas out here in the real world? Without Tom, without Harry, I have a feeling I don't exist at all.

In the end, it's Toni who shows me the way.

'Have you thought about college?' she asks.

'Nowhere will take you with two Cs,' I tell her, wearily. 'Nowhere decent, anyway.'

'Unis, maybe. But there's polys. FE colleges.'

I know this. Have still got the pile of pamphlets and glossy brochures that a well-meaning Mr Collins sent home for me when I failed to register for resits. But I don't want to do Teeline or typing. I don't want to study business or tourism. Or learn how to mind a child. How can these last resorts come close to literature? To Lawrence and Larkin? To Woolf and Wilde? How can anything they could possibly offer make up for not spending three years wrapped up in books, and in bed with the boy I love? (Loved, I remind myself.) I could write, I suppose. I used to. But even with the overconfidence of youth on my side, I know my clumsy attempts at prose showed at best promise, not accomplishment.

'Publishing,' Toni says. And her face creases with a smile so wide it is as if she has peeled the foil from a cheap chocolate egg and found Fabergé instead.

'What's that?' you demand.

'I don't know exactly. But copy-editing, proofing, publicity, I expect.'

'So not reading?' I say, suspicious.

'Yes, reading,' Toni replies. 'But with a purpose.'

I bristle, throw a quote back at her. 'All reading has a purpose,' I say.

Toni looks at you. You try to pull a *don't blame me* look. It falls flat, for we both, of course, blame you fully. 'But this would mean you could read as a job,' she says then.

And that is the line that wins her the argument, and will, eventually, win me a place on an NVQ at Anglia in Cambridge, a slim ten miles away, meaning I don't even have to leave home, leave you to the wolves, or the black dog I know still comes calling – a fact I both pity and resent you for. At least now, though, I have an escape, a new world to play in; and then, for the first time in over a decade, I allow myself to paint the first few brushstrokes, block out the opening scenes of an alternative, adult utopia. Away from the bell jar that our lives have become.

Until, two weeks before I start the course, you insinuate yourself into the picture, and feeble, foolish me, I can do nothing to stop you.

\*

You are lying on the chaise longue, poring over the prospectus with an interest I have rarely seen roused outside the borderline pornographic.

'Have you seen their studios?' you coo. 'Bloody fabulous.'

I glance at the photographs of vertiginous sculptures, strange ceramic heads, canvases that stretch two men high and a room wide. 'I don't *do* art,' I point out, a silent How many times? added on for good measure.

'I know,' you say. And then you fix me with a look that is usually reserved for menace and magic, for going to town dressed as warlocks, or scrumping apples from Mr Hegarty's house. And I feel the sharp prick of a pin to a bubble before the words even leave your lips. 'But I do.'

The words hang, tangible, touchable things in the stale air between us, before I swipe at them, try to make them disappear.

'You're not serious?'

'Deadly.'

And I can see from the set of your jaw and the wildness in your eyes that you are. You have come up with a spell, spun gold from straw, and now you are going to seize it, regardless of who might get harmed by your magic.

'But this . . . this is my life,' I protest, words – the very thing I am supposed to excel at – failing me, as if to prove your point. 'You can't just – just glom on.'

'I'm not "glomming". That's not even a bloody word.'

'Like you'd know.'

'Oh, please. Because I'm so old?'

'You're nearly forty,' I point out.

'Exactly.' You wave a hand triumphantly. 'So it's high time I went back and finished what I started. While I'm still in my prime. I don't want to be bloody Gauguin, waiting till I'm dead. Or – or Van Gogh, having to top myself to be appreciated. What's the point in that?'

'Well, you've already fucked that one up.'

You raise an eyebrow, and I can't tell if this is in disgust or appreciation that I've finally been able to mention it, the elephant that has kept us both trapped in this room, this house. But I am not apologizing. And I am not backing down.

'Who says you'll even get in?' I say, clutching at cruel straws.

'Well, thank you for the vote of confidence.' But you're not backing down either. 'If I do get in, I'm going.'

And that, it seems, is your last word on the subject, so I stamp upstairs to lock myself in my room, all the while incanting a secret prayer that you are actually shit after all, or that the course is full, or that you are deemed too oddball even for an art department.

But of course there is no genie, and none of my wishes come true. And so, on 5 September 1991, you drive us both to the campus off East Road, park your brand-new second-hand bright-yellow Beetle haphazardly and illegally in the staff car park, and then stand at the foot of the entrance wearing false eyelashes, dungarees and a lurex boob tube, while I wear black Gap, and an air of resignation as heavy as my reading list.

'Isn't this marvellous?' you gush.

'The cat's pyjamas,' I lie.

But if you know I am mocking, you ignore it. Instead, to my complete mortification, and the confounded and dumbfounded looks of our peers, you link your arm in mine.

'We'll be the Queens,' you say.

'Of what?'

You look at me then as if I must be mad, or stupid, or both. 'Of Bloody Everything, Di,' you say. 'Of Bloody Everything.'

# The Runaway

## December 1992

I expected a bang, a car crash; a year of embarrassment, tantrums and absurd entanglements that I would have to somehow extricate you from. But instead the twelve months pass with, if not a whimper, then at least remarkably less drama than I know you are capable of creating.

There were moments, of course.

The time you told a girl on my course that my father was the Aga Khan and she – all goggle-eyes and high hopes – believed you.

The time you turned up to collect me from a Hills Road house party, but instead of waiting outside as instructed, as begged, waltzed in and got hot-knife high with a boy I had kissed out of boredom in the downstairs bathroom just an hour before.

The time you posed nude in the refectory for some kind of guerrilla life drawing class, itself a level of pretension, of 'look at me, look at me' that I had come to expect and abhor from the art department, but now with the added awkwardness of listening to whispers about your arse, your tits, the slits on your wrists that, instead of hiding under beads or bangles, you bared as some kind of badge of honour.

But Toni was right, college has been good for both of us. We find new things out about ourselves, new talents. For you, a loathing of landscape, a love of sculpture; an affinity with and ability to handle clay that your tutor declares *instinctive* and *inspired*. While I find that I have an exceptional ability to copy-edit; to correct and corral the words of others. Control I feel I lack in every other aspect of my life can be exercised in the policing of punctuation marks and the balancing of poorly weighted sentences. I learn the rules of grammar: the horror of comma splicing and split infinitives. I learn the skills of rhetoric: the delicious thrill of anaphora and assonance, the satisfying click, click, click of tricolon. I learn the arcane language of typesetters: of widows and orphans, and galleys and rags. My love of books has a purpose now, no longer a mere pastime, a whimsy, a way to dream myself into another world more picturesque, more picaresque than this one. All that reading has made me, it appears, employable.

And, as we manage to make it through three terms without breaking up, or falling apart, I learn that life – albeit altered, awkward – goes on. I graduate in July with impeccable grades, a three-month unpaid placement at the university press, and a dose of chlamydia from a goth called Niall, a disease that I know now has consequences, but which, at the time, was no more irritating than a mild itch that I put down to nylon knickers and your inability, or refusal, to use the right quantity of Persil.

By Christmas, though, I am, as you predicted, climbing the walls.

My placement over, I am back in my pinafore and back stacking shelves for the season. A job made all the more unbearable by poorly worded packaging and the rogue apostrophes that taunt me from the staffroom noticeboard. At home my irritation only increases, and it is me, now, who needs her paws buttered, as I wander aimlessly from room to room, picking up porcelain ornaments and replacing them repeatedly elsewhere, as unable to settle on a mantelpiece arrangement as I am to sit on the sofa and read a book. I haven't abandoned story – far from it – but the tales I tell myself now take place in bigger towns, in brasher cities.

Here I am – will always be – Dildo, the weird kid, daughter of the drunk. Here my life is bound to yours by the strings of an apron you refuse to admit to wearing, and I am eyeing the scissor drawer with increasing ardour and regularity.

And there is another reason to flee.

Before, I had the promise of escape, of a different life, just yards away down a garden path and through a door. But there is no Narnia now, no Wonderland any more. That is London, I tell myself. Where the streets are paved, if not with gold, then at least with enough for a double room in a shared house in Zone 2.

And so, after a week of lunch hours spent in the library with a new notepad and a sharpened pencil and an out-of-date copy of the *Writers' and Artists' Yearbook*, I make a list of publishers, ranked by location, name, and whether or not they have rights to any of my preferred authors, and I send them a letter offering excellent references and my dedicated services.

I get thirty-seven rejections.

And one offer of an interview, at 11 a.m. on Christmas Eve.

The editor is called Jude, whom I imagine as some incarnation of Hardy's stonemason-turned-scholar, only more successful, and less incestuous, and it is him I think of as I call in sick to work, not even flinching as frog-faced Margaret shouts down the line, demanding if I know what day it is; it is him I think of as I pin my hair, and put on pearls – one of the few affectations I admit to borrowing from you.

'He's probably gay,' you say. 'Toni says every man in publishing is gay. Or a massive twat.'

I grit my teeth. 'I don't care if he's gay or a twat. I just want him to give me a job.'

'And anyway, you might hate it,' you continue. Then, pointedly, 'Or they'll hate you.'

I don't rise to it, know what you are trying to do anyway. And it won't work. I am doing this, I am leaving, escaping. Or attempting to. You are better now – as better as you will ever be, anyway – and I do not need to – cannot – nursemaid you any more.

And Jude – a woman, as it turns out – doesn't hate me. And I don't hate it. The job – at a small house off the Strand – pays peanuts, but it has a literary imprint and a dedicated children's division, and a vacancy in the wake of a pregnancy that became full-time motherhood.

'You're not planning children yet, are you?' Jude asks, leaning on the paper-strewn desk and peering at me from under a polished bob and over the top of expensive and elaborate tortoiseshell frames.

'Never,' I say.

She raises an eyebrow. 'They all say that.'

'I mean it,' I say. And it isn't a lie. I swallow my Marvelon every morning along with the vitamins you begrudgingly bought me, so there's no chance of accidents. No chance of fooling around then fucking up like you did. I am different, I tell myself. And this new life, this new job, will prove it.

Jude calls within an hour of me clip-clopping painfully through our door on my Dolcis heels, asking if I can start on 4 January. I accept with the same enthusiasm and speed as I accepted that embossed Christmas Eve invitation all those years ago.

That was my ticket into this small town. This – this is my ticket out. And, to your credit, you manage to swallow your pride down with two glasses of schnapps and offer me your congratulations.

'So I suppose I'll only see you at Christmas now,' you say, as we sit pretending to watch a repeat of a repeat of a *Two Ronnies* special. 'And birthdays.'

I could lie. I could say I'll be back at weekends, that I'll catch lifts with Toni and spend Sunday in the studio while you carve my bust or plaster my hands or mould me in clay, improbably perfect, and conveniently small. But I don't want to come back here. Not at Christmas, not at all.

Instead I manage only a barely truthful, 'I suppose.'

Then, a week later, the spare key to Toni's sister's flat in Clapton on a ribbon around my neck, I pack my life up into two suitcases and four black bin bags, and myself into the front seat of our car.

'We should do a grand tour!' you suggest delightedly, as if struck by the same divine inspiration that has you modelling monstrous buttocks at four in the morning. 'You know, like the Queen? You could wave at everyone. Or give them the finger.'

I jolt at that, not at your flippant suggestion but at the memory of the back seat of a Daimler, my gloved hand waggling back and forth at the war memorial, at dog walkers, at a woman with a dead turkey in her hands.

'You're all right,' I say. 'I'd rather just go.'

'Suit yourself,' you mutter, and sputter the engine into life.

There is only one place I want to see, to say goodbye to. And we are compelled to drive past it anyway, sitting, as it does, as a gatekeeper's lodge to our small world, and the last post to the wider one. But as we turn the corner, I feel my pulse quicken and my eyes prickle and I cannot look.

You reach out then, place a hand on my leg, as if a sudden need to reassure me has been woken in you. But for all the accord we have brokered, you remain unforgiven and I stiffen, then shake it off.

That's why I did it, Edie. Why I was so eager to leave, why I refused to return. It wasn't just for me, so I could escape what you'd done, what I'd lost. It was for us. Because without this, I told myself, there was no way of moving on, or forward at all. That's why I didn't call back when you said you'd locked yourself out and left the gas on.

Why I didn't come home when you turned the house into a vinyl paradise when you turned forty-five.

Why I made you meet me in cafes in obscure parts of the city, inconvenient for both of us, but far enough away from work or my home that you couldn't easily insinuate yourself into either and beg to be shown round, to stay the night, to meet, and then steal, my friends.

I did it for us, Edie.

I blocked that small town from my life with the same determination I had managed to shut out thoughts of Tom. There could be no half-measures or methadone alternative. It was all or nothing.

And I chose nothing.

# The Treasure Seekers

## May 1997

There are some people, some places, we lose from our lives without regret or even a glance in the rear-view mirror, discarding them as easily as outgrown shoes or yesterday's newspapers. The playground peers, the chemistry partners, the boy we once shared a tent, a spliff, a kiss with at a music festival – all of them slip-slide out of our lives with the same unmarked ease with which they entered.

But others we cling to, hoard in our hearts like treasures in a suitcase. Even when warned to keep our distance we are drawn like moths, all too willing to get our wings burned for the sake of a moment dancing in their bright flames. And, however hard I tried, Tom was, is – will always be – treasure.

It is April 1997 and I am a coiled spring. The country is poised, primed for newness, brilliance, and I am buoyed along by its boundless optimism and self-belief: about to be promoted, about to open a payslip that will open the door to a one-bedroom flat off the Caledonian Road, about to leave behind the world of shared showers, name-tagged cereal boxes and washing-up rotas. For I love publishing and it loves me. I love the work, I love the purpose, and, more than anything, I love getting lost in the land of story. Every new manuscript is full of promise to me, every front page a step through the wardrobe into what might be a new Narnia. Most, of course, are nothing so majestic; they are derivative, amateurish, riddled with adverbs and an astonishing lack of self-awareness: the belief that anyone can do it. They are chips of pavement mica, nothing more. But every so often there is a gem, Jude tells me, a thing so startlingly original, so wide in scope and accomplishment, so diamond-bright, that it makes up for the hours, the days lost to copycat elves and cloned wizards. And I, treasure seeker that I am, want desperately to be the one to find the Next Big Thing.

Even in Essex, something strange is afoot; an unnameable electricity prances down the narrow streets and catches on the cobbles. You crackle with it, phone calls to me filled with fine art: finished pieces, a public viewing, a private commission. And when we meet for morning tea in the Tate you are high on it, so vertiginous I wonder what else you are on, or off.

'What did you have for breakfast?' I ask cagily. 'A Bloody Mary?'

'Coffee and cigarettes,' you say, kissing me on both cheeks. 'Oh ye of little faith.'

I pull a face and pull out a chair.

'Isn't it marvellous?' you continue, a hand flapping at what could be the waiter, the white-painted walls or the world itself.

'Probably,' I say.

'Oh God, Di, cheer up, would you?'

'I am bloody cheered,' I say. 'I'm ecstatic.' And it's not a lie, just that next to you my emotions seem to pale – pastels or watercolours compared to your vivid ink.

You shake your hair, bright with henna, dismiss my insistence. 'I was listening to him on some Radio 4 thing last night.'

'You were listening to Radio 4?' My belief you must have torn up your prescription and dropped something else instead only increases with this improbability. 'I thought that was for old people.'

'It's surprisingly eclectic,' you say. 'And besides, the telly died.'

I manage not to roll my eyes.

'Anyway, I was listening to him—' you continue.

'To who?'

'Bloody hell. *Blair*. Keep up.'

'Oh, right.'

'And he actually talked about the arts. About *art*. I think it's going to happen, I really do. There's something in the air.'

I resist the temptation to remind you of your long-celebrated scepticism, of the times you told me that all politicians were the worst kind of wet public schoolboy, that anyone who even sought office was a sociopath or a narcissist or both, that what we really needed was another revolution. Because something has altered, something *is* in the air. And so we cross our fingers, hold our breath, the clock tick-tocking down until 1 May, while all about us whirls a glittering dust of change, of chance, and, above all, of second chances.

And, running lickety-split into the thick of it, I am about to get mine.

I leave you mid afternoon, after an overly liquid lunch and a minorly fraught discussion of the motives and merits of Tracey Emin, walk both off through Westminster, weaving my way behind Millbank, through Smith Square and up towards Whitehall itself. Vaguely drunk still, or just dazed and dizzy from your determined cheer, I stand at the gates of Downing Street, peer through the railings. And for the first time I feel it – the idea that life might be about to tell a story as glorious and gripping as any conjured on the page. I should read the papers, I tell myself, watch the news, stop miring myself in sub-Tolkien every night, questioning purple suns and implausible pacts and poorly timed wars. At least for an hour or so.

And so it is thanks to you I buy the *Guardian* from the kiosk outside King's Cross station. Thanks to you I turn the telly on and flick through the five channels to find something, anything on this colossal story, this election.

Thanks to you I find him.

His hair is shorter now, TV-neat, as clipped as his accent, his suit, his tie – his tie! I haven't seen him in a tie since he started sixth form. But here he is, all grown-up now – standing on College Green with a minister of something or other, speaking about identity cards and immigration and the impact of the UK Independence Party.

But still unmistakably, undeniably, Tom.

The recognition is instant and the effect profound. My

stomach contracts, my pupils dilate, my heart bursts open at this incredible, impossible thing. At him being here with me, in this room; his being tangible, his body touchable, albeit through the static of a screen. I am flooded with feeling, humming with it, while my head flicks through time-faded Polaroids of two children playing in a paddling pool on a sun-parched lawn; of the pair of us lying inches apart on beanbag beds on the day that rocked the world; of us tangle-limbed and damp-bodied, clinging to each other in the cold of a Northern morning. This is it, I tell myself. This is my sign, my portent, my magic amulet even. This will set me off on my hero's journey, see me take a new path, a better one than I had imagined possible.

I don't know quite when, yet. Or how. But Tom is my future, I know it. He is my written-in-the-stars destiny. And I will find a way back to him. I will fight off all foes this time – the wicked witches and the dragons and the ne'er-do-wells. I will be magnificent and mesmerizing, this new London me, so that he cannot ignore me now, cannot fail to see that I matter, that I am worthy. And together we will seize our second chance. Seize the day. *Carpe diem*, reads the red ink on a foolscap note that I have Blu-Tacked to my bedroom wall. *Carpe diem*, whispers Robin Williams to the Dead Poets Society that lives in my head.

'O Captain, my Captain,' I utter in reply, and turn the volume up to full.

'Do we have to watch this?'

I am sitting on the sofa, glued to my cushion and the

television screen, when my flatmate Sophia drifts in, trailed – always trailed – by the ever-wasted Jago.

'I'm interested in politics,' I insist.

'It's ITV, for God's sake,' she snorts, lifting a bottle of vodka from the mess on the table, shaking it to check its weight and contents. 'It's like saying you're interested in . . . in literature, so you read Mills & Boon.'

'Or maths, and you watch, like, *Countdown*,' adds Jago, crashing down onto the sofa next to me, so that I can smell the skunk that sneaks through the holes in his cashmere sweaters, clings to his silk-mix shirts. For somehow, by accident or atavism, I have ended up living in the equivalent of a five-hundred-a-month trust-fund squat.

'No, it isn't,' I mumble.

Because it isn't.

Yes, it's commercial television, and no, he's not Paxman, or not yet, but he's there, outside Smith Square with the party faithful; on Whitehall; on the doorstep of a white stucco house in Islington as Blair emerges for another day of campaigning. And he is everything: earnest and light-hearted, and angry and still brimming with hope, with the possibility that politics can, will, change the world.

And he is beautiful. Still.

And I am hooked.

So hooked am I that I take to watching the news three times a day, and more at weekends.

So hooked am I that I start to record bulletins on our outdated and temperamental VCR, in case I am stuck in the office, or on a train, or just need to see him again.

So hooked am I that I take to getting up at six and still have to forgo a shower and arrive to work late, offering up elaborate excuses – for I am never short of a story.

And the story I weave for Tom is supreme.

Some days I give him a girlfriend – an impatient, shrill, demanding thing. One who fails to see his brilliance, fails to support him; worse, fails to appreciate the Pink Floyd back catalogue, a sin that will sit like grit in an oyster, becoming not a pearl but a bitter pill of regret.

On other days he is single, has been bereft since that Christmas Eve. I watch him as he wakes alone, pulls on a T-shirt, pours black coffee, turns on the record player so that the room – my head – drowns in the sound of 'Wish You Were Here'.

But whatever the embellishment, every story ends the same way – with a chance meeting, a gasp, a kiss.

And always, always on 1 May.


I vote first thing, in a cramped school hall redolent of chalk and chip dinners, then take the bus to the Strand, watching the world go by, go about its business on its last recognizable day, humming REM, for this is, surely, the end of the world as we know it.

You think so. You call me early afternoon, and when I ask why you're not at work, at the art supply shop, you tell me you've quit because what with the businessman's picture commission, and now Blair the great patron of art about to take office, you feel safe, chaperoned, sugar-daddied. And besides, Great-Aunt Nina is still putting food in the fridge and pound coins in the meter so, really, why bother?

On any other day I would have had something to say. Would have reminded you that the work is to give your day shape, to get you up – at least, that's what Toni told us. But today I get it, I get that feeling of foolishness, of freedom; that sensation of standing on the brink and being brave enough, for once, to jump off. And so I sit fidgeting at my desk, clock-watching, waiting for – no, willing the hands to turn round so that I can take that leap, praying I will not be yellow-bellied, scared that here be, not dragons, but disappointment.

I have it planned. I know where he will be – he told me on the morning news. Looked straight into the camera and said he would be outside Millbank feeding live back to the studio once the polls close at ten.

So I know where to go, but I can't go then. Because then he'll be wrapped up in work, too taken up with the urgency and energy of it all, but if I wait – until the early hours, when the counts are beginning to come in, when the victory is crystallizing, when the focus will be on swing constituencies, not on commentary from campaigners (for yes, I have done my homework) – then he will see me and will tell me to wait, to meet him later, that he cannot believe this has happened and on this night of nights as well.

I leave at midnight, leave Sophia and Jago to the sofa, and the skunk, and a French film they have dismissed as no more than porn with pretensions and yet are still goggle-eyed at the gaping mouths and jiggling tits.

Don't you get it? I want to scream. This is history happening – this is as good as a book. And far better than a – a filthy film.

But they are half a bottle of Stoli gone and full of whatever.

And then, so am I.

The bus ride is buzzing. Or maybe I am buzzing – so that every glance feels laden with meaning, every smile an acknowledgement of what is about to happen. In the row across from me a woman sits chewing, a bucket of cold fried chicken in her lap.

I'm going to see Tom, I want to tell her.

Good for you, she says in my head. Seize the day.

I will, I reply. I am.

I get off at Pimlico, turn left along the river. The night is clear and cold, my skin pimpling swiftly. I should have brought a coat, I think. Or something more than the backless black dress I am barely wearing. But it is close now, his arms are close now, and so on I go, past taxis, past the Tate, until I see the building towering above me, the glint of glass, the curve of its pillared frontage, and, thank God, the camera crews assembled underneath.

I can't get close enough to find him, can't make him out in the crowd. And a rope stops me going forward, a shiny-cheeked woman with a clipboard, a lanyard and a game-show-host smile barring the way.

'I'm looking for someone,' I tell her.

'Mick, this way,' I hear.

'I'm sorry,' she says, scanning her list. 'And you are?'

'No, you don't understand,' I tell her. 'I'm not . . . I'm not trying to come in.'

'That's it,' she says to someone behind me. 'Mick's done.'

'I just want to see a reporter,' I plead. 'Tom. Tom Trevelyan. He's with ITV.'

'Tom?' She checks her list, shrugs.

I feel myself grit my teeth, turn to a photographer. 'Do you know Tom Trevelyan?' I ask. 'He's an ITV reporter. He was here a while ago. I saw him.'

The snapper in his North Face jacket shrugs. 'Think that crew went. Cutting a package, probably. Show's pretty much over here.'

'Oh,' I say, and the word catches in my mouth, fat with disappointment.

'Fancy a drink?' he says then. 'You can polish my lens if you like.'

Another snapper laughs, and I feel myself flush, not at his flippancy, but at my own folly. I turn to go, to run, to get back to my bedroom and into a book, any book where the ending is assured and always happy. And that's when I hear it. Hear him.

'Dido?'

I swing my head round, and see him standing on the other side of the rope. Short-haired, suited, smiling. Taller than I remember. And tanned too. But undeniably, unbelievably, him.

And so I let my taut jaw relax and a smile spread to match his own.

'Hello, Jimmy.'

Did you hope it would be Tom? Did you?

I should have done. I should have felt like I'd lost a pound and found a penny. And at first I do; I glance back to check the crowd. But it is still Tom-less.

And then I get it.

*This* is fate. *This.*

This is my second chance, my new beginning. Jimmy, whom I almost-loved, whom I imaginarily cheated on with Tom – would have cheated on, given half the chance – when all along he was my destiny, he was the one who truly loved me, though he never said so then, not in so many words. But I left him. Or did he leave me? I am spinning with the thrill of it and the details are hazy, blurred now, by time and six shots of Dutch courage. Anyway, it doesn't matter, because here he is. Now. In front of me.

'I don't believe it,' he says. 'Is it you?'

'Yes,' I say, smiling. 'Yes, it's me.'

'What are you doing here?'

'I don't know.' And it isn't a lie, not now. Because I have no idea how this story will play out, but play out I will let it. 'What are *you* doing here?' I say then.

'Working,' he explains. 'For Labour. I'm a press officer.'

I nod, as if this makes sense. It does make sense – of course he would work in politics. Of course for Labour. He has charm, and spins convincing, clever words, so potent he could be a politician himself one day, a prime minister, even.

'You're leaving?' I say then.

'Party,' he says. 'South Bank.' Then he clutches at something, an idea, holds it out in his hand like a jewel. 'Come.'

'Can I?'

'You have to.'

'I have to,' I agree, laughing. 'I absolutely have to.'

And just like that, I take the jewel, and his hand, and I do not look back once.

I do not check over my shoulder as he pulls me out of the melee and along the Embankment.

I do not glance into the crowd as I am whisked, a black-clad Cinderella, into the Royal Festival Hall, security assured I am with the party, a special guest.

I do not admit the thought of what might have been – if I had been five minutes earlier, or he five minutes later.

Instead, as Portillo falls, as the champagne glasses are charged, as hearts brim with hope for the new tomorrow we teeter on, I stand in the midst of strangers and I kiss this prodigal boy – man, now – like it's the last night on earth.

Two hours later, high on all of it and more, we fuck against the wall in a wood-panelled toilet, then again in the come-down and the bright morning in my single bed. Two weeks later my toothbrush is in the pint glass that sits on his toilet cistern, and my underwear nudges for drawer space with his socks and boxers. Another month after that I have given my notice to a barely sober Sophia and Jago, and turned down the offer of a mortgage because I won't be needing one any more – or not yet. And not alone.

Because, just eleven weeks after we have met, I carry my bags of clothes and my boxes of books, my suitcase of treasure and my stuffed raven, down the Clapton stairs and into the back of a black Golf GTI. Then I leave the East London hinterland for a two-bedroom repossession on a backstreet in Peckham. We paint it and carpet it and put up a shelf for his stereo and more for my books, and there we live, happily ever after.

For almost a year.

# The Tiger Who
# Came to Tea

## December 1998

He's still Jimmy, still the boy I knew. Still charming, still disarming. Still raging against the machine, the man, the dying of the light. But where once he pulsed with optimism, where he railed against Thatcher, believing that once she'd gone the world and all in it would be his for the taking, now he rails against the world itself. Against a prime minister who lacks the courage of his convictions and puts magnificent plans on hold, shelves them like porcelain to gather dust. Against the press who pull apart the ones the government does push through, picking over them like crows on carrion. Against a head of press and a political secretary who fail to recognize Jimmy's own brilliance, leaving him floundering and fire-fighting at Millbank instead of installing him at Number 10, where he belongs.

Now, instead of hope, his passion is cut with a thin, bitter impotence.

You asked me what I saw in him once. You were drunk and I was dishonest. I told you at least he had a paying job and a name that he hadn't plucked from a plant or stolen from someone else's gods.

But it wasn't that. And it wasn't just that Tom told me not to all those years ago. Nor that he was thought ugly – or conventionally so.

It was that night, of course – the hand of fate, or the gods, or mere coincidence – whichever, that was part of it; the sheer destiny of it. But something more, too. Because I did see something in him, even in the darker days. Underneath it all – underneath the control, the spite, the silence – God, the silence – I saw vulnerability, I saw hurt. And looming over him I saw the shadow of his father.

I saw the child who'd had to pull his shirtsleeves down and do his collar up to hide the bruises doled out by a brute of a man, though the eye – the result of a lost twenty-pound note that was supposed to buy cigarettes and a pools ticket – was impossible to disguise.

I saw the child who'd been told he was useless, gay, good-for-nowt because he wore clothes, used words, too fancy for the likes of him.

I saw the child who'd saved up his paper-round pounds for fourteen weeks to buy a pea coat lined in pink silk from the second-hand shop on Silver Street. A coat that was scorned, and then, when he refused to give it up, set alight on a bonfire of old magazines and a broken chair.

He said it was me and him against the world now, did I know that? And I, who had waited my whole life to hear those words, believed him.

That's why we came home. So he could show his father who he was now. Prove himself a man.

A soon-to-be-married man.

Do you remember that? We were going to get married. That's how much he loved me.

Or that's how much he hated Tom.

Tom sits spectre-like in our lives. Not silent, though, not a mute phantasm that we must not mention for fear of making it real, but one whose name is invoked with increasing regularity, thrown at me like a stone.

'I don't love Tom,' I tell him, then. 'I love *you*. I always did. I just . . . fucked up.'

But he is unconvinced, says it's spin, a sop, and he should know.

And yet still he tests me, tells me that he saw him at a launch, that he's looking fatter, balder, shagging some blonde bird off CNN, moving to the States. And then, the cherry on the cake – news that he carries home like a prize and drops in front of me to watch my face – Tom is getting married.

'Really?' I say, attempting to pour utter disinterest and only vague recognition into a single word.

'Yes, really. Doyle told me.'

I pause, calculating an answer that will get him off the subject, while implying that he has, nonetheless, won. 'Well, good for him,' I say. 'He obviously needs a certificate to prove love. Not like us.' And I reach for his face then, reach up to kiss him.

But he pulls away, distracted, taken with something.

'We should get married,' he says.

I still then, catch my breath. Is this a proposal? Do I want a proposal? Of course I do, I tell myself. That is what normal people want. What normal people do.

'At New Year,' he says, warming to the idea he has plucked from nothing more than petty jealousy or pure one-upmanship.

'What, *this* New Year? That's . . . that's in four weeks.'

He sighs. 'No, next.' He feigns patience. 'You can't plan a wedding in weeks.'

I haven't said yes, I think. But an affirmation is apparently not a requirement. 'Where?' I ask then, trying to imagine myself walking down the cold, wide aisle in St Mary's. Or will he want the Catholic church? No, he's not even religious. Hates God as much as you do, though he has more justification, for it is God who administered all those beatings, according to his stepmam.

'Here,' he says. 'London.'

I let myself loosen in relief, a sign he mistakes for something else.

'Why? Don't you want to?'

I cannot be negative, I tell myself. I cannot let even a drop of water fall onto his bonfire, his inferno of an idea.

'Of course I do,' I say. Then turn it back on him for ever doubting me. 'Why wouldn't I?'

And I am good at this, can convince us both.

So that when he opens another bottle of Moët I am already there with my empty glass, ready to toast us for the seventh time.

So that when he racks up the lines to celebrate I lower my

head over the mirror and watch myself breathe in our brilliant future.

So that when he tells me he can't be bothered with a condom, that we should stop bothering from now on, instead of panic, I make a pact with the universe that if I conceive a child tonight it will be the most golden ever born. That I will love it like you never loved me. That it will grow up in a clean house, with a neat life, and order all around.

Then maybe you will understand.

In the morning we lie, cocooned still in chemistry, heads hammering, hearts still racing as if borrowed from mice.

'We'll tell them,' he says. 'Go back and announce it.'

I open my eyes, turn to him. 'Tell who?'

He pauses. 'Our parents.'

I feel a wave of nausea slosh through me. 'Oh God. Really?'

I feel his chest stiffen under my fingers. 'Why? Changed your mind, have you?'

'No, no. Just, I didn't think you'd want to bother.'

'You've got to be fucking joking. Now he might finally get it into his thick head I'm not bent.'

'Right.'

'We'll do them all at once. One hit, get it over with.'

'In the same house?' My head fills with a Hogarthian portrait of squalor and gin.

'Are you mental? No, just on the same day. Christmas Day,' he says then, another pearl pulled from the ether. 'One for lunch, one for dinner.'

I give in then, because he has decided, it is done. But there is one final straw to be clutched at. 'Do we have to stay?'

'No, we can drive home. You won't be drinking, will you?'

I frown. Won't I? Why won't I?

Then I remember. The condoms left in the drawer. The coming hard and high up inside me.

The golden child.

I pull the sheets back frantically and fling myself out of bed.

I make it to the toilet just in time.


Lunch at the McGowans' is overcooked and underseasoned, but what it lacks in flavour, it makes up for in glutinous abundance. The anaemic bird, a turkey I assume, sits listlessly in a sea of potato products including, unusually, Alphabites.

'Noel likes them,' Siobhán tells me, nodding at one of her twins. 'But don't let him have an F or we'll never hear the end of it.'

I look at his plate, see the U, C, and K sitting there and want to laugh but my mouth is fat with claggy mash.

Later, in the kitchen, she eyes my glass of ginger ale with suspicion. 'You up the duff, then? That why you're doing it?'

'No,' I say quickly. 'God, no – I mean, just no. I'm driving, that's all.'

'I wouldn't worry if you were. I was four months gone before Darren made it legit. Mam got over it in the end. And Dad's still kidding himself the kids were premature.'

'Right.' I smile then, a bid to bond, but she raises a

painted-on eyebrow as if I've just looked right down my nose at her.

The same look her dad gave me when Jimmy told them the wedding was in London.

'Not good enough for ye, are we?'

Jimmy closes his eyes, braces himself. Just for a second, but I see it. 'It doesn't make sense to come back here. We live in London. All our friends are in London.'

'All your fancy friends,' Brendan sneers.

'Don't think you'll be getting me near Peckham,' Deirdre adds. 'Dirty place. Dirty people.'

'It'll be in town,' Jimmy tells her. 'Westminster. We can probably use the chapel at the Houses.'

My eyes widen and I have to stop my turkey-crammed mouth gaping.

He looks at me and looks away quickly. 'We'll need permission, but it's doable. It's a thing,' he insists.

Mr McGowan snorts then, red-faced, and I am unsure if it is derision, or an attempt to cover up pride. But whichever, the subject is over.

Now there is only you left to tell.


'You're overworrying,' he told me, as he sat on the sidelines and watched me dress that morning, eyeing me with the air of a referee or adjudicator.

'You don't know what she's like,' I said evasively.

'I do,' he said, taking a pair of knickers out of my hand and putting them down on the bed, taking my wrists in his hands. 'She's a fucked-up Trustafarian with a drink habit.' He pulled me towards him, kissed me roughly.

I winced at his description – my description, words that tumbled out of my mouth on the back of four lines and a bottle of Bollinger. But I still kissed him back. Because that way it's me and him tied together, do you see? Not us, Edie. Not me and you. And that is what I remind myself as the gold carriage clock on the mantelpiece counts down the time until tea.

It's gone four when we leave the McGowans', our boot heavy with unwrapped tat that will be tipped into the nearest skip when we get far enough away.

'Thank fuck that's over.' Jimmy belches and I wince without thinking. 'Christ. What's wrong with you now?' he demands.

'Nothing,' I say. 'It's just cold.' Compared to the furnace of his stepmam's front room, that saw his dad sweating dark rings into his blue shirt and Siobhán in a strappy summer top, when outside the frost still clings to the cracked concrete and hoars the Ford Cortina on the front drive.

I wait for him to offer me his coat, but instead he just climbs into the car, dropping heavily onto the seat with a groan.

'Come on then,' he goads through the windscreen. 'One down, one to go.'

I come to, hurry around the back of the car and behind the wheel.

'Quicker we get there, quicker we can get home.'

But it's getting there I am scared of.

*

As we turn onto West Road I feel unease slip down my spine and I have to clutch the steering wheel so hard my knuckles blanch.

But the Lodge is curtained; a closed eye. They are away – of course they are away, I think. In America.

'We should break in,' Jimmy says. 'Fuck for old times' sake. That would show him.'

Show him what? I want to say. And how? What will you do? Tell Doyle to tell the news crew to tell him? It's not sixth form any more.

But we are in Saffron Walden now, and different rules apply, old rules.

When I get out of the car, he pushes me against the metal, kisses me. 'You're mine, Di,' he says. 'You know that, don't you?'

It's not a question. Not really. But I have to answer anyway. 'I know,' I say. And I do know, can feel it, this desperation of his. In the way he grips me, in the way he puts his hand on the small of my back, steers me up my own front path, in the way he pushes me forward when you open the door, tells you in a single breath that we are getting married and getting pregnant, before I can change my mind, or you can change it for me.

'Really?' you say. 'Well, you'd better come in.'

And, so, steeling myself, holding a breath so deep I might be about to swim the Styx, I cross the threshold, and into this other world.

The house has changed. The kitchen sink is clogged with rice while food-dirty plates sit abandoned on the sideboard, the television, the tops of shelves; the worn linoleum floor is spattered with an arc of passata; and in the bathroom the smell of ammonia makes me gag, forcing me to flush then retreat, pulling the door to whilst cursing the environment and your fucking conscience.

But it's not just that. Underneath all the absent-minded littering and the deliberate destruction, the gingerbread house itself is crumbling, falling apart at its icing seams. The ceiling is yellowed from years of impassive smoking; the walls stamped with soil and ink handprints in increasing height and span from six to sullen teen; the guttering choked with dead leaves and live animals, so that water has been cascading down the kitchen wall causing a bloom of mould to creep above the coat rack. And without David calling round disguised as Mr Fix-It, shelves teeter, hooks dangle from Rawlplugs, a bulb buzzes and flickers off and on, off and on, and I am reminded of the kitchen disco on the day we arrived.

But I'm not seeing it through six-year-old eyes any more. I am not even seeing it through my own, but through Jimmy's.

And everywhere I am seeing an absence.

An absence of taste.

An absence of order.

An absence of discipline.

All things he has found wanting in me, and worries will return if I spend too long here, soak up too much you.

But in the end it is not that that breaks me – breaks us, Edie. It is something else entirely.

*

I see the flicker of disgust when he walks into the kitchen. But if he is truly affronted he hides it under a bright, shining cloak of wit and charm and gratitude, and you, fool that you are, drunk as you are, let him court you from your sofa throne.

'Oh, you are adorable,' you say, and I curse you again for the internal lexicon you still carry with you from Cambridge prep.

'I thought Toni was coming,' I say then.

You flap your hand, send a plume of smoke swirling, gathering dust motes as it does so. 'Away. With Susie.'

'So you were on your own?' I ask. 'For Christmas lunch.'

You shrug. 'It's only a day,' you say. 'Like any other.'

'Not any more,' Jimmy says then. 'We need a toast. To me and Dido.'

'Yes,' you blurt. 'A toast!' Though I assume your enthusiasm is more to do with wine than weddings, given your refusal to meet my eye.

'No, don't get up,' Jimmy tells you. 'I brought a bottle. Two, actually.'

'Good boy,' you praise, and watch him go out to the hall.

Then you turn to me. 'What the fuck, Di? Marrying him is one thing, but a baby?'

'And?' I say. 'You had one.'

'That's not the same.'

But there is no answer to that as Jimmy comes back in bearing two bottles, one champagne, one brandy.

'Christ, what are you two?' Jimmy demands. I bristle until

I see he is still, thankfully, smiling. 'Some kind of local coven?'

'No,' I say.

'Pretty much,' you counter, letting Jimmy pour you a sparkling glassful into a dull, tarnished tumbler. A tumbler that has clearly already seen the best part of the bottle of Scotch that sits on the stove top. 'Aren't we all?'

'That's what I say,' Jimmy agrees, sitting down next to me, and pulling me into him. 'Witches, the lot of you.'

And he kisses me then, pushing his tongue past my tight lips to prove that witches are no threat to him.

'So can I call you Mum?' he asks, leaning over to you, leering.

'You can try,' you drawl. 'But I only answer to Edie.'

He laughs. Raises his glass, elbows me to do the same, then smiles straight at you. 'To Mrs McGowan,' he says.

Then you look at me, plaster a smile on smeared lipstick, a wide, practised, fuck-the-world grin. 'To Dido,' you say.

And fuck the world we do.

By seven I have agreed to let you walk me down the aisle, though you refuse to give me away – I am not property, you remind Jimmy, though you look straight at me when you say it.

By nine I have agreed to have one glass, just a small one, and besides, by the time we get home Jimmy will be too far gone to do anything, so I won't be getting pregnant tonight.

By eleven I am drunk and not driving anywhere. I stagger upstairs for a lie-down, listening through the ceiling as you and Jimmy recalculate the Budget, recast the cabinet, redraw the world in a better light.

'Come to bed,' I plead.

'Later,' he says, then clarifies. 'You go—'

'He'll be fine,' you interrupt. 'Go on. Night-night.' And you blow me a kiss so extravagant you knock over a glass, sending a slug of brandy spattering across the carpet, though the whole thing is so stained now – with paint, with ash, with whatever – the liquid gets lost in a pattern, quite at home.

So I go.

And I lie down, and listen, and let myself imagine a wedding, an affair so precise in its detail, so exquisite in its embrace, that it will be remembered for all time by everyone who comes. Of course it is an affair woven entirely from fiction – from books and films and the *Hello* magazines I flick idly through at the doctor's and dentist, dismissing the fools who buy it, yet devouring every page of gossip like the glutton I really am. Because do you know how many weddings I've been to, Edie?

Just one. One wedding, Edie. Don't you think that's strange for a woman my age?

At first I blamed you for having the kind of friends who wouldn't, or couldn't.

Then I blamed myself for having so few friends at all.

Because despite every attempt by you to instil into me the hypocrisy of marriage – no opportunity missed to dismiss the handover as patriarchal hegemony, the flowers as environmental sabotage, the white dress as an outright lie – despite my own nascent feminism, a wedding had topped my to-do list since that hand-in-hand snapshot in someone else's garden in the summer of 1976.

I had imagined every detail, painstakingly planned it all until it ran like oiled clockwork in my mind. Not the dress, you understand, not the flowers or the favours or any fancy that might come and go with fashion or the season. But the words.

I knew exactly what he would say at every stage of our grand romance, had the dialogue down word for precious word. The proposal when, eyes brimming with pride and pathos, he would tell me I was his everything, his lodestar, his muse; that his world turned only for me. The walk down the aisle to the altar – alternately a decaying Gothic church, a sand-silted chapel skirting a beach on the Lizard, the bunting-draped back garden – when he would feel faint at my grace and beauty, the significance of my approach, before taking my own shaking hand and whispering to me that he has never loved me more. The wedding bed, where he would tremble as he undressed me, make love to me not for the first time, but with such presence I would feel we were finally, truly, one.

Not once did I realize this was Pernod-vomit-inducing pie in the sky; an adolescent confection borne of classroom Brontë and behind-the-bike-sheds Shirley Conran.

And not once did I imagine it would be Jimmy in the starring role.

*

I wake at gone one in the morning, my bed still empty; music – Carole King, I think – still murmuring below.

I sit up and the room tilts, spins. I am still no drinker, despite Jimmy's best attempts. Oh God. I should have said no, I think then. He told me to, encouraged it, but that won't matter. I should have been better behaved, been the good girl I know I am, always wanted to be. Not the one you designed.

Then I hear it. The high, affected laughter – yours – then his: lower, deeper, insistent.

Something's not right. There is a groaning sound, and the clatter of something being knocked or spilled.

My stomach drops and rises in swift succession.

Something is happening.

I stand, stagger to the door, then slowly, carefully, down the threadbare tread of the stairs until I can see far enough over the banisters.

And there you are. Both of you. You, your back against the wall, your neck tilted up, all catlike, arched, coquettish, and he leaning over you, curl-haired, a wolf in sheep's clothing, ready to devour his prey.

I could have shouted then. Could have stopped it before it happened. But I was mesmerized, gawping slack-jawed like a child at the circus.

And so I watch as he leans in, and you reach up.

I watch as your lips meet.

I watch as his hands snake around you, one around your back to keep you in place, the other pushed against what little chest you possess.

I watch as you, for a second, pull away, and I think you're

going to tell him to stop, slap him, demand to know what he's thinking.

But you don't. You laugh, let your head loll, then lift it for a second embrace.

I can't decide which is worse: that he kissed you. Or that you let him. That you kissed him back. Or that you're doing it again. Once – once would have been a mistake careless. Once, I could have believed your lies later. But twice, there is intent.

He moves a hand down then, goes to push it inside your gossamer top, and I finally find my words.

'What are you doing?' I ask. As if I am five and watching cows or sheep rut for the first time.

He looks up, sways for a second, comes to. 'Oh, fuck.'

Then, leaving you wavering, confused, he staggers to the stairs, grips me. 'I'm sorry. Shit, Di. I'm drunk. And a fool. I fucked up. I forgot – ' And then, oh, you will love this, Edie, then he says, ' – I forgot which one was you.'

'Liar,' I say.

'I'm not,' he pleads. 'Edie, tell her. Tell her I called you "Di".'

But you do not tell me that. Instead you tell me that he's a predator, a predator and a charlatan. He tells me you're pathetic, a gin-sodden armchair socialist playing at poverty. You tell him to fuck off to the council estate where he belongs. Tell me you only did it to prove what a shit he is. That you did it for me, don't you see? For me.

Maybe you did, once. But that second time wasn't for me, to prove a point. It was for you, for your fragile ego and fat ambition and indiscriminate libido. And that is all I can see, think. And so then I do something so stupid I can hardly bear to think of it now. I muster my own loud voice, but use it, to my shame, to defend him: to tell you that you started it, dancing in front of him, all eyes and tits. Then I storm out and sit in the car and refuse to come in.

'Open the bloody door,' you demand, hammering on the window, half naked and barefoot.

'No,' I say.

'You'll freeze!' you yell.

'Good,' I yell back.

'For fuck's sake,' you mutter.

Jimmy pushes you away, tries the door, then the window, then the boot. He kicks the car, his own car, leaving a dent that will cost hundreds to have beaten out.

But I do not open the door. Not then. Not at three, when he tries again. Not until five in the morning, when the alcohol and adrenaline have drained away, and I have managed a few minutes of snatched sleep. Then I wipe a circle on the fogged window and see him crouched in the porch, his legs pulled up against the cold, hands plunged between them.

And the pity I feel is overwhelming.

I wake him then, tell him we're leaving, that I'm fine to drive, that I wasn't drunk, just exhausted. And he cries as he slumps in the passenger seat, buries his head in my lap, tells me he's sorry, that he loves me, begs me not to leave him.

I lift his head, snot and salt water stringing onto my skirt, and I kiss him. 'I won't,' I say.

Then somewhere on the M11, as we leave Essex and your

filthy house and fucked-up life far behind, he will take my hand and turn to me and say, 'I'm your family now.'

And I will believe him.

And for that, Edie, and so much else, I am sorry.

# The Chocolate War

## May 1999

It happens like this. To all of us fool women who love men like him.

We slide from true romance to torment so slowly, slickly, seamlessly, that when we open our eyes one morning to discover that the rose-tinted glasses have been broken along with our nose, we are astonished to find it is us in the mirror.

I see it now, of course. I see that I am the woman on the news I used to shout at, sigh at. 'Just leave him,' I would intone, exasperated. 'How many times?'

But isn't as easy as one, two, three, is it?

We let them do it the first time because we are so shocked by the rawness of it. And because they say they are sorry. That they saw red. That it wasn't them at all, not the real them, anyway.

Then we let them do it once more, saying this time will be the last.

Then again, as we move our own goalpost to the next time. And the one after that.

Until we realize the real them *is* the one that shouts, throws, threatens; the charming doppelgänger a mirage they manage to conjure for the cameras, for public viewing only. Until we come to expect the *sorry*, come to cling to tears and make-up sex. Until we come to believe that it is our fault anyway, that we have made mistakes, provoked, goaded with the misplaced look, the wrong word, an ill-timed smile, or sneeze, or cough.

So that when he refuses to talk to me for two days straight I realize I should never have told him I was too tired for sex, even though I capitulated within seconds, let him do it anyway.

So that when he walks out on me at dinner in Mezzo I know it is because I should have agreed to dessert. Because it's his birthday, of course I should eat to bursting. And by saying no, I have spoilt the mood for him.

So that when he throws a coffee-table biography of Clement Attlee at me, cutting open my lower lip, I tell myself I should have listened to what he said the first time, instead of saying, 'Pardon?'

Stupid, stupid girl.

Our house is so thickly carpeted with eggshells that I learn to walk on permanent tiptoe.

You beg me to leave him. Phone me to plead for forgiveness, to insist again that you did it for me, to prove to me what he was capable of.

'What you're capable of,' I say.

'No,' you insist. 'This was about you. I was going to show you—'

'How? What were you going to do? Photograph the evidence with your invisible camera?'

'No. Di, please. Listen to me—'

'I can't.'

'Because he won't let you?'

'No. Because you're drunk.'

'It's nine o'clock in the bloody morning.'

'Like that's going to stop you.'

You pause. 'Are you pregnant?'

'No,' I say. And hear – or imagine, maybe – a loosening, a breath of relief. 'Not yet,' I add cruelly.

'Di.'

'No. Just . . . no.'

I cut you off with the same seemingly calm determination with which Tom and Harry exiled me. I hear you blurt out a single word and then, without registering the irony, I hang up, pull the cord out of the socket, until, eventually, Jimmy changes the number. Your letters are returned – also with no sense of irony – unopened, to sender, and, when that fails, consigned to the kitchen bin, used as receptacles for chewed gum, and, once, a desiccated mouse.

I begin to feel restless, feel a disconnect from this Dick Whittington city that I have come to call home. My concentration slips and I take to wandering. At lunchtime I walk along the Strand, across Fleet Street and into the City, imagining I am Nancy, or Oliver himself, waiting to be rescued by Mr Brownlow. After work I take the bus into Brixton and then the backstreets to Poet's Corner to search for the squat. Up and down Shakespeare Road, Chaucer, Spenser I traipse, peering in windows, trying to project myself into the picture, into that clotted-cream-painted kitchen, our bare-board bathroom, the tie-dye of Toni's bed. But all I have is a ragbag of memories and a faded snapshot of a four-year-old me standing sentinel on a gatepost, a disembodied black arm propping me up, protecting me.

When I get home, Jimmy asks where I've been. Was the Tube running late? Why didn't I call? I have no plausible explanation, none that will placate him, so, in future, I limit my wanderings to his late shifts, or his weekend duties, which have increased in proportion to his stress and my anxiety.

Until one night. One foolish, fabulous night when a piece of my past comes trip-trapping over a rickety bridge.

It is fate, I tell myself.

Fate that I left work early.

Fate that Charing Cross station is shut and the entrance to Embankment choked with complaining hordes trying to squeeze onto the Northern Line.

Fate that I don't walk north to Leicester Square but choose instead to cross Hungerford Bridge, the opening chords of 'Waterloo Sunset' striking up in my head as I see the wide, muddy river and, beyond it, the concrete bulk of the South Bank Centre, squatting on its banks.

I am stalking across, head down against the wind and the crowds, ears filled with Ray Davies, when I hear it. Hear her.

'Dido?'

I stop, feel shoulders slam into me, hear tuts, sense my heart stutter.

I know that voice, have heard it call my name a thousand times; heard it whisper secrets, dissect the past, plan gleaming futures; heard it sing this very song. A voice that used to radiate boredom and disdain in equal, practised measure, but is now edged with something else. Something harder, more chemical.

I look up as I say it. 'Harry?'

It is. It's her. All seven skinny stone of her draped in nothing but an oyster silk camisole dress and an outsized pullover – a man's pullover – so that the overall effect is of a child playing dress-up in her parents' wardrobe. And so absurd, so Harry – so you – is this, that I laugh. And as I do, the frown on her face lifts, pulling the corners of her lips with it.

'It *is* you,' she says. 'I thought . . . I didn't know you were here. In London, I mean.'

'Nor I you.'

'I . . .' she trails off and her smile slips. Because we both know that's not the reason for the silence and the stealthy avoidance.

'Do you work here?' I ask quickly. Because now that I have her, I have to keep her; I can't let her go with nothing more than a stilted hello.

'I do,' she says, her smile returning now. 'Over there.' She points to a tower to the left of the National Theatre. 'ITV,' she continues.

'You work in telly?' Her too, I think. Of course her too, because where else?

She nods. 'Producing. Well, assistant producing. On *After Hours*. Have you seen it?'

I nod. It's a magazine show – you won't have seen it, Edie, it was only on in London, and only for a year or so – celebrities on a sofa being asked anodyne questions and a boy band in the studio. Something I caught whilst Jimmy was out and I was flicking channels and couldn't face *Newsnight*, couldn't face watching a political fuck-up that I'd pay for later.

'Oh God. It's shit, isn't it?' she says.

I shake my head. 'No, I—'

'No, really, it is. But it's telly. And Max – he's the head of Light Ents – he's moving to national and I think he'll take me with him. And that means Saturday night prime time. Which, you know.'

I nod like I know, but in my head I'm thinking 'Max' and I'm looking at the jumper – grey cashmere – and putting two and two together and coming up with a perfect score.

It takes her all of a single vodka and tonic to confess.

'So where is he now?' I ask.

'Surrey.' Harry leans back against the worn green velvet of a tired pub banquette. 'With his wife.'

'Jesus.'

'I know, I know.' She pulls the sleeves down on the jumper so that her hands are hidden, wraps her arms around her knees.

'Does . . . does she know?'

'No!' she says abruptly, as if this is an impossibility. Then clarifies, 'Not yet.'

'He's leaving her?'

She nods.

'When?'

She shrugs. 'When the baby's older.'

'There's a child?'

'Alfie. He's ten months.'

'You've met it – him?'

'Kind of. They came into work. And she was passing him around. So . . .'

'You held their baby?'

'I know. It's awful. *I'm* awful.' She pulls another Marlboro Light from the soft pack on the table, flicks the Zippo, filling the booth with the smell of petrol, of adolescence, of belief. She clicks it shut, then takes a drag. 'The thing is, Di, I *love* him.'

She stresses the word like it's magic, like it can conjure away all the badness, make everything right.

Because it can. That's the thing, isn't it, Edie? However messy and inconvenient and even destructive it is, when you're inside it, love blurs these background images and casts everything inside in a circle of golden light.

'But . . . you'll be a stepmother,' I say, as I realize the implications of this.

'Well, we're not getting married,' she says. 'But, sort of.'

'Fuck.'

'Yup.'

'So what about you?' she asks then.

'What about me what?'

'Oh come on, dish.'

I feel my fingers tighten around the velveteen nap of the bench, feel myself taken back to that monkey, to the tree house, to that town. 'Jimmy,' I say.

'Jimmy?' She pauses, going through a Guess Who flip

game of prime suspects in her head. 'Wait. Not Jimmy McGowan?'

I nod, pull a face, an apology. 'He's different now.'

'He'd have to be.'

'No, he is. He's . . . grown-up.'

'God. More fool him.'

'We're getting married,' I blurt then, a desperate defence of this man I am tied to. Or about to be.

She grasps my hand, looking for diamonds, but finds only an old silver band, one you once bought me from a bra-less woman with a nose piercing at Camden Market way back when.

'He hasn't changed, then,' she says, dropping my hand onto the table.

'It's . . .' He was going to buy me a ring. But diamonds and sapphires are flashy, for fools. Better a plain platinum band and true love than H. Samuel glitter and Hallmark fakery.

'So where is it? Walden?'

I shake my head. 'Here. It won't be a big thing.' Not any more. Jimmy wants it to be just us. So our grand declaration has been whittled down to witnesses drafted from the registry office, has diminished to two people, to four walls; a goading, gloating mirror of my little life, I realize.

I shoo the thought away and change the subject to books, to work – my work. I tell her that I have edited two Carnegie longlisters, that I may have found a winner, too – a thing of beauty and brilliance that lay languishing for months in the slush pile before I, treasure seeker that I am, pulled it out and declared it a plum.

I don't tell her that the company is in flux, about to be taken over, and that my name features high on the list of possible redundancies, a placing brought about not by chance or misfortune, but by a series of Jimmy-related slips that have seen me arriving late or leaving early or not coming in at all. That have left sentences comma-spliced, infinitives split, and, worse, a character reappearing on page 137 having been killed off on 121.

'That's brilliant,' she says, then. 'You always did love books.'

She stands. 'Going to the lav,' she says. 'Want to come?'

I shake my head and watch her disappear down the wood-panelled passage at the side of the bar. Seven times she goes to the toilet that evening. And each time she comes back she is brighter, more brilliant, more . . . Harry. And it makes sense now: the words tipped out pell-mell like pick-up-sticks from a jar; the need to forgive me, or at least forget; the fact she stopped on the bridge at all.

She is high. Of course she's high. I've seen it in Jimmy – seen it in myself too, before the attempts at conception. But now I stick to slimline, even the vodka forsaken for the sake of this elusive child, while Harry, still a child herself, slips through the wooden door with her lover's cashmere wrapped around her and a gram wrap hidden in her bra.

Three hours and five double vodkas later she staggers out onto Roupell Street, clings to my arm as she sways along the cobbled bricks, under the damp-dripping railway bridge, then swerves right towards the station.

'This is me,' she says.

I look up at the bus stand number, wondering which is hers, and where it leads.

'You could come?' she says.

I shake my head. 'I have to get back,' I say.

'Of course. Jimmy. Do give him my love, won't you?' she slurs.

'I will,' I say. Then I summon it, this thing that has to be said, the Dumbo that sits on its podium performing tricks, playing to the crowd, pleading for applause, or at least an acknowledgement. 'I'm sorry,' I say.

'What for?' she asks.

'For . . . you know.' For everything. For not stopping you. For not telling her. For being your daughter.

She stares at me for a minute, trying to pluck memories out of the ether, to pull them into shape. I see the lurch then – of realization, of remembrance – and for a moment I think she's going to slap me, or spit, or worse. But instead she just shrugs and smiles. 'Fucking grown-ups,' she says. And it is so emphatic I want to hug her, this waif in a night-dress and borrowed wool.

But she hugs me first, her skinny arms flung around my shift dress. And as I hold her back, I feel the fragility of her, porcelain-thin, her limbs like sparrows' legs, as if they would snap if I squeezed too hard.

She stumbles then, pulls away. 'Here, have you got a pen?' she says.

I nod, and rummage in my Mulberry, pushing lipsticks, tissues, a tampon aside before pulling out a Parker.

She takes it, pushes up my sleeve and presses gently on the pale, translucent underbelly of my forearm, the ink tracing and crossing the blue lines of veins as it spells out a phone number.

'Call me,' she says. Then she hands back the pen and hugs me again, holding me tightly, not letting go until the bus draws up and performs its do-si-do of passengers. As a man in a black overcoat heaves himself onto the open platform, she pulls away from me and jumps up behind him, holding onto the pole as if it's a carousel horse and the bus a brilliant, luminous fairground ride.

'See you,' she calls above the traffic.

'Wouldn't want to be you,' I reply, without thinking. Because it's the obvious answer. The only answer. The . . .

'Right answer,' she says. 'You so wouldn't, Di.'

I follow the bus as it disappears down Waterloo Road into the churn of traffic, and all of a sudden I am Alice peering through the looking glass into my Wonderland again.

And you, Edie? You were there with me, of course you were. At the time I tried to deny it, pretend you weren't even worthy of being an unspoken guest. But you were in every cigarette Harry smoked, every gesture she affected. You were there in my imaginings as I tried to picture her holding an infant with the artless ease you used to hoist me onto your hip. You were there when we swore, when we sang, when we downed Smirnoff with a 'sláinte'.

But you were not there when I got home.

And Edie, I needed you.

I am late. Not by minutes, but by hours this time.

When I get home, I find that he has cooked dinner – an elaborate apology for another verbal attack in a list so long I have lost track of which is the latest or worst.

'I'm so sorry,' I blurt. 'I didn't think . . .'

'You never fucking do, Di, that's the problem. Why weren't you answering your phone?'

I pull the Nokia out of my pocket, see the eleven missed calls, the six text messages, starting with concern, then escalating to anger before signing off with disappointment and dismissal. 'Shit, I didn't hear it,' I say, fiddling with the volume. 'Sound's turned off. Sorry. I'm an idiot.'

He doesn't dissuade me. 'So who were you with?'

I flounder, try to think of someone, cannot tell him the truth of course, because that would summon the spectre of Tom who still skulks in the corners of Jimmy's mind. And mine. 'Jude,' I say. 'A work thing came up.'

He pauses, and for a moment I think he's seen through the lie, thinks I'm cheating on him. But, like he says, who else would have me? 'You missed dinner,' he says at last.

I stare at the food. Hot, it must have been magnificent, a *MasterChef*-worthy plate, the kind I would praise him for, tell him he has talent beyond politics, that he should think about opening a restaurant one day.

Now it lies cold and congealed, an unappealing mass of insipid fish and cloying sauce, and a dark chocolate tart that

I know I will have to walk to work for a week to compensate for.

'Eat it,' he says.

'I'm not—'

'Eat it.'

Each mouthful is an effort, each accompanied by an impulse to gag. But my instinct for self-defence is stronger, and so I swallow them down as he watches, impassive, and drinks his way steadily through an entire bottle of red.

Later, as he lies sweating in bed, and I in the bath, washing off shame and the smell of vomit, I realize I am that woman – the one on television; the one in the mirror.

And I know now it isn't my fault. That I shouldn't have to apologize, to say sorry. But I am. I'm sorry.

I'm sorry I didn't tell him to go fuck himself that night, or the next or for months after.

I'm sorry I didn't call you and tell you you were right all along.

And I'm sorry I put you through it at all.

But do you know what I thought the worst part was back then? That when I let the cold, clouded water run down the plughole, I let something else run out too: blue-black ink and looped, careless numerals.

I could have traced her, I suppose. Could have called LWT and asked for a girl called Harry. But I saw it as a sign again, fate. And anyway, the next day Jimmy bought me silk pyjamas and told me I looked like Lana Turner. So instead of seeking out Narnia that day, I turned my back, shut myself in my small world and prayed instead for a happy ending.

# The Party

## December 1999

D<sup>o</sup> you remember 1999?

The song, I mean. Prince in his *Purple Rain* Paisley Park finest, singing he had a lion in his pocket, a line I took to be literal, and imagined a cat nestled in the velvet of his suit as he strutted and pranced and told us to party.

And we did party – you, me and Harry; we danced in the kitchen like it was the last night of the last year of the millennium, 1999 no more than a number, a date so absurdly distant that we were sure we'd be dead or famous by then.

As if it were impossible the day would ever come.

I remember another time, too. New Year's Eve, 1986 – our last New Year's Eve together – in the Duke, drunk on cheap cider and youth and possibility, Harry with her lipstick smeared, my obsessively applied lip balm disappointingly intact, despite strategically placing myself next to Tom as the clock tick-tocked towards midnight.

The pub is packed, bodies spilling out onto the pavement and already gathering around the war memorial, plastic pint glasses and fags in hand, a spliff being passed around behind

backs before the police do their hourly check. Inside, someone puts Prince on the jukebox and another cheer goes up.

'Oh God!' Harry yells. 'I *love* this song.' And she grabs my
hand to pull me up to dance.

But as I rise I am struck by the realization that in 1999 we
won't even be here. There is uni, then work, and then, what?
So that even with my fingers clasped in hers I have the sense
of being unanchored, seasick at the prospect of an open
ocean.

'What are we going to do?' I ask. 'In 1999.'

Harry pulls a face. 'God, as if I'll be hanging round with
you two losers. I'll be in bloody – I don't know – LA or
something.'

'Bollocks you will,' Tom snorts. 'You'll be married and
living in Chipping fucking Sodbury or something.'

'Bullshit.'

'Bull true.'

I smile wanly at the back and forth, the banter that I know
by heart, could join in if I weren't so unsettled.

'We should come back here,' I say then. 'Like the cast of
*Bugsy Malone* did.'

Tom raises an eyebrow. 'They came to the Duke?'

'Oh, ha ha. They met something like ten years after the
film under the clock at Waterloo. I read it somewhere. In the
playscript, I think.'

'What, so whatever we're doing, whoever we're with, on
New Year's Eve 1999 we show up in a shitty pub in a small
town in Essex?'

'For old times' sake,' I insist.

Tom smiles. 'For auld lang syne.'

Harry rolls her eyes, expertly. 'Oh, fuck it. Fine. We'll meet back here in 1999. At this very table. But, God, can we just dance now?'

And so we do, we dance like someone's got a bomb and we could die anyway. We dance our lives away.

We dance like it's 1999.

And did we meet up?

Well, let me tell you, Edie. Because, though it wasn't the night any of us planned, it was one to remember.

They call it falling with child, like it's easy, one slip and I will be pregnant. But I cannot even do that right, and each month the evidence is there in my bloodstained knickers, in the tampons that I wrap in toilet roll and push to the bottom of the bin.

By July I become more covert with my bathroom habits, try to hide it when it comes. But he wants sex, and when he pulls out it's unmistakable. 'I'll leave you,' he threatens. 'If you don't get pregnant by next month.'

But August comes and goes, marked by red in my diary and knickers, and his threat proves empty as he simply stays and fucks me harder, as if that will force the issue.

By December he's suspicious. 'It's the drugs,' he says. 'They've fucked you up inside.'

I don't bother to point out that I never took coke until I met him. That I never took it except with him. That I only took it because if I didn't, everything seemed, would *be*, so much worse.

Besides, it's not the coke.

When I imagine a life inside me, a being I will be responsible for, I feel a clutching at my stomach, a needling, and I cannot eat, cannot breathe for the claustrophobia of it. So that when I feel the familiar cramps, see the red bloom on white satin, I feel not shame – not at first, anyway – but a flood of relief. So much so that just a month after seeing Harry, I go to the surgery on Grove Lane, sit with the fat-cheeked toddlers and the sallow-faced mothers and wait my turn to see the same doctor who, five months before that, gave me a prescription for folic acid.

'We could fit a coil,' she says, impassive. 'It's far more effective.'

The coil is also far more *there*. And it's possible, just possible, he'd be able to feel it. 'No, thanks. I'll be careful.'

And I am. So very, very careful.

The pills are foil-popped and dropped into a freezer bag which is then rolled and hidden in the toe of a pair of boots that sit, unworn, at the back of my wardrobe. He will not find them, I tell myself. But still, like Poe's telltale heart, I can feel them, hear them, see them. They pulse out their presence so that I am whelmed by panic, can barely concentrate on even the simplest of tasks.

My life is a squalid mess, I realize, ridden with lies and ripe with deceit and held together with nothing stronger than a spool of cotton. Because two weeks after that I am sacked. Jude tells me it's the cutbacks, but I know she is trying to be kind, trying to cover for my inability to spot what could have been the next Harry Potter, but which has been sold instead to Macmillan in a three-way auction. I can freelance, she tells me. I'll have to go back to copy-editing, but it's better than nothing.

Alone in the toilets, I sob. But at home, to him, fresh make-up on, fixed smile, I spin. It's perfect, I tell him. Better this way because I can work in the evenings, when the baby comes.

But there is no baby, of course.

And even without the boot-hidden pills, the chances would be dwindling. Jimmy works late and when he does get to bed he's too tired to fuck, pushing me away when I try to show willing.

'You work too much,' I tell him.

'We need the money,' he says. 'Now you're not working. We've got a wedding to pay for. Remember?'

A wedding that looms over us – less than a month away, but which we discuss almost never, still less look forward to. 'I *am* working,' I say, nodding at the three-hundred-page manuscript that sits, still in its elastic bands, on the coffee table.

'How many of those do you need to do to make your half of the mortgage?'

I shrug. I don't know. Don't want to think about it. Our mortgage runs into four figures a month as, at Jimmy's insistence, we stretched ourselves while our earning power was on the increase.

'Right. So, until you sort yourself out, I'll be doing all the overtime I can get.'

And he walks out, leaving me alone with 70,000 words of

dystopia and the needling knowledge that he doesn't get paid overtime. He's paid well, but extra hours in politics are done for love, not money.

Love.

And so it begins.

And ends.


It's 31 December 1999. The night we planned to party with lions in our pockets, party like there's no tomorrow.

Or some of us did.

'I'm working,' he says.

The lie drips bitter. But this time I'm not swallowing. This is what I've both dreaded and prayed for: a silver bullet. A kind of legitimacy. Something I can cite without implicating myself in my own pathetic situation. The possibility of it consumes me, adrenaline flooding my veins and sending my stomach into a sickly churn.

I swallow, breathe, say the line. 'I thought Blair was going to the Dome. He can't need you for that, surely?'

He snorts. 'Like you'd know.'

'I just thought we were doing something. Together,' I add, a last chance for redemption, or confirmation.

'Well, things change.'

'Really?' I am clawing now, desperate for the truth, but terrified of change.

'Yes, really. Why? Do you want to call TB and check? For fuck's sake, Di. It's not like I want to go.'

'No, I . . . What am I supposed to do now?'

'I don't know. Watch the *Hootenanny*. Call a friend.'

'I don't have any,' I want to say. 'Not any more, you've seen to that.' But instead I slip out a *maybe* and a shrug.

'Whatever,' he says, the conversation over. 'I need to shower.'

His phone is on the table. I wait until the water's running and the radio turned on, then tiptoe, heart hammering, into the bedroom, click it open, scroll down to her name in his messages, and read.

I will myself to ignore the filth along with the endearments. I need facts, that's all. A time and place.

And that is how, on Millennium Eve, I find myself standing in a shop doorway off Brick Lane, stone-cold sober but wired to all hell, waiting for my boyfriend to show up to shag some girl.


It is less than ten minutes before he rounds the corner, sees me, stops in his tracks. I can feel him thinking, trying to conjure excuses as to why he's not with Tony, not in Greenwich, why he's this side of the river at all. But he has nothing, so instead it gets turned on me.

'What the fuck?'

I should cower; every instinct is telling me to, to find an excuse, to dismiss it as coincidence, to kiss him, make it better. But I can't do it any more. Something has awoken in me, some part I had forgotten about, or disowned – the child who said *bugger* just to see the effect it had, who walked swing-hipped in your wake, flipping the bird at the world: she is here now. And others too, crowding in my consciousness – whip-smart

Becky Sharp, fearless Scout Finch, even Jane Eyre is here, stoic, determined.

So instead of making excuses, I ask for his. 'Who is she?' I counter.

I do not win the argument. I do not rise triumphant, strike a blow for female-kind. But the result is the same: we are done. I leave not with a flourish, with a final *fuck you*, but a flippant shove, dismissed, so that I trip in the litter-filled gutter, plunging a foot into a puddle of ten-pint puke. Satisfied my life cannot possibly sink any lower, I pick my way along the pavement, dodging the crowds and the cans, pushing through air thick with anticipation.

But my night is over, isn't it? My decade done.

And now what? Now where?

I need a drink. Can have one, now the charade is over.

The few pubs I can find are all closed for private parties so I walk through heaving streets until I find a corner shop, bravely unboarded and blazingly lit, its Sikh owner determined to stay the course and reap the rewards.

I point at a bottle of overpriced Smirnoff standing alone, odd in a line-up of Cherry 20/20 and Thunderbird.

'Party time?' the man says, grinning gap-toothed as I hand over a twenty, get coins back in change.

I force a smile. 'Like it's 1999.'

He smiles back blankly. 'It *is* 1999,' he says.

I take the bottle, refusing the plastic bag he holds out. 'Doesn't matter,' I say.

Cowbells clanging my exit behind me, I walk down Brick

Lane, find a windowsill, and sit and watch and listen to the hum of the world. A world on the edge of a new one, or of extinction, some say. But whichever, the anticipation thickens the air so that it is an intoxicating soup; just breathing on a night like this is a buzz. And I am doing more than that.

The bottle is almost empty now, and I need to pee. But there is nowhere open, so I squat behind a dusty Transit van and let a stream of pure alcohol piss run into the gutter. Then I stand, swaying, wondering what next. The Underground station I used earlier is shut now: understaffed, the sign says. I could get a bus, I think, but the numbers are confusing and I am unsure where I am or where I want to go.

Or who I want to see.

I want to be looked after, I think.

I want to be loved.

*I wanna be adored*, I sing in my head.

Then I see it, as a Blakean vision first, I think, before it rises before me in reality, lit up like Coleridge's pleasure-dome against a sea of slum-dirty dead ends.

Liverpool Street station.

Gateway to Essex.

I stumble to the ticket machine, fumble with change. Buy a ticket to fuck knows where, it doesn't matter as long as it gets me through the barrier. Then I'm on the platform and pelting pell-mell to make it into a carriage.

I fall into a seat as the doors sound their closing beeps, lean my hot cheek against the cool Plexiglas as we pull out and off, clickety-clacking past yellow bricks and down the track, dancing our way to the Duke and to midnight.

'Walden,' I whisper to my sorry, drunken self. 'Walden, I am coming home.'

That is the last pin-sharp memory I have. The rest of the night is a swaying haze of faces. Snapshots, really, that is all: single moments caught in time that, no matter how hard I try, I cannot fill in or fix the fading edges.

An albino-haired driver in a beat-up blue car – I must have blagged a lift from him from the station, because I don't remember paying.

The bar at the Duke – I bought a drink, or someone bought me one, because there is a glass in my hand in the picture; I can feel it cold against my hot skin, feel the curved rim against my tempted teeth.

The back of a boy – tour dates on a now-grey T-shirt, hair grown out and curling at the ends – and me calling, 'Tom!' But when he turns, his teenage eyes are glazed and his slack mouth is not one I have kissed, and I stumble out onto the high street, sticking two fingers up at Prince who is still singing, still exhorting me to party.

I tried, I tell him. But they did not come.

Next I see our house, and this is clear in my vision, Edie, you need to know that. You need to know that when I climbed the hill I wasn't looking for them, not for Tom or Harry. I was looking for you.

I was coming home.

But the door is locked and the key gone or moved and I am too drunk to scrabble under stones. So I go down the side ginnel and into our back garden. I must have been looking for another key, Edie. Or hoped that the back door would be swinging carelessly open, or at least on the latch. But you are safety-conscious, it seems, or someone is, because when I rattle the door it moves only millimetres; when I peer through the window all I can see is stillness, all I can hear is silence.

But it was *you* I came looking for – don't you see? You I wanted, needed that night. It was only accident that I ended up where I did, that I ended up doing what I did. It was foolish, I know that, not just drunk but in any state. Because I was no longer a child: no longer Heidi, nimble as a mountain goat; no longer George with knees still scabbed from climbing. I was a grown woman with a stomach full of alcohol and a head full of memories, and that, Edie, is a dangerous combination. Because together they make us do desperate things, and I must have been desperate to do this. To push my way through dead nettles. To pull myself up onto the lowest branch. To haul myself up and over a wall.

'Harry,' I shout, Queen, if not of Bloody Everything, then at least of this flint castle. 'Harry, are you home?'

A light flicks on in the big house, and I see a face in a window. A man. 'Tom?' I yell. 'Tom, it's me!'

And I raise my hand to wave.

But as I do, I feel my foot slip; feel my fingers grasping at branches but coming away clutching nothing but night air; feel myself teeter for a second, wondering if I might right myself, or, better still, fly.

And at that wondrous thought I spread my arms, an idiot

Icarus, and give myself over to the mercy of the gods and gravity.

And I topple forward off the wall and hit not a paddling pool this time, but cold, hard ground.

I wake up with Simon Le Bon staring down at me, take a second to fathom this seeming impossibility before the first rush of vomit flies up my gullet and I lean over the side of the bed and hurl.

It hits not the carpet but a bucket, spattering its pink plastic sides in a flume of orange. I am at the seaside now, though where I don't remember. Yarmouth, maybe? On a day trip. The image of the sea and the effort of thought send my insides rising on the bob and swell and I let out another burst of vodka and ginger biscuits, the only food I remember eating in the last few days.

'Better?'

I look up and see her then, her hair fanned out around her face, still golden, lit up by the sunlight that pours through the crack in the curtains.

An angel. An—

'Angela.'

She smiles, comes over to the bed, wipes my face with a wet flannel.

I open my mouth, let out not sick but a sob this time.

'Don't cry,' she says.

But I do cry. I cry for an hour, for all that has gone before, all that has been lost, and for this, this found thing, this seed of possibility, an accident of drink and timing and circumstance.

And she lets me, lets me sob and puke, hands me a glass of water, then changes her mind and holds it to my lips so I can drink, my own hands too shaky not to spill it. Old habits die hard.

'David,' she shouts. 'Can you fetch a J-cloth?'

Then she turns back to me.

'It's all going to be fine, Di. You'll see,' she says. 'It's all going to be fine.'

And I, who believe in fairy tales, in handsome princes, and happy endings, who has clutched on to these fictions as if they were tangible fact, nod and say solemnly to myself, 'It is.'

# The Incredible Journey

## February 2000

I've thought a lot about forgiveness these last few weeks; what it is that allows us to crack open our hardened carapaces, cleave our hearts to someone again. Is it the passing of time? Or distance, maybe? The clarity that comes with a sudden change in circumstances? Or a mortal threat.

For parents, perhaps, it is easier – at least to forgive a child. Even one who is not their own. Because I may not be the prodigal daughter, but I am a child in need of a parent. And though their absolution is neither full, nor immediate, David and Angela offer me clemency and grace and a bedroom decorated with *Smash Hits* posters, and I accept with the barely tempered desperation and disbelief of a wino offered a sip of Lafite.

I wake again, mouth sour, stomach sore and hair strung with flakes of vomit. I heave myself up onto my elbows and see that the bucket has been cleaned, returned – just in case – but Angela is elsewhere. Dizzy and drained, still more confused, I lie back again and try to trace the path that led me here, follow the piecemeal trail of breadcrumbs that have not been stolen by birds or soaked away by so much alcohol. In a muddled montage, lacking either strict chronology or a sweeping soundtrack, I see Jimmy's contorted face, eyes bulging, lips flecked with spittle that spatters my own already tear-damp face; I see cashmere-covered arms – baby blue – and a shoulder I bury my face into as I am carried from the garden; I feel my bewilderment when I demand to see Tom, only to be told he is in America, that Harry is in London; I see the swift look between them when I ask to see you; I see the unbodied hope that sent me climbing into the boughs of an apple tree, and the you-shaped truth that had me fall.

I slept after that, was sick, then slept some more – a cycle that must have continued for close to twenty-four hours as the thin January light is waning already, so that it seems pointless to open the curtains on a day that is almost closed, pointless almost to get up. But I am not a sick child, or a hung-over teenager; I do not have that privilege. Besides, this is not even my house, and my presence in it deserves an explanation, an apology. But there is so much to say sorry for I hardly know where to begin. My foolishness? My audacity? Or yours, all those years ago?

But when I finally summon the will to stand on shaking legs, to tread the familiar shag of landing carpet and down the stairs to the kitchen, I manage only those two little words, without any qualification or quantification, before I am silenced.

'You don't have to say anything,' David tells me.

'But . . . God, what must you think?'

323

Angela's tight face tells me she thinks I am a fool and a mess, but that I am something – someone – else too; that if she steps in now I may be rescued yet, that I am not an entirely lost cause.

'We think you must have had a terrible time,' she says. 'That's all.'

'Toast?' asks David.

I nod and he pulls out a stool so I can sit at the breakfast bar – a term and thing you scoffed at, scorned for its aspiration, its pathetic attempt to conjure New York glamour in staid small-town Essex. But that bar had once represented everything I yearned for, and as I sit there, waiting for my two rounds of sliced white with jam, I cling to it as if it is not tired melamine but a raft in the wreck of my life.

It is all I have to cling to, I think to myself, this house, these people. These people who offer me breakfast for supper; who lay out towels for me to have a shower, and fresh pyjamas for when I am clean; who tell me not even to think of leaving tonight; who let me watch television in the den until I fall asleep, then carry me to bed and leave water, aspirin and a book on the bedside table for when I wake at three, thirsty, aching and alone.

I love them, these people. I owe them. So that in the morning, while David makes eggs, I tell Angela about Jimmy. Not everything, for there are too many details that I cannot bear to have her know – cannot bear to have her think of me like that, lest she compares me to you – but the bones of it. I tell her I am bruised but not broken; jobless, homeless, but not broke. That there is money saved – for the flat that never was, the wedding that never was, the baby that never was.

'I'll be fine,' I say, as much to me as to her, then repeat it, as if it is a charm and speaking it aloud will make it come true.

'Where will you go?' David asks.

'London,' I say, as if there could be any other answer.

'But where exactly, I mean.'

'Oh. I . . .' I trail off. Because 'friends' is too vague to be believed and besides, I have already told Angela that Jimmy saw to that. 'I'll find somewhere,' I say. 'Maybe near Harry. I saw her. Did she tell you?' I laugh then at that detail, a fake, desperate sound, because it is fake, desperate – I don't even know where she lives, still less if I could afford it, given my employment status, or lack of it.

David glances at Angela and I feel it again – that tacit understanding between them, hard-won-back.

'You can stay here,' she says.

'In Saffron Walden?' I reply, as incredulous as if they were offering me Timbuctoo or Narnia itself.

'You don't need to be in London, do you?' she asks.

I shake my head. I don't, not now, I suppose. I can freelance from anywhere, after all. But—

'Only if you want,' David adds quickly. 'And only until Edie – your mum – gets back.'

'I don't even know where she is,' I say. Or that she'll want me, or I her.

He nods. 'Then stay here,' he says. 'Please.'

And there it is: my transforming potion in a glittering glass vial. This is my chance to start again, be someone new – someone better. Not by changing my name through deed poll or marriage, but by becoming a child again. Away from Jimmy, whom I only disappoint; away from a city whose streets offer up only fool's gold; back instead in Neverland. I am Peter Pan – no, a Lost Boy, I think, as I drink thick Horlicks from a Wedgwood mug, as I push my feet into slippers a size too small, as I fall asleep under the fading camera pouts of long-failed pop stars. And so safe do I feel, so content, that I fail to hear the tick-tock of the crocodile that tells me a villain is coming – this one dressed not as Hook, but instead in a black ballgown and paint-spattered boots.

A time-tattered Tinkerbell.

You.


It is a month before I see you. A month in which David has driven me to Peckham, waited reluctantly outside the flat, pacing the narrow, gum-spattered pavement while I pack, though he knows Jimmy is out, that his pleas, protests and, inevitably, insults will not have the chance to persuade me. A month in which I have hung my spoils in Harry's room: my clothes, my precious books, and, to Angela's disbelief and, I suspect, disgust, a stuffed raven in a glass dome that has somehow survived the journey. I have run away from the big, bad wolf and hidden myself in the turret of an almost-castle that I spent hours, weeks gazing at, weaving fictions about. But when I look through the glass, see the paint-peeling, tumbledown gingerbread house squatting in a forest, it is not with triumph, but a strange sense of shame, and a needling, night-whispered truth that *that* is where I truly belong.

I have called – of course I have. Did you think I wouldn't? But the door goes unanswered and the phone rings out and your mobile, I assume, is long lost or broken. So that I have become used to a town without you, without your foghorn presence dogging me, defining me. So that when I do finally bump into you, I am thrown, panicked.

I am standing outside Smith's in the sunshine, clutching a *Guardian* and a Mars bar, neither available at the Lodge, despite its bounty. You are peering into a gift shop window, staring magpie-like at the silverware, or your own reflection, and though the urge to call your name is immediate, instinctive, I find the word sticking in my throat, offering me a reprieve – the chance to double back, or run. But it is pointless, isn't it, in this small town? Where you are infamous and my return is, if not celebrated, at least noted. And so I push it out, a jagged flint of a name:

'Edie!'

Your head snaps round at the sound, and I see recognition and guileless delight sour swiftly into bristling indignation, a stubborn refusal to smile.

I cross the road because it is abundantly clear that you will not.

'Edie, I . . . it's good to see you.'

You smell of stale smoke and unwashed hair, yet your eyebrows are perfectly plucked, and you arch one in defiance. 'You're back, then?'

'Yes. I called, but—'

'Day trip, is it?' you interrupt. 'I suppose *he*'s with you.'

'No,' I blurt.

'No it's not a day trip, or no he's not here?'

'Edie,' I plead.

You look at me, see something – guilt? Or desperation, maybe. Whichever, your hard shell softens and a glimmer of Edie flickers before me. 'It's just you're the last person I expected to see,' you say.

'I know.' I drop my head – the beginnings of an apology. 'And I'm sorry,' I say. 'I can explain. I want to explain. Can I come over? Or – ' I clutch at straws, find myself grasping a nettle – 'maybe you have time for coffee now?'

'We could go for a drink.'

'It's not even eleven,' I say automatically.

'*Plus ça change*,' you sigh. 'Fine, coffee then. But I warn you I've had two already and I'll be peeing for bloody Britain.'

'Good to know,' I say.

'And I need a fag first.'

*Plus ça change*, I think.

The coffee shop is new, but then so is half the town, at least to me. This one is tiny, up a turning staircase and fugged with the steam of scalding water and hot gossip.

I order while you stub out your cigarette: a decaff latte for me – my nerves already jangled; double espresso for you – 'All that milk makes my stomach turn,' you had declared with an exaggerated shudder. 'Cow juice.'

'So you're, what, vegan now?' I asked.

'Vegetarian, vegan, whatever.'

Whatever, I thought, as I wondered whether you ate at all or existed entirely on coffee and cigarettes.

'So where is he?' you ask now as you clatter into the extruded-plastic chair, peer disappointedly at the sub-Riley prints on the off-white walls. 'Jimmy, I mean. Obviously.'

I wish then I had ignored the Pollyanna in me, ordered something stronger. 'London,' I say, then add a clarifying, 'I assume.'

You pause while this plays out in your head – the possibility, and probability.

'I left him,' I tell you before you decide otherwise. I leave out the cheating, the why that loses me the upper hand, though I am sure you have guessed.

But if you do, you don't let on. 'Well, about bloody time,' you say. 'Christ, I bet the McGowans are in conniption fits. I'm surprised you haven't been tarred and feathered and strung up on the bloody war memorial.'

'They're trying,' I admit.

For all their scorn at Jimmy and his pretensions, his *poofter's wardrobe*, he remains a McGowan, and I, therefore, have segued seamlessly from stuck-up girlfriend to sworn enemy, a status that shines as patent as their cheap church shoes when they call me names outside Cromwell Road Costcutter – a shop I swiftly learn to avoid.

'Bloody yokels,' you say, and I am grateful.

An apology sits on my lips, but I don't have a chance to offer it as your caffeine-fuelled questions pile up into a teetering tower of whens and hows and whys and what, exactly, you would have done.

'So did you take the good stuff? Did you fuck with him? You should have. I know a woman who mixed up all the CDs in her utter fucker of an ex's collection. Took him years to sort those out. He was blind, you see.'

I shake my head. I have done nothing like that, would not dare. Did not dare even take half the towels, half the bedding, half the money from the joint account, money I had earned.

'Or prawns,' you declare triumphantly. 'You can sew them into the sofa. Takes weeks to work out where the smell's coming from.'

'Nice.'

'We could still do that. Have you got keys?'

I recall posting my set back through the letter box, am thankful for its clanking closure. 'No,' I say.

'Shame,' you say. 'So when did you get here, then? I've been away, you know. Retreat in Wales. Bloody wet, and apparently you're not supposed to shag the tutors. Anyway, I only got in last night and I had to come out to get something. What was it? Oh, I'll remember later—'

'Edie.' I push in, because the more *you* you become, the more I need to tell you about who *I* am now – *where* I am. 'I've been here a while. A month, actually.' Then, as if explaining it to a small child, or slow-wit: 'I'm living here.'

But despite this addendum, I can see you still don't quite understand what I'm trying to tell you. 'Listen, Edie,' I say, and steel myself to utter a curse, as potent as the thirteenth fairy's, as damning as any dwarf's. 'I'm staying at the Lodge.'

For a moment, a strung-out, hope-clinging moment, you don't get it, or don't believe it. But then truth pricks you with its spindle, and your gaunt face contorts, becomes cold again, hard, skeletal.

'You weren't home,' I try to explain.

'So, what? You just knocked on the door and pretty pleased and they decked the fucking halls and invited you to move in?'

'No. It wasn't like that. It's not like that.'

'Well, it must be something like that.'

'You don't understand. I needed . . . help.'

You flap your hand, swatting my needs away like a fly. 'So you could have called.'

'I did. I told you that,' I insist.

'When?'

'New Year's Eve. You were gone,' I add, trying to turn it on you.

'But I was here for months before that. Why didn't you call then?'

Because I was scared you would answer. Or worse, hang up. But I don't tell you that; I just shrug, like an insolent teen.

'And there's a spare bloody key under the stone turtle thing, you know that.'

'I forgot,' I say, but it's a lie and we both know it.

You scrabble in your bag for a cigarette, pull one out with your lips, then see the *No smoking* sign and slam it down on the table, gold threads of tobacco scattering over sterile white. 'I suppose you've forgotten what they did,' you say then. 'To me. To us.'

'I don't blame them,' I say.

'No,' you say, your voice edged with contempt. 'You blame me.'

I shake my head but it's another lie and I am no actress.

'It wasn't my fault,' you snap.

When is it? I think.

'It was his fault. And hers. If she wasn't so bloody . . . seized up.'

I don't want to do this. Not now. Not ever. I have an overwhelming urge to stick my fingers in my ears, say, 'La la la, I can't hear you.' Instead I manage a more adult, 'Just stop it.'

The words slap and you are startled. 'So that's it, then?'

'What's it?'

'You've got a new home and everything's just dandy now, is it? You got your happy ending?'

'Hardly,' I say.

'Good,' you reply. Then, into the heavy silence that hangs after it, 'I didn't mean that.'

But you did. And we contemplate the weight of that against time that ticks round treacle-slow.

'How will you get to work?' you ask eventually.

'I'm freelancing,' I say. 'I can work from—' I stop myself, but you hear it anyway.

'Oh, just say it.' You almost smile. 'Home. You can work from home.'

I don't answer, instead reach for my coffee, a poor man's Dutch courage, but it has cooled to a thin, unappealing soup, and I set it down again.

This, it seems, is your cue. 'Well, this has been lovely,' you say, standing. 'We must do it again sometime.'

I try to stand but I am wedged in somehow and besides, you dismiss the gesture. 'Don't bother,' you say. 'I'm late.'

'What for?' I ask.

'Stuff,' you say, flapping your hand. 'A thing.'

I nod.

'I'd say give me your address but that would be overkill.'

'Edie,' I plead.

I see your droop then, my neediness awakening an atavistic maternalism. 'I'm sorry,' you staccato out. 'It's just a lot to take in.'

'It's a lot for me, too.'

And so the scene trails off. You leave; I stay, order another coffee, which I let grow cold while I trawl through adverts for jobs I won't apply for, at least not yet.

I'm not ready to move on. To leave the Lodge. I want to savour this time, clutch it tight in my pocket like the jewel it is.

When I get home – home! Just listen to that word! As absurd to me then as it was insulting to you – I find lunch already on the table and Angela seated, waiting.

'Anything?' she asks, nodding at the paper.

'Not today,' I reply.

She swallows her mouthful of Ryvita. 'Did you see anyone?'

'I . . .' I toy with my ham sandwich. 'No one. Not to talk to, anyway.'

'Harry rang,' she says then. 'She might come home at the weekend.'

'Oh,' I say, torn between joy and panic. 'Should I move my stuff?'

'No, she can use Tom's room,' she assures me. Then, conspiratorial now, 'She's bringing someone. A man.'

'Max?' I say.

'You've met him?'

'No,' I assure her. 'Just . . . heard about him.'

'Well, it sounds serious,' she says. 'I only hope he's less alarming than the last one. He was from Wigan. And had a tattoo of Daffy Duck on his . . . his buttock.' She shudders, though it is unclear as to which is the worst offence.

'I don't think Max will have that,' I say. 'And he's from Muswell Hill, I think.'

'Oh. Jewish,' she says then. 'Of course, you only want your children to be happy,' she adds. 'But, well, there are limits.'

We don't talk about Tom. Not really, anyway. I know he's in America. I know he has a baby – a boy called Charles, like my monkey, though this one is shortened to Charlie, I am told. I'm also told he visits rarely, his wife reluctant to bring a baby on a plane.

But I don't need to talk about him. I don't need promise, or excitement, or possibility. I need this – this humdrum lunch and, later, supper, television or Radio 4, and bed early and on my own.

No, there will be no surprises, no wonderful occurrences or adventures to which I can say a silent, secret, satisfied, 'What larks, Pip!'

Because larks are far away, over the wall and in another time, and that is where I want them to stay. Can you understand that, Edie?

Can you forgive me?

# Brighton Rock

## July 2000

Where did you imagine you'd be at thirty?

I had plans, Edie, so many plans; dreams spun from silken fiction and woven into the wide, gold fabric of a life picture-book-perfect. I was going to be a vet's wife, baking cakes and bottle-feeding orphaned lambs while my clever, patient, hardy husband tramped the unnameable moors to reach a distressed cow or trapped pony. Then, when *Dr Who* replaced the Herriots in the schedule and my imagination, I was going to be the hero's assistant, handing him the tools he needed to save the world, and keeping the Tardis tidy, preferably in tight Lycra and a borrowed body. Next up was vampire slayer, then vintage record store owner, a roster of almost limitless fancy, tempered not by lack of talent or resources, but only by the paucity of books in our library or whether or not we owned a television at that particular point.

When do we close the doors on these possible selves? On private eye or prime minister or even on a minor role in *Pretty in Pink*? When did I decide that what I really, really wanted was to turn thirty putting commas into other people's stories? Living in someone else's house, with someone else's parents; a hermit crab or changeling child. If I make it sound desperate, depressing, I exaggerate; my life is far from wretched. I have work, still, despite everything. And while the Lodge is not quite the enchanted castle I hoped for as a child, I am free to come and go as I please, I have company when I need it, and a room of my own when I don't.

But I am not making books, conjuring adventures of my own. Instead, like a brazen and bitter literature student, I am trying to force other people's words to better fit the mould I have in mind. And the Lodge – this is the life I coveted aged seven or seventeen, not one I should be playing out in the last year of my twenties.

I knew that without you having to tell me.


It's June when you hand me your brilliant idea like it's a golden egg on a platter. You text me to meet you at that cafe – a place we seem to have settled on as neutral territory, no man's land; a place where your only allowable vice is caffeine; where voices cannot be raised too high; where, over slow weeks and months, we have brokered some kind of accord, weak and unspoken though it is.

'I'm already here,' I reply. Am here most days, working in a booth in the corner, the chatter and clatter of coffee cups a white noise that doesn't interrupt my work but instead comforts me, lulling me into a sense that I am part of something, still. You, though, you come dancing into this soft fog like a Fuseli-painted Puck or Ariel, all wide, kohl-ringed eyes, skinny limbs and chiffon. A child playing dress-up, you are unignorable; you demand attention, your words scatter-gunning out, a tumble of ideas and exclamations that make me wonder, again, what you are on, or if you should be on something. But you are fine, you insisted last week, and I trust you. I am trying to trust you.

'Here,' you say, handing me a smudged and Sellotaped-down envelope, your fingers tip-tapping on the table as I turn it over, try to work out what could possibly be inside, what is the worst it could be?

'What is it?' I ask.

'Birthday present,' you say.

'It's not my birthday for three weeks.'

You roll your eyes. 'Oh, for God's sake, why are there always so many bloody rules with you? Just open it, will you?'

'Sorry,' I say, and slip a finger under the seal, pull it hard against the vellum.

I peer into the fold, looking for a crumpled twenty, or a cheque, maybe, or more likely, I think, some strange postcard you have found, a junk shop or behind-the-sideboard relic from the 1930s. Instead I see four oblongs of card edged in orange, and shake them out onto the table.

'Train tickets?'

'Yes!' you confirm, as if this is a game of bingo. 'But to where?'

I pick one up, scan the small print, pray it isn't London, or, worse, Wales – some pilgrimage to a red tent to worship our vaginas, your latest phase of self-discovery. 'Brighton?'

'Yes!' I score again, it seems. 'A road trip! Well, a train trip.

We'll stay at the Grand, of course.' You wait for a smile or a thank you, but I'm still trying to imagine us going away, being together for – I check the train times – two whole days. 'Oh, God,' you say. 'Don't tell me you don't like Brighton. Everyone likes Brighton. Especially the gays. The gays *love* Brighton. And I *love* the gays. And besides, we owe it to ourselves. You'll be thirty. And I'll be fifty next year. Fifty. Imagine that!'

I start at that, come to. If thirty is an improbable age for me to wear, fifty is impossible on you. Because, though your skin bears testament to your years of Rothmans and rollies, though there is something of the Miss Havisham about you – your insistence on wearing a dead woman's dresses, the decrepit attic in which you spend all day and night sometimes, sculpting, stalking – you still have a youth worthy of Pan or *The Picture of Dorian Gray*.

'It will be a joint celebration – you, me and Nina.'

'Nina?'

'She would have been a hundred this year. Did you know that?'

I shake my head. All I know of Great-Aunt Nina is that she paid for – pays for – almost everything; her legacy – itself inherited from her lesbian lover, an elderly American – squirrelled away in stocks and shares. So that, while she permitted herself only a meagre, cluttered existence in later life, she allowed you to raise a child, albeit in what I believed at the time to be abject poverty, our only extravagances strawberry Mivvis, cigarettes and alcohol – 'Essentials, Di,' you insisted. 'Fucking essentials!' More than that, she allowed you to paint instead of work, and even then only when the fancy took you – an act that has been either the making or breaking of you; I am yet to decide. No wonder your brother hated you.

'Well, she would have been. So, to Brighton, and to me, you and Nina.' You raise your double espresso in toast, and, resigned but smiling, I raise a tea in return. 'And to the gays!' you add.

I feel eyes on us, not for the first time. But for once I am defiant, welcome it. 'To the gays,' I repeat, and at once I am a nine-year-old, giddy with delight at the thought of going to the seaside, and a twenty-nine-year-old, sobering swiftly at the thought of what trail of havoc you might wreak.

Angela gives me a present before I leave – a necklace, a single pearl set in silver on a slender chain. 'From all of us,' she says. 'Harry and Tom, too.'

Though Harry has given me another gift – a book she had told me about last time she was home, some self-help guide she had pressed on me. 'Read it,' she said. 'It will totally change your life.'

'Do I look that needy?'

But she didn't need to dignify that with a reply. Instead, she took the book back. 'I'll get you your own copy.'

I looked at Max, eyes pleading for backup, but he had shrugged and smiled, happy to indulge her, his half-hippy slip of a girlfriend.

'Thank you,' I say to Angela now. 'I'll wear it to dinner.'

'Does Edie do dinner?' David asks. 'I thought she lived on wine and inspiration.'

I look at Angela for a tightening of the jaw, but she lets this go, lets so much go now. 'Have fun,' she says. Then clarifies it. 'But call. If you need to.'

'I'll be fine,' I say. 'It's only Edie.'

And that is when I see it, a slight purse of the lips, not at the thought of you, but at my folly. She knows me. And she knows what you are capable of.

Brighton is everything the postcards promise: tacky and brash and kiss-me-quick, but genteel too, a refined, elderly lesbian of a town, courting a young lover off the estates. And while the Pavilion is gaudy, glittering, a show-off costume piece of paste to hypnotize the crowds, the Grand – rebuilt now after the fire – still glows, a duller ruby red, but a jewel nonetheless. We leave our bags – yours an overstuffed silk-lined suitcase, mine a borrowed backpack – in our twin-bedded room, and head out immediately, too wired to have the showers and rest we had promised ourselves after a torturous train journey, the carriage July-packed. Or too nervous, for the thought of getting undressed in front of you, or lying down in the same space after so long, seems an impossibility to me right now. So instead I stave it off by asking to go shopping, play the slots on the pier, and we fly along the seafront, red-faced and sweating in our too-many clothes on this too-beautiful day, purses fat with ten-pound notes for the shops and pockets jangling with pennies for the arcade.

On North Laine you flit magpie-like from stall to stall, drawn to a heavy telephone, a string of pink pearls, a pair of sparkling ruby slippers – the kind I would wear in my Dorothy dreams, closing my eyes and clicking my heels together and chanting *there's no place like home*, hoping to wake up in technicolor Kansas instead of our faded Kodak kitchen. You buy the shoes, regardless of size, then push them into my hands.

'What are these for?' I ask.

'Your birthday,' you say. 'You are a six, aren't you?'

I nod, stunned that you remember, that you ever knew in the first place.

'Well, put them on, then.'

Without argument, I pull off my scuffed ballet flats and slip on scarlet heels. Cinderella-like, they fit, and you drop my old shoes into a bin and insist I wear these for the rest of the day: 'For ever!' Then pull me, clip-clopping along cobbled streets, back to the seafront for all the fun of the fair.

I should have taken photos, Edie – the almost-thirty- and fifty-year-old, dressed for the opera, or cocktails, but wielding not champagne flutes but plastic hammers, playing Cracky Crab and Whack-A-Mole, pushing coppers into the Tuppenny Falls and silver into the slot machines, crossing our fingers for a row of cherries or gold bars. But maybe we didn't seem strange at all, not in this town. And I could see then why you wanted to come; wondered, in fact, why you hadn't before, hadn't moved here, even, this sanctuary for the strange, for the misfits and the differently magnificent. So that my heels, and your hat – some concoction you found in a box in the attic that contrives to look like a dismembered cormorant – barely warrant a second glance.

'Nina lived here,' you tell me then. 'Well, her lover did. I visited once. She brought the two of us – me and Lawrence – on the pretext of a day at the beach. Instead we ate lemon cake and drank soda while they canoodled on the chaise longue. He – Daddy – raged when he found out.'

'Who told him? Lawrence?'

You pause then, let out a laugh, a short, incredulous sound. 'No. Me. I wanted to shock him, I think. Look how that worked out.'

Of course, you. You who stamped through life making so much noise, making your presence known, blazed through it like it was your job to light the world. 'Where?' I ask quickly. 'I mean, where did she live?'

You shrug, look around at the rows of stucco fronts and iron railings, try desperately to jog your drink- and dream-addled memory. 'There,' you say, flapping a hand towards a four-storey end of terrace. 'Yes, probably there.'

I indulge you, so taken are you with this.

'I always thought you'd be gay,' you say then, your voice tinged with disappointment. 'All that wearing shapeless clothes, and traipsing round after Harry and locking your-selves in the bathroom together.'

'Jesus, Edie. Really?'

'What? I'm just saying. Would it have been such a bad thing?'

'What, having a lesbian lover?' I pause. 'Well, you'd know.'

'Touché.' You smile wryly. 'Better than bloody Jimmy, anyway.'

'Touché,' I concede.

But when I try to imagine Harry and me, picture us, all I can see is that sterile, staid six-year-old kiss; all I can feel is the fury and fire of Tom's lips on mine, and I have to turn away, my cheeks heat-filled.

'She wrote a book, you know.'

'Who did? Nina?'

'No, her lover! God, are you even listening?'

'Yes, I . . .'

'A children's book. Surprised you haven't come across it. What was it called? Something about a fairy. She had a strange name.'

'The fairy?'

You bristle again at my idiocy, or your lack of alcohol. 'No, the lover. Porter. Or Piper – that was it – Piper Something.'

I shake my head. I don't know of any Pipers, haven't come across one stacked between Blyton and Bagnold and Dahl.

'You should write one,' you say then.

'What?' I look at you, assuming this is a joke, or a throwaway remark, another of your *you're amazing, I adore your work, you're touched* comments that you dole out like penny chews. But your eyes brim with belief, your head nods like a dashboard dog.

'Yes, you should. Write something,' you say. As if it is that easy. As if I could have said to you, all those years ago, *paint something*, and not be met with a roll call of reasons why not.

'Write what?'

'God, I don't know,' you say. 'I'm pictures, not words. Something brilliant and tragic. *Jane Eyre*,' you suggest.

'I think that one's taken.'

'You know what I mean.'

I pause, allowing this chink in. 'Maybe,' I say.

'That means no.'

'That means maybe. I haven't thought about it before.'

This is a lie, of course. I have thought about it ever since Harry made that bet. Have tried, and balled it up and pushed it to the bottom of the bin so that it can't taunt me, tell me I am a fool for even thinking I might pull this off.

'Do it,' you say. 'For me. For my birthday present.'

'That doesn't give me much time,' I say, swiftly changing the subject – your trick, I think.

'Christ, don't remind me,' you sigh. 'Fifty. I know I've said it before, but bloody hell. I need a drink.'

'You need food.'

'I'm not hungry,' you insist. 'I ate on the train.'

'You ate an apple and four Minstrels,' I point out. 'And anyway, *I* need food.'

'Fine. You eat, I'll drink.'

'Fine,' I agree. One drink, I think. One drink is nothing, in the Edie scheme of things.

*

But one Merlot turns into two, and then a bottle. Then you run out of cash and have left your card in the room, so we return to the hotel bar where we can put everything on a tab.

'We could just get a bottle in the Co-op,' I suggest. 'Take it up to the room.'

'Dear God, have I taught you nothing?' And with that you dismiss me to a bar stool, and order a bottle of Fleurie, determined to drink into the night, because your appetite is whetted and your tongue loosened and you have too much to say – everything to say.

'I mean it,' you tell me again. 'You have to bloody write.'

'I don't *have* to do anything,' I point out. Pointlessly, it seems.

'What, so you're happy as you are?'

I bristle at the truth of this. But still, seventeen again, I push it. 'And how *am* I, exactly?'

'Second-hand art,' you say. 'Like those people who paint Hirst's dots for him. You're just *help*ing, you're not *do*ing.'

'Maybe I want to just *help*.'

You shake your head. 'No, you don't. You're like me,' you insist.

I am nothing like you, I want to reply, but I swallow the thought and let you go on.

'You need to create. You think I don't know you, Di, but I do. I always have. Stories: that's all you lived for. Still do. And you're not making one of your own in the real world, so why not do it on paper?'

'What do you mean, I'm not making one?'

You pour yourself another glass. Top up a slug of mine.

'You can't tell me living at the Lodge is the stuff of fairy tales.'

'No . . . I—'

'So if you're going to stay with Terry and fucking June, at least write yourself a better ending.'

'Who said I'm going to stay there?'

You snort. 'It's been six months.'

Seven, I think. But who's counting? 'And?'

'And have you even looked at another place?'

'Yes,' I lie.

You pause, play with your rings, readjust your ridiculous hat. 'It's not normal.'

My eyes widen, incredulous. 'And living with you would be?'

You raise an eyebrow, sip your drink. 'Well, I never asked. But, yes, actually. At least it's your actual home.'

Living with you would be – was always – so far from normal I want to laugh, throw my hands up, or this drink at you; the kind of scene someone would write – that I could write. But instead I mumble that I am tired, and drunk, and need to lie down.

You pout, oblivious to my reasons. 'But you're the birthday girl.'

'Not until tomorrow,' I say, 'and I won't enjoy it if I'm hung-over.'

'Go on, then,' you sing-song. 'Run along, little Alice in Wonderland, back up the rabbit hole to the real world.'

'You're not coming?'

You dangle the bottle in mid-air. 'Still a glass left, darling.'

I smile thinly, pick up my bag, and my shoes, and tread barefoot across ornate carpet, welts on my heels, heading for the lift.

'Don't wait up,' you call after me.

I don't even bother to turn around.

I wake at four to a headache and an empty bed. I flick on the bedside lamp, but you're not in the en suite, haven't popped out for something – anything. The sheets are unrumpled, the cover still pulled up high.

You didn't come home.

I sigh, pull on a jumper and my spare trainers, pad out of the door, down the dizzying vortex of a staircase and then peer into the bar in the hope you have fallen asleep there, that I will find you propped against the pumps, or in a corner somewhere, snoring with your glass still in hand.

But the bar is closed, the chairs empty.

I know then, in one jolting moment, what Angela must have felt those nights Harry didn't show up, and didn't bother calling. The questions that must have played through her head. And for a second I wonder if you ever felt that, or would have done, had I ever given you reason. The fact that I am now here, worrying about you, suggests a negative. But this cold drip of disappointment does nothing to soothe me, offers me no solace.

What if you've been drugged?

What if you've been raped?

What if you've wandered drunk down the beach and waded in, been accidentally washed out to sea?

Or worse, on purpose.

A light flicks on and a voice – male, Polish, I think – asks, 'Can I help you?'

I turn, squinting, towards it, shake my head. 'I . . . have you seen a woman in a black dress? And a hat. She was wearing a hat.'

The man shrugs. 'I only start shift at ten. No hat lady. Maybe she take hat off?'

I want to smile, at the thought you would ever do something so obvious. But even without the hat he would remember you, I think, would know you were the kind of woman who could, would, wear a hat indoors.

'Sorry for disturbing you,' I say.

'Sure she will turn up,' he tells me, nodding.

'I'm sure she will,' I reply.

But I'm not sure. Not sure at all. Whether you're alive. Whether you'll come back. And whether it will be alone or if you'll have found another Jermaine or some other fuck-up to tag along.

I wait in the room, exhausting the individual sachets of coffee, and, when that runs out, some herbal tea that tastes like soap. But what it lacks in caffeine it makes up for in shuddering disgust, so that the result is much the same.

By six, I have written you a scene sordid and sex-filled, grateful only that, at nearly fifty, at least the morning-after pill will be redundant.

By seven, your channel-drowned body has washed up on

the shoreline of my imagination, your feathered hat no more than flotsam now.

By eight, I am poised to call the police, fumbling in your purse for a photo, cursing myself for not carrying one, for rarely carrying a camera at all, when the door rattles in its jambs. 'Di,' comes the giggling stage whisper. 'Di, are you awake?'

I drop your bag and yank open the door. 'Edie?' My instinct is to grasp you, hold you tight, the lost child returned, all the possibilities of kidnap dismissed now. But, like Angela, my relief is tempered with anger and instead I blurt out, 'Where the fuck have you been?'

Your eyes widen, at that word on my lips, and at your own derring-do. 'Di, it was marvellous,' you tell me, pushing past and flopping down onto a bed. Mine, of course. 'I met some men – some gays! I told them I was an artist – a sculptress! – and they told me they worshipped my hat and I was the new queen of their fairyland. Then we went to a club – I forget where, it was underground, or in a tunnel or something – and I danced in a cage. A cage! Bloody pooped now, though.'

I feel the adrenaline that has carried me through the last four hours now ball my fingers into fists. 'Seriously?' I say. 'You were clubbing?'

'Yes, clubbing,' you echo. 'Like the old days. Like London. Toni would have loved it.'

'Huh,' is all I manage to that. And anything else would have been overkill anyway. Because within a minute, you are deep in drunken sleep.

On *my* birthday.

My *thirtieth* birthday.

I get home early afternoon, David picking me up from the station without question. Angela looks up from her hydrangeas as the car pulls into the drive, stands to offer me a hand and a head tilt.

'I'm sorry you fought,' she says.

'It wasn't a fight,' I say. 'It was just . . . Edie.'

She smiles. Not gloating, like you assume. I know you assume. Rather understanding. 'Well, there's cake in the kitchen,' she says briskly. 'And the kettle's just boiled. Come down when you're ready.'

At this, I feel my throat tighten and tears prick my eyes.

'Happy birthday,' she says.

David touches my arm. 'Yes, happy birthday, Di.'

I could hug him. Could bury my face in the flannel shirt and his shoulder and sob. Beg him to adopt me.

But instead I swallow it down, and then later, after we have toasted my health and happiness with tea and Victoria sponge, after we have eaten crumpets for supper in front of the telly, watching the news and a game show and a rerun of something I never saw in the first place, I scrabble through the recycling for last week's *Walden Reporter*, slope to my room and search the small ads for flats to let.

Less than a month later, David helps me move into a tiny one-bedroom flat on Castle Street, the downstairs half of a cornflower-painted and pargeted terrace. The last tenants have left a bed, and I have a sofa from Sworders auction house and some old pots and pans that Angela claims she never uses. And, more than that, I have a home of my own – my first. I send out change of address cards: to Jude, to Harry, to Tom, and, pushed through the letter box after a five-minute dither on the doorstep, to you.

Two weeks later an envelope drops onto my mat – an invitation to a private preview at Kettle's Yard. I don't go to the opening, don't want to stand idly by while you preen and parade, or worse, try to parade me. Instead I view your pieces on an early Saturday when I know you will still be in bed, leave a note in the visitors' book. A week after that you text me to meet in the cafe and I agree. Our conversation is stilted for minutes, then slips back into banter, through tantrum and back again. I tell you you drink too much. You tell me I don't drink enough, live enough. I snap that I've started writing but that no, I won't show it to you. Won't show anyone until it is done. And you sulk until I let you see my notebook, and I sulk when you worry my handwriting slopes the wrong way, a sign, you claim, of psychopathy.

And so our merry dance of break-up and make-up whirligigged on, an over-loud, over-bright carousel ride. Unable to live with each other, but incapable of striking out on our own.

Angela told me once that you didn't deserve me. Harry, that we were co-dependent – a word she has learned from that self-help book and taken to heart.

Do we depend on each other? Did we?

I don't think so.

However much I tried to deny it, and you tried to destroy it, it was more than that.

It *is* more than that.

You have to believe that, Edie.

# Numbers

### September 2001

As a child, I had a list: a neatly ordered though constantly shifting ranking of who I loved the most in the world; who I would save, variously, from quicksand, from a volcano, or from the jaws of the big, bad wolf – all perils that loomed large in my imagination then and, I assumed, would take up an awful lot of time and resourcefulness in adulthood.

When I was four, in the Before days, the order was this:

1. You.
2. Toni.
3. Denzil.
4. The black lady in the corner shop who slipped me strawberry bonbons or a liquorice twist while you were calculating alcohol content per penny.
5. Chinese Clive, who had reigned at number three for seven consecutive months, but dropped two places since *a)* using up my excitingly striped Aquafresh toothpaste, leaving me with your cough-drop-tasting Euthymol, and *b)* kissing you with his minty-fresh breath.

\*

By the time I was seven you had slipped too, to a sorry fourth place behind Tom and Harry, behind even that toy monkey I clung to, whose ranking was adjusted only according to his behaviour in the stories I wove for him. Though you were, at least, above the dead raven, who lacked the poseability for games or the malleable tummy to accompany me for naps.

You knew, too. You had asked me, as you were wont to do when happy-drunk or hung-over-sad. 'Who do you love best?' you demanded. And I looked you in the eye and said, without malice, but without skipping a single beat, 'Harry'.

'Charming,' you replied.

'Then Tom,' I continued. 'Then Charles, then you.'

You fiddled with a cigarette, pulled up a slipped camisole shoulder. 'But I love *you* most of all,' you said, awaiting an adjustment.

But I had merely shrugged, not for a moment having assumed anything less, in my audacity.

'Most of the time,' you clarified.

And so the small, black seeds of doubt were sown; no more than shrivelled pips then, but ones that sprung shoots, tendrils climbing like bindweed, clutching on to every imagined slight, every evident spurn.

The affair, of course, sent my list into a whirl of uncertainty. Your transgression was an attack on all those whom I had held dear, held tight like coins in a torn pocket, so you tumbled in punishment. But when Tom and Harry voluntarily extricated themselves, who was there permanently to place at all but a long-dead bird and a plush toy?

Your restoration was slow, slight, and in any case stalled
by Jimmy, who took over management of my preferences of
friends as he did food, as he did almost everything on which
I might have held an opinion. But in all of this you were
there, if begrudgingly, at least somewhere; you were never
crossed off entirely. Others came and went – Jimmy, of
course; Jude, briefly, when I was her golden child, clay to be
moulded in her mirror image, until she realized I had other
plans, or smaller ones; a man I met in the library the Christmas after I turned thirty, and who I took home and fucked
slowly on a sofa dappled with fairy lights, who I thought
might be a gift, but two days later made clear he was promised to someone else – but you were a constant presence, a
recipient of my love and promise to pull from sinking mud
or snapping jaws even as reason told me to let you go and
save myself. Not that I would ever have told you that.

More fool me.

By the summer of 2001, you have edged your way back up
to provisional prime position, though this, I admit, is down
to lack of participants as much as anything else. But we have,
yet again, fostered a strange balance: you bring round wine
that I pretend to drink, and I cook food you push around
your plate to give the effect of eating. On my way home from
David and Angela's I call round, just to say hello, I insist.
Then you tell me to make myself at home, while you finish
whatever fat-nippled breast or buttock it is you are sculpting
right now, but instead I crouch down and pull Cif and a
squeegee from the cabinet under the sink, and begin to

rescue the kitchen from the wasteland it has become, yet again; will become, within another month.

But then someone appears; a long-lost runner crosses the Atlantic and shows up on our doorstep, bearing belated birthday gifts – saltwater taffy, a silver-dipped shell on a chain, and, best of all, a tow-headed two-year-old who goes – to his grandmother's visible disdain – by the name of Chuck.

Tom and his boy have come home. And within minutes, they are both at the top of the table.

I should pull an Angela face, recoil at this miniature, this mannequin, or at least feel nothing. But when he is handed to me on a sun-parched summer lawn – this crumpled, babbling boy – I am instantly smitten.

'You should see him,' I tell you. 'He's adorable.'

'Tom or the child?' you say, peevishly poking at oil-slicked spaghetti as if it might at any moment come alive.

'Oh, ha ha. Chuck,' I say. 'I read him some Seuss. *Fox in Socks* and *The Sneetches*. He didn't fidget at all. And I think he likes me.'

'Oh, for God's sake,' you say. 'You're turning into one of them.'

'One of who?'

'Bridget bloody Jones. All thirty-something and desperate. Like your eggs will overboil.'

'My eggs are fine,' I snap. 'And anyway, I'm not saying I want a child. I just like this one. He's . . . I don't know.'

But I do know. He's Tom. Like someone made a Shrinky Dink of him and put it in the oven. Made him small enough to hold onto, to keep. 'It's so odd,' I say. 'I thought he'd be more like her. But he's not.' Not once he's out of those bloody button-down shirts, anyway.

'What's she like?' you ask then. 'Like a boiled moose? Or is that just in your dreams?'

I ignore both your petulance and insight. 'She's like a Kennedy,' I say. 'You know, pretty. Neat. Thin.'

'Angela must love her, then.'

Not as much as she should. But then she's stolen her boy across the sea and far away, is moving him further still into upstate New York.

On this travesty, Angela and I are in seething agreement.

'It's for the children, really,' he says. 'I'd rather stay in the city.'

I miss it at first, that plural, fail to recognize its fecundity, its fat belly, so at odds with her flatness. But then it is ink on water and in the Rorschach blot I see that Hansel and Gretel snapshot perfection. Two parents, two children, and a picket-fenced house in the commutable suburbs. An all-American, and once-mine, dream.

'She's pregnant?' I blurt.

He glances over the lawn from our hideout under the tree house – for we are too shy, if not creaking-limbed, to climb it now – and looks back, red-faced. 'Don't say anything,' he says. 'I haven't told Mum. It's still early.'

'Well, congratulations,' I manage.

'It wasn't planned, exactly,' he says. And I know it should be cold comfort, not consolation, but I clutch on to it anyway, a chink in her impeccable armour.

'Chuck will be thrilled,' I say.

We watch as he totters across to Harry, gives her a hand-ful of muddy flowers torn from a pansy patch that she holds out at arm's length as if they might bite her. 'I guess,' he replies, his syntax and accent hung with hot-dog carts and Central Park.

I push it then. Need to know. 'So are you, you know . . . thrilled?' I ask.

He laughs, as if this is absurd, as if it matters. 'Enough. It's hard, I guess.'

'Having children?'

He looks at me, and I see the seventeen-year-old standing awkward in front of me, see a fifteen-year-old reflected in his eyes. 'Being grown-up,' he says.

I feel the pitter-pat of cat feet, a tickle on my spine, and have to exhale to expel them, to stop my hand reaching up to his cheek, to stopper up the words I really want to say, fumble for something else, anything to defuse this.

But he lights the touchpaper. 'Are you happy?' he asks.

The air closes in on me. Am I? I think. Am I happy? I haven't asked myself, haven't dared even to think it in case I find my life lacking. Still. 'It's good to be back here,' I say. But it comes out as a question, an upturn on the last word, and I try to substantiate it. 'London didn't . . . it wasn't . . . good for me. Jimmy—'

'I know,' he says.

'You do?'

'Mum told me.'

'Oh.' My voice has slipped from query to fear.

'It's OK. Not the gory details.' He smiles quickly.

I nod. Only because she doesn't know them, I think.

'Did he . . . no, don't tell me. I couldn't bear it. I'm . . . I'm just glad things worked out. You know, with Mum and Dad and coming back and everything.'

'Me too.'

'So you are, then?'

My face forms a question mark.

'Happy?' he repeats.

'Getting there,' I say. Then, remembering, 'And work's good. I mean, not just work, but I'm writing.'

'Really?'

I nod.

'Fuck. That's . . . I don't know why I'm surprised. I always . . . I knew you would.'

'Well . . . I am.' Or trying. I have sentences scribbled on serviettes, strange names copied out on the backs of envelopes, newspaper stories snipped from their chip-wrapper destiny, all saved and stuck down in a ring-bound notebook. I have opening lines, chapters, even, but no happy ending. No end at all.

'And . . . are you seeing anyone?'

The air closes again, so that I am swimming in soupy heat. 'I . . .' There have been men. The one from the library, another I met in John Lewis, who handed me his number in the lift between Lingerie and Homeware and then disappeared into a display of Wedgwood. And now there is another – a neighbour, Mark. A man I have not kissed, not even suggested I might. Because he is too quiet, too kind, too there. He, though, has made his feelings clear.

'No,' I say. 'No one. Are you?' I say.

'Seeing someone?'

'No.' I laugh, grateful for the easy cue. 'Happy, I mean.'

And I wait, breath held like a child who has been told to close their eyes and hold out their hands, not knowing if it is a sweet or a snake about to be placed on their palm. And it's hard to believe, Edie, but I didn't know what I wanted the answer to be, what would be more bearable. That he was happier than he had ever been, that he had found his true love's kiss and it was only the quotidian, the drudge of adulthood that was causing this pause. Or that he was miserable but staying anyway, committed because of this boy – this beautiful boy – and another on its way.

'Happy enough,' he says eventually. 'Which is all any of us can ask, isn't it?'

No, I think. No, that isn't what the stories say. That's not what I was told and believed. Still do. But, as I open my mouth to protest, Chuck places his hand on a missed thistle and his yell snatches Tom's attention and sends his bare feet running to his son's rescue.

A good thing, I think later as I flick through the TV channels, having ignored Mark's offer of dinner, or a drink down the Bells, because now I am safe and sound, back in the cynical shell I have built myself, and this version of me knows Tom to be right.

I only see him once more that visit – a chance encounter, brief, outside the launderette.

'No Mivvi?' he asks, eyeing my Magnum – a grown-up ice, and one I have forced myself to choose over Cornettos and Feasts.

I smile. 'They stopped making them, I think.'

Chuck's fat face puckers and frowns. 'What's Mivvi?' he asks.

Tom laughs. 'The best,' he says. 'Junk on a stick.'

I can tell by Chuck's confusion that he will not have a Mivvi childhood. No Fabs or cans of Fanta or fat wads of Bubblicious chewed bland and stiff on our backs on the lawn. 'You're not missing much,' I assure him. 'Honest, tofu is just as good.'

Tom raises an eyebrow. So does Chuck.

I smile, my lie outed.

'Listen, we have to go. I'm on a mission to find effing soya milk. We're running out.'

'Effing milk,' agrees Chuck.

'Good luck with that,' I say.

Tom laughs, looks at me, his face straightening now. Won't stop looking at me, so that I wonder what he might say, begin to conjure possibilities. But Chuck whines and yanks on his hand.

'Effing milk,' he repeats.

'OK, OK,' he says, his patience slipping slightly. 'Look, Di, if I don't see you again, you . . . you look after yourself, OK? Be happy.'

I feel a wash of disappointment, hear the fizz of a tinder stick being put out. 'I'll try,' I promise.

\*

I don't see him again. Despite a calculated visit to your house and a return to the launderette – a fool's errand, you would say, have said.

But then I am one, aren't I? A fool.

Two days later he is gone, back to New York and the picket-fenced, picture-perfect life he has fashioned for himself – or she has.

Three weeks later, two more planes fly across that city, but never make it to the other side. And, though I know his house is across the bay and along a railroad, and his office uptown, not down, the cloud of fire and smoke sends my fingers to the phone dial – clattering it onto the ground, once, twice, before I can steady myself to punch in the numbers I quietly copied from Angela's fridge – then, when all I get is an engaged tone, sends my feet slap-slapping up to the Lodge, my head racing with possibilities – that he might have had an appointment there this morning, an interview with someone. That he might have taken Chuck to see the Windows on the World. That he might just have been walking in the wrong place, at the wrong time.

'Tom's fine,' Angela tells me, before I even manage a hello. 'David got through from work. I can give you his number but he says everyone's ringing and he's going to take it off the hook soon. Or I can tell him you called by.'

'No, it's fine. Don't worry. I should . . . I have to . . .' But I don't finish the sentence. Just walk, dazed, into the afternoon, half relieved, half grieving for all those not-Toms, the men and women who weren't so lucky to live suburban lives; half joyous, half guilty that I am happy, that I don't live in

London, that I am in a town too small and lead a life too ordinary to be a target, to become a true story.

But you are not so self-deprecating.

When I get home you are sitting on the step, your skin skimmed milk, your eyes and tongue whisky-wet.

'Isn't it terrible?' I say, unlocking the door. Trite words, but all words are trite, too feeble, on a day as big as this.

'Terrible,' you agree, standing up, then pushing past me into the narrow hall. 'You need to stock up. Get toilet rolls and tin cans and things. Wine. God, we're going to need wine.'

'I don't think we're under siege,' I say, putting the kettle on defiantly. 'There'll be talks. The UN will do something.'

'Bollocks,' you say. 'It's war. It's like . . .' You trail off, change tack. 'Where have you been?'

'What?'

'Just now. Where were you?'

'The Lodge,' I say quickly. Too quickly. 'I . . . I wanted to check on Tom. I was worried . . . well, you know . . .'

Your face tautens, your skin translucent, tracing-paper thin, so that I can almost see the bones beneath. 'But what about me?'

'What about you?'

'Why weren't you worried about me?'

I'm confused, if unsurprised. 'Edie, you live – we live in England. In Essex. Who's going to blow *us* up?'

'*They* might.'

I am sucked back then, down the time tunnel to a Seventies sitting room, the floor full of squatting bodies, in turn full of cider, dope and nuclear war.

'Will the Germans come?' I hear myself whisper into your ear. 'Will they shoot us?'

'Don't be daft,' you tell me.

But my head is full of horrible possibilities, and I need a concrete promise. 'But *if* they do,' I continue. 'Will you rescue me?'

'Yes. Of course.' You flap your hand and turn back to Toni.

'Even if they say they'll make you do camping and have the gas and stuff?'

You turn back then, startled by the breadth of my knowledge, confused though it is, or the depth of my fear. 'Even if they say they'll make me do camping. Even,' you add, unbidden, 'if they say they will make me listen to Barry Manilow until my eardrums burst.'

I smile then, satisfied, knowing that this is true devotion, and return you to the top of my list after an earlier switch with Toni because you made me use newspaper instead of toilet roll ('It's still bloody paper, Di'). But it was thick and crackled and my bottom went black and so you lost points. But this restores you to prime position. Back where you belong.

I click the kettle off. 'Do you want a drink?' I ask. 'A proper one, I mean.'

'Don't bother,' you say. 'I'm sure you've got more important people to worry about.'

'Edie.'

You hold up a hand as if stopping traffic, or the tide. 'Just don't,' you snap. 'I've got places to be, anyway.'

'Oh, come on,' I plead. Then, when my carrot fails, I pull out the stick. 'You're being ridiculous.'

'Oh, *I'm* ridiculous?' You pause, choosing your weapon. 'He doesn't love you, you know.'

'What?'

'However much you troll around after him, he's gone. He. Doesn't. Love. You.'

It pierces, straight and true. 'I know,' I say eventually.

But you are already out of the door.

That's why I do it. That and what Tom said. 'Happy enough,' I say to myself. 'I can be happy enough.'

And so, when Mark knocks on my door at nine, red-eyed from work and worry, I let him in. I let him make pasta that neither of us will eat. I let him pour me wine that we barely taste as we swallow it down. I let him turn on the television, then turn it off an hour later, telling me we can't watch the same piece of footage any more. Then, when he says he should go, I shake my head, take his hand, and kiss the tips of his bitten fingers.

Then the crease at the crook of his neck.

Then his sad, claret-stained lips.

And he lets me.

And, though he will never be top of my list, I am happy enough.

# Snow White
# and Rose Red

## January 2003

We all turn into our mothers in the end, or so we are told.

I always thought, hoped, it was no more than a lazy cliché, or a flashed-up warning to strive for difference. I would sit at the mirror and try to see you in me, half desperate for your etiolated beauty, half scared that if I could match your high cheekbones, your rosebud lips, your baby-doll lashes, then I would be doomed to become you. But I was left both relieved and bereft; what little we shared no more than lipstick traces, forensic detail.

Then I would look for him. I thought if I could subtract what little of you there was – the flesh of our earlobes, the arch of eyebrow, the smattering of freckles that fall like fairy dust on your nose and spattergun mine – then somehow an image of my father would appear, clear and unblinking, before me. But the little I managed to piece together was no more than a hazy photofit of washed-out eyes, a too-small nose, a too-big mouth, all set on a pasty, whey-faced canvas.

Harry, though; Harry's parentage was clear. At the roots of her bottle blonde lurked David's nondescript mouse, while her daring, her hope, her brief flashes of empathy, all betrayed his part in her making. But really, she was – is – all Angela: the pursed lips that greet any argument or denial; the airbrushed perfection of her face, her wardrobe, her world; the panic that rises in her when it all threatens to tilt.

I am Sunday-morning editing when she calls – my kind of church: a new author, a big debut; rearranging words, suggesting new ones to wring a few more possible drops of magic from painterly prose. This is an important job for me, and for the publisher – a risk for all of us, given the state of the industry, given the state of me a year or so ago. But Jude has kept her word, and while at first she passed me scraps – proofreading, the worst of series fiction that will be devoured under duvets by torchlight then dropped in the recycling with the cereal boxes it so resembles – now she feeds me the real stuff: fat scripts full of ripe imagery and words to be plucked like plums, stories she knows I will understand, that will strike enough of a chord that I am able to draw out what it is the author is trying so hard to say but has mired in the mud of a first draft. Right now I am toying with the weighting of a sentence, moving a word back and forth, back and forth to see which placing brings bigger impact, will elicit the greater gasp. So that when my calculations are interrupted by the tinny ring of my mobile, I curse at the audacity of cold callers and cut it off without even checking the ID. But within seconds the landline starts up, and so insistent is its shrill tone that I have no choice but to drop the word where it is and pick up the receiver instead.

'Yes?' I ask, my voice pointed, poised like a fly swat.

But this is no accident claim, no bank or begging call; at the other end of the line is not the dull monotone of an automated message or the fake cheer of the call centre but a genuine question, and desperate hope embodied in a single word: 'Di?'

'Harry.'

'Can you come over?'

'What, now?'

'Yes.'

I look at the screen. 'I'm . . . it's . . .'

'Or I could come to you?'

I pause, confused. 'That's a long way.'

I can almost hear her rolling her eyes. 'Er, where do you think I am?'

'I don't know. Hampstead?'

'I'll be over in ten minutes.'

True to herself, if not to her word, she shows up an hour later, all bed hair and fidget. And something else as well.

'Fuck, Di,' she says.

'Fuck,' I echo.

'Yup,' she affirms.

'How?' I ask, stupidly, pointlessly.

'It's called sex, Di.' She takes another mouthful of wine I now realize she shouldn't be drinking, swallows. I flinch. 'You should try it sometime.'

'Ha ha,' I oblige, not bothering to tell her I had lengthy, heartfelt, if mediocre, sex two nights ago. 'I mean, aren't you careful?'

'Not enough, apparently.' She pulls a face. 'I missed a pill. Then I got a stomach thing from Max's kid. Missed the bloody BAFTAs. He said it wasn't the end of the world, and I told him *bollocks*, only now look.'

'This is really not the end of the world,' I say.

'Are you mad? Yes, it fucking is. It's the end of everything. My life is over and I'm only . . . what am I?' She looks at me.

'Thirty-three.'

I wait a moment for the fatness and symmetry of this number to sink in.

'Fuck. How old was Mum when she had me?'

'Twenty-eight.' I don't miss a beat, plucking the number from memory as easily as I do yours.

'Edie?'

'Nineteen.'

'Shit. I'm old, aren't I?'

I nod. 'Old enough to have a baby.'

She runs a manicured finger round the rim of her glass, smearing Ruby Woo red in its wake. 'Shit,' she repeats.

'What does Max think?' I ask.

She smiles then, looks up at me. 'He's over the fucking moon.'

'Really?'

She nods. 'Wants to ring round nurseries to check admission criteria. You have to meet criteria to get into a fucking play school, can you believe it?'

It's London. Of course I can believe it. And this is Max. Who despite all my misgivings, my *but he's married* thoughts, has come good, adores her, would do anything – does do anything – for her.

'But . . . this is good,' I tell her. 'You and Max are good. It's all worked out.'

'Right. It worked out so fucking well that I've got an inbox full of hate mail from his ex, a stepson who treats me like I'm the cleaner, and now I'm bloody pregnant, and I'll get fat and ugly, and Max will leave me for some fucking studio runner in a Wonderbra while I watch Jeremy Kyle with my tits out and slowly turn into my mother.'

You already have, I think. But I don't say it, for insults have moved on from the playground *you smell* and *lezzer* so that now there is no worse suggestion. 'Your mother would never watch Jeremy Kyle,' I say instead.

Harry smiles, takes another illicit swig. 'Not with her tits out, anyway,' she adds.

'Mine, on the other hand . . .'

'At least she has the tits to go with it.' Harry sighs and peers down her dress at her own: once braless, bee-stung, now swelling gently. 'God, once I have a kid no one will want to fuck me again.'

She leans into me then, and as I put my arm around her I am painfully aware of her fragility, of the thin skin and bones and delicate mind that have to house, to protect – no, are already protecting – another being. 'Max will,' I say. 'Max will always want to fuck you.'

'I don't know if that's better or worse. Since he got the blue pills it's like being attacked by a hammer drill. I'm downing so much cranberry juice I've given myself fucking thrush.'

'Good to know.'

'Sorry.'

And then I ask it. The only question that really matters. 'But do you love him?'

At that, I feel her nod, hear her murmur a *yeah*.

So I take the glass of wine and tip it down the sink; make her a cup of tea and a sandwich instead.

'I'm not eating for two, if that's what you think,' she insists. 'Wait, no pickle! Jesus, Di, do you want me to throw up on the rug?'

'What does Angela think?' I ask as she manages a bird-sized bite.

'Are you insane? I haven't told her. Not yet. That's a three-vodka job, which kind of limits my chances right now.'

'Then why are you here?' I wonder aloud, confused, as her visits home are a rarely elicited event, duty not desire, as she had always promised.

'Oh.' Harry frowns. 'Mum insisted. She rang and said she was doing family lunch and I had to be here. She said you were coming – clearly not. When I showed up she was still in her bloody dressing gown cleaning the microwave.'

'Sounds par for the course,' I say.

Harry shrugs. 'Anyway, she had a total spaz-out and sent Dad to Waitrose. They're doing duck at six. Will you come?'

I nod. 'Duck?'

Harry rolls her eyes. 'Don't even ask.'

'Sounds divine, darling.'

'Sounds bearable. Or at least it would if I could bloody drink. Though I suppose if I'm sober I won't have to stay the sodding night.'

'Every cloud.'

But we are wrong. So very wrong.

Dinner is a strange and strained affair from the moment I arrive. Angela is distracted by celeriac, which she insists is the *new potato*.

'You'll be telling us cucumber is the new KitKat next,' David tries to joke.

Harry and I roll our eyes, but Angela snaps.

'Oh, do stop being so obtuse and do something useful like lay the bloody table.'

I start, haven't heard her swear since that night. David reddens, though, embarrassed. 'I'm so sorry,' he says.

I look at Harry, who shrugs and shakes her head.

'What?' Angela demands. 'What's the matter?'

'Nothing.' David smiles tightly.

'Good. Then go on, shoo.' She flaps us out of the kitchen with a tea towel. 'It'll be another ten minutes. Have a drink or something.'

Obligingly we troop to the dining room, where David cack-handedly uncorks a bottle of Côtes du Rhône. 'Oh bugger,' he says, as he drips claret onto cream carpet.

'It's only a drop,' Harry says.

But practised, prepared, he finds the soda siphon and sprays away the evidence.

'What's up with her anyway?' Harry asks. 'She's especially . . . Mum tonight.'

David goes to pour Harry a glass but she covers it swiftly. 'What's up with you?' he asks. 'That's more the question.'

'I need to get home later,' Harry lies. 'Anyway, don't change the subject. She's being . . . weird.'

'I think it's . . . the change,' he says, reddening again. 'You know. Lady stuff.'

'Menopause?' Harry demands. 'You can say it. It's not a dirty word. Anyway, didn't she go through that years ago?'

'She had pills,' David says. 'Maybe they're wearing off. Or maybe she's stopped taking them.'

'Christ. I'll be taking them until they carry me out in a coffin. I'm not growing a bloody moustache or giving up sex.'

I think of you then, wonder if you're starting it – the change. Or staving it off. Wonder if I'll even be able to tell, given your mood swings, your erratic behaviour.

'It's sexist as well,' Harry continues. 'Women have to have periods, and then babies, and then just when the fuckers bugger off and you get a life back you dry up and grow a beard and no one would want to do it with you even if you could. Men just carry on shagging willy-nilly.'

'That's not true,' I say. 'Well, not all of it.'

'I've already got chin hair,' Harry protests. 'It's vile. Promise me when I'm old and blind you'll pluck them out for me.'

'I promise,' I say. 'I will always be your wing woman.'

'Men have their problems too,' David says.

'I don't even want to know.' Harry shudders.

And thankfully, David doesn't get a chance to elaborate anyway because the duck arrives, borne on a silver platter by a sweaty Angela.

'I . . . can you clear a space?' She teeters slightly, swaying to the left.

'Are you all right?' David asks.

'Yes. I'm absolutely fine. I'm just—'

But she is not fine. She is not *just* anything. Because then, in what now plays out as a strange, slow-motion sequence, but which cannot have taken more than a few seconds, she slips again and buckles, the duck arcing onto the table, while the platter clatters to the floor, arriving only a moment after Angela.

'Oh, fuck!' Harry yells. 'Fuck!'

David stumbles around the chairs, crouches next to her. 'Call an ambulance,' he tells her.

But Harry does not move. 'Fuck!' she repeats.

'Harry!'

'I'll do it,' I say, fumbling for my mobile phone, sucked back in time to another night, another emergency call. This time, though, I am practised, know what they will ask. What I need to say.

I hang up. 'They're coming,' I say.

Angela groans then, a guttural, animal sound.

'What's wrong with her?' Harry wails. 'Dad?'

'She's – she's—'

'She's having a seizure,' I finish. 'An epileptic fit.'

'She's not epileptic.' Harry looks at me. 'She's not!'

'I know,' I say, panic rising. 'I know. You need to – we should talk to her. Shouldn't we?'

David reaches to touch her juddering body, then pulls his hand back. Not disgusted – afraid. 'It's all right,' he tells her then. 'You'll be fine. You're going to be absolutely fine.'

But if she could hear him, she'd hear in his voice that he doesn't believe it. None of us do.

And for once, we are right.


Angela is taken to Addenbrooke's where she has a second seizure, then a third. By the time she is taken for a scan she is grey, exhausted, and confused. The clarity that comes afterwards, though, is far more debilitating.

Less than twenty-four hours after she was wrestling vegetables, Angela is diagnosed with a brain tumour, aggressive and inoperable. She is given a matter of weeks to live. Angela being Angela, she will eke those out to months, but this will not, does not, lessen the pain for David, Harry or Tom. Or for me.

And for you, it exacerbates everything.

'Why are you always there?' you demand. 'I suppose Tom's back, is he?'

I smart at this. At the cruel accusation, and the truth at the heart of it. 'He was, but he had to go back.' Back to the kids and their demands. Back to his wife and hers.

'Then why? She's got Harry. And . . . *him*.' You cannot bring yourself to say his name. 'She doesn't need you as well.'

'*He* needs me,' I say. 'It's not easy.'

'It never is with her. Even her death has to be bloody difficult.'

'Jesus, Edie.'

'Sorry.'

'No, you're not.'

You don't argue, just pour another glass – a glass I can't even be bothered to tell you you shouldn't have. Not any more. If you want to ruin your body, your life, that's your call, I tell myself. If you have so little to live for, go right ahead.

The unfairness of it slaps me, and not for the first time I slam the door on you and walk to where I am wanted, needed, welcomed.

Life *is* unfair, that's what you would say – do say, now. But back then it felt needle-sharp, acute, that she, who hardly drank, never smoked, barely even swore, was being consumed by a tumour, while you, who abused yourself and others on an alarmingly regular basis and with such wild abandon, were still tottering around the cottage with a fag in one hand and a vodka in the other. It wasn't that I wanted it the other way, was trying to do a deal with the devil – whatever you might have thought; whatever you might think now. I've not for one second revelled in the bitter justice that has brought you to the same stark hospital. But with you, we knew it was coming; it has been a long, slow process of inevitability. With her, it happened so swiftly, and so decisively. Or so it seemed.

She'd had a headache for months, David told me one

evening – *years*, the you in my head muttered uncharitably – which he'd told her to get checked. But there were other symptoms too: misplacing objects so that David would find a shoe brush in the freezer, her wedding ring in the medicine cabinet; forgetting the time, the day, her own children. And, incredible though it seems, she became demonstrably happy. No longer snapping or sniping but laughing at the smallest, oddest thing. Brushing off the pain like it was no more than tiresome. Telling David she loved him. This, he said, was the saddest thing of all: because when she said that, he knew something was really wrong.

But I believe, or like to believe he's wrong, underestimating her. She told me things, too, you know, when she was deep in the confusion of drugs and damage. Strange, improbable things: that as a teenager she had been a ballroom dancing champion and danced the cha-cha-cha with a man called Johnny Rockets. That her father was a fairground gypsy with a greasy quiff and slicker words, that he rode into town on the waltzers for three nights and went by the name of Elvis. That she once lived for a week on glacé cherries and cocktail olives, because that was all that was in the cupboard.

But there were moments of clarity too, of absolute truth.

That her saving grace had been Sunday school, where her mother dumped her so she could worship down the slots, and where she was taught to read and glimpsed a better life in the shape of a childless woman called Bible Pat.

That David was the making of her; that he had plucked

her from secretarial college and put a ring on her finger and made sure she would never have to live on bar snacks again.

That she saw herself in me. But then we both guessed that already, didn't we?

She got to see the baby, though she barely knew who it belonged to by then. It was a girl: Martha Evangeline; as close to *Angela* as Harry would allow herself, could bear. And though the child was – is – all Max in looks – dark curls, conker eyes – she is all Harry and all Angela in every other way imaginable.

'I suppose you want one now,' you say when I show you a photo. 'Now that Tom and Harry have them.'

I think back to Mark, and his question two months ago, as we lay under the covers in my bed – always my bed. 'No,' I said to him, say to you, too. But then it was a truth, and now it is a fat, sugar-coated lie.

I want a child. I want new life. I want something to hold on to now that she is gone, and you are God knows where.

I just don't want it to be his.

I just don't want it to end up like me.

Lest I end up like you.

# Tom-All-Alone

## October 2003

I'm jumping ahead, because we're running out of time, or
so I've just been told. And I don't suppose it will matter
too much; I've already missed out so many scenes in our
story, all of them significant in their own small way. And I
need to explain this, because this is the last pebble in our
trail. This is how we got here. *Why* we're here, even. So
listen, Edie. Listen hard.

I watched a film a few years ago, and again last night; flick-
ering Super 8 footage shot in a garden – the squat's, I suppose.
But the location is an irrelevance, a blurred background,
because what matters, what is sharp, focused, is me. On you.

You are talking to me – or singing, perhaps; there was no
sound, just the whir of Toni's projector – but I don't think
that is important either. Because you could have been reading a cereal packet or reciting the books of the Bible, and I
would have still hung on every word, savoured it as if it were
gospel.

It was gospel, to me, then.

I'd ask where that adoration went (or to whom), but I
think we both know the answer to that.

Oh, Edie. I should have kept my eyes on you. Not because you were a glitterball, a glimmering sun, the star who commanded, demanded attention. But because of the times when you knew you were not. Those dull fog-grey days, or, worse, the slick ink-black ones, those were when I should have watched your every move, listened to every word, to make sure you were still here, stop you slipping through a crack in the floorboards.

But I failed. Too wrapped up in my own drama was I to have to suffer yours being played out on repeat. So I ignored the signs, even ignored your spelled-out pleas; swept them under the carpet with the dust and the cigarette ends.

I should have listened, Edie. I should have looked. I should have seen.

Angela died a month after Martha was born, and in Addenbrooke's: the same hospital Tom and Harry were born in, the same one Tom was taken to aged eight with a fractured femur, the same one you took Harry to aged sixteen for another reason entirely.

Her funeral was on the thirteenth of October. A Monday when the mercury tipped temperatures rarely seen in high summer, let alone in a month when the air should be sharp with sloe-picking frost. It felt blasphemous, somehow, unseemly to be wearing thin linen to church, to have to push on sunglasses for their intended purpose rather than to conceal our grief.

Did *I* grieve? Of course I did.

I missed her, this bone-dry, bone-thin woman. This *Good*

*Housekeeping* angel who mended her world, her children, not with kisses but with antiseptic and kaolin – offers I leapt at, would feign stomach ache for. While your medicine – television, a homework ban, a day on the chaise wrapped in moth-eaten mink and hand-fed dusty Muscat grapes – was met with, if not outright derision, then a sigh and a stomp to my room to read about mothers who might better meet my requirements, in sickness and in health.

So wrapped up in them, and her, was I that I barely had time to wonder what you were thinking, still less care. So if you have ever silently asked if I blame myself, you can be sure that the answer is, yes, on bad days – today, for instance – I do blame myself.

I ask you to come. Foolishly, I know, but I feel I should at least make the offer – or David does. But as soon as I step into the fly-filled kitchen I know I have made a mistake, that I am wasting my time and what little energy I have. The air is treacle-thick and cloying-sweet; rotting fruit lying in a pile on the table, once a still life, possibly, but now crawling, heaving with insects.

'I don't have time,' you dismiss, your hand flapping frantically.

'To clean, or to come with me?'

'I'm not coming,' you snap. 'Why would I come? Why are *you* even going?'

'You know why I'm going,' I say, determined not to have to spell it out, aware that that will only make things difficult – more difficult than they already are.

But you have less willpower. Or more. 'Because you love

her,' you say. 'You love her more than me. You always bloody did. He always bloody did.'

'Edie—'

'You said it.'

'What?' I demand. 'When?'

'Once.'

That night. I jolt at the memory. 'I wish Angela was my mother,' I'd said. 'Or I wish you'd never had me. Then we'd both be better off.'

'Edie, I was a child, then,' I plead. 'I didn't mean it.'

'Yes, you did,' you snap back. 'Because . . . because I'm a nuisance, aren't I? A, a—' You flap your hand again, sending a bluebottle into a buzzing arc. 'A fly. That's all. A fucking fly that you wish you could swat, swish-swish.' You swipe the air. 'Then I'll be gone.'

'I don't wish that,' I insist. Not without guilt, anyway, great steaming reams of sobbing guilt that I want a better past, a future that is not even glittering, but just clean. Calm.

Your hand stills and you clutch instead at the table.

'Edie?'

'I don't feel well,' you say.

I stiffen as I think of the boy who cried wolf, an allegory I have woven into a story of my own, one that sits on an editor's desk right now, awaiting judgement, my agent prodding gently, nudging for a deal.

'You probably just need to eat.' I look around me again, at the wreck our kitchen has become. 'Off a clean plate,' I add.

'I'm busy,' you say.

'You just said you were ill.'

'I *am* ill,' you insist, your black-ringed eyes wide with alarm. 'I'm dying,' you say, your voice rich, fat with drama.

I sigh. 'You're not dying, Edie.'

You pout, a sulking child. 'I might be.'

'Please, just stop it. I have to go or I'll be late.'

'Well, go on then. Go to them. Fuck off.'

'Edie.' But it's pointless, and so I sigh silently, ready to concede defeat, or a portion at least. 'I'll come round later.'

'Do you promise?'

'I promise.'

So I leave under a cloud, but in bright autumn sun, and I walk solemnly to St Mary's Church, retreading my six-, seven-, eight-year-old footsteps to harvest festivals, to carol services; then, at David's insistence, take my seat in the very first pew, my bare knee pressed against the sheer sheen of Harry's on one side and the black wool of Max's on the other, Martha in his lap, her sausage-fat fingers clutching his tie.

Tom is two seats away, conspicuously alone. He came home again two months ago, to help David and me care for her when it got to the very end. We took it in turns to take her magazines she had never once read before, music she had never listened to; took it in turns to hold her hand when the pain became too much, so much she needed to transfer some of it with her clutching fingers. We didn't talk, though, not properly, or not about us, anyway. Though I know things are difficult with Caroline. And he knows they are non-existent with Mark.

Of course they are non-existent. He was at once too much, and never going to be enough. He was too David – too kind, too eager, too compliant – and not enough Tom. Never enough Tom. And so I chose work, words, and to care for a sick woman to whom I owe, not my life, but *a* life.

The service is elegant, neat, befitting. The elegies are strained, both in voice and content, David stoic as he talks of the woman who raised his two fine children, her precision, her attention to detail; Tom, sleep-deprived, lapsing into laughter as he recalls the time she thought Harry was dying after she came home jaundiced from a food-colouring bath – yours, of course, though he doesn't mention your name.

The wake is packed, the living room as full as it ever was on Christmas Eve, fuller than it has been in years: the same faces, but lined now, less devil-may-care. Self-conscious, aware of my status – my supporting role in the headline drama the last time they saw me – I cling onto a tray of canapés, hand out ham sandwiches Tom and I cut this morning, sausage rolls that I can see Angela grimace at, the pastry flaking onto her carpet and leaving smears of grease even after we have vacuumed.

I watch David struggle with drinks, not finding enough, or the right glasses, not having thought to line them up this morning. Which she would have done. I see Harry, glowing with motherhood, pale with grief, clinging grimly onto Martha as if she, too, might disintegrate, dissipate into the swirl of dust motes if she were to let her go. And I see Tom. Tom all alone. His wife too stubborn to come, his sons too small. I listen to him recount the same story – that he has taken sick leave, a sabbatical from CNN, but that he hopes to be moved to Washington soon – a promotion. That, yes, Caroline is well, his sons are well. Look! Here's a photo of them all, standing proud with her parents on a clipped and sprinkled lawn. But I hear, too, what he doesn't say – that the move to DC will be without them. That he will go home only on weekends. If that.

And so late afternoon slip-slides into evening, which dissolves into night. Guests leave in dribs and drabs, offering promises of dinner dates, or dropped-off casseroles. Martha is prised from Harry and put to bed, while Max, drunk on cognac, falls asleep beside her. David says he will turn in too, that there's a programme on Radio 4 about cricket he's been meaning to catch. And, though we know it is a lie, we nod, and kiss him goodnight in turn like good children, breathe in his dad smell of faint cigar smoke and faded aftershave.

And we three? We musketeers? We sit at the kitchen table, like we did a decade and more ago, and we talk about life, and death, and try to solve the sorry world we have been left with.

'Shitty way to go,' Harry says. 'Painful. And so bloody drawn-out. Worse, she knew what was happening.'

'Not all the time,' I point out.

'Still, if I had to pick, it would definitely be something quicker. Car crash. Or trampled to death by hippos. It's quite common, apparently.'

I fidget, uncomfortable despite the familiar ground, familiar company. Taken back to another conversation, about how we'd do it, if we were going to. 'Should we be talking about this, so . . . glibly?' I ask. 'Or at all?'

'Better than ignoring the elephant in the room,' Harry says.

'God, Harry. When will you get it?' Tom says then. 'The elephant isn't death. It's life. That's the real bloody torture. You two live in fantasy land. You're still acting like you're seventeen. Like there's a happy ending. When we all know the truth – that it just gets harder.'

'Jesus.' Harry exhales. 'Trouble in Paradise?'

'That's my point.' He lets a whisky glass clatter down on the counter. 'There is no paradise. Why, is your life perfect?'

Harry snorts. 'Hardly. My tits are leaking, I've got fourteen stitches in my fanny and our mother just died, or had you forgotten?'

Tom closes his eyes. 'Shit. Sorry. I'm sorry. It's just . . . this is a weird day.'

She shrugs. 'I know. I haven't even cried yet. What the fuck is that about?'

'You will,' he tells her. 'It will come.'

'Oh goody,' she says. 'Well, that's something to look forward to. And on that note, I'm going to bed.' She stands, kisses the top of Tom's head, then mine. 'Then maybe I can have at least an hour's uninterrupted sleep before my services are required.' She squeezes her swollen breasts, sighs as she trails out of the room. 'I'd declare her an utter fucker if I didn't bloody love her so much.'

Tom dangles the bottle of Jack Daniels at me. 'Nightcap?'

'I should go,' I say. 'It's late.' And I promised to call in on you.

But I don't remember that then, do I? Or maybe I do and I don't care. Whichever, when he says, 'Go on. Just one for the road,' I cave and nod. When he says, 'Let's go to the den,' I slip off my heels and stand them in the hallway, a skinny ghost of eight-hole cherry-red Docs, then tread softly in his footsteps towards a sliver of light seeping under a door.

He lies on the sofa. I slide down onto the floor in front of him. His arm drops and pulls me back and he kisses the top of my head, on the very spot Harry's lips touched a moment ago. But hers didn't send my heart hammering, my stomach swirling, alive with butterfly wings.

'I didn't mean what I said,' he whispers into my hair.

'Yes, you did,' I say. 'And you were right.'

'No.' I feel him shake his head. 'You should never give up on all that. On . . . on stories. Harry was right. This is about me. Things are shit. It's not just the Washington thing. I asked her to come home. Come here. It seemed obvious. She could be here with Dad and I could commute to the London bureau. But she's refusing to leave the States.'

I take a breath, force the question. 'So what are you going to do? Take the Washington job?'

'I was, but . . .'

'. . . but what?'

'I can't leave Dad. Harry's too busy, and—'

'I'm here,' I blurt. 'I mean . . . I don't mean that's a reason to stay. But to not to. Shit. This isn't coming out right.' I try to find the words. Better words. 'I can look in on him. If that's what you're worried about.'

'He doesn't need someone to look in on him. No disrespect. He needs someone. Full stop.'

'So you're going to stay?'

'I think so.'

'For how long?'

'For good.'

'Oh.'

'I know.'

We stay like that, in the semblance of silence, for a few minutes. Feeling the velveteen nap of the couch that Angela brushed on a daily basis, smelling Glade and underneath it the fust of old feathers and hardback books; hearing the heavy tock-tock of David's gilded retirement gift and the light rise and fall of our own breathing.

My phone rings. I pull it out, glance at the number, see it is you.

Jesus, Edie, I think. What is wrong with you? Why can't you just . . . be? Just . . . work? You, you are our elephant in the room, your life, or the mess of it. I shouldn't have to check in on you. Shouldn't have to clean up after you. And yet I do it, time after time. You are right, you are a fly right now. A fly that I wish I could swish-swish away.

Then you'd be gone.

'Answer it,' he tells me.

'No.' I decline the call, then switch the phone to silent, stow it away under the side table.

'Do you remember Live Aid?' I say then. 'We slept in here.'

'Did we?'

I look round at him, stunned at his forgetting. Not because it meant so much to me, but to the world.

He sees my surprise, smiles. 'I'm joking,' he says. 'I do remember.' I let my head turn again, lean back against him. 'You kissed me,' he adds.

'I . . .' I feel it then, the heat of shame, of memory. But only momentarily. Because what does that matter now? What does that matter in the face of what came after?

'You left,' I said.

'I did.' He slides off the sofa so that we are shoulder to shoulder, legs aligned, hands touching. 'I won't tonight.'

And he doesn't. When I wake at five he is still there, his lips just inches from mine, his breath fuggy now, morning-tainted, but his, still.

I could kiss him again, I think. Kiss him now like I did last night, like he kissed me. Could start it again, cling on to us, to something, in all this wreckage.

But life isn't a fairy tale.

And he is still married.

And I am fooling myself in every possible way.

'Di?' Tom stirs, reaches for me.

I pull away. 'I have to go.'

'Not now.'

'Yes,' I say, softly. 'Now.'

Before Martha wakes and brings Harry, bleary-eyed and bloat-breasted, stamping downstairs for coffee.

Before David knocks to offer tea and toast.

Before I do something, say something I can't take back, only to end up empty-handed again.

It is better this way. Best.

I fumble for my clothes – find only a funeral dress, and pull it on as I pad down the hallway, pick up my shoes, and step swiftly, silently out of the front door, like a cat burglar from the scene of the crime.

I should take a left at the gate, head down the hill and home. To bathe, to sleep, to wait for an agent who promised to call. But as I flick on my phone, see the missed calls – fourteen of them, the last only two hours ago – I remember, reluctantly, my promise. And so it is duty, not love, that turns me to the right, to the gingerbread house.

But it is love – God, Edie, it is love that kicks in when I round the corner and find myself bathed in light.

The house is a jack-o'-lantern: every lamp switched on, the door ajar. From over the road, flashes of anglepoises behind twitching curtains. And across it all, the hypnotic wash of blue from the ambulance.

And I slip as if through quicksand to a long-gone Christmas Eve, to hot, spiteful words, spat out like grape seeds. Then to the drip-drip of a cold tap and a pool of pink-ribboned water.

You do not like being upstaged. Not by her.

Or ditched. By me.

'Fuck.'

I burst barefoot, knickerless, into the hallway, head straight for the stairs, treading on shoes, coats, a plate as I go. 'Edie? What have you done?'

'In here.'

I trip, turn. The voice – not yours – is coming from down-stairs, from the kitchen.

Oh God. Not the bath, then. Not slit wrists. But some-thing else. Pills? A gun? I rack my memory for Harry's roll call of other options, better options, but they all end the same way, however painlessly or quickly.

Fuck.

I stumble back down, fling myself towards the front room, and find myself in the arms of an ambulance man – para-medic, that's what they call them now, but he was an ambulance man to me then, a knight on a shining white steed – and behind him, you prone on the sofa, your eyes closed, your body still, another ambulance man bent over you.

'What has she done?' I demand, trying to push past. 'Tell me. Edie. What have you done?'

He blocks my path, bullish but calm. 'Are you Di?'

I nod. 'Dido. I'm . . .' Say it, I think. Tell him who you are. 'I'm her daughter.'

He nods. 'She's been asking for you.'

'Is she . . . is she . . . ?'

'She had a heart attack.'

'A heart attack?' I think back. To you clutching the coun-ter. To your 'I'm dying' – a declaration I dismissed as no more than a cry for help of the fairy-tale kind. I feel my legs buckle; feel this stranger brace himself to take my weight.

'OK, OK,' he soothes. 'It's a shock, I know. But she's alive.'

'How alive?' I ask stupidly. 'Enough?'

'I don't know,' he says. 'We're taking her in.'

And so I watch as your body is carried out on a stretcher, your face gaunt, distorted behind the plastic of an oxygen mask, but still I see your fear, see the tracks of tears traced in Max Factor black.

'You should come,' he says, as you are loaded like a black bin bag, like a box, into the back of a van.

I nod, clamber up, the floor cold metal on my still-bare feet.

'Do you need to call anyone else?'

'No,' I say, quickly. 'There's no one. Just me and her.'

Then I hear it. His voice. My hero. My Prince Charming. Here to rescue us. Rescue you.

'Di? Is it Edie? Is she—'

'She's alive,' I say. 'David, she's alive.'

# Forever

## December 2004

D id you ever get lonely, Edie?

You seemed so self-sufficient, or self-obsessed maybe; so wrapped up in your own cultivated weirdness and wonder that even when the men stuck around they seemed more like minions, hangers-on. 'Never let them change you, Di,' you warned me once, after the estate agent, or maybe the yoga teacher. 'If they try, then run for the fucking hills.'

But we all alter: metamorphose from caterpillar to chrysalis to butterfly and back again the moment we meet someone new. And that is how it has to be, it seems. I read a piece – in a newspaper, I think – that said the self is not contained in hard casing, unbreachable like a nut or a pearl, but is rather a piece of Plasticine, a shape-shifter that forms and reforms in the company of others. We all do it, mould ourselves like clay to fit around the shape of other people, other people's lives, because we need them to do the same for us. We crave company, contact; without it we simply do not exist. Except you, I remember thinking. You were the exception that proved the rule. Or so it seemed to me.

Do you remember that one wedding? Denzil's? You and

me, we stayed up late into the night in our twin-bedded, shared-bathroom, no-room-service hotel room. We lay on the thin sheets and candlewick covers, dizzyingly drunk from cheap Cava and the rich cavalcade of old friends and absurd strangers we had danced with in that hall in Shoreditch, me staring at the slow turn of the ceiling carousel, you defying the warning sticker on the plywood door by lighting up a last rollie begged from a woman called Bob.

'I want that,' I had said to you, a rare, heartfelt confession.

'A fag or a wedding?' you replied, unable to walk the line yet somehow still managing to summon sarcasm. 'The first will kill you, the second is probably only worth it for the floor show.'

'God, Edie, do you have to?'

'What?' you demanded. Then, seeing my face, half-heartedly flapped a hand in the smoke, as ineffective as it was irritating

'Not that,' I said. 'I . . . don't you want to be with someone like that? Like Denzil and Marie. Not even the whole *to have and to hold* thing, but just to be with that person, I don't know, completely?'

'I'd rather be alone or dead than wed to a woman who thinks no bra is an option when you're a bloody D cup and pushing fifty.'

And I had sighed and dismissed you as belligerent. Your refusal to believe in love, true or otherwise. But maybe it is just that you had tasted it, and had it taken away.

I heard once, or read it maybe, that unrequited love is the only truly pure form. Because it can never be sullied, dimmed with the dull tarnish of reality. But to those of us who have loved, and loved, and loved with no return, it is dirty, desperate; springing from bright-eyed hope, but cloaked, by the end, in humiliation. An exercise only endured because what is the alternative?

Heartbreak.

Not the fey melancholy we imagine when we are children, but a snarling, slicing, blackened cancer of a thing that comes to us in the end anyway.

And all from a lack of three little words.

I love you.

Did you ever say those words, Edie? To him, I mean. You've let them slip from your tongue as slickly as if they were no more than a *hello* to friends, to acquaintances, to anyone, everyone who wandered into our lives. 'God, I just love you!' you would exclaim to Harry, to Mrs Housden who found your purse under a table at the Duke of York, to the bread man. I can't do that, be flippant with language, foolish with it. Those three words carry such weight, such heaving, electric possibility within eight letters, loaded as they are with atavistic meaning, with expectation plucked from films, television, books and some deeper collective consciousness. And when I summon up the daring to let them fall, finally, from my lips – these full, fat, ripe cherries – only an absolute echo will measure up in return.

What do I want with an *I care about you*? What does it matter if he *really likes* me? There is nothing to be done with those replies. Not even silver-medalled, they are poor runners-up; they are also-rans. Because what he's really saying is that

I will do for now. But love? I was not enough to be worthy of love: not pretty enough, not funny enough, not clever enough.

Or so I told myself.

Was that what you told yourself too?

David and Angela called time on their Christmas Eve party long before the tumour began to swell. Old friends had moved, or had grandchildren of their own to set out stockings for. And new neighbours, airdropped from faceless London suburbs, were wary of anyone even saying hello; and an invitation in for cheese and wine is too reminiscent of a scene from a Seventies sitcom to be taken seriously, let alone taken up.

But this year David is determined to do something, if not for Christmas itself, then for New Year. 'I want to mark it,' he says on the phone. 'A new beginning. For all of us. You will come, won't you? I know Edie wants you to be there.'

I know that too, because you have asked me yourself not once but three times. And each time I have told you yes, of course I will come. No, it isn't because I have nothing else to do – though that is true, I don't – but because I want to be there. Because it matters.

'Come here first,' you say, your voice girlish now, free of fag smoke and alcohol, instead edged with guileless delight at this new chance you've been given – we've been given. 'Then we can get ready together.'

So we do. We dress in your room from a bed piled high with a flotsam and jetsam of cast-offs and collectables, from vintage Chanel to voguish charity-shop finds; paint our faces side by side in a lipstick-smeared mirror; spray ourselves with scent from the same stoppered bottle that has sat for years – for a lifetime – on a dressing table found in a skip on Coldharbour Lane and dragged home by you and Toni, with me marching at the rear.

'Ready?' I say as we stand at the foot of the stairs, shoes on but coats left hanging from their hooks, for the walk we have to make is so short, and our excitement will make it swifter still.

'Ready,' you say, then salute me.

I take a breath and turn towards the front door. 'Where are you going?' you ask. 'This way.'

And taking my arm, you lead me out of the back door, through the weed tangle and dead leaves of our path and to the gate in the wall.

'It's open?' I ask.

'Abracadabra,' you say and turn the handle.

As if by magic, Narnia appears. A frost-sparkled scape of fir trees and lawn bathed pale by a luminous moon, then warmed at the far edge by the glow of a street lamp fastened to red brick. And underneath it, my own Mr Tumnus, putting out the last of the party peanuts for the birds.

Tom.

'I'll see you inside, then,' you say, knowing what I am thinking before I do.

'Thanks,' I reply, then watch as you walk to him, tilt your cheek up for a kiss, then slip through the door and into the heart of your new world.

*

We talk outside until our fingers blanch and then blue, and the chattering of our teeth drowns our whispered words – about the boys, about his new job back at ITV, about the bloody commute, but he's still not ready for London, might never be; about my new book deal – a series this time, 'Enid Blyton for the modern age,' Jude claims. 'Inevitable,' he calls it, but both I take as compliments.

In the kitchen we are conjoined twins, Chang and Eng, our hips touching, my head leaning on his shoulder, my high laugh blending with his as Martha lies defiantly across our feet and crosses her arms because she is not sleepy and will not go to bed. Then, when Harry takes Milo back upstairs from his fifth foray into the land of the grown-ups and slips into bed with him instead; when Max falls asleep on the sofa with a glass of brandy in one hand and an unlit cigar in the other; when you and David head back to the gingerbread house, because you will do most things – all things – but you will not sleep in her bed, we follow our two-sizes-smaller footsteps, our teenage selves, to the den, pull the beanbags from behind the chesterfield, and lie on our backs, heads spinning in our own private carousel.

'You don't believe in fairy tales,' I say, as his hand cups my face.

'Some I do.'

'Well, I don't believe in drunk kisses.'

'Dido Jones, are you seriously giving me the brush-off?'

'Just for now. Ask me tomorrow.'

'Tomorrow never comes.'

'Yes, it does. There is always tomorrow.'

'What if you run away in the night?'

'I won't.'

'What if a witch casts a spell in the night, or a goblin curses you, or a wall of thorns grows up around your house and you don't wake up for a hundred years?'

I put my hand over his, pull his fingers to my lips and kiss them. 'Meet me at the gate. At eight.'

'Because it rhymes?

'No, because it's early and then I'll know you mean it.'

It is the hope, they say, that ruins you, for hope rides bare-back on disappointment, blows raspberries and jeers *I told you so.*

And I know this to be true: I held on to a tiny flicker of hope for so long it finally burned my fingers, and I had to drop it, scalded, shamed.

It was the fear of that sent me scuttling away from him that night, the night you nearly died for the second time.

But now it is hope that takes me to him. That sees me, at five to eight in the morning, still in pyjamas but with my teeth brushed, and the faintest trace of last night's perfume on my still-glittering skin; sees me slip across the landing and down the stairs, careful not to tread on the floorboards that David hasn't got round to fixing. I don't want to wake you, or him. Then I slip, light as a will-o'-the-wisp, through the door and down the garden path, brambles snagging silk, damp soaking through the wool of a pair of your socks. For a single, dazzling second I consider climbing the apple tree, dropping down beside him like I did nearly thirty years ago.

But as I pull on a branch to see if the calloused wood will bear my weight, I hear a handle being turned, and the gate opens, and he is there, in pyjamas too, and a frayed dressing gown, and with slippers on his pale, bare feet.

'I didn't know if you'd come,' he said.

'Yes, you did,' I reply. 'You've always known.'

'I love you,' he says then. 'Dido Sylvia Jones, I love you.'

'I love you, Tom Trevelyan.'

And then he nods. And then there are no more words.

There is just me and him in this glorious bloody Wonderland.

## Now

So that, Edie, is the story of you and me. How we came here. To this point, to this room. Like Hansel and Gretel I have followed this trail of breadcrumbs from the gingerbread house, only to find they led back there all along. That perfect snapshot? It wasn't me in the Lodge garden, in a polyester dress with someone else's mother standing rigid behind me. But here, today, in this room.

This is it. This is our Kodak moment. So smile, and say cheese. Because we are all here. Our fucked-up, cobbled-together family. Me and Tom. David and Harry. And Toni, too.

I'd hoped there would be more of us. Hoped I would have children to tear round the room, for you to swear at but secretly adore. We tried, Tom and I, but after four years of assumption, three rounds of IVF and a decade of fading hope, we have finally accepted this is never going to be. All those pills, those panics, for nothing; every threat Jimmy made pointless. Like telling a legless man you will kill him if he can't walk tomorrow.

The truth is that thanks to chlamydia, and a goth called

Niall, I cannot have children, at least not of my own. But I have two splendid stepsons who visit us in the summer and we them in the fall. And every other Christmas our small house stretches at the seams as two strapping boys take over the spare rooms and the sofa, and use words like *faucet* and *sidewalk*; who call me *ma'am*, and even, sometimes, to my secret delight, *Mom*.

And I am a godless-mother to Harry's youngest, Min, though I fear this is unfair as her two older siblings have a game show host and a former girl band member to guide them down the righteous path, whereas authors are not as lucrative in either actual money terms or the strange stock market that is still played out on hopscotch-painted tarmac and in the queue for the lower-school toilets. But then I remember that Milo and Martha have their own share of bad luck. Because their godmothers won't teach them how to fake a sick note, or fend off a boy with a knee to the balls, or pour the perfect gin and tonic. Nor any of the useless, brilliant things you taught me.

Oh, Edie, you did teach me. So very much. And I never said thank you. I just rolled my eyes and slammed doors and swore under my breath that the sooner and the further I was away from you the better. All those days spent lying on a single bed rereading *Othello*, wishing I was black, or star-crossed, or just anyone but me. Scared that somehow, without trying, without even knowing it, I would manage to squeeze myself into your ragtag coat – the one that you wear to all your fuck-ups and faux pas.

How foolish I was, because we, Edie, we were the Queens of Bloody Everything. But only you could see it.

But here I am. Here we are. We had a second chance – more than a decade together, done properly this time. But the past is still in us, some of it diamond, some of it mica. And there are only so many things you can undo, mend. And years of drinking, a rotten liver, is not one of them.

So this is it, Edie. They're coming to take you down to pre-op in a few minutes. And I know the others want to come in before that. So I'm going to say it now because you can't raise a hand or your voice to stop me. And because, with the odds Dr Rowland has given us, I know I may not have the chance to say it again.

It's been a fairy tale.

An enchanted-wood, gingerbread-house, handsome-prince fairy tale.

And you and me, Edie? We are the queens of the story. We are the Queens of Bloody Everything.

Thanks, Mum.

# Acknowledgements

With thanks first to Fox Benwell, who kept each chapter safe as soon as it was written in case I pressed delete; next to my agent Judith Murray who fell in love with Edie and Dido from the very first page, and to Sam and everyone at Mantle who felt the same; to Nicola Murphy and Adrian McMenamin who filled in the blanks in my hazy memory of 1 May 1997; to Nicola Watkins and my friends from Saffron Walden who did the same for Essex in the 1970s and 80s – if you recognize yourselves or anyone from town, it is accident not design; to the Manatees for endless virtual cups of tea, and to Sarah Geraghty, Wendy Meddour, and Helen Stringfellow for actual ones; and lastly to Michael, for always believing I could do it.